Spires of Arenthyl

Ryan D Gebhart

Other Books by

RYAN D GEBHART

THE JEWEL OF LIFE

SPLENDOR OF DAWN

HIDDEN WITHIN

FADING LIGHTS

BURNING DESIRE

SHADOW OF THE LOST:
A NOVEL IN THE JEWEL OF LIFE SERIES

SPIRES OF ARENTHYL

PART FIVE

OF

THE JEWEL OF LIFE

RYAN D GEBHART

Hardcover ISBN 979-8-9853738-1-3

Paperback ISBN 979-8-9853738-2-0

Distributed by Ingram Publisher Services

Printed in the United States of America

Cover design by Fiona Jayde Media

In Memory of Melissa McPhail,

a Brilliant Light

TABLE OF CONTENTS

Skrein Sea
Wooded Hills of Thellion
PERRIEN
PARENDIOR
Gneal
The Verpien Mountains
Oern
Belina Wich
Cyril
Cirillean Pass
Selma
Lewis
Lake Saeryndol
Septyl
Reinyl
Mount Verinien
Arenthyl
Evenir
Stellantis
River Illiael
The Eldin Wood
Audun
Delmira Wood
City1
Winstyl
KRYSINA
Verenthyl
EVELLION
Overen
Brunst
Plains of Mindale
Harnl
Wexly
Binton
Farenton
Nedil Wood
The Purged Desert of Dwonia
MINDALE
Jopht
Achton Wood
River Zendar
New Castle
Freiton
River Kras
Houll Wood
YANL
Dwota's Gap
Nyner
Nuntol
The Shadow Mountains
Lankor
Dornal Marsh
Mount Cyngol
Zorik
Hannly
Kinzdol Islands
Tempestien Sea

The Unarian Sea
River Barbyl
The Loudien Mountain
Givoll
The Illumined Wood
Mount Saecrien
Kweil Aitch
Ceurenyl
Enthel
Lucilla
Raselan
SORENTHIL
Myrium
Ruins of Quellion
Peran
Daerinth
Plains of Orithil
River Myrien
GISTORIA
RSI2
Hendil
Dead Wood
Brie
River Reifel
TIEL
Harding's Crossing
Eddle Port
Nairin
Josque
Aulen
Ja'mare
Irynien Bay
Jahro Islands
Suderil
Jadien
Map of the Continent
EKLEAN
Inscribed in Ink
by the Hand of
RDG
N
S
E
W

Desolate

An unwelcome wind buffeted Abbie Wintyr's face. Wind did not belong in this place, but neither did the ever-growing storm clouds above. Their eerie presence here was all the warning that the druids needed to confirm the troubling days to come. Entering Somnaeniel was now restricted, and Abbie could only enter if her brother, Eagan, agreed to accompany her. And he was late.

She had promised to not venture far if she arrived first, but the wind was making it difficult to keep both feet planted on the ground. Dark ooze bubbled about the Dream, no longer confined to small puddles. Lakes had formed as it pooled over and swallowed everything in sight.

Stepping back from the encroaching lake, Abbie wondered if the ooze had a mind of its own, for it edged closer to her as though it could sense her. She had not been that close to the lake when she had entered the Dream. Perhaps it was just expanding, but it felt otherwise; it felt conscious.

Her eyes darted up to the sky as she moved, ever cautious of where she stepped, but wary of what was happening above. Clouds swirled in a cyclone, and from her perspective, they appeared motionless, but the winds against her face said otherwise.

"You promised you weren't going to move," Eagan said, coming up behind Abbie.

"I didn't have a choice; that ooze nearly reached my toes."

Eagan bent down, his nose only a handspan above the ooze.

"Are you trying to actually smell it? You know you can't smell anything here unless…" Abbie could not finish her sentence. She looked from her brother to the ooze. "Get away from that!" She didn't intend to scream, but Eagan's idiocy outweighed her ability to control her voice.

Eagan straightened and stepped away.

"Have you lost every last bit of your mind? What were you thinking? Coming here in the fle…"

Eagan calmly pressed his hand over her lips.

His solid fingers upon her incorporeal mouth felt wrong.

It was wrong. He should not be here as he was. Visiting the Dream at all was dangerous at present. But physically coming here was another matter entirely.

"It's not wise to say it out loud; the risk is grave enough."

"Then explain why." Abbie crossed her arms, unable to determine whether she was more scared for her brother or angry at him.

"I was asked to."

Eagan turned from his sister to reexamine the sludge. His nose neared it once again, uncomfortably close in Abbie's opinion. When he pulled a stick from his pocket, Abbie instantly recognized it as a verathn, the type the ei'ana called wands. It had a linear shape with smooth edges, but the color and material identified it.

Eagan swirled the verathn in the ooze. Nothing happened at first, but then the dark ooze bubbled and hungrily clung to the verathn's sides.

Abbie held her breath, hoping her brother was not stupid enough to hold on to the verathn longer than necessary. She knew he was more experienced in the Dream, but only because he was older. Still, seeing him perform such a foolish action took every bit of her to not yell at him again.

When the ooze neared his fingers, Abbie gave her brother a desperate look, silently pleading him to forget about the verathn and abandon it to whatever that sludge was.

The ooze crept ever closer to his fingers and Abbie felt her heart pounding within her chest, finding it more and more difficult to contain herself.

"Drop it!" Her voice pleaded in a tone she was ashamed of. The verathn fell from Eagan's fingers, his expression unconcerned and vacant. "And what did you learn from this folly?"

Eagan continued to examine the place where the verathn had been swallowed by the ooze.

"It's called dorthl."

"And what *is* dorthl?" she said, lips pursed by her fury at her brother's stupidity just to discover a name for the ooze.

"It acts similarly to tenebrys. Our assumption that it originates from the Void is likely correct," Eagan said, still staring into it.

Abbie stepped further away from the dorthl.

"Is the Dream turning into dorthl?"

"There is a consumptive attribute to it, but I can't say whether the Dream is becoming it or being consumed by it." Eagan's emerald eyes continued to stare at it. "I'm afraid it won't be long until the entire Dream is blanketed with it though—we'll be entirely barred from entering before long."

"But what of the…"

Eagan pressed his hand over her mouth again, more firmly this time.

"There is still a glimmer of hope that it has remained a secret here," said Eagan, unapologetic for his action. "We should leave."

"What will you tell the others?"

"I won't be telling them in person, not today. I did not take such a risk to return to Kweil Aitch in the same breath."

"Where will you go?"

"With you. We no longer have the luxury of time. Come, let's return to Teraeniel."

The predawn half-light in her room washed across her face. Abbie looked to see if her brother had left the Dream, and whether he had found it fit to enter directly into her chambers. Appearing out of a foggy cloud would startle anyone foolish enough to be looking when a druid left the Dream.

Quickly dressing in her leathers, Abbie left her room and walked through the castle corridors looking for Eagan. She was tired of having to stay in Gneal's castle while Alex repeatedly abandoned her for his reckless missions, knowing full well that Devlyn was just as involved and careless as Alex. Even if they were not directly related, Abbie found their similarities, especially their weaknesses, all too troublesome.

Eagan had yet to reveal himself and she would turn the castle upside down to find him. She knew little about walking the Dream in the flesh, only that the druid elders highly discouraged its practice. That hadn't always been the case though and it was only due to the weakening of the Evil One's prison following the fall of Krysenthiel that the druids had abandoned the practice entirely.

Assuming that Eagan knew what he was doing, Abbie made her way to the most logical place she thought her brother would go—the stable. She knew he had no intention of staying in Gneal and even less to explore the city. No, he had only come to Gneal for her and together they would likely travel south to find Devlyn. Time was running out and Devlyn was wasting what little of it they had on this silly war.

Abbie pushed open the castle doors and turned toward the stable just off the bailey. She could easily hear the stable hands speaking in raised voices all the while trying to calm down the horses. She had no doubt about who had roused them. Sure enough, her brother waited inside, baffled by the stable hands' reactions. "We already told you, you can't just take the king's horses." Abbie overheard one of them say.

"There's no reason to get upset over it. I need two horses. I believe those will do fine." Eagan pointed to the far stalls where the grey coursers were kept. Perrien prized those horses above all else.

"And who are you to demand the use of the king's grey coursers? They are restricted to the king's directive."

"Excuse my brother," Abbie started.

"And who are you?" The stable hand asked, clearly frustrated.

"Abbie Wintyr. I've been staying in the castle since Alex liberated it from that council." She crossed her arms.

"There are plenty of servants in the castle that I don't know and I wouldn't lend any of them a horse!"

If they had known who she was, they would have also known that was the wrong thing to say to Abbie Wintyr. "I am not one of Alex's servants!"

"No reason to get upset, sister. Who do we have to ask to borrow two of the horses?"

"His Majesty is fighting a war in Evellion. I thought you would've known that since you're living in castle and all."

"Who *else* can grant us permission to borrow the horses?" Abbie growled.

"Only the king."

"I thought we already covered that the king isn't present." Eagan looked back at the horses he wanted to borrow. "Can we ask someone else? Perhaps a representative?"

"Closest thing to a representative would be the Queen Mother."

"Let's find the Queen Mother then." Eagan's vacant expression contrasted sharply with the daggers Abbie's eyes were shooting at the two stable hands.

Familiar with his lack of outward emotion, Abbie caught and held her brother's gaze. It was odd how different they were from each other. She could not imagine holding back her reactions as he did. She didn't think it was healthy and he had to be constantly constipated due to everything he held inside.

Abbie led the way back through the castle; the stone walls pressed against her, and the windows provided little relief. It was the middle of spring and grey clouds hung in the sky. They were not as threatening as the storm clouds in the Dream, but Abbie was sure there was a connection between them. She was no native to Gneal or Perrien, but even she could tell that those clouds and the snow had overstayed their welcome.

Refusing to inquire as to the Queen Mother's location in the castle, Abbie followed her instincts and strode through the corridors with Eagan on her heels. The sound of swords clashing rung in her ears, a sound she always enjoyed, but it was not quite the same if she did not hold a sword herself. She loved the feeling of the reverberations pulsing through her fingers and up her arms to her shoulders and stabilizing in her back and legs. She was half tempted to abandon her search for Alex's mother, and demand that one of the recruits pick up a sword for a quick duel with her. She might have, if her brother was not present; he had little patience for sword play.

Abbie's impatience reached a point of relief when she spotted Vine Vaerin in the far arcade of the courtyard. A noblewoman stood beside her and the two likely chatted about something meaningless, something that didn't matter in the current circumstances.

Vine looked up at Abbie, and from her to Eagan. "I didn't realize we were expecting a visitor." Vine had made it her priority to know everything going on in the castle, something she had insisted on after Alex had left for Evellion.

"This is Eagan, my brother."

Vine extended her hand in greeting, but Eagan looked at it oddly.

"He's never left Kweil Aitch before," said Abbie, trying to ease the awkward encounter. She did not want to get on Vine's bad side, especially since Eagan wanted to borrow the king's horses.

"Of course, I have; there're few places I haven't been to," said Eagan, his protest sounding childish.

"And in how many of those places did you interact with the people there?" The places that Eagan referred to were all in the Dream. Gneal was the first place outside of their island home beyond the Illumined Wood he had ever visited in the flesh.

Eagan kept his mouth closed.

"I'm not familiar with it," Vine said

"It was never part of Thellion," Abbie supplied. She didn't feel like explaining to Vine who the druids were.

"And how did you get here, from wherever it is you're from? I don't recall any envoys arriving last night or this morning." Vine looked over the red haired and freckled pair.

"I came alone," Eagan said.

"Not the wisest choice with the Daer seizing every Perrien they come across," the noblewoman accompanying Vine said.

"It wasn't the Daer that concerned me on my journey here," Eagan said.

"Well, they should have; whole villages have been forced into slavery. Including the ones with a half decent guard too." The noblewoman appraised Eagan anew, clearly having changed her opinion of him.

Abbie blanched at the direction this conversation was taking. "Anyway, even though Eagan has only just arrived, we need to borrow a couple horses to leave."

"Leave? Well I don't see any problem with that, but why doesn't your brother just use the horse that he came here on?"

"I didn't come here on a horse." Eagan said it plainly and Abbie thought he might tell Vine exactly how he came to be in Gneal.

"How peculiar," the noblewoman said.

"Indeed. Well, I'm sure you're aware that we don't just lend out grey coursers. They've been reserved for military campaigns for a number of years now. They'll be critical in the days ahead when we confront the Daer."

"I understand, but we're needed elsewhere."

"And where exactly are you needed?" Vine asked.

Abbie looked from Vine to her brother; he hadn't mentioned where they were going.

"Devlyn needs to learn to walk the Dream more proficiently. A narrow window is closing, and if he doesn't act soon, it's difficult to determine the consequences," Eagan said.

"Is he expecting you?" Vine asked, a single eyebrow raised.

"No."

"And do you know where he is?"

"Sleeping comfortably in a bed in Everin with his dreams warded. He won't be there much longer though."

"Well that explains it," said Abbie, more to herself than the others. She had tried to reach Devlyn on countless occasions with little success.

"What of the giants and renegade Perrien militia?" the noblewoman asked.

"They've been defeated," Eagan said.

"And my brother?" Vine asked.

"I don't know who your brother is."

"Of course," Vine said, her voice strained. "Do you know the manner of the victory?"

"I'll be sure to ask Devlyn when I see him," said Eagan, his face expressionless.

So, we're not that different. Abbie smirked at her brother's reply to the Queen Mother, a title she had taken after Alex had left for Everin.

Vine looked to the noblewoman; an understanding passed between them that made Abbie want to kick them both in the shins. They thought she was unaware of what they said about her.

"About those horses," Abbie pressed.

"It's quite out of the ordinary, but I suppose it's acceptable," Vine said. "Give Devlyn my regards."

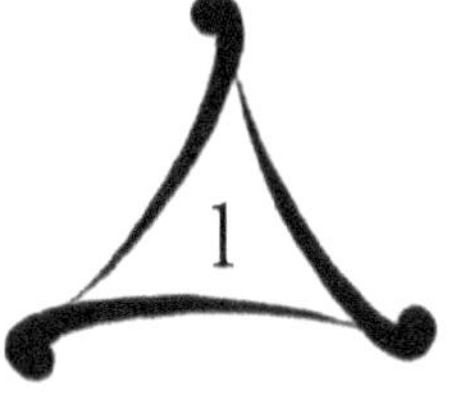

TREATY

It had taken some time, much discussion, dissension, contention, and posturing before a treaty had finally been hammered out. The treaty papers now sat unattended in Everin's throne room as everyone prepared for the official signing ceremony.

As Queen of Evellion, Lara had enacted the necessary steps to place Evellion under a Thellion suzerainty. Evellion had stood as a proud independent nation for thousands of years. Its first citizens had fled the Thellish civil war, along with the rightful King of Thellion at the time. King Evellion Thellion had placed the people of Elothkar first and fled the besieged capital. Those people had built the proud nation of Evellion, and within a few hours, the descendants of those same refugees would formally fall under Thellish rule once again.

When Devlyn had told Ellendren about the state of affairs, he had expected her to tell him to return to the Luminari—to her. He had been away far too long as it was. Perrien's renegade army had been defeated and the giants driven back, but the Luminari elves waited for their Lorenthien aryl to return and fulfill his promise to destroy the Shroud. While he had complied with Ellendren's request that he return to the Luminari camp, it had only been for a brief visit. In less than an hour, he had found himself shifting back to Everin with a small party of Luminari aryls and Guardian knights that Ellendren had organized, herself included. Ellendren Lorenthien, daughter to the last king and queen of

Lucillia, and now Devlyn's wife, had no intention of missing one of the most consequential political decisions in an age.

Evellion's nobility had swarmed their capital in the weeks following the siege on Everin. The only nobles not accounted for were those from Cyril. Everin's castle was filled to capacity as nobles debated their kingdom's future. They had all conceded that Everin would have fallen without Thellion's assistance, but they had also blamed their northeastern neighbors for the long siege in the first place; the invading militia had been from Perrien, led by Lex Telvin, a former Perrien general and the Thellish king's uncle. Even if Perrien was now under a new rule, the Evellions worried about the sort of treatment they might receive as subjects to a foreign crown.

Devlyn agreed with most of their concerns and critiques and it certainly hadn't helped when he was asked to bring three of the deposed councilors from Gneal to Everin. Alex had failed to mention that he had reinstated some of the deposed councilors to act as advisors on a trial basis.

While the treaty was supposed to have been drawn up, finalized, signed, and sealed a week after Everin's victory, twice that time had passed. Aurenth was drawing to a close and a new moon hung hidden in the sky.

Devlyn had thought to wear his blue lierathnil for the occasion now that the treaty was finished and ready to be signed, the same outfit he had worn for the victory feast two weeks ago. Ellendren had quickly pointed out that choosing to wear blue could be misconstrued as him supporting an independent Evellion. His outfit could show his objection to an expanded Thellion. Devlyn didn't understand how his clothing could be a slight against anyone. Still, he bowed to Elle's judgement and wore the purple lierathnil set. She had said it shouldn't offend anyone present.

"You're certain no one will be upset with me for wearing purple?" Devlyn asked, winking.

"Only if they try to connect it to the purple doe of Parendior and it means you're supporting Thellion's claim over Evellion. Everyone knows you were born in Cor'lera, but there's no reason to remind anyone," Ellendren said.

"But I thought we did support that?"

"We do." Ellendren straightened his outer garment, her hand resting against his chest. "Best not to mention it though. We can't be perceived to be forcing this treaty. Eklean has to see this as Evellion's own choice."

"You make it sound like it would've been better if we weren't here," Devlyn pulled Elle into a hug, her lips close enough to kiss.

"That would have sent an entirely different message." Ellendren leaned against him, her breath mingling with his own. "A set of golden lierathnil with Kryseniels embroidered on it would have been ideal. Then we would have been seen as a neutral ally. That's something we'll have to figure out in the coming months."

"How do you mean?" Devlyn asked, suddenly wishing that they were somewhere more private than the castle garden they had stopped in. There was still an hour before they were expected in the throne room to witness the treaty signing.

"Devlyn, we're to be the Exalted Aryl of Krysenthiel and with any luck, the Guardian Senate will be reinstated with us as that august body's prefect. If we want it to survive past its first year, we'll have to have a fair and appraising eye in all matters requiring our judgement. To put it simply, we cannot turn a blind eye if your cousin oversteps himself."

"You don't think Alex is capable of that do you? And I doubt Diana would lead him astray."

"She's not the one who concerns me. You realize he's reinstated members of the deposed council, yes? What if they have hidden agendas aligned with Erynor? I understand they're most familiar with how Perrien was run over the past decades and their expertise will be invaluable, but who knows what sort of mischief they're capable of. Never take for granted the tongue of a trusted advisor who has the ear of a powerful leader."

"How much sway can a deposed councilor actually have? Alex isn't likely to forget their role while Perrien was aligned with the Erynien Empire."

Ellendren turned to invite Viren's opinion; the Guardian had been keeping a circumspect distance. "Would you like to educate the future Exalted Aryl or should I continue?"

"I believe you're doing just fine. I assume you're referring to Pelanu," Viren said.

"I was. You should tell the story though. I have to keep my mind clear for tonight."

"Very well. Pelanu Relien was a trusted advisor to Ei'denai Faerndryn Lorenthien. He repeatedly spoke against the hostile tactics of the Cyndinari elves before the Ceurendol War started with the sack of Septyl. It was clear that the only future Erynor vied for was a violent one. The members of the Guardian Senate fought among themselves with no agreed resolutions. As prefects, Faerndryn and Ithendryl could have directed the debate toward action, but Pelanu's voice stayed their hand and Septyl was sacked. Thousands of ei'ana were slaughtered at Septyl and countless verathn were repurposed for the Evil One's desires."

"So, to answer your question, a lot of harm can be done if the wrong person is whispering into Alex's ear," Ellendren said.

"I thought you didn't want to clog your mind?" Devlyn smirked.

Ellendren shot him a stern look. "You do realize the importance of this treaty, don't you?"

"Of course, I do, Elle. I'm just teasing you." He squeezed her hand.

"Forgive me; I know you do. Tonight has me worked up and I can't stop thinking about what it will be like when we return to the Luminari after this is all finalized."

"Still trying to figure out the best way to inform the aryls that we're married?"

"Yes. I should have made an announcement after returning from Ceurenyl, but it didn't feel right to do it alone."

"It'll be fine. It's not like we planned it or anything."

"That's what concerns me most. What if the Luminari perceive that negatively? What if they interpret our lack of preparation as a flaw in our own foresight and therefore an inability to rule?"

"Give Silvia an hour and she'll manage that and more." Devlyn pulled Ellendren into a kiss, not caring that Viren was even closer to them. "I love you. I love that I'm your spouse and that together we're the Aryl of Arenthyl. And to be honest, I couldn't have asked for a better wedding."

"It's not how I imagined my wedding." She smiled against his lips.

"Really? Because from the moment I met you, I only wanted one other person at my wedding."

"You are quite the flirt." Ellendren twisted her fingers in Devlyn's. Time seemed to suspend for a moment. It felt as though Aliel and Tariel had frozen time around them, allowing the fresh newlyweds to enjoy their imagined seclusion. That stopped as soon as it started when Viren coughed to remind them of the time.

"Already?" Devlyn growled, his forehead pressed against Ellendren's. She touched his cheek and they smiled at each other.

"It is why we are still here," Ellendren said as she pulled away. They continued to hold hands while walking through the garden and back into the castle. Every chandelier and candelabra had been lit along the grand corridor, the light blue marble on the walls polished to a bright sheen. Mirrors were inlaid in some of the marble behind the candelabras, brightening the space all the more. They came to the great gilded doors to the throne room. The doors were open wide and a pair of Evellion knights stood guard, the white eagle emblazoned on their blue tunics.

Evellion nobles circulated among Thellish dignitaries, Luminari and Eldinari aryls, and ei'ana councilors to both monarchs in the crowded room. The treaty papers that were to be signed lay on a small table directly in front of the throne.

Devlyn and Ellendren had sat in on many of the negotiation sessions. Rights and titles were to be maintained among Evellion's monarchy and nobility, along with a certain clause of Evellion's distinguished status among the reforged Thellion. While Alex was a direct descendent of Thellion, the Evellion monarchy had maintained its royal line from eldest son to eldest son through the millennia, all the way back to Thellion himself. As a reminder to the world, the royal house of Evellion still bore Thellion's name.

A clause that Devlyn had not expected was that Evellion was to maintain a majority of Elothkar's population. The people of Evellion had never ceased to lament the lost Thellish capital. It seemed they longed to return to Elothkar as strongly as the Luminari desired to return to Arenthyl.

After the dozens of meetings and lively discussions, it felt odd to see all the nobles assembled and the treaty of their design lying passively on the table. Devlyn and Ellendren took their place at the front of the Luminari representatives, Arlyn having saved their place. Other than the two monarchs, it appeared that everyone had arrived.

Princess Diana stood nearest the treaty. In truth, Diana *was* the treaty. The marriage between the first Thellish king in an age and the Princess of Evellion was the string that would tie the two kingdoms together better than any parchment could. Because of Evellion's archaic laws over succession, Diana, as a female, could not sit on Evellion's throne. Only a male heir could ascend to the Eagle Throne. Her betrothal to Alex was the next best thing for Evellion's nobility, who would prefer someone from Evellion ascending to the Winged Throne of Thellion. Diana's children would reign over the reunified Thellion. The Evellion nobility thought it a poetic justice that the strongest blood line of Thellion's descendants would marry the Thellish king.

Horns began to sound from the balcony and Queen Lara strode into her throne room, followed by a wet nurse carrying the two-week-old Amryian II, the future King of Evellion. This treaty would see him crowned king of a Thellish province. Lara took her place at one side of the table. The horns continued as Alex entered the throne room after her, taking his place at the table as he smiled at Diana. Both monarchs wore their respective crowns.

The horns stopped but the procession into the throne room continued as a royal scribe entered, holding a feathered quill on a plump pillow. He offered the quill to Lara first. With a single swish, she signed the treaty. Devlyn could feel the tension in the room. Even though it was a fair treaty and the Evellion court had agreed to it, they were still forfeiting their independence. They hadn't lost any battle and Alex wasn't a conqueror storming their city. Instead, they had willingly offered to join the renewed Thellion. The quill was returned to the pillow in a ceremonial show, and Alex took it next. He signed the treaty and the agreement was finalized. Evellion was now a province of Thellion.

The horns started anew in a jubilant tune. As the suzerain of Evellion, Alex had every right to sit on the Eagle Throne. His advisors had argued at length about it, most of them in favor. Alex looked to the throne and then to Lara and the infant, Amryian. "I vow to serve you and your people to the best of my ability." Alex bowed, then took Diana's hand and left the throne room. Lara followed and soon the entire room was empty. Colored lights flashed over the city, setting off the celebrations that would last throughout the night.

Devlyn and Ellendren met up with Wyn and Sanjin and made their way to a private room to meet with Alex and Diana. Now that the treaty was signed, Devlyn and Ellendren could no longer put off their return to the Luminari. They had not received any discouraging news since they had left, but they knew that Erynor would not sit idly by for much longer, especially while the Luminari were vulnerable.

Devlyn clapped Alex on the shoulder. "Thank the Light you decided to stay the entire time!" Alex said as he hugged Devlyn. "I had thought planning Everin's defense had been complicated, but I would prefer that over the past two weeks of politicking any day."

"I have to admit, you surprised me, Alex, or should I call you Alexander?" Ellendren teased.

"It seems that's all the ei'ana will address me as now, not that Velaria ever called me anything else. My own mother—forgive me, the *Queen Mother*—has even taken to calling me by my full name and I can't help thinking that every time she does, I've gotten into some sort of trouble!" The group laughed as Alex looked at the three elves. "So, how much longer will you remain in Everin?"

"We'll have to leave in the morning. We've been away for too long," Ellendren said.

"That's a shame, although it has been nice to spend so much time together again. It's almost like old times," Alex said.

"Almost. I can't say I miss sharing a room with you. Does Diana know about your snoring yet?" Devlyn chuckled.

Diana smiled but did not answer.

"What about yourself? Will you stay here much longer?" Ellendren asked.

"Perhaps a week or so. We have to find out what's going on in Cyril before dealing with the Daer on the Skrein coast."

"The Duke of Cyril's absence was particularly noticeable during the deliberations and signing. My uncle would never have stayed away from such an historic event," Diana said, concern heavy in her voice.

"What if you find that shadow elves are holding Cyril? How will you confront them?" Ellendren asked.

"Fendryl has agreed to join our escort with some of his star wardens. We're hoping the battle of Everin drew them all out though," Alex said, turning toward Wyn. "Are you certain you aren't able to join us?"

"I have put off returning to Stellantis for too long. I must deliver my account of Alethea's disappearance to my people."

"Well, you'll be missed," Alex said.

"I'll second that notion," Devlyn said, not looking forward to returning to the Luminari without Wyn. The Luminari aryls were bound to be as much of a challenge as the twelve shadow elves he had fought in Everin. Still, twelve seemed like a small number, especially in comparison to at least ten times that number who had sieged Myrium. Had Erynor truly only devoted a dozen shadow elves to raze Everin? Were there more holding out in the north somewhere, biding their time to strike? Devlyn tried to not worry about Erynor's next promised assault. Moving on to happier thoughts, he asked, "Has a date been scheduled for the wedding?"

"The Evellion nobility would prefer to see us wed at once. But we've agreed that a ceremony in Elothkar would be most appropriate," Diana said.

"Does any of it still stand? Elothkar had been abandoned even before the elves migrated from the skylands," Ellendren said.

"Aewen led me to believe that the palace does. Who knows what sort of condition we'll find it in though. As for the state of the rest of the city, we'll just have to go there and find out," Alex said.

"It's those unknown factors that make determining a date rather difficult. We might find the city as though no one has left it or it could be a pile of crumbling ruins. A number of builders and architects have agreed to make the journey. Some of them claim to still hold the traditions of those old days—knowledge passed down through the ages. I'm a little skeptical, but their work here in Everin speaks for itself," Diana said.

"Speaking of reclaiming cities, Alex leaned forward. "Do you think you'll really be able to remove the Shroud?"

"We have no reason to think otherwise," Ellendren said, more confidently than Devlyn felt.

"I'm curious about this Shroud. Is anyone actually familiar with its origins and how it came to be?" Sanjin asked.

"It's somehow linked to the Void and was brought about by those who are now Deurghol. Legend says they only became Deurghol by bringing the Shroud into existence. Aside from that, we know precious little about it," Devlyn said.

"Curious. I would like to see what it hides before I return to Karithel. I too have been away from my people for too long." Sanjin gave Alex an appraising look, making Devlyn wonder if they had some sort of agreement. Had Alex agreed to travel to Charren on a military campaign? Surely, he wasn't considering that while the Erynien Empire had its clutches over Eklean.

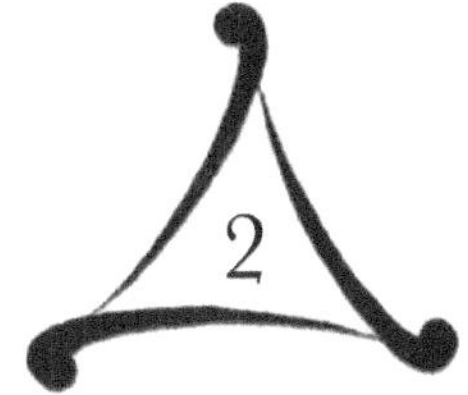

SPRINGTIME FÊTE

Devlyn and Ellendren had bid their farewells to the Evellion and Thellish courts, wishing them all the best in the trying times ahead. Devlyn had enjoyed spending time with his cousin, but Ellendren was right to be concerned over how long he had been away from the Luminari.

The Luminari who had come to Everin stood in a circle with their hands joined. Once Devlyn bonded with Aliel, he sought out the camp. The Luminari had moved since he had left them; the camp was now much closer to the Shroud. He fully believed that the only reason he had been able to shift there before was because Ellendren had been there, serving as a beacon for his mind to latch onto. She was here with him now, holding his hand, Arlyn on her other side. They did not have time to travel back to the Luminari camp in any other way. And the longer they were away, the longer the Shroud would remain. Devlyn had to get back and begin probing it with lumenys. The Luminari elves' only hope to survive the migration from their faded home along the Illumined Wood would be to reach a defensive position from where they could stand against the Erynien Empire. If Erynor's forces attacked them while they were vulnerable, there might not be any Luminari elves left to take back Krysenthiel.

After taking a final look at Everin's castle gardens, lingering briefly on the slender marble tower rising above the rest of the castle, Devlyn closed his eyes. He brought forth the memory of Ellendren at the Luminari camp and willed himself and the others linked to him back east.

Shifting to just outside the camp, snow-covered plains greeted them. Northern Sorenthil was noticeably warmer than it had been in Everin. Tufts of grass had broken through the snow after a longer than usual winter. In the near distance, tents stood in the circular layout favored by the elves. Liara, the red dragon, soared over their heads. They'd made it back! Devlyn let out what he hoped was an inaudible sigh. He didn't want the others to think that he wasn't confident about shifting.

Three months had passed since he had left his people. Three months since he had first told Ellendren that he would return as quickly as possible. He hadn't imagined that he would be gone for a quarter of a year or even considered that any number of issues could have arisen while he was gone. Just thinking of what the other elves were likely saying about his prolonged absence made his stomach turn upside down. Without their future aryl and Phaedryn, the Luminari were ripe fodder for an attack. It didn't matter that a red dragon and a draelyn scouted the sky or that the last contingent of Guardian knights had come to them. All that mattered was that Devlyn Lorenthien had left them to go assist their allies, leaving his own people with only canvas tents and packed snow drifts to defend themselves.

As he prepared to withdraw from Aliel, the phoenix stopped him.

They need to see us like this.

You're certain? Devlyn conveyed. It felt odd to show off; something inside him repulsed the idea.

They need to see who you are.

Even though he was uncomfortable with the idea, Devlyn remained bonded to Aliel in their Phaedryn form. The camp was not far from where he stood with the others. The guards and watchmen would have noticed their arrival by now; his luminous form was difficult to hide, especially with nothing but snow and dense clouds beyond the camp. He would be a flare. He moved toward the camp beside Ellendren, the rest of the party falling in behind him. He would have liked to take Ellendren's hand, but for now, their marriage was still a secret.

In the distance, the Shroud over Krysenthiel remained, looming. Devlyn was no closer to figuring out how to remove it than that single occasion when he had extended all his energy so long ago, barely piercing a hole large enough for one elf to walk in a circle.

The sound of horns filled what had been a still evening as the group approached the camp. Lifting his spirit, the tune filled him with hope and courage as it permeated his body, reaching his heart and making his skin tingle. Not expecting a fanfare, Devlyn looked over the camp, to assure himself that they were in fact Luminari horns and not in the possession of an enemy announcing its presence. But horns with this beautiful, uplifting quality that inspired him to face any difficulty could not belong to an enemy, especially not to the Erynien Empire.

A wall of packed snow and ice shielded the encampment; although it wouldn't stand much of a chance against fire or giants, it stood twice as tall as himself and looked sturdy enough for a decent defense.

Two Guardian knights stood in the opened gate. They wore armor similar to Viren's, glittering in the torchlight. A third Guardian knight came out of the gate. She stood in the center wearing a confident expression, her hands clasped behind her back, her shoulders squared. The sword at her side was clearly a verathn.

"Ei'denai Lorenthien," she greeted them, her hand raised to her chest as she bowed. The metallic ribbons of her armor moved flawlessly with her body. "I am Jeanne Darkel, First of the Guardians, or as we have come to be known in this age, Eklean knights. Welcome back, Ei'terel."

Raising his fist to his chest, Devlyn bowed, missing Ellendren's shock. "It is a pleasure to meet you, Jeanne. I would very much appreciate, among other things, to learn a fuller history of your order. As a Lorenthien, I feel my lack of knowledge shames me and the family that came before me." Devlyn's head remained inclined as he spoke.

"You are kind to say so. I knew much would be forgotten, but I never dared to believe the extent would be so wide and complete."

There was no proper manner to respond to that statement. Devlyn felt as though he had just admitted that he was an idiot.

"Have there been any difficulties in or around the camp?" Devlyn asked, raising his head and steering the conversation away from his ignorance.

"Unprecedentedly quiet," Jeanne replied. "I know we are within Sorenthil and near Krysenthiel, but that the Erynien Empire has not pushed an offensive is unlike their usual tactics."

"Would they fortify their positions in the south?" Ellendren asked.

"I don't expect it," Jeanne replied.

"What's our best chance at holding them off?" Devlyn asked, his anxiety rising at the specter of an impending attack from the Erynien Empire on the horizon.

"Arenthyl."

Removing the Shroud and reaching Arenthyl had always been the goal, but if he failed, the entire population of Luminari elves would once again be at the mercy of Erynor, forced into slavery.

One of the knights guarding the gate stepped forward and bowed to Devlyn. "Ei'denai, I am Elayne Thenrel. I had the pleasure of meeting your brother in the temple several years ago. I'm sorry to hear that he's fallen captive."

"Thank you, Elayne," Devlyn said, unprepared to think of his brother as a prisoner again. "That would make you the other Guardian knight who had left the citadel with the news of Aliel's hatching."

"That's correct. I trust Viren has been more than a protector." Elayne smiled as she nodded to Viren.

"It's good to see you again, Elayne," Viren said.

"As for your brother, I would not concern yourself too much; Jaerol will not sleep until Liam is rescued," Elayne said.

Devlyn managed a weak smile as Elayne stepped back to her post.

He kept his thoughts to himself while Jeanne led him and the other elves into the camp—well, Devlyn thought they remained private, other than to Ellendren. He knew Viren was aware of others' thoughts, and if he was capable of it, the chances of Jeanne Darkel having that same sensitivity were quite high.

Devlyn eventually withdrew from Aliel and the two phoenix fluttered away to fly with Liara. As the elves moved further into the encampment, a gathering of elves, many of them aryls both high and minor, approached. Naesiv and Valerie Aerquin stood near the center, holding a bouquet of flowers; greenery dribbled down from it to the ground. All the aryls held similar arrangements.

"What do you think this is about?" Devlyn whispered as he leaned close to Ellendren.

"Those are matrimonial flowers. Either they intend to see us married here and now, or they've discovered our secret. And considering how Jeanne addressed us, they know." Ellendren took Devlyn's hand as they bravely continued forward. The aryls who had come to Everin and had now returned with Devlyn and Ellendren, muttered confusedly about this reception. Devlyn and Ellendren had agreed to keep their unexpected wedding in the Empyrean Sphere and their new status as the Lorenthien aryl a secret until they could inform all the Luminari aryls together.

"How could they have found out? Not that I'm upset about it…"

"It must have been Kaela. She somehow knew the moment I came back from Ceurenyl with Tariel."

Valerie broke from the crowd with a broad smile. "What incredible news you've kept from us. Your sister has kept us busy these past weeks after she told us you two had been secretly married. How has this come to be? Surely, you know there was no reason to be married in private. You both have the full support of the aryls and people. A larger public wedding would have been a blessing in these dark times."

"Agreed." Silvia stepped forward with her own bouquet, although the way she held it seemed to indicate that she was convinced it was poisonous. "What reason did you have for getting married away from us? Your late mother and father would have never permitted it."

More aryls stepped forth, all with questions tinted with a hint of accusation for the young and newly married aryl. Despite Devlyn's presence, the aryls directed their concerns to Ellendren, as they clearly believed she should have known better.

"Respected aryls," Ellendren started loudly, her cheeks flushed by the unexpected onslaught. For someone who prepared for every outcome, this had caught her off guard. Devlyn knew that she had been thinking of how to reveal the news to the Luminari but they had both thought they had more time, at least until the following morning. Attending to Evellion and Thellion's treaty had left little time to consider the politics at home. Surely, they wouldn't have to explain themselves the instant they returned to the Luminari camp. "We are happy to answer all your questions, but I am sure there is a better place than on our camp's outskirts."

Valerie nodded. "Of course, Ei'terel." Devlyn caught the title this time, signifying Ellendren's status as a married elf and head of her house. "You understand our impatience though, as this is quite irregular. We merely wanted some details before escorting you and Devlyn to your delayed fête. The question on all our minds is how delayed is this fête?"

"Yes, when was the joyous and *private* occasion?" Silvia asked.

"A party? Is there really time for that? What about the Shroud?" Ellendren blinked in surprise.

"The Shroud will still be there tomorrow. The Lorenthien aryl will not be introduced to the Luminari without proper customs being upheld," Fyona Lauriel said.

Kaela pushed through the aryls with her bouquet of matrimonial flowers. She seemed to be the only elf present who was smiling ear to ear. "We talked about this, Fyona. You were supposed to escort them to their tents so they can prepare for the festivities." She turned on the aryls.

"Questions can wait for later; tonight is for dancing!"

Before either Devlyn or Ellendren could stage a protest or answer the simplest question of exactly when they had been married, they were pulled away from each other as the women dragged Ellendren in one direction and the men ushered Devlyn away in another. Kaela latched her arm around Ellendren's to make sure she didn't run off.

The men cared little about Kaela's insistence on holding off any questions, for once she'd disappeared around a bend, the men renewed the onslaught. Each question had an air of condemnation to it. Secret weddings were particularly intolerable among the Luminari and it seemed that after spending the whole winter traveling away from the faded Lucillia, they all desired some reason to celebrate. Tensions were high and the Luminari had agreed that they would not be denied a wedding fête.

The elven lords pulled Devlyn into a tent and pushed him toward a privacy screen in the corner where Lyren waited with a change of garments. What Devlyn could see of it was spun in intricate, lacy designs, as though only a spider could weave such a spectacular thing. Devlyn immediately recognized them as wedding garments. "But we're already married," he protested as he was shoved behind the screen.

"Either you change your clothing on your own, or we'll see to it," Therrin said, amusement in his voice.

The gathered men laughed. Traditions would be upheld, and the most sacred of those traditions were the customs connected to weddings. "You'll have to forgive us, Ei'denai, but this is as unavoidable as the sun rising in the east. We might not yet know all the details of how you two were married, but we will always stop what we're doing to celebrate a new marriage, especially when that marriage involves the future Exalted Aryl of Krysenthiel," Kyiel said.

"But what about the camp's defenses? Surely there are more important matters that we need to see to," Devlyn said as he changed his clothes, placing the pouch with the lucilliae in an inner pocket he was pleased to find included in the special tunic. Devlyn mouthed "thank you" to Lyren, who smiled in gratitude.

"The Guardian knights and that red dragon are seeing to our safety. The First of the Guardians insisted the party take place. Now, do you intend to tell us the manner of your marriage?" Kyiel asked, receiving a round of agreement from the other men.

Realizing that he was powerless in this situation, he abandoned any further objections and allowed Lyren to help him change as he told the other ei'denai about his and Ellendren's experience in the Empyrean Sphere and the seraph declaring them wed. Small flowers were placed in his hair and all the gathered men hugged Devlyn one by one before he was led out. The whole affair left him feeling uneasy, unsure about his role in it all.

The men ushered Devlyn through the maze of tents until they reached a large clearing. Devlyn's breath caught in his chest. Tiny lights sparkled in the air just above the grass like morning dew. Flowers of every sort had been woven into a latticework above the clearing, crafted specifically for garland. Hundreds of elves filled the space, all smiling and laughing, putting the past months of hardship behind them for now.

Somewhere, a harp sent beautiful, delicate sounds into the air. The gathered crowd cleared a path and his remaining breath was stolen away when he caught sight of Ellendren, her eyes sparkling in the light. She wore a wedding garment similar to his. She too had flowers in her hair, woven into slender braids. She smiled at him from across the clearing and his knees quivered. The women ushered her forward, and his feet felt heavy as he moved toward her, every other sight or sound suspended. The clouds blocking out the sun could not block the inner light of Ellendren Lorenthien.

"You're beautiful." He tried to say something else—something more, but his mind had been wiped blank.

"As are you," Ellendren said.

Devlyn forgot about the gathered elves and leaned in to kiss Ellendren, causing the crowd to cheer, drowning out the harp. When the music came back, Devlyn bowed to Ellendren and extended his hand. He had never been so bold in front of others, least of all the Luminari aryls. He supposed that didn't matter anymore. He and Ellendren were married. They were the Lorenthien aryl; the Aryl of Arenthyl and future Exalted Aryl of Krysenthiel.

Ellendren took his hand and they began to dance to the tune of the harp. They twirled about the clearing, various elves congratulating them as their dance carried them across the space. Devlyn felt Aliel and Tariel replicating their dance above, contributing their own mystical light to the sky. Devlyn and Ellendren gazed upward to watch, their well-wishers ooh-ing and aah-ing at the sight of the phoenix.

While the music continued, Devlyn and Ellendren were guided to a space beneath one of the pergolas wrapped in garlands and flowers. "Kaela organized this entire party for us."

"How did she manage all this?" Devlyn asked.

"I learned at a young age to never underestimate my sister." Ellendren laughed, holding his hand. "She also asked for Wyn and wanted to know when he was coming back."

"Oh, did she?" Devlyn paused, remembering the last time he had seen Wyn and Kaela together. "They did seem cozy with each other, didn't they?"

"Perceptive of you," she said with a mischievous twinkle in her eye.

"What's that supposed to mean?" Devlyn squeezed her hand.

"Oh, nothing. Did you tell the ei'denai the manner of our marriage?"

"They pulled it out of me," Devlyn said, not quite ready to switch topics. "They wouldn't let me leave until I did."

"The ei'terel were the same, even with Kaela there. They said if they hadn't approved of the manner we were wed, they would have insisted on another ceremony, which, incredibly, was all prepared."

The gathered elves continued to dance even as a line formed to greet and congratulate the Lorenthien aryl. In no time, Devlyn's cheeks ached from smiling.

His smile vanished when he saw who stood next in the receiving line. He had hoped he would never see her again after he'd been imprisoned in the box that had severed him from Aliel and the erendinth. But there she stood, wearing more jewelry than he had ever seen on a single person. Only dwarves were more weighed down by gold.

"Queen Alesei," Ellendren acknowledged the woman curtly.

"My dear Ellendren. A pleasure to see you again. I believe the last time was at the Lucillian palace—your parents were hosting a banquet of some sort."

"To what do we owe the pleasure?" Devlyn wanted to cut the reminiscence short.

"And people wonder why no one likes the Luminari. There was once a time where even your people would have invited foreign monarchs to their wedding."

"You locked me in box to offer as a betrothal gift to Erynor."

"And this futile war might have ended if I had been successful. But no, you're far too content to allow the bloodshed to continue."

"What do you want?" Devlyn asked, trying to control his anger at the Tieli queen who would fashion herself empress.

"To congratulate you, of course. Is it not customary for royalty to bear gifts to fellow royal blood on such happy occasions?"

"And what sort of *gift* have you brought?" Devlyn asked, expecting a viper to snap at his neck.

"There's no reason for that sort of tone. It's a shame your mother couldn't attend your wedding. Perhaps she would have taught you better manners."

"What do you know of my mother?"

"Only that Erynor tires of her. He knows now who she truly is."

"Where is she?" Devlyn growled.

"If you would like to see her alive, you will abandon this folly here.

The Shroud is dear to our emperor. He will not be pleased if you destroy her. He might have the need to destroy someone you care for if you do."

"Where is my mother?" Devlyn leapt forward and gripped the neckline of the Tieli queen's gown.

"You will never see her again if you threaten me," Alesei shrieked in return, her voice deadly. "You have until Meridephaen to deliver yourself to Broid."

Devlyn hadn't noticed the minum accompanying Alesei until she turned to leave. The Tieli queen and the minum disappeared through a seguian. *Was that Jax?* he thought. Few of the gathered elves realized what had happened. Ellendren gripped Devlyn's hand. "Oh, Devlyn."

Devlyn swallowed hard, tucking away his virulent emotions. Leaving this fête was not possible, but it was the last place he wanted to be.

Devlyn paced inside the tent he now shared with Ellendren. Although he was relieved to have finally found a moment of quiet, away from everyone who wanted to celebrate the Lorenthien aryl's marriage, he was feeling an anxiety that had nothing to do with Alesei's appearance.

Although their tent had a single, although roomy, bed, Devlyn couldn't think of that just yet. They had thought they would keep their marriage a secret for a while, so had yet to share a room, let alone a mattress, since they had needed to uphold appearances before making their announcement. He didn't want to think of what would be expected of him as Ellendren's husband. He certainly wanted what that involved, yet he was still quite nervous about it.

Their shared bed didn't matter right now. He had been reminded that Erynor still had his mother. In a single breath, he had been relieved to hear that she was alive, but also tortured at the knowledge that she was Erynor's prisoner.

He went to the folding desk and picked up the creased picture of his family. His mother looked lovingly at the toddler version of himself.

Those two figures in the portrait were locked in an eternal gaze, just as the artist had captured them, while the other three figures looked toward the artist. Devlyn's mind went black as he looked at the image. His mother was beautiful and her eyes were warm and kind. How could anyone imprison her, accuse her of killing her husband, and then allow the Erynien Emperor take her into his clutches? How could anyone wish harm on Evellyn Lorenthien?

"Devlyn?" Ellendren spoke from behind him. He had lost track of time and had no idea how long he had been staring at the picture.

"I'm here, Elle." He turned to her and saw that she was still dressed for the celebration.

"Oh, Dev." She pulled him toward a small settee, and they sat side by side, turned toward each other while she rubbed his back, offering whatever encouragement she could.

"I'm not sure what to do, Elle. You heard Alesei—you heard what Erynor would do to her if we brought the Shroud down."

"I think we should take a step back and analyze what she said."

"Do you think she was lying?"

"I think she's trying to catch you in another trap. She knows she won't be able to ensnare you like she did the first time—abducting someone from a military camp is quite different than taking a sleeping person from a stone room in a castle filled with secret passages."

"So, she's baiting me. What difference does it make? They have my mother."

"Erynor has your mother, not Alesei. Tiel is part of the Erynien Empire, but Erynor was never known to trust non-Cyndinari as emissaries."

"What are you suggesting? Pretend that Alesei never came here? Pretend that she didn't just threaten to have my mother killed?"

"Meridephaen is two and half months away. We have time to figure this out. We will figure this out. I promise."

Devlyn dropped his head onto Ellendren's shoulder and closed his eyes while she continued to rub his back. They sat like that for a while until Viren cleared his throat outside the tent.

"Ei'denai, Ei'terel. Arlyn is here," Viren said through the canvas.

"Send him in." Devlyn composed himself but remained sitting beside Ellendren on the settee.

"I'm sorry to interrupt," Arlyn said, bowing. "I wanted to let you know that those nearby—no small number—overheard Alesei." Devlyn didn't reply. He didn't know what there was to say. "I came here because I thought we could talk about your mother—my sister."

Devlyn looked up at that, wondering if Arlyn had a plan. "Okay."

"You should know that Evellyn is the bravest elf I know. She'd look Lucillia and Ithendryl in the eye and rebuke them if she thought they were in the wrong. I'm not saying either ever were, but I think it's important that you be aware of your mother's character." Arlyn paused to collect his thoughts, smiling at a memory.

"She wouldn't want me to hand myself over for her sake."

"She would not. She would never forgive herself if any harm came to you on her account."

"So, we just leave her with Erynor?"

"I recommend that we find another way to bring her back to us while going through with our plan to remove the Shroud. It's what she would want."

"What if Erynor hurts her more?"

"Evellyn would not hold her life as dearer than the entirety of the Luminari population—not even over a single elf, especially that of her child."

"Right. I need to get some air." Devlyn threw Ellendren and Arlyn a weak smile before leaving the tent. Viren followed him as he walked away and Aliel fluttered somewhere above with Tariel.

REGRET

Shivering in the mountain chill and knee-deep snow, Jaerol swiped at the icy tears that rolled down his cheeks as he gazed at the sight of Gwilnor Academy rising from the city of Ceurenyl for the first time in weeks.

It had been an agonizing wait for the last stragglers of the planned escape to reach the final checkpoint by the tapestry that hid a secret passageway. It led to the cavern where the ei'ana who remained true to Gwilnor had taken sanctuary. The escapees had had a few harrowing incidents—the group he'd led had been infiltrated by two Tenebrae ei'ana—but most had made it safely, and he had kept hoping that Liam and his group would join them, even as Mother Selenya insisted that it was time to leave. When it became obvious that Liam had been captured, Jaerol had desperately wanted to rescue him, and had argued to stay behind. Gwilnor needed him—Liam needed him. Selenya had told him that Septyl needed him too. Other than the Eldinari who had been part of the escape from the castle, Jaerol was the most experienced kien wielder. Balance between kien and kiara wielders had to be reestablished if they were to survive this war. The events at Gwilnor had delayed the eventual return of Balance. The Tenebrae School did not want Balance to return among the ei'ana. Erynor did not want a strengthened Septyl and had successfully sabotaged the ei'ana. He would ensure that they remained weak and divided, barely capable of reaching half their potential.

For the good of Septyl, Jaerol had conceded to Selenya and had left Gwilnor Academy and Liam in the Tenebrae School's custody. He had left the cavern in a defeated daze and had continued in that state, following the other escapees through the mountain passes. As though Liam's captivity wasn't enough to bear, Velaria was also missing. She had been the one who had put the events into motion to get as many students and ei'ana out of the castle as possible, but, as Jaerol had learned from Selenya, she had sacrificed her own freedom to do so.

When Jaerol stopped to look at Ceurenyl in the distance, Trethien bumped into him from behind. "Sorry about that; I was trying to shield my eyes from the wind and snow." Trethien looked up and saw what Jaerol was looking at and patted his back in consolation. "He'll be okay, Jaerol."

"I left him. I promised I never would."

"We'll get him back; we'll get everyone back."

"What if we're too late? It's not just the Tenebrae in the castle, there are shadow elves too."

"I know and it won't be too late. Besides, not all the Eldinari came with us. Fyreh and Myrah are still there. They won't let anyone be killed." Trethien made to continue walking but paused when Jaerol didn't budge, staring at Gwilnor's towers rising in the distance.

Velaria had urged the other Chairs to flee Gwilnor and make for the palace-city of Septyl. She was convinced that the Shroud would soon be a thing of the past and reclaiming the city of the ei'ana was their best chance at defeating Erynor and confronting the Evil One if he returned. Jaerol agreed with her thinking but still could not fight the feeling that he had made the wrong choice. Septyl very well might need him in restoring the balance between kien and kiara wielders, but Selenya was wrong; Liam needed him more. As he looked over the mountain valleys and river and at Gwilnor Academy, he knew in his heart what he had to do.

The sense of wrongness resonated in his chest and as Jaerol stood there gazing at the castle, Trethien saw the determination on his expression. "You're going back, aren't you?"

"I have to."

"I'm coming too then. Anything to get out of this cold—it's freezing." Trethien seemed to force his jaw shut to stop the clattering teeth that his shivers were causing. "Will you tell Selenya? She seems to have taken a liking to you." Despite his effort, his teeth clattered anyway and he rubbed his arms to warm them.

"Tell Selenya what?" Danielle, one of the student wielders asked. She and Fiona were Trethien's friends and had approached while they'd been talking.

"Nothing." Jaerol glared at Trethien as though to will his lips sealed.

"Not the most convincing. You do realize that Fyreh was actively trying to awaken our inner senses, yes? And I'm sure you know what that entails." Danielle smiled and batted her eyelashes at Trethien. "Don't make me bring your fib to light, Trethien."

"Might as well tell them. It'll be pretty clear soon enough anyway," Trethien said.

"Fine," Jaerol said. "I'm going back to save Liam."

"*We're* going back to save Liam. And the others of course," Trethien said.

"Well, in the name of returning Balance, you'll need some kiara wielders in your company. Did you think you could be successful with just the two of you?" Fiona scoffed.

"I was hoping to be successful with only myself." Jaerol crossed his arms and held back a curse for Trethien.

"Even more foolish," Danielle said. "So, what's the plan?"

"Get out of the cold so we can stop shivering and actually think clearly again," Trethien said.

"Well, we should start by informing the Chairs. They won't approve, but I don't think they'll stop us either. Paurel and Selenya both think highly of you; I doubt they could deny you even if they wanted to," Danielle said.

"We are still student wielders though; they could deny us to their hearts' content and still be in the right," Fiona said.

"True, but they worry about Velaria—how could they not? When do you intend to head back to the castle?" Danielle asked.

"Preferably yesterday," Jaerol said.

"Well, if that's the case, we should speak to them now. I think we're done trekking through the mountains for today. I doubt we'll find a better camping spot than here," Fiona said, and she waited for Jaerol to move toward the Chairs.

"Fine." Jaerol turned away from the picturesque view of the castle. Despite how lovely the castle appeared in the snow, it felt wrong, for the frigid weather had lingered longer than usual this year. The snow that was falling should have turned to rain by now and while the ground might not have started to thaw further up in the mountains where the Gwilnor refugees currently were, the weather gave no sign of relenting.

Fiona and Danielle led the way around small clusters of students, ei'ana, and knights. No one was moving any longer, all of them too cold and too tired to continue their journey toward Septyl. At their current pace, it would take years before they reached the palace-city of the Ei'ana. By the time they reached Septyl, the war with the Erynien Empire might well be over with a large population of ei'ana lost in the mountains and unable to support the free peoples of Eklean. Velaria was right in wanting to reach Septyl, but Jaerol worried that they might never make it. Eklean needed the ei'ana more than an abandoned city did.

Jaerol groaned inwardly as their little group reached the Chairs. He had hoped that he might only have to talk to one of them and im-mediately take his leave. Instead, other than Velaria, all the Chairs were gathered in conference. Fiona and Danielle fell back and allowed Jaerol to approach the leaders of the Ei'ana.

"Ah, Jaerol," Paurel said when Jaerol cleared his throat to get their attention.

He bowed before speaking and kept his eyes lowered as he did. "I have to go back." With the words, the weight he had felt since first leaving the cavern beneath the castle finally lifted, confirming the rightness of this decision. Leaving Liam behind had been a mistake, one that he would never forgive himself for if anything bad happened to him.

"We've already spoken of this. I thought the matter closed," Selenya said.

"We have, and your arguments for me staying with you are logical and sound. But I cannot leave Liam with the Tenebrae—I cannot leave him with Razcul. Razcul—Danyol—will hurt Liam in order to hurt me."

"Razcul is the shadow elf that was disguised as an Eldinari, yes; the one assisting Yvonne's art of wielding class?" Loretta asked.

"That's right. He's practically rotting from the inside out from all the souls he's stolen over the years," Phendien said.

"Why would a shadow elf want to hurt you more than others?" Agnelle asked.

"We were classmates at the Imperium. We've…never gotten along. It's been worse since he found out that I didn't take Kiron's soul to become a shadow elf myself." Jaerol waited in the silence that followed. The Chairs knew of his past but that didn't mean they were any more comfortable with someone who had been raised in the heart of the Erynien Empire and had attended its most prestigious school, the very school that trained shadow elves.

"Do you think your mission has a chance of success?" Paurel asked.

"I'd rather fail than not try."

"A shame you're set on becoming an Azurelle; you'd make a fine Vyoletryn." Paurel smiled and the skin around her eyes crinkled.

"Thank you, Mother Paurel." Jaerol blushed at the rare compliment from the Purple Eagle.

"Forgive me, but we're not actually considering giving this fool's errand our blessing, are we? Returning to the castle in its current state is madness! You might as well hand yourself over to this Razcul or Hannah and be tossed in a cell with your lover," Melanie said.

"Peace, Melanie," Agnelle said. "We all know how much stronger love is than hate."

"That might be so." Selenya had been quiet for a time, but Jaerol felt her eyes on him. "I agree with Melanie though. Returning to the castle in its current state is an unnecessary sacrifice." Jaerol felt his heart plummet at the declaration.

"What do you recommend?" Paurel asked.

Jaerol looked between the White Owl and the Purple Eagle, confused. Did he miss something? What else could Selenya have meant? He looked pleadingly at the Chair of Albien, hopeful that she had a plan.

"Exactly what I said. If you hope for any success, you must wait to enter the castle until its state has changed."

"How will it change if we're here? Who has the ability to oust the Tenebrae?" Melanie asked.

"I believe the young and indecisive Kevn Weyvien is currently residing at the Temple of Ceur with the ei'ceuril. Go to him and tell him to research an ei'ceuril named Benedetto. An answer might be hidden in his diaries."

Cold air filtered into Velaria's lungs. She tried to warm the air by wielding ignys, but whenever she attempted it, someone would come into her cell and strike her over the head. She'd wake hours later, still cold, and with an aching head. Velaria couldn't recall the last time in recorded history that Gwilnor had used these cells. A school simply did not need a dungeon.

Weak and fatigued, Velaria shivered as she wrapped her arms around her bare skin. The shock she'd felt that first morning when she'd realized that while she had been unconscious, her leafy appendages had been snipped from her body still stung. The pruning had not been gentle; even in the dim light of her cell, she could see the fresh scars left behind by the knives they had used. They'd also shaved her head since they could not remove the flowers from her hair properly. Not that there were any mirrors here, but she could feel the bristly and uneven stubble of her hair.

Feeling as though she had disgraced Tera by her failure to prevent others from removing her gift, she thought back to the mystical night in the Illumined Wood when she had found a dress unlike any other. Shortly after Velaria had started her novitiate, she had entered the comforting embrace of a willow tree and found the gift graced to her by Tera.

Velaria had never felt opposed to Uriel, shepherd of the enthiel who guided the elves, but she did not trust the enthiel of the Cyndinari, Meridiel, who was known to have abandoned Anaweh long ago. Instead, ever since she had been a small girl growing up on the edge of the Illumined Wood, she had felt a certain affinity for Tera. The anadel had not appeared physically, but their bond had been cemented when Tera had named her as her own with the gift of the leafy dress. Shortly after that, she had met Yelaris.

At least two months had passed since she had been tossed into this cell, although she was only guessing at the amount of time. There was no certain way of telling the passing of days let alone weeks. She knew it had been Uraen when Devlyn had returned to Gwilnor but since she'd been captured, she had lost all track of time. She did her best to keep a mental tally of the days that had passed. If she had enough energy, she might be able to calculate which day of the week it was, and perhaps even the date.

Velaria wasn't the only captive. Fewer than half of the students had escaped Gwilnor that night, something the Tenebrae enjoyed reminding her of. Most of the ones who had been caught had simply been sent back to their dormitories, but any knight or ei'ana who had been part of the escape had been tossed into Gwilnor's cells. With the intent of crushing her spirit, the Tenebrae had bragged about the failed escape. Velaria had no idea who the other captives were or how many were down here in the other cells. Asking her jailers about specific knights and ei'ana would only give them more details about what had happened that night. She only knew that Liam was a special prisoner of Razcul, because the shadow elf liked to gloat about it, in hopes of luring Jaerol into a rescue mission. The shadow elf didn't have to lure Jaerol into anything. Velaria knew without a hint of doubt that Jaerol would rescue Liam, and if they were lucky, rid Eklean of Razcul.

She had yet to discover whether the other Chairs of Septyl had also been captured. She held on to her hope that they were safe and far from the Tenebrae. Velaria hoped they had heeded her and escaped the castle and were keeping the students who had managed to escape with them safe. Before she had been knocked unconscious, she had told them to make their way for Septyl. By the time they reached the abandoned palace-city, the Shroud should be gone.

Shivering uncontrollably in the cold, she held onto herself. She would not cry, not here, not as their prisoner. She was the Blue Dragon, the Chair of Azurelle. She would not give the Tenebrae the satisfaction of seeing her defeated, even if she felt that she was. Her hand stopped at her side, just below her ribcage where there was something more than the goosebumps that dotted her skin. Her fingers brushed against it. It was warm and it took her back to the Illumined Wood and her thoughts returned to Mother Tera.

The dark cell limited her vision, so with her fingers she outlined the shape of a tiny leaf, so small that it would look like nothing more than a green stem, sprouting from her side. She hoped all would grow back in time, just as she knew her hair would. She cared less about her red hair than Tera's gift though.

Rusty hinges creaked and a flood of light washed into the room blocked only by a silhouette standing in the doorway. Velaria felt the woman embrace the erendinth, filling her and making Velaria thirst for that touch as well. A small globe appeared from nothing, casting light on Hannah's aging face.

"How long before professing your Counsels did you abandon Azurelle? Were you ever truly one of us?" Velaria asked, surprised with her own courage in speaking to this woman.

"Do not presume you have the privilege to question my motives." Hannah held a knife.

"What harm is it?" Velaria asked, hearing the plea in her voice. How many had forsaken Septyl?

Hannah smacked Velaria hard across the face. "I would love to find out." Hannah showed her teeth as she smiled down on Velaria.

"What do you want?"

"It's been quite some time since the students and ei'ana have seen one of their illustrious Chairs. There's to be a mandatory dinner tonight and your presence is requested."

"By whom?"

"Mine, the Chancellor of Gwilnor Academy, of course."

"You are neither chancellor nor an Azurelle. You shame us all."

Hannah smacked her again, but Velaria refused to let out any sound. She had suffered under this woman's disdain her entire life. It had started out as a simple prejudice because Velaria was a Cyndinari elf, but later, it evolved into a jealous hatred, particularly when Velaria had been named the Chair of Azurelle, something Hannah had long desired.

"It's time for those here to know who is in charge of Septyl. If you so much as speak a single lie this evening, you will never part your pretty lips again. Understood?" Hannah asked, her grandmotherly voice almost sweet and comforting.

Velaria didn't respond but held Hannah's glare. Hannah spun around and two men came into the cell as she left and pulled Velaria to her feet. They pulled her out and dumped her into a tub of freezing water, which did produce a yelp from Velaria. The two men, likely kien wielders who had helped overthrow the castle, scrubbed stiff brushes against her skin, bathing her for the first time since she had been captured. Velaria looked in horror at the bath water as the muck and dirt came off while her skin was rubbed red. If she had not been so exhausted, it would have been embarrassing to be bathed by men. But Velaria Treyven had suffered worse than shame these past months.

"Chancellor," one of them said. "There's some sort of leaf on her."

Velaria flushed at her stupidity. She should have tried to conceal it somehow.

Hannah came over and lifted her knife. "Where?"

The man pointed to Velaria's side where the tiny leaf had just started to sprout. In a single quick slice, Hannah severed it. Hannah watched it float to the surface of the water and plucked it up and twirled it between her fingers before crushing it.

Once bathed, the two men dried her off, their hands lingering on her body longer than anyone should uninvited. They dressed her in a fine blue dress and roughly pinned her brooch to her chest. She looked down at the crest of Azurelle, saddened by something that had always brought her pride. Now, she felt that she had failed and the Tenebrae would use her as a puppet.

TAINTED

The morning after the Luminari had celebrated his and Ellendren's marriage, Devlyn had left the camp before the sun rose. He was still tired, but eager for solitude.

The Luminari camp had continued to grow since he had last had the chance to inspect it; elves had arrived in droves from the various settlements along the Illumined Wood, but none had come from north of the Laudien Mountains. He and Arlyn were the only elves from Cor'lera in the encampment. Devlyn wondered whether the Cor'lerans even knew that the larger population of Luminari elves were camped along the edge of the Shroud. Had anyone traveled north to tell them?

The pressure he felt about the elves still in the north didn't compare to what he had learned the previous night regarding his mother's whereabouts. Ever since he had first met Velaria, he had known, or at least assumed, that Evellyn was Erynor's prisoner in Broid. However, hearing it confirmed by Alesei was quite different. He no longer had to speculate about Evellyn's whereabouts. The Tieli queen telling him where his mother was and also putting conditions on her safety had changed everything.

Ellendren wanted to talk to him about what he was going through; he loved her for it. But just now, he needed to be alone with his thoughts. Alone, and without anyone listening in on them either. He didn't intend to keep secrets from Ellendren, but in truth, he didn't know how to digest

Alesei's news. As he sat with his emotions, he could only identify anger and frustration. And as if the news about his mother wasn't enough to cause those emotions, the Shroud loomed in front of him, mocking him with its seeming permanence. The weight pressing down on his shoulders got heavier by the second.

He had left the camp early to come to the Shroud on his own, however, Viren and Aliel were with him. Aliel was part of him, always present and Devlyn had thought better than trying to elude the Guardian knight at this hour. Viren had joined him as a silent shadow, respecting Devlyn's request for solitude.

The pre-dawn sky prevented Devlyn from seeing the Shroud properly, yet he felt it mere paces before him. He wanted to draw closer still, but Aliel insisted that he had gone close enough. Whorls of corruption and death were abundant here as flashes of something more sinister streaked about inside the gaseous mass. Gruesome clouds loomed overhead, melding seamlessly with the Shroud. The change in color was minor, but the Shroud and the clouds were too similar to not be related somehow.

Few ventured beyond the relative safety of the camp; the Shroud and clouds could be observed at a much safer distance. Not that anyone other than Devlyn cared to risk examining the Shroud. No one was prevented from leaving the camp, but the dangers of both the Shroud and a possible attack weighed on everyone's mind. In a single blow, Erynor had wrought the Shroud and brought the greatest realm to her knees fourteen hundred years ago. The Luminari elves had grown up hearing tales of Krysenthiel and the Shroud that plagued their realm.

Only brief accounts of the Shroud's nature existed, and even they were incomplete. Ei'ana who had dabbled with the Shroud to study its nature were never the same after their research was complete. Therril would have the best knowledge, having traveled through it at his own peril to see his sons, Roendryn and Feolyn. As wise as the old elf was, Devlyn doubted he could provide any insight for removing it.

He wished he knew when he would be ready to confront the Shroud. Rumors had spread like wildfire through the camp: he didn't have a plan; he had no idea how to destroy it. As awful as the rumors were, Devlyn was beginning to fear they were true. He had encouraged an entire civilization to leave their homes and follow him. Even though Lucillia no longer existed, he still felt a pang of guilt for forcing them to live in tents throughout the too-long winter. Fortunately, the chilled weather was finally giving way and the ground was wet and slick from snowmelt.

There was only one way to diffuse the rumors spreading through the camp—destroy the Shroud. He didn't feel any nearer to doing that than he had before he had learned to wield lumenys. To make matters worse, he still didn't understand how lumenys worked. The erendinth were intrinsically different from each other, and if there hadn't been seven of them, Devlyn would have claimed that they were all each other's opposites. Alethea would have taught him how wield lumenys. But that was no longer an option; she was gone. Arlyn was Devlyn's next best option here in the camp. He would have to arrange a meeting with his uncle who was likely the only person who could help him learn how to wield lumenys.

Brushing against the dark place within his heart, Devlyn felt the little light at the center. Breathing life into the tiny flickering flame, he was comforted by the light that blossomed outward as he bonded with Aliel, transforming the world and illuminating everything but the Shroud, which stood in abomination, contrary to the world it did not belong in.

Without wielding, Devlyn could feel the erendinth thrum around him, eager to bend to his will. Embracing animys and umbrys, Devlyn felt his surroundings intimately—the very aether danced and skipped, alive in its own fashion. Everything felt different standing along the edge of the Shroud. Even this close to it, he could easily see that the erendinth swirling around him were part of the fabric of creation. A taint was also there, a taint that threatened to expand and dominate that which it had not already consumed, like the smell of waste wafting through the air.

Bound to the world as he was, Devlyn wielded animys and umbrys toward the Shroud. His wield explored the outer limits of the Shroud, not penetrating into its depths, more like an exploratory tap. There was nothing special about his wield; it would accomplish little when it came to the Shroud's immensity, but it might reveal something, something yet to be discovered. Kevn might have already read volumes of research dedicated to the cause of the Luminari elves' despair, but Devlyn doubted anything useful for destroying the Shroud would be found in those tomes. *I hope he hasn't stopped his research*, Devlyn thought to himself, despite his own ineffectual experience with research.

Might as well ask him to stop breathing first, Aliel conveyed, a fresh sense of amusement about Kevn passing between them.

Aliel was right, of course. Kevn might have difficulty figuring out in what capacity he wanted to live his life, but whatever he chose, he would never be far from a library.

Daring to penetrate the Shroud, Devlyn felt a violent and malevolent storm meet his cursory wield as the Shroud tried to expel it. An incredible and awful force lashed against the intrusion, destroying Devlyn's preconception that the Shroud was nothing more than an evil-looking cloud. Whenever he saw the Shroud from a distance, all he could see was the stagnant mist on the surface, never the storm within.

Do you think it only reacts violently when disturbed? Devlyn conveyed to Aliel. Their minds were connected so intimately that he didn't have to form the thoughts completely, and Aliel would know his intent.

It's possible. Little is known of the Shroud, even among anadel. It is foreign to Lumaeniel where we come from, Aliel conveyed.

Arms extended with his feet planted on the cold, slushy ground, Devlyn maintained a firm grip of his wield, pushing deeper into the Shroud. The resistance grew more violent the more he pushed, and his wield now resembled a pillar, standing in opposition to the Shroud. With every new step he pushed the Shroud back, the more area he provided for the elves.

A northern breeze blew out of the Shroud, the stench alone making his stomach turn. As it encircled his body, he thought he heard a woman screaming. No louder than a whisper, but so distinct that Devlyn almost ran into the Shroud to pull her out.

His wield evaporated at the shock of the scream, what he was sure was an actual sound and not a figment of his imagination.

The scream faded, ending as quickly as it began. His surroundings became quiet again, the air still. No longer embracing animys and umbrys, his senses returned to normal—as normal as they were while bonded with Aliel. The taint of the Shroud no longer affronted his every sense. Relieved to be free of it, he also felt troubled at the memory of it.

What was that? Devlyn conveyed to Aliel. A soft golden light illuminated the ground around them.

Who, is the better question.

That was a person?

A Cyndinari.

Grasping the significance, Devlyn kept his eyes on the Shroud, trying to see whoever had screamed. The sound had been so faint that he doubted he would ever be able to see her, but the thought of someone lost in the Shroud was too terrible to conceive. Cyndinari elves were not evil by nature; Velaria and Jaerol had proved that time and time again.

Devlyn waited for another breeze that never came. The first hour of the day had come and gone, the sun still trapped behind the clouds that had ripped Alethea from Teraeniel. The world dimmed as he withdrew from Aliel, as though the world wasn't dim enough without Alethea Lenwyn in it any longer. He turned and saw Viren watching him.

"Are you ready to head back?" Viren asked.

"I suppose so."

"Walk with me," Viren said.

They crossed the barren plain between the Shroud and the camp, the melting snow sloshing beneath their feet as Aliel flew just above them. Brisk winds struck his face. Dynenth, the first month of summer was only a matter of weeks away and the unnatural wintery weather had only started to ease its grip over the land. Devlyn wondered, and not for the first time, if the Evil One was involved.

They reached the camp soon enough and continued their walk along the pathway formed by the tents. Devlyn kept his head held high, following Ellendren's instructions, even though his eyes often fell to the slush of snow and mud beneath his feet. He smiled and acknowledged anyone he passed, more often than not, not recognizing them. He had started to learn the names and faces of the minor Luminari aryls and their heirs when he last stayed with the Luminari. There were many more minor aryls than high aryls and he doubted he would be comfortable recognizing them all anytime soon.

Eventually, they reached the far side of the camp where the knights had their quarters. The sound of metal clashing against metal filled his ears and his heart skipped a few beats as recent memories of Everin flooded his thoughts. Brushing against his connection with Aliel, Devlyn followed the sound; goosebumps covered his skin. A long exhale escaped as he came to the training ground for the first time.

Knights from Lucillia and Guardian knights were already sparring with each other. The impressive warriors moved flawlessly as they dueled with the considerably younger elves. Jeanne Darkel walked through the sparring, untouched by the swords swishing past near enough that she should feel the wind of their passing.

Devlyn avoided the sparring as he made his way across the field. "You're not joining them?" he asked Viren.

"I was not assigned a squire," Viren said.

Devlyn could not tell whether he was upset by this or not. "Why? Not enough volunteers?"

Viren chuckled. Devlyn rarely ever heard him laugh or even smile. "I already made a vow; a vow that the First Guardian was not happy to hear of."

"The vow you made to me?"

Nodding, Viren turned to look Devlyn in the eyes. "The Lorenthiens were thought extinct. I would make my vow anew today if I had not already made it."

"What will you do while the others practice?"

"You presume you're exempt from training?" Viren's hand was on the hilt of his sword. He was actually smirking.

"Kyrendal convinced me that I should not take a sword for a verathn, but a staff—a scepter."

"You jest."

"Well, I asked for a sword after fighting a Deurghol and Aren in Lankor, but Kyrendal had other ideas."

"Kyrendal vanished from Krysenthiel thousands of years before I was even born; every Guardian knight dreams of receiving a verathn crafted by him."

"What of your sword? It's still a verathn; isn't it?"

"Kyrendal's verathn would shatter the imitations created after his departure," Viren said.

"Actually, Kyrendal isn't crafting my verathn. The draelyn gave me two seeds that will become verathn on Vespephaen; one for me and one for Ellendren."

"Is that where you learned jienzu?"

"The draelyn said that you and Alethea were already teaching it to me without my knowledge."

"It's more that we were preparing you for it; we had to ensure your body and mind wouldn't break if you weren't ready." Viren said with a smile, walking away as he spoke.

Uncertain whether he should follow, Devlyn watched Viren disappear into a nondescript tent, then reemerge after several moments with a slender staff of polished wood.

"If you are to have a staff as a verathn, then you'll have to learn to use it. As you know, the erendinth can't stop every attack," Viren said, tossing it through the air for Devlyn to catch. Catching the staff with both hands, he felt it wobble and thought he might drop it. Viren unsheathed his translucent sword and held it aloft.

"You're not using a wooden sword?" Devlyn asked.

"Did the Deathless drop his verathn when he saw you carried no weapon?"

Distraught at the memory, Devlyn gripped the staff anew, pointing it at Viren. Taking a step forward, he moved toward the Guardian knight, calculating his moves. This was not the first time they had sparred, but it was the first time that Devlyn held a staff instead of a sword. He always liked how swords would slice through the air, their balance offering little resistance. Yet now, he stood with an elongated staff, something not necessarily designed to be a weapon.

Viren's verathn fell to his side, a tactic he favored with Devlyn, making him think there was an opening. Devlyn knew that trick though.

Lifting his staff toward the clouds, Devlyn watched Viren flick his sword effortlessly to meet the staff. Changing stances, Devlyn swept the staff toward Viren's knees. He smiled, thinking he had finally gotten through the knight's defenses.

The next thing he knew, he was lying on the cold ground, blinking, and the clouds had moved. A painful knot dug into his back. He had not felt the sword strike him, but somehow, the staff was beneath him, pressing against his lower back.

"How do you expect to learn with your eyes closed?" Jeanne asked, having approached without Devlyn noticing.

Pushing himself back onto his feet, Devlyn rubbed his lower back then bent to pick up the staff.

"Have you ever used a staff before?" Jeanne asked.

"Never."

"Give it here."

"Pardon me?"

Closing the distance between them, Jeanne stood in front of Devlyn, her nose inches from his own. "Give me the staff. I've never seen anyone so clumsy with one." He glumly handed it to her.

Devlyn watched as Jeanne and Viren moved to face one another. Viren maintained his starting position, while Jeanne stood in a similar stance but holding the staff so that it extended along her arm at a downward angle. What was the bottom, now rose behind her to just below her head.

"Keep your eyes open, Phaedryn." Jeanne did not move her gaze from Viren as she spoke.

The staff whirled around in a great arc, flashing through the cold air to meet Viren's verathn, which Devlyn could barely see move. The sword appeared invisible as it swung through the air, meeting the wooden staff.

Watching the two Guardian knights spar, Devlyn came to the realization that Viren had gone easy on him in their training sessions. Granted, he had never gotten the better of Viren, but he had been able to see the movements of Viren's sword. Now, eyes straining, he could only see where the sword and staff touched, but never the motions. They were a blur of the two materials.

The staff was easier to follow, if only because it was longer than Viren's verathn. The two Guardians moved at dizzying speeds, neither showing any weakness. Just as quickly as it began, the bout stopped. Confused, as he had not heard an impact, Devlyn noted the still elves, Jeanne's staff resting next to Viren's neck, his sword too slow to stop her.

Jeanne took a step away from Viren, lowered the staff and the two bowed to one another. Devlyn had to make sure that his mouth wasn't hanging open when Jeanne turned back to him to return his staff.

"Did you learn anything?" Jeanne asked.

"Never to get on your bad side, that's for certain."

"I hope that was not all, Ei'denai." Jeanne walked away to resume her surveillance of the knights, none of whom had paused their training to watch the impromptu duel.

Bartering

Devlyn fell into one of the more complicated jienzu forms that Viren was teaching him. While his time with the draelyn in Tenethyl had taught him much, he had only had a week to learn from them. Vivien had done her best to ensure that Devlyn knew the basics before he left. She did not have time to teach him anything more advanced and even if she had tried, Devlyn's body would not have been ready for it. He had been more likely to hurt himself than learn something beneficial.

But Devlyn had made a commitment to regularly practice the jienzu forms. His body, mind, and heart had strengthened through those months of daily discipline and Viren felt Devlyn was now ready to move on to some of the more advanced forms. Every time Devlyn learned a new jienzu form, it felt like every previously unused muscle in his body would rip apart. Throughout their early morning session, Viren reminded him that it was also a meditative exercise and if done properly, would strengthen his inner sense.

Devlyn fell into another form, trying to quiet his mind as he imagined two interconnected water wheels gently turning. It felt like he rotated the wheels in an infinite slow loop. Lost in the form as he held it, Devlyn almost missed the images that appeared. They weren't necessarily in his own mind, but he was aware of them. They were quiet and Devlyn watched what had to be a young and carefree Viren receiving the news of Septyl under attack. Images of loss and pain transformed into determination as a young Viren trained with the Guardian knights while also learning more advanced jienzu forms. Devlyn couldn't tell if he was feeling Viren's pain from the memory or if it was his own body in agony over the form he was holding as he watched.

Hundreds of years passed in a few memories as Viren's past unfolded. A kind and beautiful face bloomed in Devlyn's mind, a face that he recognized as someone he had seen in another of Viren's memories. The memories linked to that face were a mix of carefree youth and grief and loss. Devlyn opened his eyes and relaxed his body out of the jienzu form, the images fading as he did.

"You never intended to be a Guardian knight," Devlyn said, surprising himself at the revelation.

"I thought that was you." Viren straightened and rounded his shoulders to ease them, turning to look at the Shroud in the distance. "He was at Septyl that day when everything changed—when Erynor began his war."

"The one with the kind eyes?"

Viren nodded. "Reinyn Lorenthien was Faerndryn and Ithendryl's nephew. His mother was a Phaedryn and his father was an ei'ana. We had made so many plans together. He wanted to visit every continent and learn what each culture knew of wielding: whether they understood the erendinth as we did mattered little to Reinyn." Viren chucked. "He was to begin his studies at Gwilnor within the next decade and I was to join him."

Viren dabbed a tear as his smile faded. "After I learned that he had not survived the attack on Septyl, in my grief, I went to the Guardian knights and enlisted. I had to wait several years before I was mature enough; the wait was likely because I was still grieving, though. The recruiters knew I needed more time. When the war took a grim turn and our defeat was all but guaranteed, Ithendryl selected me to be one of the protectors of the phoenix egg. She remembered me from the times Reinyn and I had been to Arenthyl's palace. She confided in me that she had not stopped grieving for Reinyn and the rest of her family who had already been slain. She never told me whether she thought her house would survive the war, but she did tell me that I would find the one who the phoenix had chosen."

Devlyn listened to the sad tale, not sure how to comfort Viren. Saying he was sorry didn't feel right, but neither could he think of an appropriate substitute. Devlyn knew that the Ceurendol War had accounted for a long list of casualties, but he didn't know how those casualties had affected the people who had lived at that time. And who, like Viren, had survived with scars following the losses. The Luminari had only lost their immortality once the war was over and the Shroud covered Krysenthiel. What would it have been like to know and love someone for decades— centuries—anticipating sharing thousands of years together only to have that person stolen from you too early?

"Those dark days have yet to pass." Viren must have heard Devlyn's thoughts. "You remind me of Reinyn. It seems that every Lorenthien shares that spark. When we first met in that wagon, I had a suspicion that you might belong to House Lorenthien, but only because you reminded me of Reinyn. I had told myself that it was merely a coincidence and didn't let myself hope that House Lorenthien had survived. When I found out that you were indeed a Lorenthien, I could not help but make my oath to you—for Ithendryl and Reinyn and for their memory."

"Viren, I don't know what to say."

"You don't have to say anything. Come, Lyren will want to see you washed and properly dressed for the chamber meeting."

The meeting today was to be one of the larger gatherings and every Luminari aryl was expected to attend, both high and minor aryls. He had only attended a meeting with the entire court once before and was thankful that, given the large attendance, he was only expected to speak once since everyone else demanded the floor. This meeting was bound to be the same, but he still had to ready his resolve. Unlike the other meetings that focused on reclaiming Krysenthiel, this meeting's focus was his mother.

"How do you think the aryls will respond?" Devlyn asked.

"Your mother is a Lorenthien. They will not recommend abandoning her to Erynor's will."

Devlyn took a final look at the Shroud before turning away and returning to his tent where a tub filled with hot water waited. Lyren knew Devlyn's routine and schedule better than Devlyn did and had likely only just finished filling the water a moment before Devlyn returned. Practicing jienzu had been a welcome relief in preparation for today's chamber meeting. Now, Devlyn happily discarded his clothing and slipped into the soothing heat. He soaked longer than he should have, but finally pressed into ignys to warm the chilled water before scrubbing himself clean.

He got dressed in the blue lierathnil that Lyren had laid out for him and was out of the tent shortly after, heading for the meeting. Somewhere above, he sensed Aliel flying with Tariel. They had joined Liara in keeping an eye on the skies and the distant land for approaching enemies, something every elf in their camp knew was inevitable. Erynor wasn't going to sit idly by until they reclaimed Krysenthiel.

Once at the noisy chamber tent, Devlyn took his seat at the makeshift ring of tables meant for the high aryls—the minor aryls were expected to stand around the tables. He'd lost count of how many of these meetings there had been, each one focused on their position and a strategy for reclaiming the lost cities of Krysenthiel, Arenthyl and Septyl holding the most concern. Devlyn wasn't sure why everyone had to rediscuss their strategy since everyone now assumed that Devlyn could quickly remove the Shroud.

Arlyn was the only elf in the entire encampment who knew Evellyn, who had spoken with her and had shared memories with her. None of the other elves had known of her existence before Devlyn first showed up in Lucillia and the Roendryn aryl had revealed that a second branch of Lucillia's descendants had survived through the line of Feolyn. They hadn't intentionally kept it a secret; rather, the elves had simply forgotten with the passing centuries.

Aryls now filled the tent and Ellendren was one of the last to arrive, surrounded by advisors and scribes. She had not stopped working since they had returned to the Luminari and Devlyn wondered how she found any time to train with Tariel. The gathered aryls quieted as Naesiv, who usually chaired the proceedings and set the agenda for each meeting, rose to begin this one.

"Good morning, respected Aryls." Naesiv gestured broadly across the very crowded tent. "Today's meeting shall begin with a formal recognition of the reinstated Kingdom of Thellion and its acquisition of Perrien, Parendior, and most recently, Evellion."

"Can we say in good faith that this Thellish king didn't bully Queen Lara into signing that treaty?" Silvia asked, stirring a round of commotion from the assembled aryls who called out their comments without being acknowledged by Naesiv.

"I too would like that verified. The events in the north unfolded far too quickly for it to be a mutual and well executed merge."

"Agreed. And treaties of such magnitude are not composed of in a manner of weeks."

The aryls quickly dissolved into dozens of individual debates. Devlyn sat patiently beside Ellendren. They had to play a delicate game to garner the cooperation of the aryls and prevent any factions from splitting off, something that seemed more likely with every night where Silvia had to sleep in a tent. Ellendren had explained that the aryls had to discuss every matter and that it was best to wait them out. Often, during her parents' reign, the aryls would reach the right consensus without their interference and it was always a much more popular resolution when that happened.

Naesiv spoke over the gathering, calling them to order and finally quieting them enough to be heard. "I was present for the treaty deliberations and signing, as were several others from this very assembly. Queen

Lara was of sound mind throughout and not once did I take note of any sort of aggression from the Thellish king. I believe it is our responsibility to acknowledge the reforged Kingdom of Thellion. Besides, our present alliance with Thellion and the relationship between Ei'denai Devlyn Lorenthien and King Alexander Vaerin is already sending that very message."

The arguments renewed but Naesiv's reasoning for acknowledging the knitted and expanding Kingdom of Thellion won out. Ellendren smiled. They had both hoped for that resolution but had been careful to not show their hand. The Lorenthien aryl's voice might be needed later and it couldn't seem that they were throwing their weight around too much, especially since they were not yet the Exalted Aryl.

The meeting agenda shifted through a number of topics and the aryls had an opportunity to address any complaints, which were many. The Shroud was mentioned only briefly before the topic finally turned to Evellyn Lorenthien. Devlyn's palms grew sweaty when Naesiv introduced the sensitive topic. Fortunately, the gathering didn't fall into another argument, everyone remaining quiet. Ellendren held Devlyn's hand in support.

"For those unaware of the situation, Queen Alesei of Tiel recently came to our encampment by way of a seguian. We're under the impression that the same minum who opened the seguian in the Temple of Ceur, leading to Ceurtriarch Ealyndol's assassination, is responsible for bringing Alesei here." As soon as Naesiv paused, a flurry of questions rose from the gathering.

"Have the time wardens forsaken us?"

"How are we to protect ourselves if Erynor has the time wardens?"

"As far as I know, Erynor only has one minum, and it is by no means Jax's choice. In order to protect the larger minum population, Jax is forced to do as Erynor bids," Devlyn said, having met Jax briefly just before a Deurghol had showed up.

"Thank you, Ei'denai. We can discuss the time wardens at a later date; their safety and wellbeing must remain a priority. We must focus on Evellyn Lorenthien just now." Naesiv cleared his throat before continuing. "Alesei claimed to bring a message from the emperor. A scribe was not present to record the message in its entirety, but the meaning was clear. Abandon the Shroud or forfeit Evellyn Lorenthien's life. Alesei also required Devlyn to deliver himself to Broid if he wished to see his mother alive again. I know this will not be an easy conversation, so I invite Devlyn and Arlyn, her family here, to speak first about what they believe is an appropriate action. Our broader discussion can continue after they've said their share."

Despite the burden he felt, Devlyn stood and walked to the center of the tent. Elves looked at him from every side and he wondered if they could hear his heart thumping in his chest. He took in the dozens of faces, many of whom were becoming familiar, before catching Ellendren's eye, her calm smile giving him the strength to speak.

"Evellyn Lorenthien, my mother, was stolen away from Cor'lera after witnessing Erynor's servants slaughter her husband and injure her daughter. Other than myself and my sister Leilyn, her entire family was rounded up and carted to Gneal, where shadow elves tortured them with the intent of gaining information on the location of a fabled weapon, then stealing their souls. She was forced to watch her family suffer under the Shadow's malice.

"Eager to interrogate Evellyn personally, Erynor had her brought to Broid, while the shadow elves in Gneal continued their long interrogation and torture of my family. Erynor believed that Cor'lera hid a powerful weapon of some sort, one that could ruin him, and that my family knew its secrets. As many of you know, Cor'lera translates to king's cradle in High Aelish. The village I was born in never held a concealed weapon, but rather, kept a blood line hidden. As far as I know, my mother knew she was a descendant of Feolyn, but I cannot say whether she knew that Feolyn's wife, Gwendolyn, was a Lorenthien. Whether the village's name refers to Feolyn or Gwendolyn, I have no idea.

"My mother has been Erynor's prisoner for fifteen years. Initially, that was because he thought my family was hiding that non-existent weapon, but I fear the emperor's cruelty will be exacerbated now that he knows that Evellyn descends from both Lucillia and House Lorenthien. Erynor will use my mother as bait to draw me to Broid. He will use her as a bargaining chip to control us. I know that we cannot negotiate with Erynor in this matter, nor can we halt our study of the Shroud. And I also know that I cannot go to Broid to save my mother. I promised you that I would remove the Shroud, and so I will not jeopardize our future. That being said, I am open to any suggestions anyone has that would help rescue my mother." Devlyn turned to Arlyn. "Uncle?"

Arlyn stepped forward, his conflicted emotions barely disguised behind a veil of an ei'ceuril's practiced calm. Devlyn knew how much this affected his uncle; it was his family too that had been tortured and killed. Only Evellyn and Liam had managed to leave Gneal's dungeons alive.

"Evellyn has always been a bright spark; she lit any room she walked into. I'd say she never had the need to travel to the Temple of Ceur to learn how to wield lumenys but already had the ability embedded into her very nature, a gift she no doubt would have passed on to her children." Arlyn paused and took a deep breath. "We will be forever disadvantaged if Erynor holds one such as my sister as his captive. Devlyn and I have already discussed this at great length and are agreed that he cannot go to Broid. To do so would play into Erynor's hands and we would never reclaim Krysenthiel. I do not know why Erynor wants the Shroud to remain intact, but it greatly worries me; the Shroud must be destroyed and that must be our priority."

Devlyn's mind flashed to Thien, his very distant ancestor, who with Loren was the namesake for his house. Perhaps Evellyn was capable of harnessing lumenys. Like Devlyn, she wasn't only a Luminari elf. House Lorenthien had been sired by a draelyn of the Gold House. Devlyn wondered how his connection to the Gold Dragon Flight might assist him in removing the Shroud. Even though he had already pierced the Shroud once before, he did not know what he had done or how he had done it. Even now that he had entered the Empyrean Sphere, he still didn't know exactly what to do.

His attention snapped back to the discussion in the chamber tent. He didn't necessarily expect the aryls to argue about Evellyn, but he certainly didn't anticipate them fully supporting a rescue attempt.

"Rescuing Evellyn Lorenthien from Broid must become a priority," Iridil Taerinior said, startling Devlyn with this overwhelming support since Iridil was normally one of the loudest dissenters, aligned with the Narielles and one of the biggest skeptics when Devlyn had first revealed his ancestry.

"Yes, but how do we penetrate the heart of the Erynien Empire?" Ciraenth asked.

"We've been in discussions with the Goblin Guild," Silvia started, her voice demanding the assembly's attention. "Their interests are determinedly one sided. They hope to acquire our renewed currency within their control. They care most for favorable exchange rates between their long-standing monetary system and the fortune that our ancestors had left behind in Krysenthiel. Naturally, our lumols are much more valuable than their crowns; historically, one lumol equaled three crowns."

"You don't recommend using that as a base for bartering, do you?" Valerie asked.

"Absolutely not; if anything the rate should be higher," Silvia said. "It's absolutely ridiculous to exchange a lumol for three measly crowns. We can however use their piqued interest to establish a friendship and perhaps take advantage of their residence on the Kinzdol Islands and close proximity to Broid to stage a rescue mission. We need access to someone on the inside."

"Even if we could get into Broid undetected, Erynor will no doubt have Evellyn under a watchful eye. If he did not know before that she was a Lorenthien, he certainly knows now," Kyiel said.

"That does not mean that we should prolong devising a plan for her rescue," Iridil said.

Devlyn found himself looking dazedly around the room, as though he had only understood for the first time who the Luminari aryls truly were. He did not know if they were playing a political game, but he did not care. The aryls, even those who had initially opposed him, wanted to rescue his mother.

"I can't thank you enough," said Devlyn, choking on his words.

"Your mother is a Lorenthien," Toral said, without a doubt in his tone. "We will not stand for the enemy holding a Lorenthien prisoner. If we're to reclaim our previous glory, we cannot permit it to begin with the way we initially lost it."

Devlyn's eyes began to water at the declaration. For the first time, he had complete confidence in the Luminari aryls, in all of them. He longed for his mother, and the song she had hummed to him as a toddler sprung in his heart.

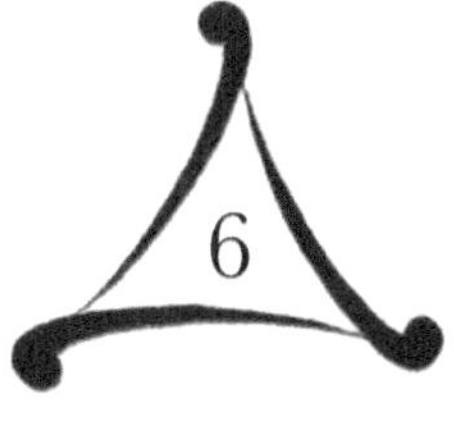

SEVERED

Spent, Jaerol banged his head on the desk. He knew he should grab the next book in the pile, but he was pretty sure he had glossed over something in the diary he had just tossed aside.

He, Danielle, Fiona, and Trethien had returned to the Temple of Ceur, leaving the other escapees from Gwilnor to find their way to the Luminari elves who were said to be encamped somewhere along the Shroud in northern Sorenthil. Fortunately, they had all been given rooms to stay in, an uncommon occurrence since none of them had an official role in the temple, something which was a prerequisite to enter its cloisters, let alone board there. But, given the circumstances, where Gwilnor stood, and what Jaerol hoped to achieve, Aaron had lifted the usual requirements and allowed them to stay.

While Jaerol had no interest in ever living in the temple again, he was happy to reunite with his old bunkmates, Renaud and Stephen, and his old instructors, Bastien and Daphnel. They had immediately agreed to help when Jaerol had explained that Liam was a prisoner at Gwilnor. Stephen had given every impression of wanting to break into Gwilnor that very night, which quickly led to Daphnel calling him a fool without a plan. Renaud and Stephen had soon joined the others to go through Benedetto's diaries when they weren't on duty as temple knights.

Seeing his friends again was nice but stepping foot inside the temple without Liam felt wrong. His history with Liam hadn't started in the temple, but it was where everything changed between them. Jaerol had only been able to walk through the grief of Kiron's death because of Liam.

Since they'd been back, Jaerol had spent every waking hour devouring Benedetto's diaries. All the ei'ceuril's available diaries had been delivered to the Ceurtriarch's private library for a thorough review by their little group. When Jaerol had told Selenya of his intention to return to rescue Liam, she had accepted his decision but had also referenced those particular diaries without being specific about why they might be important. Jaerol had been somewhat surprised. He was already familiar with them from when he had been living in the temple and had already read many of Benedetto's entries. But when Jaerol had told Kevn that the diaries might hold some critical information, Kevn had seemed skeptical since the diaries had never been classified as a reputable source. Benedetto had been a lowly ei'ceuril from Lankor who had enjoyed a very long life because of Ceurendol, the Jewel of Life, before the Erynien Empire won the war fourteen hundred years ago and everyone had been severed from its life-extending effects.

While Kevn was familiar with the diaries, he had never gone to the trouble to study them until he was told of Selenya's recommendation. Aware that only a fool would ignore the White Owl, and despite trusting the others' researching capabilities, Kevn would sneak away any book that the others had finished and go through it himself, since he could read at an incredible pace. Unlike Jaerol, who now slumped at the desk, his head a bit sore from being banged on it. More diaries awaited, but he was tired and couldn't help the gaping yawn that overtook him.

"Going well?" Renaud asked, yawning himself.

"What could Selenya have possibly referred to? And why didn't she just say it?" Jaerol asked.

"I have a suspicion about why she didn't say it plainly," Aaron said from behind his large desk.

"Only the Chairs were around her to hear. You don't think she suspects one of them to have betrayed Septyl, do you?” Fiona asked.

“That’s a strong accusation,” Renaud said.

“Only the Chairs knew the details about the planned escape and none of them knew the timing until Velaria signaled it and still, only half the students managed to escape Gwilnor. The Tenebrae knew about the plan,” Jaerol said.

“So, she fears Tenebrae among the refugees. What hope is there if they can’t get away from that corruption?” Danielle placed her own book down, exhausted and saddened.

“We can’t think of that just now,” Trethien said, passing the diary he’d just finished reading to Kevn, well aware of Kevn’s secret rereading of everything. Kevn blushed and thanked Trethien even as he grabbed the diary eagerly.

Bastien and Daphnel came into the Ceurtriarch’s private library.

“You all look exhausted,” Daphnel said, quickly appraising the room.

“I agree and I think you all deserve a night off,” Bastien said. Nearly everyone immediately stood to leave, but Kevn and Jaerol stayed at their desks. Jaerol felt his exhaustion and knew that he’d be little help if he picked up another book. He’d just as likely pass over something important without realizing it but couldn’t bring himself to stop looking.

“Come on, Jaerol, you won’t be much use tonight anyway,” Renaud said.

Jaerol agreed, somewhat begrudgingly, and turned to Kevn. “If I have to go *relax*, so do you. Those diaries can go an evening without our attention.”

“I suppose you’re right. I can’t help feeling that my time here at the temple is limited though,” Kevn said.

“How do you mean?” Stephen asked.

“I can’t quite place my finger on it, but it feels like something, or someone is trying to pull me somewhere else.”

“Is it getting stronger?” Aaron asked, clearly familiar with whatever Kevn was experiencing.

"I believe so," Kevn said.

"If that's the case, then we definitely need to take you down to the tavern before you leave." Renaud smiled. "Will you join us, Aaron?"

Kevn shook his head. "Only his secretary knows his schedule. Still, you'd probably have to schedule it a month in advance."

Aaron laughed and shrugged. "Jehn will have my head if I sneak out for a drink without telling him."

"All the more reason to join us," Kevn said.

"His holiness will do no such thing." Jehn, easily the oldest person in the room, hobbled forward, leaning heavily on the cane supporting him. He had served as Ealyndol's secretary before Aaron had been selected by Ealyndol to replace him. "A tavern is no place for the Ceurtriarch. Not even when Ealyndol was a young Ceurtriarch would he have considered it."

"I'm not arguing, Jehn." Aaron turned to the rest of the group. "You'll have to enjoy the tavern without me."

The group chorused their farewells to Aaron and left the library. They passed through the rest of the Ceurtriarch's extensive apartment before making their way through the Chamber of Light and then the cloisters. Bastien and Daphnel led the way down through the temple, leaving the ei'ceuril quarters behind, past the temple knights' residences and to where the lay votaries had dwelled. Most of them were gone now, having left either to become student wielders or tossed their lot in with the Erynien Empire and helped to seize Gwilnor Academy for the Tenebrae.

When they finally reached the tavern, Jaerol recognized it at once. He flinched at the memory of coming to this very place as Bastien and Daphnel's guest, recalling how rude he had been to them both.

Due to the greatly diminished numbers of lay votaries, they had no trouble finding a table large enough for them all to sit around. There was a bit of a stir at the appearance of two women—even though there were female ei'ceuril, they were likely the first females to set foot in the tavern since before the Ceurendol War. The first round of drinks came quickly. Jaerol knew to stay away from the wine down here and happily sipped his mead.

The group from Gwilnor melded easily with the group from the temple. While they had already spent a significant amount of time together, it had been to read the diaries which was not conducive to getting to know each other. With the more relaxed atmosphere after their first drinks had disappeared, they were soon all laughing together. Jaerol sat closest to Renaud and Stephen, eager to find out what his friends had been up to since he had left the temple. Despite living in the same city, Jaerol had never returned for a visit since he had started studying with the ei'ana.

"So, what have you two been up to since Liam and I left?"

"Well, it has been nice to have our room to ourselves again. Neither of us has to sleep on the top bunk any longer," Stephen said, stretching to emphasize how much space they now had.

"Don't let him fool you; Stephen insisted on staying in that room with Renaud after he was knighted. He could have had his own room like all the other knights if he'd wished," Daphnel said.

"Another room without a window," Stephen said. "Besides, Renaud won't be here forever, and who knows when I'll get to see him after he leaves. Former temple knights tend to avoid the temple after they leave."

"You're leaving?" Jaerol asked, surprised at the revelation and choosing to ignore the gibe.

"I've written to my cousin, Queen Myranda, and she accepted my request to return to court. There's simply no reason for me to stay in the temple any longer. I might not be as advanced as the kien wielders who were able to study at Gwilnor, but I've managed enough control to not be a danger to anyone," Renaud said.

"You're Myranda's cousin?" Danielle said as Fiona leaned in.

"That's right. I suppose you would have gotten to know her at Gwilnor."

"Danielle, Trethien, and I spent most of our free time with her before she returned to Myrium. We miss her dearly; both she and Ellendren went off to lead their kingdoms," Fiona said.

"My condolences for the loss of your aunt," Trethien said. "I never had the pleasure to meet Karina, but I understood she was a remarkable queen."

"Indeed. My late uncle could not have found a more suitable woman to bring into the monarchy. Her legacy will only be diminished by Myranda's great deeds," Renaud said.

"To the late queen and to Myranda's health." Bastien, another Sorenth, raised his goblet and everyone followed.

"When will you return to Myrium?" Danielle asked.

"I've been asked to remain in Ceurenyl until things settle down at Gwilnor," Renaud said before lowering his voice. "The queen is understandably concerned about what's happening in the castle and feels better having someone she trusts still in the city to send news."

"So, you're a foreign spy now, are you?" Daphnel huffed, then looked abashed at the glare Renaud sent him.

For the rest of the evening, they veered away from any discussion of Gwilnor and their task. They all knew that the temple was not as secure as it was once believed. Servants of shadow were hiding in every darkened crevice across Eklean, and those places which had once been thought safe, such as Gwilnor, had fallen the hardest.

Another leaf had sprouted since the first one had been clipped off and Velaria knew to conceal this one as she was roughly bathed by kien wielders. She was aware that the only reason Hannah was having them bathe her was to embarrass her and break her down. Velaria wouldn't give her the satisfaction. With every public meal she was required to attend, she sat with her back straight and her shoulders squared. The students and ei'ana still loyal to Septyl would know she had not broken. She considered refusing the food, a sign that she did not support the Tenebrae.

She discarded that thought though, for she needed her strength. If Velaria wanted to make a difference and take back Gwilnor Academy, she would not be able to do so if she was weak from hunger. So again, she ate her meal with everyone in the dining hall throwing glances at the Chair of Azurelle between bites. At first, the attention was discouraging. They all knew, especially the students who had been involved in the escape plan and hadn't made it out, that Velaria was a prisoner. She might not be dressed as a captive, but they all knew, given that she was always accompanied by kien wielders when she came in. Even if Hannah had made an excuse for Velaria's shaved head, no one believed that the Chair of Azurelle willingly sat among them.

The high table was lined with Hannah's new magisters. Only Kai and Yvonne had been among the faculty before the Tenebrae had seized Gwilnor. Velaria took note of the others, furious as she recognized them as sisters she had once trusted. The most insulting was Indryl. Not only was she also an Azurelle, but she had been entrusted to train Devlyn when he first came to Gwilnor. Velaria couldn't believe that she had miscalculated so badly.

Liam sat at the other end of the high table, next to Razcul, more like Razcul's pet than his prisoner. Liam's face was bruised and one eye was swollen shut. Velaria worried about the extent of whatever injuries his clothing hid if his visible wounds were that terrible. Her heart broke for him. She wasn't much older than he was but seeing him in his current state took her back to when she had rescued him from Gneal's dungeon. She knew he had a strong will and would survive this. Still, he had gone through enough pain.

The meal ended and everyone left the dining hall, the students for their dormitories and the ei'ana back to their apartments. Velaria knew to wait until instructed to leave. She would not give her captors a reason to abuse her publicly. The only thing she could give those in the castle who were still loyal to Septyl was her resolve. She would not let the Tenebrae humble her further.

As she waited and the dining hall emptied, an envoy of twelve men entered, two of them carrying a small chest between them. They bowed curtly to Hannah. Stunned, Velaria couldn't believe her eyes. These men were Sons of Yanil, a knightly order that protected the Yanilean. Not in her wildest imagination had she ever expected them to set foot in Gwilnor. These men despised ei'ana and sent their own wielders to work camps.

Velaria didn't notice at first, but in the center of the column was a dwarf. His skin was pale as though he had never stepped out into the sunlight.

Yvonne grinned at the men, her eyes set on the man at the front as she moved toward him.

"Hello, sister," he said. "I've brought you a gift."

"Sandro, you are too kind, dear brother." Yvonne embraced him. The other Sons of Yanil seemed uncomfortable with the exchange. They were aware that Yvonne was a wielder. Velaria was suddenly very curious about Yvonne's history. If her brother was a Son of Yanil, that meant that she had been born into nobility. It would have been impossible to keep her ability to wield a secret from the authorities. Velaria wondered how she had managed to come to Gwilnor. Was she even an ei'ana? Had she taken any of the counsels?

"Our friend apologizes for the delay." Sandro stepped aside and the dwarf stepped forward.

"Mistress," the dwarf started, "I bring you gifts from Zorik Schtam at our Master's request. He says you have need of rings crafted from dorthl—rings that will bind and sever the wearer from the seven erendinth of creation." Velaria's shock and dismay increased at hearing the name Zorik Schtam. The dwarves of the Shadow Mountains had long ago cast their lot with the ancient Cyndinari and had served the

Sha'ghol.

The knights carrying the chest stepped forward and opened it. The contents seemed to suck in the light around the chest.

"Perfect." Hannah leaned over the table to look down into the chest. "Test them on our *guests*."

Velaria was roughly pulled from her seat and shoved toward the chest and the dwarf. A quick glance around showed that Liam had also been pushed toward the chest.

The dwarf plucked out one of the obsidian rings, his features revealing nothing of his motives. Without explaining what he meant to do, he took one of Velaria's hands and placed the ring on her finger. The dwarf had been gentle, but the ring burned as a thousand fiery needles lanced her finger. She screamed at the shock of it and imagined that the needles would go right through her finger. The fire spread through her entire body, then seemed to turn to ice. She could still feel the erendinth, but couldn't access them, just as though someone held a wield over her to prevent her from wielding.

She didn't see the dwarf place a ring on Liam, but she did hear him scream even as her vision blurred. She fought to maintain consciousness against the unrelenting pain in her finger. At one moment it was fire and the next ice, the needles constant. Her body shook from the jarring experience.

"Can we remove our nullifying wields from them?" a Tenebrae ei'ana asked. She had been maintaining the wield over Velaria during dinner, annoyed at having to do such a menial task.

"They can do no harm, unless they desire to wield tenebrys," the dwarf said.

"How many rings did you bring?" Hannah asked, pleased with the result.

"Fifty. A gift from our Master in appreciation for your work," the dwarf said.

"I know just the fifty fingers for them." Hannah smiled, her grandmotherly tone jarring.

"Do know, while these nullify access to the creative erendinth, it has the opposite effect for our Master's touch," the dwarf said. Despite her agony, Velaria realized that the dwarf was not referring to Erynor as his master. The dwarf of Zorik Schtam referred to Ramiel.

"How do you mean?" Hannah asked.

"These rings weaken our Master's enemy but become a strength to those who would serve him."

Razcul laughed and stepped forward. "Give one to me, dwarf."

The dwarf bowed to Razcul—still in the guise of Danyol, an Eldinari elf—and lifted one of the rings up to the shadow elf who shoved it on his finger and roared with eerie delight. Velaria couldn't tell if he suffered from the pain or relished it. With the ring on his finger, his connection to the creative erendinth was severed, and with it, his disguise vanished. The shadow elf's blistered and decaying skin was revealed and a shadowy presence spilled out from him. He roared again.

"How do you feel?" Hannah asked, clearly nonplussed by the transformation.

"Invigorated." His voice terrified Velaria. "Give my gratitude to our Master." Razcul bowed to the dwarf.

DEFEATED

Where Everin had escaped an Erynien occupation, Cyril had spent the past four years under the empire's oppressive thumb. Alex had always known that the Erynien Empire was evil, but he had never imagined the extent of their vileness. The stench alone in Cyril was enough to keep him from passing through the city gate, which curiously had been bolted from the outside. After the gates had been pried open, the reason for the outer bolts had become clear. The city had transformed into a prison and it smelled of the rot and decay of death.

Following the four-year occupation, the people of Cyril, the ones who had not died from assault, disease, or starvation, appeared to be walking corpses, stripped of their will to live. No one in the city seemed to have eaten a proper meal in years and neither did it look like the water supply was sufficient for hygiene or even staying hydrated. The number of injuries that Alex saw during their slow march through Cyril was overwhelming. None of these people looked like the proud Evellions that Alex had come to know and respect in Everin. These were a vanquished people and Alex couldn't say whether they would ever recover from the atrocities committed against them. The same brutality and disrepair he saw in the city streets was also evident in the palace. Like most of the city, it too had been pillaged.

Alex held Diana's hand as they passed through yet another looted corridor of the palace. It looked as though whoever had ransacked it, had held a deep hatred for Evellion and everything the kingdom stood for. Stone crests on the walls had been scratched out and the banners had been torn down and soiled. Diana held a perfumed cloth to her nose to mute the worst of the stench but determinedly pushed on next to him.

Before they had entered the city, Alex had asked her whether she wanted to wait outside. The look she had given him at the question meant that he had no intention of asking her again as they had passed through the city and now the palace, despite being tempted time and time again. Diana was by no means fragile, but surely, she would want to be spared the stench. She hadn't flinched when they had come across the first corpse in the streets. None of the dead had been dealt with; they had been simply left to rot where they had fallen, even in the palace. The sight made Alex's stomach turn. Cyril was not just a prison; it had become a tomb where the living walked among their dead.

Diana did blanch when they entered the throne room. The doors had been ripped off their hinges and smashed to pieces at the entry. A lone figure occupied the bloody throne and Diana rushed forward to the dead man. By the stench and state of decay, he had been dead for quite some time. Diana wailed as she collapsed at the feet of the Duke of Cyril, her father's uncle, an Evellion prince. The sound echoed off the dirty stone walls and Alex stayed back for a time, allowing the woman he loved to grieve another loss in her family.

When he finally stepped forward, he saw a small filthy head poke through a doorway on the far side of the room. The child seemed to recognize Diana and rushed to her as other children came out from the doorway. One of them called out, "Demetri, you can't go in there; Grandmother has forbidden it."

Diana turned at the sound and had little time to prepare for the boy named Demetri launching himself at her. He clung to her with a visceral grip and she rubbed his back. "Is it really you, Demetri? Look how big you've grown." She tried not to cry for the child's sake. Like everyone else in the city, he was too thin and could have been mistaken for a corpse.

Alex came closer and heard the boy sniveling into Diana's tunic. "One of your cousins?" he asked, placing what he hoped was a comforting hand on her back.

Diana nodded and then noticed the other children by the door. "Olivia, Colin, Desmond, Kara," she called to them, but they stayed back for a moment, uncertain whether they could trust her. They all seemed younger than Demetri and might not remember Diana. They could have been too young to remember the last time they had seen her. Given their current malnourishment, determining any of their ages was impossible. Diana held their faces in turn as they eventually came to her. "Is anyone else here? Is anyone else…" she choked before finishing, "alive?"

"We're not supposed to leave the residence," Olivia squeaked.

"Will you take me there?" Diana asked gently, not wanting to frighten the children. They nodded and before they led the way, Diana unbuckled her cloak and placed it over the late duke.

"You can't do that," Desmond shrieked. "The bad ones will come back and hurt us more." The boy started to cry and the other children looked just as anxious, especially Demetri.

"The bad people are gone and they aren't coming back." Diana hugged Desmond tightly in an effort to calm him.

"Do you promise?" Olivia asked.

"I promise. You're safe now. Can you take me to the others?"

Comforted by Diana, the children nodded again and Desmond wiped his tears away on his dirty sleeve. They pulled her away from the throne room through the door they had used. Alex followed, trailed by the retainer that accompanied him and Diana. They passed through the private quarters of the ducal palace and it was much the same as what they had already seen. The entire place had been ransacked and then abandoned. Alex doubted that anything of value was left.

They came to a quiet room where two women sat together, not

talking, just sitting in shared silence. The older one looked at them, and Alex noticed her dirty face and filthy clothes.

"Diana?" the woman asked tentatively, rising slowly and raising her arms to Diana.

"Great Aunt Mildred." Diana went forward and hugged the older woman—the duchess.

"Diana, what are you doing here? How are you here?" Mildred asked, frantic.

"Has Everin fallen too?" the younger woman asked.

"No, Aunt Jenna, we've survived a siege, giants, and shadow elves. Everin remains standing, thanks to our allies and new suzerain."

"Suzerain? We might have been brought low, but who would dare claim suzerainty over Evellion?" Mildred asked, her will clearly unbent despite her sorry state.

"Alexander Vaerin, the King of Thellion and also my betrothed." Diana gestured for Alex to come forward to meet the two women.

"Your Grace." Alex inclined his head and took Mildred's hand to press a kiss to it.

"A Thellish king? Now of all times? What gives a Vaerin a stronger claim to Thellion's crown than those who sat on the Eagle Throne?" Mildred asked.

"I claimed nothing and neither did I seek any crown. I'm the youngest child of the family of Perrien's exiled monarchs. Thellion's crown was placed on my brow by Aewen herself."

"Thellion's wife? Surely, she can't still be alive," Jenna said.

"Indeed, she is. She's preparing Elothkar for our return. Our wedding is to be held there," Diana said.

"So, you're the reason Evellion still stands? Not that it matters anymore, the royal line has ended. I doubt Amry, my husband, or my sons had any bastards," Mildred said.

"I'm sorry? I don't understand. I saw Demetri and Desmond. Even if Clavian and Rhys were killed with Duke Talyian, your grandsons still live," Diana said.

"You've seen the state they left my husband in." Mildred kept her voice level and impassive. "Before they murdered Talyian in front of the entire court, those vermin castrated Clavian and his two sons for all to see, including my husband. Those wretches delivered the same punishment to Clavian's brother, Rhys, despite his never marrying nor showing any inclination to sire any children of his own. They drove a spear through Talyian's heart after they announced that King Amry was also dead and without a male heir."

Alex understood now why the two boys were so terrified.

"Before my father died, my mother became pregnant." Diana held Mildred's hands. "She gave birth to a son, Amryian II."

"Evellion's line continues?" Mildred whispered.

"Forgive me," Alex cut in, puzzled. Having grown up in a small village away from Evellion's customs, he never understood the reason Evellion held that their house's lines could only continue through male heirs. "It never ended. Even without Lara's new son, there are women enough in this family who are quite capable of continuing that legacy."

"Evellion's line is maintained through the male descendants," Jenna said.

"But why? I mean, sure, Aewen placed a crown on my head, but I can guarantee that she didn't do so because of what dangled between my legs."

The three women looked at each other, uncertain how to answer. "Are you recommending overturning tradition that has been maintained since the time of Thellion?" Jenna asked.

"As the Thellish king, tradition be damned. Whichever is the most capable of my—our—children will wear the crown after we both pass," Alex said.

"I always knew you would choose your match wisely," Mildred said to Diana.

"So, what exactly are you suggesting?" Jenna asked again.

"I suggest that Lara remains the Queen of Evellion, not simply as regent for an infant, and that you, Mildred, continue on as Duchess of Cyril. Your children can take that mantle whenever you choose to pass it on."

"The other dukes and lords will be in an uproar over this," Mildred said.

"They'll come around. I'm pretty sure they're all married and wouldn't want to offend their spouses trying to defend tradition for the sake of tradition. Besides, look at Sorenthil. Their first monarch after Thellion's civil war was a queen and since then, they've had more queens than kings and they've managed just fine."

Mildred cracked a smile and Jenna laughed. "I suppose a Vaerin wearing Thellion's crown isn't the worst thing to have happened in this age," Mildred said.

"Evellion's descendants will have to wear it after I'm done with it." Alex squeezed Diana's hand.

"But Diana, I ask again. How are you here?" Mildred asked.

"After the siege was lifted from Everin and Evellion became a province of Thellion, Alex brought his army here, accompanied by Eldinari elves and dwarves of Oern Schtam. The Erynien Empire must have focused their entire northern effort on Everin, for we didn't come across any resistance on our journey here," Diana said.

"And how long ago was this decisive battle at Everin?" Mildred asked.

"About a month," Diana said.

"Perhaps not all is resolved. Chaia has been here since then. She had been staying here in the palace before the city fell. I never thought I would meet a shadow elf, but she was what I had imagined they would be like. She's been gone longer than usual, so perhaps she has fled back south," Mildred said.

"Or she's still hiding—watching us and biding her time." Jenna shivered as she looked over her shoulder.

"If she is, she won't be able to hide from Fendryl and his star wardens," Alex said.

"Who?" Mildred asked.

"An elven lord—sorry, they don't like to be called that. He and his spouse are the Lierafen aryl. He's a wielder and is still immortal, as are the star wardens. They'll comb through this city before they head south to join up with Devlyn and the Luminari," Alex said. Mildred and Jenna shared a look, neither knowing who or what Alex was referring to.

"I'll bring you up to speed on everything that has happened in the past years, but first, what happened here? How did Cyril fall so quickly?" Diana asked.

Mildred pursed her lips, clearly not wanting to relive those events. "Demetri, please take your siblings away and ask your father and uncle to come join us." The children darted away at her word. "They were already here inside the city walls. We had no reason to turn anyone away from our gates. Chaia even had a place in our court. Granted, she wore a different face and pretended to be Lady Jasnil of House Renfry. We only realized who she was after Cyril had fallen and Erynor's flags flew above our gates and palace.

"She wasn't the only shadow elf either. They stole the souls of hundreds and those scoundrels from Perrien and Dwonia slaughtered anyone who wore armor. It all happened so quickly and the city was filled with enemy troops before the sun dipped behind the Vespien Mountains. I will not speak of the atrocities they committed against our people."

Diana held Mildred's hand as Jenna rubbed the duchess' back.

"They threatened to burn the city and slaughter every civilian if we didn't open the palace gates. Knowing that the city was lost, we let them in. They abused us all and paraded us through the streets. The people learned that the duke had been killed and what had been done to my sons and grandsons. When the brutes started to randomly kill again, they forbade anyone to care for the bodies. Anyone caught doing so received the same treatment as the dead. It's why we haven't…" Mildred choked up as her eyes watered.

"That's all in the past now. The dead will receive proper burials," Diana said.

"Thank you. Now that the enemy is gone, it will be nice to clean this place up again and restore the water flow more fully into the city." Mildred flattened her dirty threadbare skirt and took a deep breath in and straightened her posture just as two haggard looking men came into the room. They were as dirty as the women and children and their clothing was just as filthy and ragged.

"Clavian, Rhys." Mildred opened her arms to her sons. They shuffled forward, then noticed who else was in the room.

"Diana?" the two men said together, and Alex noted the panic that overtook them at what her presence here might mean.

"Be calm, uncles. I am here freely and no prisoner. The enemy has been defeated, the north is free, and Thellion's banners have returned."

"How is this possible?" Rhys asked, his haunted look fading as hope rose.

Diana told Clavian and Rhys what she had already told Mildred and Jenna. The brothers now looked at Alex quite differently.

"We like him," Mildred said.

"Already?" Clavian arched an eyebrow.

Jenna grabbed her husband's hand and smiled at him. "It's a good match and Evellion only survived because of Thellion."

"Is it true—is Cyril free of the Erynien Empire?" Clavian gripped the back of Jenna's chair.

"If any shadow elves were foolish enough to remain, the Eldinari will find them," Alex said.

"Now that that's settled, we need to release the water from the mountain back into the city and start washing the filth from it." Mildred stood as though she had every intention to trek up the mountain herself.

"We'll show the Thellish soldiers the way, Mother. It might be wise to bring one of those Eldinari wielders as well. There's no saying what sort of traps might be waiting for us," Clavian said.

"The Eldinari and ei'ana are scattered throughout the city, helping anyone they can and most of our troops are distributing food and water. We didn't think the situation would be as dire here as we found it. Once we had those gates opened and took our first glimpse inside, the nature of our mission became clear," Alex said.

"I never thought a Vaerin would be so kind to Evellions and I certainly never thought I'd be happy to see one wearing Thellion's crown," Clavian said.

Alex thought Clavian's opinion of Vaerins might change after meeting Alex's mother. "Fendryl will be more help than I can be—he and the other wielders will see the people here restored," Alex said.

"He?" Rhys said, sparing a cautious look with his mother and brother. "Are you saying he's a kien wielder and can wield with control?"

"The Eldinari elves had never lost their balance—their kien wielders were never a threat like the others in Eklean. That being said, I suppose you wouldn't have received the news. Balance is returning between kien and kiara wielders. It started with Devlyn Lorenthien, but now there are a number of men who can wield safely," Diana said.

"It seems we have more to learn about the state of Eklean than we thought if a Lorenthien walks these lands again," Mildred said, stunned.

"They never left us. Whether they knew who they were is another question entirely. Devlyn only found out because of his bond with a phoenix, or something along those lines—elf magic or something. His family has been in Cor'lera for twelve hundred years," Alex said, uncomfortably remembering his uncle's involvement in nearly destroying that family.

"We should start restoring this city before we waste any more time here. Diana, you stay with me and tell me everything that's happened since Cyril fell. If I'm to be Cyril's duchess, I'll need to be informed."

"Mother?" Clavian asked.

"Your mother still has some fight in her and would see this city returned to its former glory while being a thorn in the empire's side. King Alexander here has lifted the sexist rules of succession." Mildred patted Diana's forearm. "Come, let's start in the throne room and finally put my poor husband to rest."

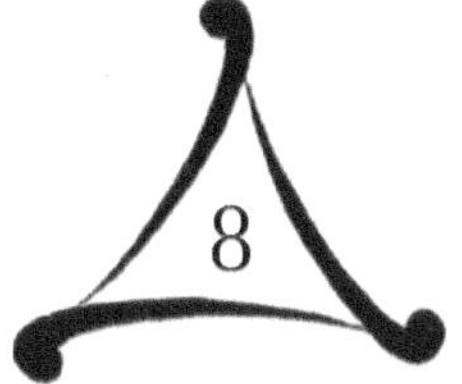

BACK AND FORTH

Devlyn, Ellendren, and Arlyn sat in silence, cross-legged in a triangle on the floor of Arlyn's tent. There was little to distract them for the furnishings were simple and limited to a mattress and a folding desk and chair designed to be broken down for travel. The mattress was thin and the chair looked wobbly. Arlyn was by no means an elderly elf, but neither would anyone consider him youthful enough to be comfortable on a threadbare mattress.

Devlyn and Ellendren were there to learn to wield lumenys so Aliel and Tariel kept their distance from the tent, choosing to enjoy the morning sky instead. Their presence too easily obscured lumenys. Arlyn was the only elf currently at the Luminari encampment capable of teaching them. They had considered inviting Clara or one of the Eldinari to help them, but Arlyn reminded them that lumenys was not something that was taught, but rather a gift—a gift they had already received. The wielder had to discover how to harness that power in themselves.

Based on their seating arrangement, Devlyn assumed that Arlyn had to have studied with Therril, for they had been sitting together in the silence for a long while. Surely Arlyn wasn't old enough to adopt the passive and meditative teaching style that Therril and Alethea favored.

"I'm going to assume that your bond with the phoenix, along with your already established comfort with the other erendinth will make this session rather short." Arlyn smiled and Devlyn felt something alter.

The change wasn't anything physical. It felt like a small droplet of the Chamber of Light had been transported to Arlyn's tent, and it now appeared before them in the shape of a melon-sized globe. Following his and Ellendren's visit to the Empyrean Sphere, Devlyn had realized that the incredible light in the Temple of Ceur was not lumenys. As impossible as it sounded, that brilliance was a droplet of Lumaeniel in Teraeniel. The light was not a single erendinth, but so much more.

"As an ei'ceuril steward, my influence over lumenys will be quite different from your own experience. While you are both able to wield that transcendental erendinth, I am also connected to the temple—every ei'ceuril is."

"What have you been able to do with the light only an ei'ceuril can wield?" Ellendren asked.

"For the first time since the last stewards died out following the Ceurendol War, I rekindled the Light and performed our sacred rituals in Gneal's and Everin's cathedrals, a task typically carried out by a city's archsteward. The faithful who are unable to visit Ceurenyl and the Temple of Ceur can bask in Anaweh's Light once more. Eklean's cathedrals have been dark long enough," Arlyn said.

"Does that mean that this light you wielded is part of the Chamber of Light?" Ellendren asked, reaching out to the illumination as though she could touch it.

"Indeed, it is. The ei'ceuril have studied the light in the temple since all the way back to Theseryn. We know it is connected to Lumaeniel, but we also speculate that it might be connected to Anaweh as well. We've yet to come to an agreeable consensus as an institution and it is likely that some lowly and forgotten ei'ceuril from long ago has already answered it."

Devlyn saw the gears turning in Ellendren's mind, her determination to research that light evident. Arlyn shifted the conversation away from academia and back to wielding.

"According to Theseryn's account of creation, Uriel was the fourth anadel to journey beyond Lumaeniel and he brought lumenys with him to this world-below. Lumenys is most like Anaweh and ties all creation—it's the pin that holds everything together in the center."

Recalling the trials at Tenethyl and his experience of Thien's memories, Devlyn asked, "Is it possible to heal someone with lumenys?" He had experienced Thien's healing of a woman, but Devlyn wasn't thinking of healing a person. Could he heal Krysenthiel of the desolation caused by the Shroud? What if they had been looking wrongly at the Shroud this entire time? Rather than something to be fought, what if it was a physical disease that needed to be healed?

"I've never seen it done myself, but in principle, lumenys should be a highly effective healing agent. The very nature of lumenys is to bring light to all creation, not just to illumine, but to reveal it as it truly is—as it was meant to be." Devlyn immediately thought of how he saw the world when he and Aliel were bonded. Even the darkest of nights appeared as though a hundred suns lit the sky when he looked through the phoenix's golden eyes.

"So arguably, lumenys perfects creation." Ellendren tapped her fingers on her leg, doubtless trying to riddle something out.

"I recommend we start with a simple wield before you both leap to something more exotic." Arlyn had already come too familiar with their ambition. "I want you both to examine the wield I currently have in place. You'll recognize it easily enough and should be able to replicate it shortly."

Devlyn and Ellendren both reached out to the wield, not physically, but in the same manner that they would examine one of their own wields. Simply by interacting with lumenys, Devlyn wanted to embrace it and bring that erendinth into himself to wield it in return. Without intending to, he realized that Ellendren was thinking the same, only while he had to embrace the transcendental erendinth, she had to exert her being and press into it, in the same manner that he wielded the elemental erendinth. A balance existed between kien and kiara wielders.

That Balance had been thrown out of order when Erynor had assaulted Septyl. While Balance was finally returning, the Erynien Empire and its Tenebrae School were trying to stop that—they did not want a whole and strong Septyl reformed. The ei'ana had been Erynor's first target when he had started his war fourteen hundred years ago. They might not have been able to stop his empire, but they would have been a commendable adversary.

Devlyn couldn't think about Septyl just now. He returned his attention to the wield in front of him. It didn't give off any heat like ignys would, but it did make him feel warm on the inside. Simply by interacting with Arlyn's wield, it managed to penetrate to his core, and he again wondered if the erendinth were alive. Were they active and intelligible beings set in Teraeniel?

A second globe bloomed in the tent. Devlyn turned to Ellendren and realized that she had already replicated Arlyn's wield while he had been lost in thought. Feeling as though he was falling behind and not wanting to stall their session any longer because of his wandering mind, Devlyn embraced lumenys. The experience reminded him of bonding with Aliel. Everything in the tent appeared more real as he held that erendinth within himself. His knowledge of Ellendren and Arlyn deepened, nothing new, but he saw them more perfectly as who they were in that moment.

As he internally massaged lumenys, learning as much as he could while he interacted with it, he wondered what sort of wields he could create in conjunction with the other erendinth. He had previously only been able to wield six of the erendinth together before and those had been some of the most powerful wields he had ever used. His mind drowned in the endless possibilities, not just to defend the Luminari, but also the ability to create with countless new wields.

At last, Devlyn wielded a globe, the same as the other two already hovering in the tent. The three globes were very different from the lighted spheres that the ei'ana wielded; in fact, calling these globes was misleading. Their source was focused on a central node, but unlike the globes of light wielded with the elemental erendinth, these did not have a defined shell. These weren't wielded of fire and air; this light did not have to be contained. These wields were brighter at their centers but the light diffused the further it went from that center.

With finally knowingly wielding lumenys for the first time, Devlyn had a strong urge to go to the edge of the camp and visit the Shroud. Ellendren must have sensed his desire and placed her hand on his. They shared a look and without speaking, agreed it was time to test the Shroud.

"Determined?" Arlyn asked as he smiled. "Good. I'll come with you."

The three wields faded and the elves stood, ready to leave the tent. Devlyn reached out to Aliel who seemed excited, no doubt aware that Devlyn had managed to wield lumenys. Devlyn saw Aliel and Tariel flying toward the Shroud as their song filled the camp. Elves poked their heads out of their tents to see Devlyn, Ellendren, and Arlyn walking toward the Shroud, beckoned by the phoenix's tune. Viren trailed behind them and before long they stood outside the camp with a broad plain between them and the Shroud. While their camp lay near the edge of the Shroud, the Luminari did not dare sleep any closer than they already did. So much about the Shroud was unknown; all they could say for certain was that it hungrily reached out as it tried to expand and consume more of Teraeniel.

The tents now well behind them, Devlyn and Ellendren bonded with their phoenix and formed a link between themselves and Arlyn. Devlyn embraced lumenys and led the wield as Ellendren and Arlyn lent him their strength through their connection. He began to probe the diseased mist and fog with the lumenys wield, immediately sickened by their proximity to it. The Shroud congealed like a thunderous storm clap. For the first time, Devlyn saw streaks of what had to be tenebrys lightning inside the Shroud. He had never before come close enough to it to see the sinister bolts hidden in the mass.

He felt the Shroud lash out at him in a vicious reaction to his wield. Somehow the Shroud knew who wielded and was capable of defending itself. Embracing the other transcendental erendinth and pressing into the elemental erendinth, Devlyn allowed his instincts to take control as he formed a new wield. It felt familiar somehow, but also wholly different at the same time. He built up the wield, holding it as he poured more power into it.

Bolts lashed out from the Shroud, some haphazardly outward, but one came straight for Devlyn. He sensed its direction as his heart chilled and the reminder of the wound he'd received in Lankor flashed through his body. Without knowing what his wield would do, he unleashed it in a burst of energy. The wield latched onto the tenebrys bolts and swallowed them, as though they were dust caught in a breeze.

Something screamed from within the Shroud and Devlyn wondered if it was the Shroud itself screaming. Maintaining his wield, he released a second burst, not toward any oncoming lighting, but at the Shroud itself. His wield exploded against its edge. It felt like he pushed against a solid wall. Pouring more energy into his wield, thankful for Ellendren and Arlyn lending their strength as he was nearing the brink of collapse, he continued to heave against the wall of disease and death as thunder cracked inside it. He stepped forward and continued to push. He lost count of how many steps he had taken, simply feeling ice crunch beneath his feet with each one.

With a final exertion, he unleashed the powerful wield. Thunder clapped in response, but he thought it might have been his wield smashing against the Shroud. He didn't have the opportunity to investigate. His vision blackened and he didn't feel his body smack against the frozen ground.

Toryn heard the thunder explode in the distance and only spared a glance to see the Shroud's violent reaction. In her opinion, the Shroud was a beast—a monster from the stories told to frighten children. The monsters that the Evil One had unleashed on Teraeniel in the Elder Days, now locked away with their master. She had no idea what had so aggravated the Shroud, but it seemed the beast was angry. Toryn couldn't do anything about that though. She was needed. What the Luminari had long feared had finally come to pass. A small force of Cyndinari had been spotted only moments before they attacked and Toryn was still exhausted from the skirmish that had followed.

It ended just as quickly as it started and the Cyndinari retreated immediately after their first and only strike. It seemed that they weren't meant to break through the Luminari lines and while the victory was appreciated, it also had a stench of something more devious in the works, like it had been nothing more than a test of the Luminari elves' defenses. Toryn didn't know if they had learned anything, but it did worry her. If that was only an exploratory strike, what would a real offensive measure look like?

She replayed her small role in the battle; oddly enough she hadn't come across any shadow elves. The enemy carried slender curved swords and knew how to use them. While it had only been a small force, their expertise with swords made it feel like they were fighting a force twice as large. Fortunately, Toryn hadn't heard of any casualties yet. That would not be the case when the Erynien Empire sent their full force and she shivered at the thought. People died during wars and battles, but what if the enemy got past their defensive lines or went around them to reach the civilians in the camp? The entire Luminari population was here in the open. If Erynor wanted to, he could erase them off the face of Teraeniel if he brought enough might to see the job done.

Toryn walked with Jeanne and Byron through the defensive lines, content to let the other two do most of the talking. They had extensive military experience that Toryn dreamed of having herself. While Jeanne had thousands of years over Byron, the former Lord Knight of Lucillia's knowledge of the Luminari military capabilities was invaluable. Jeanne spoke with all the lieutenants and captains on the front lines, determining their weak points. Their lack of any defensive walls worried everyone present. All they had were the mounds of packed dirt, snow, and ice. They weren't particularly high, offering only a token of resistance to slow down the enemy.

Toryn noticed that a large gathering huddled together toward the end of the patrol route, near the far end of their defensive lines. The closer Toryn, Jeanne, and Byron came, the louder the group grew. The Luminari parted quickly for Jeanne and Byron, barely acknowledging Toryn despite her previous role as Lady of the Watch. She no longer had that title and had only briefly held it, so her position was largely forgotten. She cared little about the lost title but wasn't thrilled about being seen as a squire. Byron was in a similar situation and if it was difficult for her, she imagined the transition was all the more so for him. He was the late queen's brother, while Toryn was the daughter of a man who attended House Narielle. If Byron Roendryn held a grudge about becoming a squire again he never mentioned it, at least not to Toryn.

Once they made it through the gathering, Toryn was surprised to see a scowling elf with cinnamon hair—a Cyndinari. The enemy had retreated so quickly that Toryn didn't think it would be possible to take any captives. The prisoner's armor was mostly stripped from him and his sword was piled on top of it, a safe distance away. He looked at Jeanne with such a deep loathing that Toryn wondered whether the Guardian knight and the Cyndinari had a past. That was impossible since Jeanne had only recently left the Guardian's Citadel. Still, the Cyndinari looked as though he was ready to lash out at Jeanne.

"What has he said so far?" Jeanne asked the gathered elves.

"Not much. He's been tight lipped nearly the entire time," Elayne replied, the only other Guardian knight present.

Jeanne stepped closer to the prisoner. On his knees with his arms bound behind his back, he was now avoiding eye contact with the First of the Guardians. "Where is your army hiding?"

"They will kill you," he said, his tone venomous. "They will right the sin of your people and wipe your filth from memory. Erynor is not interested in slaves this time."

"What were you hoping to learn with this folly of an attack?" Jeanne ignored the threat.

"Both our people are mortal because of your ancestors. You destroyed the natural balance and we were all brought low to waste away as mortals."

"Take him away. We won't be getting much more out of this one." Jeanne remained steady as two Luminari pulled the Cyndinari to his feet and took him away under Elayne's watchful eye.

Toryn's mind still swirled in response to the battle and now the ramblings of a seemingly crazed elf added to the whirling thoughts. None of what he said made any sense to her. The Luminari had created Ceurendol to share their Life immortal. The Cyndinari were the ones who ruined everything. If the Erynien Empire hadn't started the Ceurendol War and placed the Shroud over the entirety of Krysenthiel thereby severing the Luminari from the Jewel of Life, neither elven kin would have lost their immortality.

Lost in her thoughts, Toryn almost didn't hear Jeanne call for her to follow. Toryn had somewhat assumed that she wouldn't be required to practice jienzu this evening. Surely there had been enough excitement for one day. She was wrong in that assumption and she joined Byron and the other squires for their evening jienzu and meditation. At least the forms should relax her after the rigors of the battle—her shoulders were still sore from the fighting.

REPORTS

Devlyn's dreams had been fuzzy with light and dark swirling about and the Shroud laughing at him. He finally woke when he felt an inward pull, a pull he recognized. Someone was trying to bring him into Somnaeniel. He'd promised Eagan and Abbey that he wouldn't stop his training with the World-in-Between, but the Void was consuming that realm and Devlyn did not trust himself to venture there alone. So much of it had been consumed by oily puddles.

So the moment he felt that pull, his body jarred him awake and he found himself alone on the bed in his tent. He didn't recall falling asleep nor going to the tent in the first place. It certainly wasn't late enough for bed. The dull glow against the canvas had the look of evening, and he questioned why he was lying in bed at this hour. Before the question could fully form, Aliel appeared in a flash of light and flapped about before settling on Devlyn's chest, the phoenix's talons scratching his bare skin. Aliel nuzzled Devlyn's cheek with his own.

You need to stop scaring me like this, Aliel conveyed.

Sorry. I'm still trying to remember exactly what happened. How reckless and careless is Elle going to accuse me of being this time?

Tariel says it's all that's on her mind, but she has kept it hidden from the aryls. She's spent the entire afternoon spinning the story to make it seem intentional.

Make what seem intentional?

Before Aliel could respond, Ellendren came in. Devlyn immediately felt her warring emotions. She was rather worried over his wellbeing yet also somewhat angry with him for endangering himself. Aliel retreated to a perch as Devlyn sat up.

"Thank the Light you're awake," she said plainly, keeping her true thoughts to herself for the moment. "I'll call a chamber meeting at once. A number of things have happened and I'm afraid I wasn't inclined to wait much longer for you to wake before summoning the aryls. Some of them were insisting on coming here whether you awoke from overtaxing yourself or not."

"What's happened?" Devlyn asked, gently patting the tender scratches on his chest.

"Lyren?" Ellendren called without answering Devlyn. "Please assist Devlyn in getting ready for a chamber meeting. And Pevrel, can you please have the summons delivered to the high aryls?"

Lyren already had a set of lierathnil ready for Devlyn and handed him the trousers even as he helped him out of bed.

Ellendren paced as she waited for him to dress. "We'll get more details at the chamber meeting, but it seems that your willful ignorance of your own limits has indeed pushed the Shroud back. We aren't sure yet how much. I've sent a few Guardian knights and ei'ana to investigate just how far the boundary has been moved. I hope they'll return before the chamber meeting is over."

"That's fantastic news," Devlyn said moving his arms back to slide them into the shirt Lyren held out.

"That's not all." Ellendren paced some more. "The Cyndinari led a surprise attack while we were occupied with the Shroud. There aren't any reported casualties and we've captured one of the enemy. It's too early to tell, but Jeanne believes it was to test our defenses. I've only spoken with her briefly, but she said she hasn't learned anything helpful from the prisoner."

Devlyn pulled the outer garment over his shoulders, ready to leave. He considered Ellendren's words. Either of these two pieces of news could stand alone and require a week's worth of chamber meetings. Dealing with them both at the same time was sure to be a challenge. As they left their tent and made their way to the chamber tent, Devlyn went through what happened earlier at the Shroud—what he could remember of it. He had to be ready for the aryls' interrogation and Ellendren clarified the parts that were fuzzy in his memory. The first thing they would ask was how long would it take to remove all the Shroud. Devlyn dreaded that question. He had no idea how long it would take; he didn't even know how far he had pushed the Shroud back today.

When they reached the chamber tent, most of the high aryls were already present, and while the minor aryls were not invited to this meeting, a number of them had gathered outside the chamber tent to be the first to hear of what was discussed inside. They all knew about the attack and some of them might even know about the Shroud already. Surely, they had all heard it groan earlier.

Taking their seats at the ring of tables, Devlyn waited for Naesiv to begin the meeting, but he remained seated while Ellendren cleared her throat and rose to her feet. Devlyn wondered whether she was leading this meeting because she had been the one to summon the aryls.

"Distinguished aryls, by now, I'm positive that you are aware of today's events. The Erynien Empire in the form of a Cyndinari advance exploratory force has finally caught up to us. We suffered no casualties and we've taken one of them prisoner. The First of the Guardians is having him interrogated. However, she fears that his mind is broken and that we won't learn much from him. It appears he has been given a fabricated version of history, one that vilifies our people and holds our ancestors accountable for our shared loss of Life immortal." Ellendren sighed and her gaze briefly lowered. "Going forward, it will be prudent to assume that the Cyndinari elves truly blame us for the loss of their immortality and still despise us for that."

"How could they possibly deign to blame us? They're the fools who started the Ceurendol War all those years ago and placed the Shroud over Krysenthiel, severing us from Ceurendol while condemning themselves," Aegian argued.

"Surely they are deranged and have been fed nothing but Erynien propaganda. Do they also blame us for depriving them of their heinous emperor for twelve hundred years?" Kyiel asked.

"I'm sure that is the case. I've invited the First of the Guardians to deliver a report to us." Ellendren returned to her seat as Jeanne walked into the chamber tent, as though she had been waiting for Ellendren's signal.

She walked to the center of the tent and bowed to the gathered aryls. "Respected aryls. Earlier today, between the seventh and eighth hour, a small contingent of Cyndinari attacked our southern defenses. This force was no larger than fifty elves and given their numbers and the brevity of the strike, we surmise that the attack was simply to test our defenses and gather information. Whether it was meant to determine where our fortifications stand or what our defensive capabilities are, I cannot say. Nor can I say if they've learned what they sought. They very well could have attacked to discover whether the news of Guardian knights returning was accurate."

"So Erynor has finally unleashed his legions against us," Ciraenth said.

"No. The legions do not attack in small forays. Our losses would have been higher if even only one of the Erynien legions was set against us. We would likely still be fighting for our lives if they were involved," Jeanne said. The tent quieted at the weight of Jeanne's information.

"How is it that we weren't prepared for this attack?" Enoria asked, breaking the silence.

"Forgive me, Ei'terel, in what manner were we unprepared?" Jeanne asked, obviously feeling slighted.

"My household had no warning of the attack—we had no time nor means to protect ourselves."

"Visibility is quite limited this close to the Shroud. While the

Shroud does not extend into the rest of Eklean, dense fog here is quite common. The Cyndinari would be knowledgeable about manipulating the fog and clouds to conceal their movement, especially if there is a wielder among them. But I assure you, we were not unprepared. We met the enemy and pushed them back," Jeanne said.

"What of that red dragon and its rider? I thought they were supposed to be able to alert us to dangers such as these," Iridil said.

"Liara and Prya did alert us to the approaching Cyndinari, giving us precious moments to organize before they attacked," Jeanne said.

"Do you think a shadow elf was involved in manipulating the fog?" Binoral asked.

"Not every Cyndinari wielder is a shadow elf. If there were wielders among their numbers, they did not engage themselves or their abilities in the fight. As to the force that we did confront, they were skilled sword fighters. I believe they still utilize a form of jienzu, although it is a corrupted form bent on power."

"Jienzu?" Therrin asked, stirring similar questions from the aryls at the forgotten word.

"It is a way in which anacordel balance themselves; its origins date back to the First Era and before all was lost, the Luminari practiced the forms daily," Jeanne said impassively.

"Is it an exercise?" Toral asked.

"This is likely not the appropriate time to introduce you to jienzu. I invite you all to the Guardian knights' training grounds; we practice jienzu twice a day." Jeanne appraised the aryls as though she truly hoped they would all learn jienzu. "Perhaps classes could be offered."

"Do we know where the Cyndinari forces are hiding? Where have they set up their camp?" Binoral asked, steering the meeting away from exercise and back to the point.

"Our scouts have maintained a large perimeter since we moved to this location and they have yet to find any evidence of a large camp. It's possible that they are intentionally staying outside our perimeter, or they've discovered a way to cloak their entire camp," Jeanne said.

"We should expand our patrols then. We can't allow a repeat of what happened today. Surprise attacks simply cannot be tolerated," Silvia said snippily.

"Given our current numbers, expanding our patrol will only lead to our scouts going missing. Our perimeter is as large as we can safely maintain it, especially now that we've been asked to form a different sort of patrol," Jeanne said.

"And what sort of patrol is this? We have not been consulted," Ciraenth said. Jeanne looked to Ellendren.

"That is the other reason for this chamber meeting." Ellendren returned to her feet. "Thank you for your report, Jeanne. Before you go, have your scouts returned yet?"

"Afraid not. I held off sending them until I was confident our defenses were secure and another attack wasn't likely."

"Of course, thank you. We eagerly await their report."

"As do I." Jeanne bowed and left the aryls, all of them now staring at Ellendren.

"Before the Cyndinari attacked, Devlyn, Arlyn, and I went to the edge of the Shroud. We believed it was time to test what we have learned. The little that we know of our endeavor at this time is that we have successfully pushed the Shroud back some. We will not know the full extent of the distance until the Guardians and ei'ana return," Ellendren said.

"How long have they been gone? Is it such a great distance that it's taking them longer than expected?" Enithil asked.

"Jeanne would have been the person to ask for how long the scouts have been gone. As for the distance the Shroud has been pushed back, we'll have to wait for the scouts to return. Truly, we don't even know if the Shroud will reclaim the territory lost," Ellendren said.

"I don't think that's likely," Devlyn piped up, stifling a yawn. "When Aliel and I pierced the Shroud four years ago, I don't know how

I knew, but something told me that the Shroud could not take back that land once it was freed."

"Is there any proof of that? The Cyndinari are on our doorstep; sooner or later we will be forced to retreat into the lands freed from the Shroud. We must have the utmost certainty that it will not swallow us if we do."

"Agreed, the Shroud and its boundary should be monitored before we consider crossing into Krysenthiel," Fyona said.

The gathered aryls fell into deliberations among themselves of how to best observe the Shroud. It seemed that they all had their own idea of how to do so, which was odd since few of them were wielders. As Devlyn listened, he noticed that the Clarion aryl, Enithil and Binoral were speaking privately, their tone hushed; they seemed to care little about the discussion surrounding them. Then Enithil stood, still holding Binoral's hand and cleared his throat as a signal to the aryls who hadn't realized he wished to speak. The other aryls looked surprised and annoyed as they all believed their ideas would be better than anything Enithil had to say on the matter.

"How close are we to Eandyl?" Enithil looked from Devlyn to Ellendren and then to the gathered aryls, all the while holding Binoral's hand.

"I beg your pardon?" Silvia said. "We are all eager to reclaim our ancestral cities, but surely now is not the time to focus on your own."

"My grandfather told me stories of Eandyl. He likely heard them from his grandparents and they from theirs, all the way back to the time our people were slaves. My ancestors refused to let their descendants forget who they were. They knew their descendants would live short mortal lives and die. When my grandfather first told me about Eandyl, I felt as though I could actually see it, as though I was there or had been there before. He said the entire city glowed in a golden light from the lumaryl. I can even see how the spires of the palace and the rest of the city caught the sunlight and magnified it. It seems an impossible image."

"Enithil, we were all told similar stories—we only know of our titles and place among the Luminari because those tales were preserved in living memories," Therrin said.

"Of course, forgive me." Enithil shared a warm smile. "When my grandfather told me of Eandyl, he said it stood in the southeast of Krysenthiel, the nearest of our cities to Sorenthil. An ancient road once connected Myrium and Eandyl. If we can find that road and Eandyl's location, the Lorenthien aryl can focus their efforts in removing the Shroud from Eandyl. We could have a fortified position the next time the Erynien Empire attacks."

"Eandyl can't be far from us," Ellendren said, her eyes unfocused as though she was mentally tracing out the cartography.

"Someone send a page for some maps. I would like to see just how close we are to Eandyl. I would very much like to no longer sleep in a tent," Toral said.

The aryls continued to discuss their new focus on Eandyl after several maps were brought in, crowding around the table the maps had been spread out on. The most helpful one showed only Krysenthiel with all its cities and landmarks penned across the vellum. Curiously though, there weren't any roads connecting the cities. Roads came in from the south and into Krysenthiel, such as the road that Enithil mentioned leading to Myrium.

"The roads," Toral commented, "it's curious that none of them go past the border cities."

Devlyn looked back at the maps and quickly saw that Toral was correct, none of the roads went further than the outer cities. He turned to Viren, the only elf still in the chamber tent who had lived in Krysenthiel during those days, and asked, "How did everyone travel through Krysenthiel without roads?"

Viren's face showed his surprise that Devlyn didn't know. "You're accustomed to seguians."

"Well, yes, but… minums wouldn't create them constantly."

"Only rarely did they do it themselves, Ei'denai. Did you not see the lumaryl arches at Gwilnor?"

Realization flashed across Devlyn's eyes, as he remembered the opened seguians used by the Eldinari elves in the Eldin Wood. "The cities are connected by seguians?" he said in disbelief, looking at the maps anew.

"Those portals have long been closed," Viren said.

"How do we reopen them?" Ellendren asked.

"They cannot be reopened until the Shroud is gone and the cities are unsealed by their aryls," Viren replied.

"Enough about roads; I still can't find Eandyl, where is it?" Aegian asked. Devlyn pointed to it.

"Are we really that close to Eandyl?" Valerie asked.

"We should consult with the First of the Guardians about our trajectory; this will doubtless require their planning as well as our own," Toral replied.

"We can schedule a meeting when their scouts return to brief us. The information they bring back will be invaluable to our next steps," Zara said.

"Do we know where this road is located? It would lead us directly to Eandyl if found," Naesiv said.

"It's been unused for fourteen hundred years. Surely, it's grown over by now. We could be standing on top of it and have no idea." Aegian said.

"We could start asking around the camp; this is quite a large settlement. If we are on top of it, surely someone has noticed it. And if no one in the camp has, perhaps scouts have noticed it during their patrols," Binoral said.

An excitement took hold over the aryls and they all seemed ready to start the search for the road to Eandyl, none caring that it wasn't their own ancestral city.

While everyone had been examining the maps, Devlyn had felt an impulsive impatience come over him. He didn't understand why they had to wait for the scouting party to return. Flying there on his own would require significantly less time. He could easily bond with Aliel and fly there and back.

You forget that you recently passed out from overexerting yourself today, Ellendren shared. She placed a hand on his, as though to hold him in place. *We don't have to do everything. Besides, you need to rest.*

Forgotten Passages

Kevn stayed awake after everyone else had gone to sleep and was now alone in the Ceurtriarch's private library. A single candle flickered beside him to light the book he was reading. He had grown comfortable with the space and its neatly lined bookshelves. Unlike the temple's main library with a dozen unconnected rooms each holding collections that were even less connected and organized, this small library had a clear order to it that Kevn appreciated. The only books that were seemingly out of place were the scattered stacks of Benedetto's diaries that he and the others had brought here to study. Together, they had read through most of the available collection and had yet to find anything useful toward retaking Gwilnor Academy.

He wondered again at what Selenya had meant about changing the status at the castle before attempting any sort of rescue mission. What could they possibly change?

He stood to stretch and then took the candlestick to light the books on one of the shelves. He enjoyed reading the titles when they were lined up next to each other. It relaxed him and allowed him to refocus before returning to his task or settling his mind enough to sleep. He had looked at these shelves hundreds of times in this very manner but had not appraised them with a critical eye. Not expecting to find anything useful on the shelves, he instead mused about the lettering on the spines. The Ceurtriarch's personal collection had been selected by each of the successive Ceurtriarchs. Aaron had yet to review the current selection, so his predecessor's collection remained on the shelves. Ealyndol had been a wise elf and Kevn liked to think that he had spent most of his free time reading. Given the tomes available in what had been his personal library, Ealyndol had been either incredibly intelligent or had never removed a single book placed by his predecessors from the shelves.

As Kevn went down a line of books, one caught his attention. The brown leather spine was free of any lettering and it was much thinner than the other books accompanying it. Kevn had read dozens of similar books and wondered if Ealyndol had kept a diary of his own. Kevn hesitated before reaching for the diary, unsure about whether or not he had the right to read the private entries of Ealyndol. Pushing that thought aside, he grabbed the thin book and opened it to the first page. His eyes lit up when he read the familiar opening words of Benedetto marveling about his advanced age due to Ceurendol. Kevn flipped through the pages, quickly realizing that the earliest passages of this diary were written in the year 7530.3E, thirty-three years before the fall of Krysenthiel.

Kevn had read other documents from during the Ceurendol War but considering that Eklean had been fighting for its survival at the time, scholarship had plummeted and nothing of note had been published during the period. However, this diary provided an in-depth view of someone living during the war. As Kevn pored through the diary, too excited to sit down, he learned that Benedetto and the others in the temple had been living with Ceurtriarch Daeryn's decision. Benedetto lamented about the consequences of that decision and hoped it would one day be reversed.

Despite the lateness of the hour, Kevn read through the entire diary. While it didn't provide any definitive answer, it was clear that something had been done and that something had affected the entire city. Kevn surmised it had to do with extending the temple ward beyond its current boundary. How was such a thing even possible? Surely no one could control that much power.

Set on a new purpose, Kevn returned to searching the shelves for another diary, hoping that Ealyndol had kept other diaries from years long past. Had Ceurtriarch Daeryn kept a diary during the Ceurendol War?

Tired, Kevn rubbed his eyes. They were well past their straining point and he knew that he had to get some sleep, but he pushed on. That diary had to be in here and he didn't want to have to wait until morning to access the temple's main library. As he continued his search, something scratched at his ear. It tickled and he turned to find no one. Dismissing the itch, he turned back to the shelves. His mind was too focused to divide his attention but the scratching at his ear persisted. Calming his mind, he looked around the library again.

"Is someone there?" he asked.

It is time.

Kevn didn't recognize that voice, not even as his own mind telling him he should sleep. That the voice he'd heard did not speak in the Common Tongue, but rather in a form of Aelish, possibly High Aelish did not occur to him. "Time for what?" he asked the empty room, clearly delirious and needing sleep.

You've felt my call before now. Come to me.

"Where are you?"

The voice didn't answer but images flooded into Kevn's mind and he saw a city he had only dreamt of. The entire city was a single palatial complex, with courtyards and gardens and water features throughout. Seven towers rose from the complex and a large dome rose from the center of the palace-city of Septyl.

"What about the Shroud?" Kevn's heart thrummed in his chest as he still held that image in his mind. He had seen tapestries and depictions of Septyl before, but none had done it justice.

She is not as powerful as I am. I will keep you safe. I have slept long enough.

"Who *are* you?"

Come to me.

Kevn felt the presence retreat from his mind although he still could feel her far to the west and knew that she originated in Septyl. The chances of someone surviving the sack of Septyl was impossible. Erynor had had every ei'ana residing there slaughtered. Weighing his options, Kevn wondered whether he could just leave Ceurenyl. Ellendren had left him her alicorn for this very purpose. He knew deep in his heart that he was meant to go to Septyl, but that didn't mean he should go now. Devlyn and Ellendren were actively pushing the Shroud back, but he didn't think they had made any significant progress in that endeavor. Had they freed even one city yet?

The voice's promise to protect him resonated in his mind. Not sure of what he needed to reach Septyl, he resumed his search and located a second diary, then read through until he found what they had been seeking, wrote a note for Aaron and Jaerol before finally leaving the library.

"What do you mean, he left?" Jaerol asked, enraged that Kevn had abandoned their task. Kevn knew how important their mission was and Jaerol could not believe that he had simply left them.

"It's all in this note. He's gone to Septyl, as he always said he would." Aaron handed the note to Jaerol. They were alone for the time being. "Curious that he left in the middle of the night though. I've reached out to the stable hands and they're still upset that Kevn woke them and had them saddle the alicorn for him. They also had to give him a cloak since he hadn't dressed for travel."

"Has he ever traveled before?" Jaerol asked, still upset, but now also worried for Kevn's safety.

"Only from Lucillia to Ceurenyl. I doubt he knows the first thing about providing for himself in the wilderness."

"Hopefully he'll reach his destination quickly." Jaerol read through the note and glanced at the two books neatly set on the writing desk. "He figured it out?"

"It appears so."

Jaerol sighed as his frustration eased slightly. He flipped through the pages of Benedetto's diary and then picked up the other diary that had a slip of paper marking a certain page.

...Jaerith pestered me about the ward again. If anything, he is persistent—a trait all too common among the wise ones here in the temple. I've tried to send him forth from the temple, but he has an unwillingness that I've never seen before. I understand the fear to serve Anaweh's children in these uncertain times, but still, he made a vow. We all made that vow.

Even so, Ineya returned to us. Ithendryl herself demanded that she vacate Arenthyl's cathedral. She wasn't the first archsteward to return to the temple in the past years, only the most recent. After poor Tomaso died in the destruction of Lankor and Desmynd was dragged from Nairin, I couldn't blame the others for wanting to return home to the temple.

Still, how will we ever recover from this? Archstewards abandoning their cathedrals in the midst of war...will the faithful ever forgive us?

And now Jaerith is pressuring me to extend the temple ward to cover the entire city. I thought having it extended to the entire temple was a stretch. Now we'll have to go outside the city to wield anything!

"Is that what Selenya meant?" Jaerol asked once he finished the excerpt that Kevn had marked.

"I believe so. That same diary has a passage shortly after Ceurtriarch Daeryn extended the ward. It describes how he managed it. Only the Ceurtriarch has the ability to manipulate the ward."

Jaerol slumped down on the sofa. "Do you know how to do it?"

"I understand the mechanics, thanks to Kevn leaving his notes behind, but that's quite different than actually achieving it. That being said, if I extend the ward to cover the entire city, Gwilnor will be largely undefended. The Tenebrae School is only holding on to their authority because of the threat of wielding tenebrys. Not even a shadow elf can wield under the temple's ward."

"What are you suggesting?" Jaerol asked.

"A much larger plan in conjunction with yours to rescue Liam."

"What do you need from me?" Jaerol asked.

"Nothing in the meantime. I must speak with the captains of the temple knights first. You should take advantage of the pause and spend some time in the valley. The snow is finally gone and it's a safe place to wield and practice jienzu."

"Thank you, Aaron."

"Of course."

Jaerol left the Ceurtriarch's apartment and decided to follow Aaron's recommendation. The valley was no longer a secret now that Aaron had revealed its location and the passage connecting it to the temple in order to train kien wielders among the ei'ceuril and temple knights. While Jaerol thought revealing a secret entrance to the entire temple community was rather foolish, he understood the reasoning. The ei'ceuril needed to learn how to wield again if they ever hoped to return to their cathedrals and chapels scattered across the continent.

He was delighted to find that, as Aaron had said, the snow had all but melted in the valley. The sparkling white had retreated to the highest reaches of the surrounding mountains. Inhaling the crisp morning air, Jaerol was happy to be alone. For the first time since he had learned that Liam had been captured, he allowed himself a breath of relief. He was going to save him and no one, not even Razcul, was going to stop him.

Without thinking, he fell into one of the jienzu forms, his body stretching to achieve perfect form. He knew he should have been practicing the forms more often but had not been able to concentrate in the past months. His shirt soon clung to his torso as he sweated from the exercise, and he berated himself. He knew better than to leave his shirt on while performing jienzu and tore it off as he moved into another form.

His mind emptied into a meditative state. He was more aware of his surroundings, yet also less so. He felt the ground rumble but kept his eyes closed, absorbed by the jienzu form until he felt a presence beside him and heard a voice.

"Odd," he heard someone say.

Jaerol lost his focus and opened his eyes. Standing beside him was a very large, very strong-looking, and very naked man. Unable to maintain his form, Jaerol collapsed onto the ground.

"I didn't mean to interrupt you. I'm Rusyl." The large man with azure eyes and matching hair extended a hand to help Jaerol stand.

"Jaerol Solaris."

"I find it odd that a Cyndinari knows jienzu forms favored by the Luminari—specifically, by the Guardian knights if I'm not mistaken."

"Well, the forms I had learned from my own people weren't the most helpful for achieving Balance."

Rusyl roared with laughter, eventually composing himself. "When's the last time someone led you through the forms? Forgive me for saying, but you seem more advanced and practiced than the forms you're using suggest."

"It's been a few years. Elayne Thenrel, a Guardian knight, introduced me to the proper way of jienzu. It was quite different than what I had been taught at the Imperium."

"Well, would you be interested in learning some advanced forms?" Rusyl asked.

"Sure."

Rusyl rolled his shoulders back and stretched some before entering one of the forms. The first form wasn't too difficult and Jaerol imitated Rusyl's movements. They held that form for thirty breaths then transitioned to a more difficult one which made unknown muscles scream. He had thought that Elayne's instruction had revealed all those unknown and previously unused muscles.

They continued like that for the next hour before Jaerol was finally too exhausted to continue. His body ached but his mind swam in a calm sea, almost euphoric.

"Not bad for someone who only knew the basics," Rusyl said.

"Not that I'm complaining, but I take it you're not a fan of clothing." While Jaerol's body glistened in sweat from the exercise, Rusyl's didn't even show a droplet, as though the exercise hadn't strained him.

"The young Ceurtriarch is having some made for my sister and me. Most tailors don't have anything near our sizes."

"Are you half giant or something?" Jaerol sized Rusyl up again, noting the striking azure hair and eyes on the massive body. His ears were pointed like an elf's, but Jaerol didn't know of any elves as large as Rusyl.

"I'm not half anything. And you're only seeing my smaller form." Rusyl winked.

"Smaller form of what?"

Rusyl didn't answer, just stepped away from Jaerol. His body began to shift, and Jaerol's mouth gaped when he saw sapphire scales flurrying across Rusyl's skin as he grew and kept on growing. Jaerol fell back again, gawking up at the blue dragon now towering over him. He had of course seen dragons before for they had been a common sight in Broid. Granted, none of them were as colorful as Rusyl, since the dragons in the Erynien Empire's service all belonged to the Dark Flight or had been subjugated to it.

"I didn't realize that dragons could change their form." Jaerol stood up and Rusyl's sapphire eyes watched Jaerol as he walked around the dragon's impressive girth. Then Rusyl changed back to his *smaller* form. While the form was certainly smaller than a dragon's, Jaerol thought that only giants and ogres might be bigger. "So, what are you doing here in Ceurenyl?"

"The one my sister has bonded to has been captured by the worms in the castle. Aaron insists that we wait before rescuing her."

"Is your sister Yelaris?" Until meeting Rusyl, Yelaris was the only dragon Jaerol knew of in the area. He'd thought she was the only one.

"She is and she's growing impatient. Yelaris says that Velaria is being tortured."

"Well, you might be in luck. We might have finally come up with a plan to take back the castle."

"Someone you care for is also a prisoner?"

"Yes. He is also being tortured, no doubt to bait me into recklessly trying to rescue him. Liam would never forgive me if I rushed headfirst into the castle to save him to only get captured myself."

"Smart of him to think so." Rusyl scanned the sky as though he was expecting something. "So, what's this plan of yours?"

"It's still undefined, and best to run it by the Ceurtriarch first."

"You don't trust me yet?" One of Rusyl's blue eyebrows rose.

"We've only just met. I don't think you're lying, but I did grow up in Broid. Trusting anyone doesn't come easy to me."

"I suppose that's fair. Let's go to the young Ceurtriarch then, for as I said, my sister's patience is thinning."

Jaerol shrugged his shoulders. He had wanted to spend more time in the valley to also practice wielding, but he supposed practicing jienzu would have to suffice. He wouldn't be able to wield when the time came to rescue Liam, and he had been open to the erendinth while executing the forms. Jaerol grabbed his shirt and turned away to head to the tunnel back to the castle when he once again felt the ground beneath his feet quake.

Rusyl had returned to his larger form and was scratching at the ground with his front claws. Images flashed into Jaerol's mind of the absurdity of a dragon, even in his smaller form, walking through a tunnel. Rusyl seemed to communicate that caves were only for sleeping.

"You want me to ride you?" Jaerol asked, recalling Yelaris carrying him in her claws when he was believed to be a shadow elf and attacking Gwilnor four years ago, when the shadow elf he'd accompanied had killed the Chair of Arantiulyn. There was nothing memorable about that experience and Yelaris' claws had not been particularly gentle.

Rusyl sent another image to Jaerol, assuring him that riding a dragon and being carried by one were quite different experiences. Jaerol had never flown on a dragon before—he had never flown on anything before. He had been amazed when the Eldinari had arrived at Gwilnor with their griffins, to say nothing of seeing Devlyn as a Phaedryn soaring above the castle while bonded with Aliel. He hesitated for only a moment. This was a blue dragon and they were inseparable from the sigil of the School he hoped to join as an ei'ana one day.

Climbing up Rusyl's leg was less difficult than he had previously imagined. Before he could securely position himself between the dragon's neck and shoulders, Rusyl launched into the sky. In a blink of an eye they were hundreds of feet above the valley, soaring higher until they crested the peaks of the mountains. Rusyl didn't seem to care about hiding from the people of Ceurenyl. Dragons were meant to be seen.

Jaerol took in the sight of the city from this perspective, losing his breath as he did. The temple, castle, and city wall with its towers were most distinguishable. As he gazed down, it looked as though he was examining a parchment map of the city spread out on a table. They were too high up for Jaerol to see any people walking the curvilinear streets of Ceurenyl, but he knew that they all had their heads tilted back as they gazed up at the sky to watch the dragon fly above them.

Rusyl angled down, speeding toward the canyon behind the temple, his tail directly above his head as he plummeted down before swooping back up. Jaerol's heart raced. Rusyl thumped onto a large balcony and Jaerol grinned from the exhilaration. He didn't make a move to get off the dragon, trying to catch his breath from the excitement of the ride.

He took too long and Rusyl must have thought he had gotten off for the dragon shifted to his smaller size and they both tumbled over. Jaerol laughed and Rusyl joined him as they scrambled to their feet.

"Who's out there?" Jehn poked his ancient head out the door to find Jaerol and a naked Rusyl. "That will not do in the Temple of Ceur!"

"It's not what you think," Jaerol said through bits of laughter.

"I'm sure. You're in luck, Rusyl, the tailors have finished the first outfit for you and you *will* be expected to don it while a guest in the temple," Jehn said before going back inside.

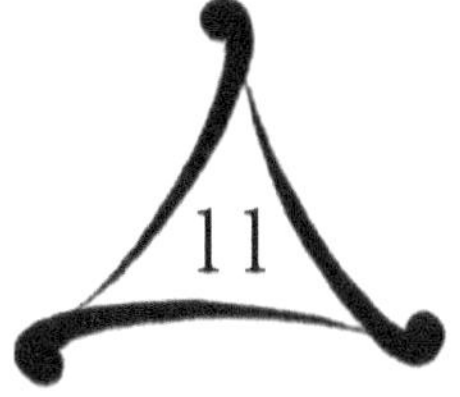

RUINS

Devlyn soared over the empty plains, Prya and Liara a short distance behind him and Viren on a griffin borrowed from the Eldinari trailing behind them. The air was finally warming with the approaching summer. The meadow below showed hints of green and the first sign of flowers that should have bloomed two months ago. Nothing about the prolonged wintery weather was natural. Elves much wiser than himself feared that Ramiel's weakening prison had caused the long winter.

They were flying toward Myrium in search of the road that led to Eandyl. After dozens of failed attempts to find the road near the Luminari camp, the aryls concluded that the only place they knew for certain where the road might be, was where it terminated—Myrium. Devlyn didn't think they would have to fly the entire way to the Sorenth capital, but they had already flown over two thirds of that distance and he could just make out a silvery line breaking the plains. The River Meyien shimmered in the sunlight and Devlyn thought he could see the city rising from in that sheen. It seemed like a jewel on a ring and was aptly named the Jewel of the River.

Angling south, and already open to his inner senses, Devlyn pressed into terys, hoping to find something that would not normally be part of a soft meadow. He barely had to press into the erendinth before finding something not too deep into the soil that was hard and long but not wide. His eyesight was useless in this case, and as he pressed further into terys, he discovered that there was indeed a road buried beneath the meadow. He hovered directly above it. They no longer had to fly any further—they'd found what they were looking for.

Devlyn dipped toward the ground. Even as he came closer to it, there was no indication that the road was there. His senses did feel something solid though and it was linear and ran both north toward the Shroud and south toward Myrium. Devlyn landed, immediately followed by Liara thumping down, and Viren's griffin landing without a sound, just in a flurry of wings.

Prya watched from Liara's back as the dragon dug a red claw into the dirt, energetically swiping away a mound of dirt and sending it flying.

"We could have just wielded the soil off." Devlyn flicked a patch of grass and mud off his chest.

"You want to tell a dragon when to use her talons? I assure you, that never ends well," Prya said.

"Not particularly." Devlyn craned his neck to see into the shallow pit. Despite the dirt and overgrowth, something glimmered in the cleared area below. "Viren, is that what I think it is?"

"Lumaryl—even our roads were paved with golden light made solid," Viren said.

"And I thought we draelyn had a love for beauty and jewels. But we never paved our roads with lumaryl," Prya said.

"It's not as refined as the lumaryl used for buildings and nowhere near the quality chosen for jewels and currency," Viren said.

"Lumaryl comes in different qualities?" Devlyn asked.

"Doesn't all stone? Some is suitable for building, other for sculpture and decoration, and the rarest for jewels." Viren looked down into the shallow pit as though the lumaryl road was simply another road. "Thelyn and Laeris Lorenthien, the Exalted Aryl who founded Arenthyl had intended to replace all Eklean's roads with lumaryl. They saw the constant upkeep of the continent's road network as a waste of time. However, Eklean was at war with itself. The wounds and power vacuum left from the collapse and division of Thellion had still not healed. Some of those wounds and prejudices remain to this day, perhaps softened somewhat over the ages that have passed, nearly an era by most counting."

The road had inlaid grooves and channels that created patterns of flowers, vines, and trees. Devlyn had never seen flowers and trees quite like those before.

"Pray that they too have endured," Viren said, aware of Devlyn's thoughts.

"What are they?" Devlyn crouched by the exposed road to run his fingers over the design.

"The flowers are kryseniels, the same flower that gave us the means to create the fabric for lierathnil. The trees are kirenae. When our ancestors fled Luminare, they brought as much of our Skyland to this land below, so it too could be preserved. While the trees and flowers could be found throughout Krysenthiel, the Delmira Wood was once a great forest on the western coast of Lake Saeryndol and stretched to our border with Evellion."

"Do you think there's a chance they survived?" Devlyn asked.

"I hope they have. It would be a great loss if Teraeniel lost two of her most beautiful creations. Anaweh must have thought we Luminari were special if we were given gifts such as those."

Devlyn remembered stepping on something frozen when he had pushed the Shroud back with Ellendren and Arlyn. It had crunched beneath his feet. The ei'ana had theorized that the Shroud had frozen everything inside its poisonous mist. Was it also possible that that permafrost had protected Krysenthiel's vegetation from the mist?

Liara dug at the dirt again, not to reveal more of the road, but to show her impatience and readiness to move on.

"We should be able to follow the road without any difficulty now that we've found it," Prya said. "Are we ready?"

"Let's go." Devlyn took a last look at the road, taking in its signature before they all took off again, flying north toward the Shroud this time.

The Shroud had made that road all but useless. Fourteen hundred years had passed since it was last used to travel between Myrium and Eandyl. Villages and a small city once sat along that road, but their wealth and prosperity had been built on trade with Krysenthiel. Those places had dwindled over the years and were now largely abandoned. The Sorenth city could have had a chance to survive on its own, but its citizens had likely fled out of fear of the Shroud expanding. A place that was once a thriving metropolis had likely been reduced to ruins. Curiously though, Devlyn hadn't noticed any ruins while they'd been searching for the road. Perhaps their estimate of the road's location was further off than they had anticipated. That, or the city had not survived the Ceurendol War and had been razed.

The newly-revealed section of the road was soon behind them as they continued northward. Maintaining his connection and sense to the road was simple now and he knew that the unbroken strip of lumaryl stretched toward the Shroud. The grass soon gave way to a small, wooded area that to Devlyn felt like much more than trees and bushes. Something was hidden in its shadows. Still pressed into terys, he noticed that the lumaryl road wove through the center of the wooded area. He dipped toward it, aware that he was going to have to apologize for this detour after they returned to the camp.

The first look around the area revealed crumbling ruins covered in overgrowth. This had to be the Sorenth city that had been abandoned following Krysenthiel's fall. Devlyn could feel the lumaryl road below fourteen hundred years of overgrowth and soil. The road wound through the city in a slight curve before marching onward to the north. While Devlyn was curious to explore, Viren, Prya, and Liara seemed more hesitant to do so, their anxiety oozing off them.

Nudging his bond with Aliel, Devlyn asked, *Do you think it's safe here? Whether it is or isn't matters little now. I would not fly out of this place—we are being observed*, Aliel conveyed.

Viren walked forward, verathn in hand. "We are not alone here."

"I feel it too," Prya said. She had leapt off of Liara and the red dragon had taken on her smaller form. A dragon would hardly go unnoticed, and discretion was probably wise.

Crumbling buildings lined the road. They'd be lucky to find even one that still had a roof to protect anyone seeking shelter against the elements. Despite the unease they'd all acknowledged, the ruins were eerily silent. The abandoned city was too quiet, no birds sang, no tree branches sighed, and no leaves stirred in the very still air. Only their own feet made any noticeable sounds. The stillness reminded Devlyn of a graveyard. Moving forward through the quiet, they came upon a crescent of wagons in what had once been a plaza. The colorful wagons seemed at first to have been abandoned, but as they drew near, they saw the bodies. Their deaths seemed recent, no more than a few days ago. From their clothing, it was clear that the wagons had belonged to Sojourners and Devlyn wondered if it was the same band that had taken him away from Ceurenyl when he had met Viren for the first time.

They went from one dead Sojourner to the next and Devlyn was saddened to see that the peaceful and nonviolent people all had sword wounds. It didn't seem that any of them had tried to fight back, not that they could have as the Sojourners never carried weapons.

"Why would anyone kill Sojourners?" Devlyn asked.

"Likely because they knew who else was hiding here. By the looks of their wounds, we've found the base of the Cyndinari that attacked us." Viren crouched over a dead woman.

"Do you think they are still here? Watching us?" Devlyn asked, expanding his inner sense to search for signs of life.

"Likely so, but they are concealing themselves from us. We should keep moving."

They moved onward, Devlyn still in his Phaedryn form, less concerned about the light he gave off than being vulnerable without Aliel.

The ruins grew denser the further into the abandoned city they went. The Sojourners had stayed near the edge of the ruins and the wooded area, making Devlyn wonder if they knew trouble lurked here. The other alternative was that they had fled from someone into the supposed safety of the forest. As the options piled on, Devlyn's senses finally caught something, although it was nothing more than a slight tingle on his shoulders. He still couldn't hear anything, but he decided he should be prepared and once he embraced animys for a defensive wield, he became even more attuned to his surroundings. His wield was not the only one in effect.

His breath caught in his throat as he tapped the foreign wield. It reverberated, sending a shimmer through the air. The trees no longer looked real but appeared as though they were an illusion. When Devlyn thrummed against the wield again, harder this time, the woods snapped out of existence, leaving only the ruins. Devlyn and the others stopped, taking in their new surroundings.

"Did either of you do that?" Viren asked.

"I felt the wield in place but didn't realize it was an illusion." Devlyn spun his head about, expecting a surprise attack at any moment.

"Someone is definitely hiding from us." Prya went through an opening in the ruins.

Viren moved to pull her back but stopped himself. "We can't divide right now."

"She'll be fine. She'll find whoever it is before they spot her," Liara said.

"And if we're ambushed while she's gone?" Viren turned to the dragon in her smaller form. "We still haven't found the Cyndinari that attacked us."

"I don't think any of us here are still questioning their hiding place," Liara said.

"Do you think we'll be able to get away?" Devlyn asked.

"If anything turns sour, you need to shift back to the camp," Viren said.

"I'm not leaving without any of you."

"And we don't intend for that to happen either," Viren said.

Before Devlyn could reply, the sound of footsteps drew near. His heart rate quickened and he pressed into aerys to blast away whoever it was. Pressing more forcefully into the wield, he nearly unleashed it just as Prya appeared in the opening she'd gone into, holding a child's hand. The trembling girl wore the colorful clothing of a Sojourner. Prya turned as though to soothe her, but even as she turned, the draelyn had her sword unsheathed and sticking through the gut of a Cyndinari who'd appeared behind her. The elf looked at Prya in shock.

"You dare betray your own kin?" he gasped.

"Forgetful fool," Prya said, pulling her sword out to let the elf collapse. "Child, stay in the center of us, you'll be safe." The girl uneasily moved between them but stayed closest to Prya. Even the griffin joined in forming the protective barrier around the girl as increasing sounds of clattering and raised voices from all around reached them.

Not for the first time, Devlyn wished that he had a weapon to defend himself. He understood Kyrendal's reasoning for forsaking a sword, but surely the ancient elf understood that when they were fighting for their very existence, swords were rather useful. He instead pressed into the erendinth as a wave of Cyndinari leapt from the ruins.

Ignys sprung into Devlyn's palm and he launched it at the nearest assailant. The Cyndinari screamed and collapsed, his place immediately taken by another elf. He could hear the others fighting behind him but couldn't spare a look for how they were faring. There were screaming and yelling Cyndinari all around them. As he pushed back another elf with a blast of aerys, his heart froze at the sound of a deep roar from somewhere in the ruins. Their attackers pulled back a bit, laughing derisively.

Sparing a look over his shoulder, Liara furrowed her brow. "One of the betrayers—a dragon of the Dark Flight." She moved off a bit, giving herself enough space to transform into her larger form, then leapt into the sky, buffeting those below with the current created by her massive wings. Prya screamed after Liara to come back, but the dragon was already gone.

Another dragon with blood red scales that seemed to have been dipped in Darkness flew out of the ruins. It was more beastly, more vicious-looking than the dragons Devlyn knew. Both dragons sent loud mental images out, each accusing the other of betraying their ways and being enslaved—no more than puppets to their master, while roaring and screaming loudly enough that anyone within a league would be aware of the battle overhead.

Devlyn's little band couldn't watch the battle. They had to refocus their energies on the Cyndinari who were renewing their attack, pressing in on their group again. Clearly, the Cyndinari hadn't expected that one of them was also a dragon and had been sure that their dark dragon would finish the little group.

Viren's sword flashed in front of Devlyn, striking down a Cyndinari who had gotten too close. Prya's sword was flashing too, and Devlyn's wields caught many of the attackers by surprise, slowing their advance. Cyndinari bodies soon littered the ground in a circle around them and the rest of the fairly large group retreated deeper into the ruins. Devlyn was finally able to catch his breath. He glanced up to see Liara flapping her wings above, alone and clearly wounded, with the other dragon off in the distance, heading south. Liara shared an image of her biting into his neck, making him too weak to continue the fight. The skirmish was over, the ruins returned to their eerie silence despite the bodies on the ground.

"We need to get out of here," Prya said, still breathing a bit heavily.

"Agreed. Let's follow that road to the Shroud and return to the camp. The sooner the better," Viren said, with a nod at the girl Prya had found.

Prya bent down to the girl's level. "What's your name? I am Prya, this is Devlyn, Viren, and the dragon above is Liara."

The girl trembled, shocked by the events and the recent battle she'd endured while in their midst but managed to mutter her name. "Twil."

"Come with us, Twil; we'll keep you safe." Prya held out a waterskin to the girl; she nodded and reached for it gratefully.

They were soon back in the air, Twil joining Prya on Liara, leaving the ruins behind. Looking back, Devlyn watched the wooded illusion return and the ruins disappear beneath a canopy of fake trees. Had a wielder recreated that wield already or had Devlyn's interference only been temporary? If there were wielders in the ruins, they had avoided the fight.

As they followed the lumaryl road, Devlyn wondered why the Cyndinari had retreated again, in a similar manner to when they had attacked the camp. There were more of them and they would have probably overwhelmed Devlyn and the others. Were their orders limited to taking on minor engagements only? Perhaps they had only attacked because he had found the wielded enchantment. Still, if they didn't intend to continue fighting, why reveal that there was a dragon among them? They could have had a stronger strategic advantage if they had kept their dragon a secret for a larger assault.

Devlyn had to stop thinking about the skirmish as they neared the ever-present clouds and mist along the Shroud's edge that blocked out the sun he'd enjoyed while they'd been away. They landed as close to the Shroud as they dared, the lumaryl road still beneath them.

Eandyl was not far into the Shroud and whether or not it was real or a trick of his imagination, he thought he could see the city. They stood silently, looking into the miasma that was the Shroud, each lost in their thoughts until Viren spoke quietly.

"It would be wise to hold off removing the Shroud from Eandyl until we are prepared to reclaim the city and defend it. We don't want anyone else taking up residence in the meantime," he warned.

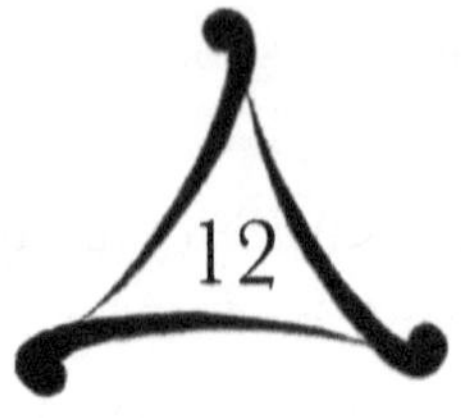

REFUGEES

The clouds darkened as they returned to the encampment. While Devlyn was relieved to have found the road leading to Eandyl, the bodies of the Sojourners haunted him. Why would anyone attack a people who had vowed to never lift a weapon again? Twil, the only survivor of the massacre, seemed less frightened than she had been when they'd first come across her. She now sat snuggly in Prya's arms on Liara, likely the first Sojourner to fly on a dragon.

Twil's entire family had been killed so that they couldn't expose the Cyndinari hiding in the Sorenth ruins. Their deaths had seemed recent; they couldn't have been dead for more than a few days. Twil didn't know how many days had passed; she was still in shock. That the deaths of her family had been for the Cyndinari's vile purposes made Devlyn sick at such a waste of life.

The sprawling Luminari camp was soon below them as the last bit of daylight disappeared and torches and wielded lights began to glow in the deepening gloom. Devlyn thought there were more wielded globes than he'd seen there before. While the ei'ana had been a constant presence in Lucillia, Devlyn didn't think that there were more than forty who had been residing there before the city had faded back into the Illumined Wood. That number didn't comply with the number of wielded lights that he now saw in the camp. Ei'ana, and especially the ei'ana of Lucillia, didn't go around providing light for people. Half of them belonged to a Luminari noble house, preferring to live among their families' wealth and comforts—severely lacking in the camp—than at Gwilnor. The rest of the ei'ana served as advisors to various aryls or carried out their own missions linked to their Schools.

After they landed, Prya and Liara left with Twil and Devlyn knew that the draelyn would see to her getting cleaned up and fed and possibly lodged with a family. Devlyn didn't need to be in his Phaedryn form any longer—the camp was bright enough without his own light spilling out—so Aliel flew above Devlyn and Viren as they made their way toward the chamber tent. Devlyn noticed a large crowd gathering outside it and he immediately felt tense. What could that possibly mean? Had a meeting been scheduled without him, or worse, had he forgotten about a meeting? Surely, someone would have reminded him before he had left to search for the road that led to Eandyl. Trying to keep himself calm, he saw that the crowd was largely made up of women, grouped in pairs, and dressed in only seven colors, each one representing a School of Septyl. The rest were teenagers and a few men, Septyl knights by their clothing. The escapees from Gwilnor!

Devlyn looked from the ei'ana to the students to the Septyl knights, hoping to find a familiar face, but also knowing that Velaria and Liam would not be here. Velaria had sacrificed herself so that this group could escape. It looked like two hundred people were gathered here—two hundred people who were now safe and free of the Tenebrae School, all thanks to Velaria. Devlyn still blamed himself for the events of that night and for leaving Velaria behind when he had shifted to escape Razcul, Hannah, and Yvonne. Velaria had made her choice and even if Devlyn had wanted to, she would not have permitted him to alter it.

The crowd parted for him and Viren, Aliel leaving them to dance among the stars of the night sky. Familiar yet dirty and exhausted faces smiled at him. Devlyn wondered how they had traveled from Ceurenyl to here. He had not seen most of these faces since he had been abducted from his bedchamber two years ago and locked in a box. Although he wanted to reconnect with his old classmates, he also had to find out what was happening in the chamber tent. Had the aryls gathered to determine whether to shelter the ei'ana and their students? Or were they discussing something else?

Pushing the tent flap back, Devlyn saw that the tent's interior was just as crowded as outside. Both high and minor aryls had gathered and were listening to Mother Paurel Roendryn give a report on Gwilnor Academy's dire state. Paurel, sitting near Ellendren with Selenya beside her, was speaking for the Chairs; she appeared exhausted, as though she had not slept in many nights. Devlyn headed for his seat beside Ellendren, half listening to Paurel as he maneuvered through the crowded tent.

"Before executing our plan to escape, we were betrayed. The Tenebrae knew. We barely managed to get half the number we had hoped for out of the castle. The original number we'd planned for was already only a fraction of Gwilnor's residents. The students were our priority, so many more ei'ana and knights loyal to Septyl are still in the castle and under surveillance." Paurel paused to catch her breath. Devlyn expected the aryls to start asking questions, but none of them did. He had never heard the chamber tent so quiet before. Paurel was clearly respected by everyone in attendance. "We dared not take the roads or any known path out of Ceurenyl and even when we were safely away from the Tenebrae's reaches, we feared discovery."

Paurel paused, letting out a sigh as she did. The gathered aryls sat in silence, digesting the impossible news. Gwilnor had not only fallen, it was now in the hands of those loyal only to the Erynien Empire. Whether every Tenebrae ei'ana knew it or not, that School answered only to Erynor. Whispered conversations arose in the chamber. Many of those present had children or grandchildren attending Gwilnor. Devlyn noted that Silvia and Toral didn't speak, sitting still and quiet after Paurel's report.

Selenya stood as the volume increased. "We understand that you all have questions and rightly deserve answers, but there is little else we can tell you just now."

"Is there a plan to retake the castle?" Valerie, Danielle's grandmother, asked. "Our granddaughter isn't here."

"Gwilnor is lost," Selenya said, stoic. The Chair of Albien had a reputation of saying as little as necessary. "We will try to rescue more students and ei'ana, but as it currently stands, we have no idea who is still loyal to Septyl. Spiders have been feeding in Septyl's shadows longer than any of us care to know." Selenya returned to her seat and this time the crowd grew louder and Devlyn thought rightly so.

"So, we're abandoning Gwilnor to the Tenebrae? My brother is there, as is Mother Velaria." Devlyn burst out, angrily rising to his feet. Ellendren placed her hand on Devlyn's wrist to calm him.

"I'm sorry, Ei'denai, there is nothing we can do. We, the Seven Chairs, Velaria included, agreed that our best chance to fight in this war was by reclaiming Septyl. The palace-city has power and we will not be blind to Erynor's schemes again. We will be ready," Selenya said, which did nothing to placate him.

Just as he opened his mouth to speak out again, he heard Selenya's voice in his mind. *Not all is lost—there is still hope.* She was not looking at him, but had turned to answer someone else's question, speaking in a level and collected tone despite her exhaustion.

What hope? Devlyn thought. He had fought against the Tenebrae when he had gone to retrieve the two lucilliae in his old bedchamber at Gwilnor. Razcul, Hannah, and Yvonne had easily overpowered him and Devlyn had only just managed to escape. But doubting Selenya was never a good idea. If she had reason to believe that there was hope for Gwilnor and those still loyal to Septyl there, then Devlyn would have to trust her. Still, he wondered why she didn't speak plainly in front of the aryls. Was she trying to hide something from them? Did she suspect that some of the aryls were servants of shadow? Devlyn scanned the tent anew. If there were servants of shadow hiding here, he wanted to find them and root them out.

His gaze fell again on the Narielle aryl. Silvia and Toral sitting quietly was suspicious. Devlyn had not seen Trethien in the crowd outside the tent and wondered if he was still at Gwilnor.

Devlyn tried to pay attention to the aryl's discussion. Each of the aryls thought they knew how to best liberate Gwilnor, which was ridiculous since not only were most of the aryls unfamiliar with the castle, they had never seen tenebrys wielded before. They had no idea what that destructive and negating power was like—they couldn't. Devlyn knew he had to stay focused on the meeting, but he was more interested in talking to the Chairs privately. He knew they would be busy getting Gwilnor's refugees settled, but they were clearly withholding information.

When the meeting finally adjourned, Devlyn had learned precious little. He walked out with Ellendren to find Viren waiting for them. The crowd outside the tent had greatly diminished as efforts had been made to find accommodations for Gwilnor's refugees. As Devlyn and Ellendren made their way to their own tent, Viren close behind, a young woman approached them and Viren stepped closer to monitor her. She was plainly dressed in simple clothing, but held an open hand out to Devlyn, offering a coin. Devlyn recognized Vyoletryn's purple sigil on it. She was one of the observants of the Vyoletryn School, their infamous eyes and ears throughout Eklean. From her rested appearance, Devlyn realized that she did not look like she had come with Gwilnor's refugees. She was certainly old enough to be an ei'ana, but it seemed that she had kept her identity a secret from the other ei'ana who had been staying in Lucillia. Devlyn had met with them all on various occasions, mostly in relation to protecting the camp from enemy forces. But a Vyoletryn observant would not have presented herself; they functioned in secret and only answered to their School.

Once she was sure that Devlyn and Ellendren recognized the coin, she put it in her pocket without offering her name. "The Purple Eagle would like to meet with you."

"When?" Ellendren asked.

"Now, if you can."

"Take us to her." They followed her away from their original path, Viren dropping back but following too. Gauging their direction and destination became difficult as there weren't any markers although the way was lit with torches and wielded globes of light. Given the increased wielded lights, Devlyn assumed they were near the area designated for the ei'ana. They would have likely been placed near the edge of the camp; only a fool would openly attack ei'ana.

They eventually came to an empty and unlit path. The tents were closer together here, the path narrower. An itch in the back of his neck cautioned him—they didn't even know this woman's name and they had allowed her to take them away from the center of the camp. This would be an easy place to ambush the Lorenthien aryl. There was no way of knowing how many servants of shadow were in the camp, but Devlyn knew they were here, just as he knew that they had been at Lucillia.

Finally, the woman stopped in front of a tent and indicated that they should enter, and Devlyn was surprised to find Mother Paurel sitting at a desk piled with reports. Devlyn had no idea how she had managed to have her belongings unpacked already.

"Mother Paurel, you've settled in quickly," Ellendren said.

Paurel looked up from the report she'd been reading and smiled. "Ellendren." As Paurel moved forward to hug her younger relative, she wielded aerys to prevent their conversation from being heard outside the tent. "Alas, this is not my tent. It is the headquarters for Vyoletryn's observants. They've been here all along."

"Of course," Ellendren said. "I can't begin to describe how relieved I am to see you here. When I had heard what had happened at Gwilnor, I didn't want to believe it."

"A tragedy. Sadly, our family has not been immune to grief either. I wept when I learned of your father's passing. First your mother, then Ealyndol, and now your father." Paurel held Ellendren's face. "But amid the sorrow, there is still reason for joy." She smiled at Devlyn. "Be good to each other. I said the same to your parents and they had a very happy marriage, although it was cut too short."

"Thank you, Paurel. I'm sure you've already heard of how it happened so unexpectedly," Ellendren said.

"Indeed, but not a moment too soon. You two might be young, but we could not go another day without the Lorenthien aryl. My observants are everywhere and if my calculations are accurate, I knew before the aryls here did. Has Kaela found herself a match yet? It's not why I wanted to speak with you, but it does need to be resolved. I'd rather avoid having the other aryls grow accustomed to a Roendryn aryl's absence in court."

"It's at the front of her mind. She's not interested in the nobles from Lucillia though—she finds them quite boring," Ellendren said.

"That they are. It was no different before I left as a young girl. She'll find someone; she's a clever elf and a cunning politician." Paurel gestured at the folding chairs and they all took seats. "You'll have to forgive these old bones of mine. The journey here was not an easy one for us older ei'ana."

"Of course. Paurel, if you don't mind my asking, what's really going on? I know you didn't lie to the aryls, but I also know that there was a lot left unsaid," Devlyn said.

"A necessary evil, I'm afraid. I'll tell you everything, but to start, we no longer know who we can trust. One of my own wise ones, a woman I've trusted for decades with sensitive information, turned out to belong to that wretched School." Paurel sighed before continuing, clearly still hurt by the betrayal. "I trust you know about the fire that was set to the East Tower at Gwilnor. That was no accident and its purpose wasn't solely to kill all the Vyoletryns at Gwilnor. We were conducting an extensive investigation into the Tenebrae School. Publicly, we denied its existence, hoping that our investigation could remain a secret. If only I had known then what I know now. We would have likely been betrayed either way, but at least I could have preserved some of the investigation's findings. It's all burned to a crisp now. Who's to say how much of it was reliable though—Tenebrae in my own School. They could have been sabotaging the investigation from the onset."

"Forgive me, but how long have you known about the Tenebrae?" Ellendren asked. Devlyn clearly remembered her yelling at him for suggesting there were duplicitous ei'ana only a couple years ago.

"We first suspected they existed when it was rumored that Erynor had returned. The Chair of Vyoletryn before me feared it and set me on the task of discovering more many springs ago. Decades-worth of research was destroyed the night the East Tower burned. I believe we were getting close to discovering the location of their initiation ceremony. Every School has their own private ceremony. None of them are the same and they're kept secret from the other Schools. No doubt that the Tenebrae now has those secrets as the women who later joined all belonged to one of the seven Schools. Erynor was rumored to be the Chair of Tenebrae during the Ceurendol War, but I doubt that's the case today. It has to be someone at Gwilnor—someone so entrenched in Septyl's hierarchy that she's managed to fool us all. She is likely the only one of that School who knows the identity of the others. It's why we were eager to find where they held their initiation ceremony. If we can find her, we can cut that infection out of Septyl."

"Have you ruled out Hannah or Yvonne?" Devlyn asked. He fought down his memory of them; just thinking of them made him angry.

"Of course not. If they are not the Chair, then they are certainly wise ones."

"And what about Gwilnor? Is there any news about Liam and Velaria?" Devlyn asked, desperate.

"Selenya believes there is a way to extend the temple ward to cover the entire city, thereby cutting the Tenebrae off from tenebrys. Before Jaerol left us with some of the other students, she gave him a hint of where to look to find a solution. I wouldn't worry about your brother too much; Jaerol will pull every stone from the castle if necessary to save him."

"A hint? Why didn't Selenya speak openly?" Ellendren asked.

"Again, we don't know who we can trust, even among those closest to us."

"You suspect a Chair," Ellendren whispered.

"Only the Chairs were aware of every detail of our escape."

"What will you do now? Will you stay with us here or will you travel to Septyl?" Devlyn asked.

"Reaching Septyl will be our priority. That being said, we need to regain our strength before we set out again. While we are here, do know that our services are available to you."

"Jeanne will be happy to hear that," Devlyn said.

"I look forward to meeting her. If she is half the elf my informants tell me she is, then she is a formidable woman, indeed."

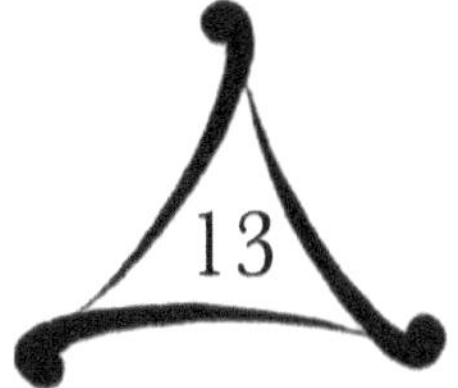

BENEATH THE COWL

The ring on Velaria's finger stung, like a thousand needles poking into her skin. She couldn't understand how Razcul took such delight in wearing it, cackling as though he was intoxicated by the power running through him. Did he really not feel the pain? Perhaps being a shadow elf altered the feeling given by the ring. Velaria had yet to witness his improved strength over tenebrys and hoped she never would. The more she saw him—the real him—the more unhinged he appeared. Velaria didn't know what terrified her more, a stronger Razcul or an unstable Razcul. Unfortunately, it seemed that both were inevitable now that the shadow elf walked plainly through Gwilnor's halls.

The door to Velaria's cell opened and she immediately shrank back. It had become almost instinctual, since whenever the door opened, she would have to undergo some cruel torture or humiliation. Velaria couldn't prevent herself from flinching. She was terrified of what the Tenebrae would do to her next.

"Look how the mighty have fallen." A cowl hid the woman's face but Velaria knew she had heard that voice before, although without the taunting tone. "You had such a promising future ahead of you. I scouted you out personally, you know. I thought a Cyndinari would be the ideal candidate. We all saw your talent and potential while you were a student here. I even thought that you might usurp me one day. Erynor would certainly give our School the attention and respect it is due if the next in line for the Chair had cinnamon hair like himself; he's never pretended to hide his prejudice."

Velaria tried to connect the woman's voice to someone she knew. She definitely recognized it, but something about it sounded different, as though this woman had intentionally altered the tone before. It wasn't so much that she sounded confident now, but rather that she was convinced that she pulled every string and had ultimate control of every situation. She spoke with a surety that was rare even among ei'ana.

"You do realize that you can harness that ring's power, yes? All you have to do is abandon those childish ideals of yours and join us, Velaria."

It clicked. Hearing the woman say her name brought back a memory from long ago. This woman had said the same thing to her before, only Velaria had been a child living in Lucillia at the time. The descendants of the Cyndinari guards who had abandoned Erynor lived a meager life in the Luminari capital. While the Luminari publicly accepted them, the Cyndinari were never fully embraced, only tolerated, and many were poor as it was difficult for them to make a living. Velaria had wanted to get away from that life; she wanted to be someone. She didn't want people always reminding her that her Cyndinari kin would destroy the world if given the chance. Then one day, a woman came to their home and spoke to Velaria and her parents about Velaria enrolling at Gwilnor Academy. They couldn't dream of affording Gwilnor's tuition, but the woman had offered to cover it for them. She claimed to see great potential in Velaria.

"Nadia," Velaria breathed. Nadia Dasuani had brought Velaria to Gwilnor, had comforted her when her parents had died an early death, and had seen to her wellbeing throughout her studies. Nadia had stopped asking Velaria to visit her after her novitiate though and they had rarely seen one another since. Velaria had thought that Nadia had moved out of the castle without saying goodbye.

"So, you do remember me?"

"How could I not? You were always there for me. You comforted me."

"I had hoped your parents' death might reveal a darker side of you. But instead of wanting revenge over their untimely deaths, you cried like a child. I knew I wouldn't be able to recruit you after that."

"Revenge?"

Nadia laughed. "You still haven't realized it, have you? *I* killed your parents. Still the foolish child, I see."

Velaria scooted back, nauseated and terrified at the revelation. Nadia had always had a commanding presence, but this side of her was different—twisted. Velaria's hands stole to touch the burgeoning vines under her arms and she reminded herself of who she was. She wasn't the scared girl being teased in Lucillia for her red hair anymore. She was the Chair of Azurelle, the Blue Dragon.

Her demeanor shifted. She was still a prisoner and still wore that excruciatingly painful ring, but she also knew who she was. "So, you're the Chair of Tenebrae that we've been looking for. Have you ever been loyal to your School?"

"I took my vow as a Tenebrae ei'ana when the night was darkest, hours after taking my vow as an Arantiulyn. I told the Tenebrae Chair before me that I did not want to spend a single day as an ei'ana of another School. Tabitha delighted in my dedication. She quickly named me a wise one and I was seen as her natural successor. Granted, the woman refused to die in her old age, so I quickened the process for her." Nadia smiled as she flicked her hand. "She was a weak woman, lacking vision and drive. Because of me, the Tenebrae School is larger than any of your pathetic individual Schools. Join us, Velaria. Join the real power in Septyl. You're fooling yourself if you think it hasn't always been that way. Embrace the ring you wear—feel for the first time what power truly feels like."

Velaria glanced at the dorthl ring on her hand. She knew it had power, just as her stolen verathn did. If she ignored the pain, she could feel its corruptive power waiting to be unleashed. She didn't have to betray Septyl to wield tenebrys. She could claim the ring's power and fight Nadia. The woman she had trusted as a child had not only admitted to grooming her to join the Tenebrae School but had also admitted to killing her parents and then others who had stood in her way. She deserved to die. How many ei'ana had she stolen from their Schools? How many broken counsels was this woman responsible for? How many more would follow?

Rage bubbled in Velaria's chest. She could feel her blood boiling inside and as she reached the precipice of action that she could never return from, a memory bloomed. It started small, but she remembered what it had been like to behold the lucilliae of justice. The seven lucilliae were imbued with the Luminari's more cherished virtues. Velaria might not be a Luminari, but she cherished those virtues just the same. If the Cyndinari hadn't lost their way, perhaps they would also have settled on those seven.

Nadia deserved to meet justice and meet it she would. Velaria vowed that she would personally deliver whatever that justice was to this woman who sought to destroy Septyl from within.

"Septyl is stronger than the Tenebrae School."

"Your Seven Schools will crumble beneath us," Nadia said, her voice low and filled with venom. "I gave you a chance. After tonight, I will be the only Chair the ei'ana will recognize." Nadia spun away and the sound of the lock on the cell door resounded.

Velaria wondered what the Chair of Tenebrae meant. Did she intend to kill Velaria tonight? Had Velaria's usefulness to the Tenebrae finally run out? She worried about the other Chairs and whether the Tenebrae would kill them too. Had the Tenebrae managed to track down the people who had gotten out of Gwilnor? Velaria prayed that hadn't happened—the ei'ana's future depended on them reclaiming the palace-city of Septyl and ensuring that the Tenebrae never gained entrance or control.

Velaria didn't have to wait long before a Tenebrae ei'ana came to escort her to the dining hall. The castle's corridors were quiet but she kept her back straight and shoulders back as inspiration for those still loyal to Septyl. Velaria refused to let them see one of the Seven Chairs of Septyl defeated. She would not give the Tenebrae School that pleasure.

Velaria went through the large double doors and into a very crowded dining hall. She couldn't remember the last time she had seen so many people in the space. It looked as though every ei'ana, knight, and student had been forced to attend. Most notable were the women sitting at the high table. Hannah and Yvonne were there, but they were the only magisters. Hannah was not sitting in the center, the traditional place for the chancellor. Instead, Nadia sat in that place of honor as though she were a marble statue, still wearing the black outfit she'd had on earlier, her cowl still hiding her face.

Ei'ana, knights, and students still loyal to Septyl risked whispering to each other. No one knew what was going on, least of all the ei'ana and knights who had been captured trying to escape. This was the first time that Velaria had seen any of them. The Tenebrae likely had them under a form of house arrest, only permitting them to leave their apartments for the lavatory if they didn't have their own. Velaria shuddered at the thought of Gwilnor's residents being forced to use a chamber pot like herself.

Scared faces watched Velaria walk to the front of the hall. They all seemed to have the same fear as Velaria that the Tenebrae intended to kill her. Others avoided looking over at her, and Velaria wondered if they were Tenebrae and wanted to see her killed in front of the assembly.

As Velaria reached the front, she took note of the women seated on either side of Nadia at the high table. Only Nadia had her face hidden so Velaria easily recognized the seven others. Each woman had belonged to a different School. Every School of Septyl was accounted for on that dais. The Chair of Tenebrae and her wise ones sat poised like vultures over Gwilnor's residents. The sight made Velaria sick. Velaria's escort led her to the single chair that waited in front of and below the high table, her back to it and facing the rest of the room.

Velaria took her seat, making every effort to present herself as holding power, refusing to allow the position imposed on her by the Tenebrae diminish her authority here at Gwilnor. She held an image of every other Chair of Septyl before her in mind, remembering how intimidating they could appear. The castle might have fallen into the hands of the Tenebrae, but Velaria's posture would remind those in the assembly of its true caretakers. Regardless of whatever happened next, those in attendance would see the Chair of Azurelle—the Blue Dragon—as the imposing figure that she was.

Near the front of the dining hall, Velaria noticed Razcul, the shadow elf staring hungrily at Velaria, a badly beaten Liam beside him. She knew that Razcul wanted to steal her soul, seeing her, a Cyndinari, as a stain on their people that had to be eliminated. Velaria didn't know who had authority over a shadow elf here, but he had yet to touch her.

"Ei'ana and knights of Septyl," Nadia began, "and students of Gwilnor Academy. You have been deceived. For fourteen hundred years you have been led by weak women; ei'ana who could only pretend at the true power they had lost. These inadequate Chairs claimed that our strength was lost when the Balance between kien and kiara was lost, but they lied to you all. They kept us weak and refused, no, they failed to grasp the true power—they still do."

The room darkened and Velaria could see the hum of tenebrys behind her reflected on the faces of everyone watching Nadia. She was relieved to see that some looked on in horror despite far too many others lusting for the power that Nadia wielded. Few of the students looked eager; most of them looked away. Velaria's heart lifted slightly; the students were not yet lost to the Tenebrae.

The air shifted, as did the darkness behind her. Velaria could still sense the erendinth and could feel Nadia creating a wield of tenebrys. Lightning crackled behind her, its negating presence dancing across the faces in the hall. The air seemed to still for a moment before glass shattered in an explosion and bits of the colorful stained glass window that depicted Gwilnor's crest of all the creatures from the Seven Schools flew past. A burst of dark flames flew over Velaria's head, incinerating the banners of the Seven Schools of Septyl hanging from the rafters. The crowd tried to control their outcry as the Tenebrae ei'ana cackled in delight at the destruction.

"The Seven Schools of Septyl are no more. As Chair of the sole School of Septyl, I strip Velaria of her rank and position among the ei'ana. Every ei'ana will have to pledge themselves to the Tenebrae School. Until that time, you are no longer ei'ana and will be kept locked away."

Velaria was shocked when a voice unlike her own roared from her mouth. She felt herself lifted from her seat into the air and spun around to face the high table.

"I, Cyrelle Azurelle, and the other Founders, forsake you. You have no power or authority here. The power you flaunt leads only to death. Ramiel will feast on your souls. You Tenebrae are ei'ana no longer. My successor remains in my Chair."

A rush of wind blew through the dining hall as Velaria fell to the floor and tenebrys lashed through the hall. People were shouting and screaming, Nadia's scream the loudest. Velaria could only look around in a daze as people fought. There were still ei'ana and knights loyal to Septyl. Even though she knew they could not possibly overcome the Tenebrae just now, it made her smile. Septyl had not fallen and would not unless every last ei'ana and knight were killed. And even then, the Founders would still guide it from their place in Lumaeniel.

Two of the Tenebrae women dragged Velaria out of the dining hall, repeatedly beating her as they pulled her back to her cell. Even as she unsuccessfully tried to dodge the blows, she reflected on the curious occurrence. Had Cyrelle Azurelle truly spoken through her? Those had not been her words and the voice had been masculine. She thought back to the ritual of her elevation to the Chair of Azurelle. The ceremony had been filled with symbolism and had been recited entirely in High Aelish. She had always thought that the wording was purely symbolic, especially when she had been called the mouthpiece for Cyrelle Azurelle. She never imagined that the founder of her School would one day speak through her. She had always assumed that as Chair, she spoke with his authority as the leader of the Azurelle School.

Before shoving her back into her dank cell, one of the two women escorting her, no longer ei'ana by Cyrelle's decree, wrestled her hand up to ensure the dorthl ring was still on her finger then slammed and locked the door. Velaria had no idea when she would be permitted out of it again after what had happened tonight. The Tenebrae would try to convince Gwilnor's residents that what they had seen and heard was only a deceptive illusion—a trick and nothing more.

Velaria wondered how Nadia and the others would deny their connection to Ramiel. Cyrelle had condemned them as accomplices of the Evil One. Had all the women who had joined that School—stolen from other Schools—fully known what they were doing? The Tenebrae School wasn't just a political force or an ideology propounding that a single School was superior to seven. Without understanding why, she knew that it was part of Ramiel's schemes to break free of his prison and claim the realms for himself. If left unchecked, the Void would swallow Teraeniel and Somnaeniel. Velaria didn't know how she knew any of that. She had never read it and nor had anyone ever told her.

An image of Cyrelle Azurelle flashed in her mind. *My knowledge and wisdom are yours. What I was capable of, now you are too.*

The image disappeared. Most striking about the man were his unusual eyes and hair. He had pointed ears like every other elf, but she had never seen an elf with eyes like sapphires and azure hair before. She had assumed that Cyrelle, and the other Founders, had all been Luminari elves.

LOST

The gentle lights of Stellantis embraced Wyn, easing his anguished heart. His people had now heard his account. But he also wanted answers.

When he had followed his cousin out of the Eldin Wood, he had grown accustomed to the bright sun and then the lack of sun as the Evil One's influence over Teraeniel had grown. Readjusting not only to the softer lighting but also to the slower pace of his kin was more difficult than he had envisioned. The Eldin Wood was his home, and with the exception of the past few years, he had only known the Eldinari's way of life. He had never had a reason to hurry or view something as urgent. But that had all changed when he had followed his cousin Devlyn into the world beyond his people's borders.

Alethea had warned him that journeying beyond their forest would have its challenges. She must have always known what was happening beyond the Eldin Wood, for she had prepared him as best she could for his eventual departure. But Alethea was gone now, ripped violently from Teraeniel and into the Void. Her disappearance was the reason for his return here.

Wyn thought he could feel her, as though an echo of her had survived. The elves, particularly those who still had Life immortal, viewed death differently than the mortal races did. For elves, death was merely a transition from Teraeniel to Lumaeniel. But Alethea had not migrated to the blessed realm of Anaweh's Light. No, she had been stolen away to the Void where the Evil One reigned as a god.

Fendryl had told Wyn and Devlyn that Alethea was lost there. Rescuing anyone from the Void simply wasn't feasible. Not only was entering that realm incredibly dangerous, escaping it was an impossible feat. Any would-be rescuers might as well surrender their body, soul, and spirit to the Evil One and save themselves the trouble. An even more depressing thought was that if the free people of Teraeniel didn't figure out how to stop the Evil One, there wouldn't be a need to find a way into the Void; Somnaeniel and Teraeniel would be swallowed and severed from Anaweh, damning everyone trapped in those two realms. Wyn didn't know what sort of life that would be. Would he even have the mental acuity to seek out Alethea? Or would he just waste away, barely cognizant?

Wyn squeezed his already closed eyes at the thought. He was supposed to be meditating, not wallowing in fear of what the undefined future might hold. The shrine that held the Verathel, a sprout of the Tree of Life, was otherwise empty, which suited Wyn. He wanted to be alone. Informing the Eldinari here in Stellantis that Alethea had been taken had been unbearable. He felt like a failure and a disappointment. So many elves had envied his relationship with her. For centuries, she had refused to take on new students, even among her own family, but she had taken on Wyn.

Everything he knew had been passed down from her. And now that she was gone, Wyn didn't know who to go to with his questions. What was he supposed to do now? Deep down, he knew he had to find a way into the Void and rescue her. But even if he survived the journey there, what promise did he have that he would escape alive? Alethea would not have abandoned him to suffer in the Evil One's domain.

The crystalline tree seemed to shimmer at Wyn's resolve. Did it approve of his course of action? Would Anaweh protect Wyn on this foolish venture? He stilled his mind and opened himself to whatever answers the tree would provide.

The quiet of his interior ebbed as more thoughts fought their way to the surface, bringing doubt and despair. Those were not his own thoughts. Contemplating the Void while meditating was risky. Wyn had been careful to guard his thoughts and omit the Evil One's name, but that didn't explain this inner battle. Sweat beaded on his brow as he struggled. Something had taken him—someone. Whatever or whoever it was, they were trying to strip him of his faculties. He could feel the assault attacking his mind and will.

Too afraid to ask or even wonder what was happening, he cried out as the pain started to overwhelm him before everything went black.

He blinked, hoping the surroundings would brighten. It felt like a dark fog hung over his eyes, as though wherever he was had no trace of light. There were no shadows here—shadows needed light. This was different—this was simply darkness. He was no longer in Stellantis where he had closed his eyes.

Something flashed in the distance, a flash that was somehow darker than its surroundings. It looked like an even darker scar, shooting through the dark land.

Wyn hoped he was dreaming. He prayed to Anaweh that he wasn't where he feared he was. Even the deepest caverns of Teraeniel where sunlight couldn't reach weren't so oppressively dark. He had never once wondered what absolute darkness would be like; had never cared to see a world without light—a world without Anaweh. But now he didn't have to wonder. It felt like the Void had swallowed him, as though it was a giant beast that had eaten him whole.

Looking around to get a sense of his location and bearings proved impossible. Oddly, he felt weightless here, similar to the feeling in Somnaeniel, but noticeably different too.

"It's rare that we get a visitor."

Wyn spun around to see who had spoken. That proved useless since he couldn't see anything. Instead of relying on his sight, he tapped his interior sense. That was a mistake.

He was far from alone. He not only felt the stranger who had spoken, he also felt himself in the midst of many people inside a vast city. Everything had been wrought by the Void, in a similar way to cities that were constructed of the substances of Teraeniel, only there wasn't any variation here. Everything of this city was of the Void. Like every other city, thousands—tens of thousands—of people occupied it. It was not a desolate wasteland as Wyn had assumed the Void would be.

"You see the sublime beauty now, yes?" asked the stranger. "Tosk is only one of our cities. It is not weighed down and forced into a singular dead form like the cities you are used to. Even your Stellantis is dead compared to Tosk—Tosk is alive. Dorthl is similar to what formed our Skylands, but it is not troubled in the same way as substance is. Nothing here is corrupted by solidity and the intrusion of the erendinth. This place is the last bastion of how existence was intended. It remains pure."

Wyn didn't trust himself to speak, afraid he would give this stranger what he wanted. He realized that this was not the first time he had come across dorthl. Somnaeniel was actively being consumed by it. But in the World-in-Between, to have contact with the oily puddles was to die. Wyn wanted to ask Alethea if dorthl was different in the different realms. How would it materialize in Teraeniel?

In the silence that followed, Wyn took note of the city. This dorthl non-substance was as similar to eldaryl as dark was to light. He didn't think they were opposites or negatives of each other, but nor did they have anything in common. While eldaryl was one of the many substances that formed Teraeniel, this dorthl seemed to be the only non-substance here in the Void. He couldn't understand how a singular substance was able to distinguish between something built and not built. Even the spaces between the buildings were dorthl. There was no air or space between what was built and what was left open. Everything was dorthl. Perhaps the dorthl was thickened in certain locations to replicate habitable buildings.

"You're a curious one. The other is the same."

Alethea! Wyn broadened his interior senses, hoping to find her.

"I could take you to her, but you would have to actually come to this place."

"I'm not actually here?" Wyn said, more relieved than he had thought he could be.

"You would not be as relaxed if you were. Visiting this place for the first time can be jarring and often painful."

"Who are you?"

"Jaris."

"Jaris Iln Desaris." Wyn didn't say it as a question. The truth of this elf's identity sang through him as he spoke the name.

"So, the Sha'ghol haven't been completely forgotten."

"Not completely."

"We thought you Eldinari would be our strongest allies, seeing how much you all admired the night. Your high feast day was even on the longest night."

"Not for the sake of darkness though. It's the stars—they shine brightest on Borephaen."

"Yes, we discovered that the hard way. Well, if you'll accept any advice from one of our kind, don't fall in love—they'll only kill you in the end, and I don't mean figuratively." Jaris seemed to examine Wyn. Wyn couldn't say how, but it felt like Jaris was looking through him. "Ah, you know Yloran. And you were with the young Lorenthien and the Lenwyn from our own era. I had expected someone of her wisdom to understand the futility of trying to resist the Void."

"She only tried to save us." Wyn cringed at the memory. He could still hear Alethea shrieking that they must not engage with the violent clouds but let them steal her away to the Void.

"Curious. I'll never understand why people sacrifice themselves for the sake of others. Love never demands such a price."

"Are you certain you understand love?"

"Words of a child. I am older than your Alethea. Don't presume to question me." Jaris' voice took on a dangerous edge.

"The people who are here now…how are they here?" Wyn tried to shift the conversation to safer waters. "Are they dead?"

A roar echoed from somewhere in the darkness. The sound reverberated inside Wyn's chest. How was that possible if he was only here in a dream?

"Not all who are here have died. And what is death anyway? My body was destroyed and I died, but here I am—different but not entirely. I am still me—I'm still Jaris Iln Desaris, am I not? But to answer your question, those who you would identify as anacordel can only come here through what you call death. A great many other beings were trapped here when the Tree of Life's roots made this place a prison. If not for Anaweh's interference, Ramiel would have been lord of all existence. Our Master still believes he can usurp the Creating Light and return existence to its primal and pure state of being."

"Does that mean that Alethea has died?" Part of Wyn didn't want to hear the answer.

"It depends how you look at it. She didn't come to this place as the others have and she still has a body. But if you consider anyone dwelling in the Void as dead, then she is dead."

Wyn didn't know how to determine whether Alethea was dead or not from that explanation. "If I too come here, will I die?"

"Again, depends how you describe death. I am dead, but I still exist much as who I was. I just don't dwell in Teraeniel with a body anymore." His tone indicated that he had grown bored and started to fade. "Come here or don't; it matters little in the end. The Master will cut through the barrier and extend his realm. Sooner or later, you will be swallowed by the Void, young Lierafen.

Wyn woke with a start. He patted himself to make sure that he was still alive—that he still had a body. He no longer sat in the Verathel shrine but lay in his bed in the Lierafen district of Stellantis. He could see clearly once more and that all-encompassing darkness was gone, replaced by the quiet lights of Stellantis.

The realization of what had just happened weighed on him. He had spoken with one of the Sha'ghol in the Void. How was that even possible? Was the Void similar to Somnaeniel in that people could travel there in their dreams? How much of that had been real? It certainly felt real and he knew he hadn't imagined any of that conversation. Or had he?

Before he had the opportunity to figure out how he had gotten to his bed, his grandmother Dalenya walked through the doorway. "You had us worried."

"What happened?" Wyn asked.

"We were hoping you could tell us. You went into a trance of some sort. It was quite different from any other meditation we're familiar with. It seemed similar to entering Somnaeniel, but we could tell that that's not where you had gone." Dalenya looked worried. "Where did you go, Wyn? We feared you might have died."

He looked down at his hands lying on the bed covers. Death wouldn't touch Wyn or any other Eldinari as it did mortals. The Eldinari elves had never lost their Life immortal. They would choose when to heed Anaweh's call to the World-Beyond. "I think I know how to save Alethea."

"She is lost to us, Wyn. She would not want you to risk your life to venture into the Void."

"We can't leave her there."

Dalenya remained quiet for a moment, her lips pursed in thought. "Only the Sha'ghol have ever crossed into the Void and returned."

"I spoke with Jaris Iln Desaris in my dream. He's dead now, killed by Yloran Eth Gnashar."

"You believe that Yloran might help you find a way? She might no longer serve the Evil One, but that doesn't make her a trusted ally. She'll have her own agenda if you seek her out."

"We can't abandon Alethea to the Void though."

Dalenya turned as though to leave. "After you told us about that awful night, we risked reaching out to her."

Wyn practically leapt from his bed at the news. "Were you successful? Why am I just learning of this?"

"We were." Dalenya turned back to face Wyn. "She's the one who told us she was lost. She told us not to pursue her."

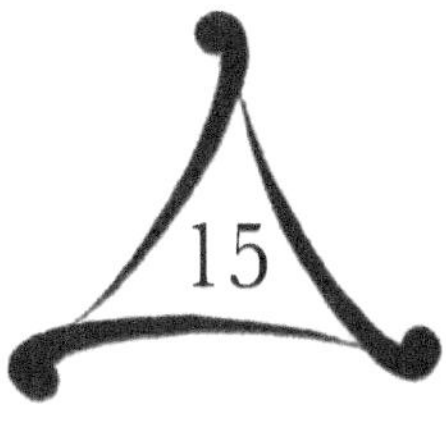

Chamber

Devlyn studied Jeanne Darkel's stance, balanced on the balls of her feet, knees bent as her body swayed. She held a staff similar to his, but she carried it with an in-depth familiarity, reminding him of his near-novice state with a staff.

Hands placed where Jeanne had instructed, Devlyn gripped the slender staff of polished wood, wondering if the verathn would resemble it in weight and balance. He swung the staff toward her, forming an intersecting loop with it. His hands vibrated as Jeanne's staff struck his; she had barely moved, yet her swift and powerful response left Devlyn bounding backward from the shock.

"If you're not bendable, you will shatter," she said, her feet still planted exactly where they had been.

"How is a wooden stick supposed to bend?"

"I said nothing about the staff." Jeanne sprang toward him, staff extended over her head.

Raising his own horizontally, Devlyn braced for the impact as Jeanne slammed down against his defensive stance. The reverberations went through his hands and up his arms to his shoulders.

"You'll break an arm if you continue like that." Jeanne swung toward Devlyn's midsection.

Angling his own staff to meet the attack, Devlyn tried to take the hit in a more *bendable* manner. He felt the strike, but instead of using his strength to remain immovable, he allowed his own staff to have some give.

There were no vibrations when the two staffs connected, but Devlyn immediately realized he had provided too much flexibility, as Jeanne's staff ended up whacking his ribs. He felt the purple and black bruise forming even before she withdrew. Instinct brought his free hand to the bruise—a mistake, for Jeanne capitalized on his vulnerability.

Blinking through a headache and looking at the cloudy sky above, Devlyn pushed himself onto his elbows. "I didn't even see that one."

"Don't make that a habit." Jeanne squatted next to Devlyn. She never offered her hand to help him up, simply came down to his level. "I understand that you're still young, even among mortal standards, but if you wish to see more springs and sunrises, you'll have to leave these youthful follies behind."

"I know."

"Now, do you need a break or are you ready to try again?"

"Actually, I wanted to ask you something." Devlyn rubbed his head with one hand, propping himself up with the other.

"Concerning what?"

"The Guardian Senate. How did it work?"

"Ah—an admirable administration. They did wonderful things for Eklean and all Teraeniel. While the Guardian knights will always have a special connection to the Luminari, we answer only to the Guardian Senate."

"But *how* did it work?"

"Well, each nation maintained its autonomy, and were fairly represented in Chamber. At its inception, we called it the Eklean Council and its defenders were called Eklean knights. Even in those days when Eklean desperately longed for peace and stability, your ancestors dreamed that it would become an intercontinental chamber. For an all too brief time, Teraeniel came together. Such unity has not happened since before we left the Valley of Saeryndol and the elder ones became different races."

"Do you think it's possible to reinstate it?"

"It won't be an easy task. For the Guardian Senate to function properly, all Teraeniel must be involved."

"Do you think it can start small again and grow over time?"

"Possibly, but there is a risk of it appearing as an empire."

"We would just make it clear that it's not—that it's a council with the best interests of every anacordel."

"And you think that Erynor doesn't use the same rhetoric?"

Devlyn didn't respond; he didn't know what to say.

"Forgive my asking, but what brought this to your attention?" Jeanne asked.

"My time with the dwarven schtams. Dwarves, humans, and elves were all represented before the battle of Everin. Also, during my time in Myrium and Lankor, I saw their connections with the merpeople. Seeing all these races work together made me want to see the return of an official body."

"Teraeniel is weaker when divided. Erynor is not our only enemy—we face much worse than a power-hungry elf. The sooner *you* reinstall the senate, the better." The corners of Jeanne's lips twitched into a smile as she repositioned her staff. "That will have to wait though. We have an additional hour of training together, and if you don't start learning to bend properly, you won't survive to reinstall the Guardian Senate. And before you think that having a verathn will benefit you, you'll be left wanting if you can't bend. Don't forget the jienzu forms that you've already learned. Adapt them to the staff—the forms were never meant to be stagnant."

Devlyn pushed himself to his feet and readied himself for an additional bout. By the time the training concluded, he felt slightly more confident but his body ached in places he had never felt before. He looked forward to seeing Ellendren and relaxing a bit with her. But her training schedule was different than his and he wasted little time searching for her among the Guardian knights.

Reaching their tent, he was surprised to see an Eldinari waiting outside. Devlyn smiled and nodded at the star warden and went in to find Ellendren and Fendryl sharing a cup of tea.

"Good afternoon, Devlyn," Fendryl rose to greet him.

"It's nice to see you again, Fendryl, although not as nice as the last time, considering the circumstances." Devlyn brushed a hand through his hair as he recalled the battle in Everin and the subsequent weeks of negotiations leading to the treaty. "Has everything settled in Evellion?"

"As well as we can hope for. There are still some supporters of the Erynien Empire running around, but we're confident Thellion can manage without us."

"That's great news!"

"It truly is. If only the state of affairs in Cyril were better. I have never seen so much unwarranted destruction and unnecessary death. The people there are safe now and are being nursed back to health, but I worry more for their spirit than their bodily injuries."

Devlyn took a seat to join them, briefly reaching out to clasp Ellendren's hand before pouring himself a cup of tea. The news of Cyril left him distraught. "Is there anything we can do to help?"

"You are already well occupied." Fendryl smiled and sipped his tea. "The Eldinari stayed as long as we thought necessary and Cyril is in the capable hands of Evellion and Thellion now."

"Has there been any news about Alethea?" Ellendren asked. Devlyn dreaded the response. He had watched Alethea disappear into the clouds, her entire presence consumed by them.

"Afraid not. Wyn has provided his account and seems determined to rescue her. But there is no way to locate her—she is indeed in the Void. And to enter the Void is to die."

Devlyn shivered. Like Wyn, he too blamed himself for Alethea's disappearance. They should have done something; they should have fought. Frustrated with himself and not wanting to deal with those emotions, he asked, "What of the other Eldinari elves from Everin? Did they all travel here with you?"

"A sizable force did accompany me, but we divided into three groups, each settling at a different location on Krysenthiel's borders. One remained within Evellion's borders, just south of the Laudien Mountains, and west of the Delmira Wood, at least, what was the Delmira Wood. It would be a tragic loss if those trees no longer breathed."

"Why wait there?" Devlyn asked.

"When the Shroud falls, Septyl and the Delmira Wood will be vulnerable to attack. Indryn Allandis is leading the expedition there. Naerelle Shendielle and Elialen Illia are directly south of Verenthyl, while my force is here."

"Truly?" Devlyn wanted to hug Fendryl at the news.

"The Eldinari are committed to seeing the Luminari returned to Krysenthiel. And Ellendren has already told me that you located the old Eandyl road."

Devlyn turned to Ellendren, his mind already shifting to strategy.

"It shouldn't take long to make preparations—dividing our own numbers that is," Ellendren said, knowing Devlyn's thoughts. "We were already planning to move our camp closer to Eandyl."

"Imagine the benefit of having Eandyl and Verenthyl both occupied and fortified," Devlyn said. Now that the Eldinari had arrived, there wasn't any reason to hold off their next move.

"I can arrange for a chamber meeting. As it is, I can barely go outside without being hounded by an aryl about your recent expedition," Ellendren said.

"I've been experiencing that too, especially with Silvia and her allies." Devlyn took another sip of tea, trying to calm himself. Thinking about a chamber meeting with the aryls was certainly sobering enough.

"Difficulties with the other aryls?" Fendryl asked, cocking an eyebrow.

"In small ways. Things have gotten better since we became an aryl ourselves, but we are still seen as children in their eyes despite constantly placing ourselves in harm's way for their benefit," Ellendren said, rising to prepare a summons that she then handed to her attendant for distribution. Like Lyren, Pevrel was a constant presence in Devlyn and Ellendren's tent.

"By necessity, mortals age differently, but given that none of them have seen a hundred winters, I would have once considered them all still children. Thirty or fifty years of life over someone else seems like a trifle to me," Fendryl said.

"In time, hopefully we will see it that way too," Ellendren said. "I think it best to have a full chamber today and we should also invite the Chairs, Guardian knights, and generals, since we'll need their help to co-ordinate our next steps. Also, the aryls will want you to lead this meeting, Devlyn. They haven't seen you in that capacity yet and I think that it's important that they do, especially in regard to removing the Shroud and getting ourselves in place."

Devlyn nodded, not sure how he felt about leading a chamber meeting in front of such a large gathering. Not only did they have to discuss what they intended to happen next, but he also had to provide a briefing about the discovery of the Sorenth ruins, the Cyndinari hiding there and the murdered Sojourners.

A couple of hours later, Devlyn walked toward the makeshift chamber tent once again. He had taken the time to bathe and had donned his lierathnil, complete with the robe and all the unnecessary sashes. He had taken to only wearing the inner pieces of the outfit recently as the weather warmed.

Devlyn was one of the first to enter the chamber tent; Kyiel and Fyona, the Lauriel aryl, were the only others.

They returned his greeting of inclined head and raised opened palm to chest.

"Is it true, Ei'denai? Are we coming closer to reclaiming Krysenthiel?" Fyona asked.

Devlyn knew little about Kyiel and Fyona, only that their ancestral seat was in Verenthyl. Even though they were not the oldest aryl among the Luminari elves, they reminded him of what he imagined grandparents would be like.

"It is. Ellendren and I will share what we've discussed with Fendryl regarding the Eldinari elves assisting us."

"Imagine that; I never thought I'd see the day where I would meet elves who were still immortal," Fyona said.

"You've met Wyn and Alethea, right?" Devlyn asked.

"We have, but they were only two elves; comparing them to an entire population is something different entirely," Kyiel said.

"With any luck, we'll regain the Jewel of Life and our Life immortal with it," Fyona added encouragingly.

Devlyn took his seat to collect his thoughts and ended up counting the empty chairs to distract himself. The tent filled quickly and unlike prior chamber meetings, this one was not restricted to the high aryls nor the minor aryls. Guardian knights, ei'ana, and generals were also present. Byron stood at Jeanne's side, a young woman—Toryn if he remembered correctly—to her other side.

As he idly scanned the tent, Devlyn waited for Naesiv to officially begin the meeting as usual, forgetting that Ellendren had said he should lead it. She sat beside him, her hands resting on her lap, a slight smile on her lips as she too scanned the tent.

When he realized that every eye in the tent was focused on him, he remembered that it was his turn to begin this meeting. "Thank you for coming on short notice," he said as he stood, smiling nervously. "As I'm sure you're all aware, we're here to discuss our plans moving forward. The other day, Viren, Prya, Liara, and I sought out the Eandyl road. We did find it and followed it along its northern route until we came across the ruins of a Sorenth city. The Cyndinari elves that had attacked us here are hiding in those ruins. There is a dragon of the Dark Flight with them and also a strong wielder who has created an illusion over the ruins, disguising it as a forest."

Questions and comments quickly filled the chamber tent, derailing his presentation and preventing him from sharing the Eldinari's involvement in their plans for reclaiming the land held by the Shroud.

"How close are these ruins to Eandyl?" Enithil asked, breaking the soft commotion of private conversations.

"Too close to the Shroud for comfort. I imagine the city was initially abandoned for that very reason," Devlyn said.

"How vulnerable will Eandyl be to an attack once the Shroud is pushed back far enough for us to reclaim it?" Enithil asked.

"An attack is highly probable and the sooner we can push the Shroud away from Eandyl and get our people behind its walls, the better," Devlyn said.

"About time; I can't bear living in a tent another day," Sylvia commented.

"We don't even know the condition of Eandyl or any of our cities for that matter," Aegian scoffed. "We very well might continue sleeping in tents and on threadbare mattresses for some time still."

"Actually," Jeanne said, politely interrupting, "the stone wielded from Luminare to construct Krysenthiel's cities, lumaryl, is incorruptible. I can't speak for the furniture left behind since those days, but the buildings themselves will display no form of ruin or deterioration."

Hushed whispers rushed through the tent; such a resilient substance was inconceivable to the mortal-minded Luminari, especially since Lucillia had returned to the Illumined Wood. Only the statue of the woman the city was named after and mother of Feolyn and Roendryn remained of their former capital.

"It truly is a remarkable substance, but we need to shift our focus on ensuring that the Erynien Empire does not take advantage of the empty cities once the Shroud is destroyed," Devlyn said, raising his voice to be heard above the whispers.

"And how do you intend to do that?" Iridil asked.

"We have to start thinking about dividing our camp into three groups and positioning ourselves as close to the vacant cities as possible before pushing the Shroud back," Devlyn said, annoyed by the interruption.

"Won't that only make us more vulnerable? Erynor could start picking us off, starting with our smaller and weaker groups. The Erynien Empire could wipe out a third of our entire population in a single sweep and then target the next vulnerable group," Valerie said.

"I agree and I think it's prudent we stay together until we reach Eandyl. But after that, we will have to divide to retake the other cities," Devlyn said.

Fendryl rose then to address the gathering. "When Erynor last threatened Teraeniel and before we knew he was in league with the Evil One, Auriel bade my people withdraw from the conflict. With his foresight, he knew our part in this war would be better served at a later time. The Eldinari waited, secluded in our forest as our friends and allies first perished at the hands of Erynien Empire and later to mortality without access to Ceurendol. While Auriel and Uriel have yet to reveal themselves, Boriel has revealed that we cannot remain hidden away in our forest. The Luminari have the full support of the Eldinari." Relief flooded through Devlyn again as he listened to Fendryl speak, removing some of the pressure from himself. "We've already stationed ourselves in three strategic locations near Krysenthiel's border cities. Our star wardens and ei'ana await your arrival."

"Verenthyl and Eandyl will serve as our first bulwarks against any future Erynien invasion," Jeanne said. "The cities are strongly fortified and could withstand any siege for a number of years. If the Shroud had never been wrought, we would never have lost any cities. While the coastal lake cities are also fortified, Verenthyl and Eandyl will allow us to easily move our forces to our allies beyond Krysenthiel when needed. If we could enliven the old riverbeds, we could move even faster with watercraft."

"What riverbeds are these?" Ellendren asked.

"Lake Saeryndol is a massive body of water that receives constant snow melt from the surrounding mountains. Where do you imagine that excess water once went before everything froze under the Shroud?"

"How are there empty riverbeds? Surely the Shroud can't prevent water from flowing," Kyiel said.

"Krysenthiel is entirely frozen," Devlyn said. "I felt the ice when I first breached the Shroud and again when we more recently pushed it back."

"What of Reinyl? I've heard no mention of reclaiming my city," Therrin said.

"Reinyl is protected by the lake to its south and mountains to the north. Only Thellion and the dwarves neighbor it; surely you must see the advantages of restoring the cities separating us from the Erynien Empire first," Toral said.

"And what do you expect will happen when Reinyl is taken in our absence? Only Winstyl is closer to Arenthyl. If we don't reclaim and defend Reinyl, Erynor could seize the city and launch a full-scale attack on Arenthyl from it. Who knows if all his supporters in Perrien have been rooted out? For all we know, they could have fled into the mountain passes."

"Won't Undol Schtam will be monitoring those passes? I doubt dwarves take kindly to unwanted visitors in their mountains," Valerie said.

"I wouldn't exactly call them eager to help, but they were adamant about fulfilling old promises in regard to Ceurendol," Devlyn said, recalling what the Matriarch of Undol Schtam had said. "I'll send a messenger to Everin, to Matriarch Miurel IV, once this meeting is done. We'll have a fair bit of time before we can clear the Shroud away from Reinyl. We've only been able to remove a small segment so far."

Therrin and Zara Reyndien appeared satisfied with that.

"So, it's agreed. We'll divide our forces to retake our cities. Now, explain how you intend to deal with the Shroud. We've yet to receive a full report on how far you managed to push it back. At our current pace, do you imagine we'll reclaim Krysenthiel in its entirety within a month, or are we looking at years before we can return to our cities?" Iridil asked.

"We've investigated the area that had been freed of the Shroud," Jeanne said, relieving Devlyn of some of the pressure of addressing the aryls. "As Ei'denai Lorenthien has already mentioned, it is entirely frozen and without the sun reaching it, will remain so. The further we push the Shroud, the further its mist and clouds will also be forced back. That being said, the liberated area is quite large, but still only a tiny fraction of Krysenthiel. I do worry about the required time and energy if this is the chosen method of removing the Shroud. The two Phaedryn cannot repeatedly be incapacitated by overextending themselves with each attempt. They will be needed in the battles to come. Ultimately, Erynor will not let us remove his precious Shroud without pushing back. Hopefully, his forces won't be prepared until we at least have secured Eandyl."

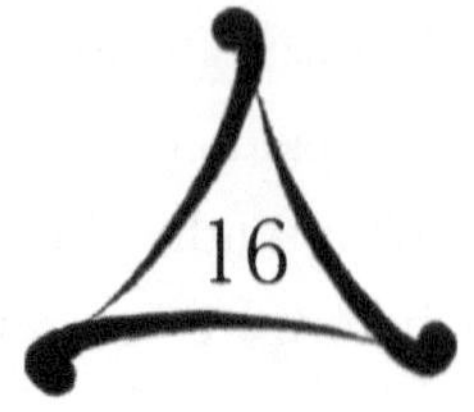

LUMARYL GATES

By the time Devlyn, Ellendren, Arlyn, and Viren left to follow the buried lumaryl road that disappeared into the Shroud, the Luminari camp was entirely packed and on the road. A line of wagons crawled west, slower than Devlyn could have imagined possible. The soft, muddy ground repeatedly mired wagon wheels and only wielding seemed able to dislodge them. But if everything went according to plan, some of them wouldn't need to pitch their tents at day's end; they'd be staying in Eandyl.

The Guardian knights had told the aryls that Eandyl wasn't large enough for the entire Luminari camp, but they could squeeze people into the city in the event of an attack. Devlyn knew that if they managed to free Eandyl from the Shroud today, the aryls would soon pressure him to free the next city. The only problem with that was that it wouldn't allow him, Ellendren, or Arlyn much rest since Verenthyl was still quite far away with many leagues of the Shroud standing between the two border cities. The other cities were buried deep in the Shroud and a wave of fatigue fell over Devlyn just thinking about it. The next few months promised to be exhausting.

As Devlyn flew off with the others, he fretted about the caravan's safety. They would be passing near the Sorenth ruins where the Cyndinari had been hiding out, so an attack was almost guaranteed. Liara and Prya would be staying aloft to survey the area and warn the Guardians as soon as an enemy force was sighted. Fendryl and his star wardens added another line of defense, patrolling along the length of the caravan. While Devlyn knew that he couldn't do everything, he did feel a pang of guilt that he wasn't also watching over them. What if something happened and Erynor sent more troops while they were vulnerable? They still had not seen any shadow elves near the Shroud, which only made Devlyn more concerned. Were the shadow elves waiting for a full-scale battle before making themselves known? Aliel tried to soothe Devlyn through their bond, but too much could go wrong today and they both knew it.

The caravan was soon behind Devlyn, Ellendren, Arlyn, and Viren as they flew west. Devlyn opened his interior sense to the lumaryl road and it stood out like a blaze beneath the muddy ground. Devlyn angled toward it and toward the edge of the Shroud. They landed, Devlyn and Ellendren remaining in their Phaedryn forms to illuminate the area, standing out against the Shroud. Viren had unsheathed his verathn the moment he and Arlyn had dismounted from the griffin. He would be their only defense once they began the process of pushing back the Shroud.

"Are we ready?" Devlyn asked. He had no idea how long this would take, but he hoped that they would be able to push the Shroud back far enough from Eandyl without having to have the caravan stop and wait before reaching the safety of the city.

"I'll alert you the moment there's danger," Viren said, looking south toward the open plains while the others looked north and into the Shroud.

"Let's hope the Cyndinari haven't realized what we're up to. The fog and clouds should have kept us hidden," Arlyn said.

"They would not have missed us breaking camp. I imagine they'll surmise our intent from the caravan's trajectory," Ellendren said.

Forming the wield he had used previously, Devlyn held it as he bonded with Ellendren and Arlyn. With two phoenix and three elves, Devlyn felt like he could do anything with the amount of power flowing through him. He built up the wield's strength, wielding all seven erend-inth, but principally lumenys, and he reached out to the Shroud.

Gently at first, Devlyn probed the Shroud and was reminded of its long taint on Eklean. It felt as though he had placed both hands on an immovable stone wall, like a solid cliff rather than a poisonous mist. His being pressed against it and he channeled his wield forward. Interacting with the Shroud this time brought forth an unexpected nausea and he swallowed back the bile and tried to ignore the diseased nature of the Shroud. He didn't ram the wield against it, but slowly tilted the enormity of his strength forward until the full weight of his wield pushed against the Shroud, forcing it back.

The Shroud thundered and something inside it screamed as Devlyn took a step forward onto the frozen ground that was now freed of the poisonous mist. He was already starting to sweat from the exertion. He didn't feel fatigued yet, but a tiny doubt arose about whether he could push the Shroud back far enough to free Eandyl. He took another step forward, then another. As the frozen vegetation crunched beneath his feet, the Shroud thundered deafeningly in revolt, covering any other sound.

Blinking against the flashing of tenebrys, Devlyn thought he saw a figure in the mist. It faded, winking in and out of existence, as though it could only be seen in the presence of tenebrys. Each flash left an after-image of a woman, her features indistinguishable. She seemed ethereal, as though she would blow away on a light breeze or disappear if sunlight touched her.

He took another step forward and heard her laugh. "You dare try to destroy me?"

Devlyn pushed forward again. Part of him wanted to engage the woman, to find out who she was. Ellendren gave him a mental nudge that suggested otherwise. The woman was dangerous and Ellendren urged him to keep his focus on their wield and not get distracted.

"I have seen and conquered death. A child of House Lorenthien who hasn't even seen twenty summers is powerless against me. Ithendryl couldn't stop me nor could she prevent my Master's designs. What chance do you think you have against me?"

———————————

Toryn marched forward in diligent watchfulness but also in some disgruntlement. Her role as Jeanne's squire meant she had to stay with Jeanne and away from the vulnerable rear of their caravan where she was quite sure she could be more useful if they were attacked.

The thunder coming from the Shroud unnerved her. The last time the Lorenthien aryl had tried to push back the Shroud, the Luminari camp had been attacked. They had at least had defenses then. Minor though they were, the packed snow and dirt had slowed the Cyndinari attack and had prevented them from killing any civilians. If the Cyndinari attacked now though, they would have their choice of any of the many weak points along the caravan. While there were guards stationed along the entire caravan, it would not be difficult to exploit the weaknesses. Even the extra security details around the aryls wouldn't be enough if the Cyndinari targeted them.

A shiver ran down her spine as the thunder pealed again, penetrating deep into her being. The Shroud stormed violently and its misty and cloudy form folded in on itself to double down again. Toryn tried not to pay too much attention to the Shroud. There was nothing she could do about it. From what she had overheard, not even the ei'ana could help with that beast. It was up to the two Phaedryn and an ei'ceuril, all of whom were Lorenthiens.

As she slogged on, she wondered how far they would have to march. Promises had been made about staying in Eandyl tonight. She wondered if it would be anything like Lucillia. Like all the Luminari, she missed the only home she had ever known. Lucillia and all the other Luminari settlements along the Illumined Wood were gone and there was no going back. She knew that. Even if some of the elves complained about their current lack of defenses, they would have been just as poorly defended without their homes along the edge of the Illumined Wood. Still, half a year had passed since they'd left the Illumined Wood and Toryn missed sleeping in the shadows of the tall trees.

She was snapped back to the present when the horns blew. The first warning had come from the west and Jeanne had already given orders on how to deal with an attack. Annoyed that she had to maintain her position near Jeanne, Toryn knew they couldn't redirect their entire defense to the one place the caravan was being attacked, but she really didn't want to stay behind while others fought. Jeanne and Byron frenziedly directed the defense from the middle of the caravan as messengers dashed away with Jeanne's orders. Toryn thought their position a mistake. They should be closer to the fighting—they should be involved in the defense and not simply leading it from a distance.

The frenzy intensified when a second horn blared from the east. Jeanne must have known about the second attack, for she had already sent runners in that direction before Toryn heard the horn. The dragon and her rider had to be sending information directly to Jeanne, but how were they doing that? She had assumed that they would have to land to give a report, but they hadn't, not once. They hadn't even dipped down to yell the report to Jeanne.

Waiting impatiently for her chance to prove herself, she heard Jeanne curse under her breath before she addressed the nearest unit.

"Two more waves are coming toward us, and as we feared, they'll hit this position the hardest," Jeanne said. Now Toryn understood why her company hadn't been sent to the other two attack points and smiled. Jeanne had expected this and had kept Toryn where the heat of the battle would be. The Cyndinari had tried to pull their attention away from the middle of the caravan by attacking the front and rear. It hadn't worked though. "Ei'ana are already forming bulwarks to slow the enemy. Under no circumstance is the caravan to stop. The Erynien Empire will continue to send reinforcements if we stay here in the open. That being the case, only some of us will remain to engage the enemy, while the rest will continue to defend the caravan."

Toryn waited eagerly to hear where she was needed and was sorely disappointed when she found out that she would be staying with the caravan. While the decision infuriated her, she knew better than to argue with Jeanne Darkel. She bit back what she had wanted to say and instead followed her orders. Jeanne didn't have the time to deal with an unruly squire just now.

The caravan continued its slow crawl forward, Toryn with it, as a larger portion of the Luminari defense tore away from the wagons. They would want to get as far away from the civilians as possible before the battle commenced. Toryn had to remind herself that her role was still important. She could still prove herself in this capacity. The Cyndinari would try to break through their lines and attack the civilians. She was part of the last line of defense for people who had never lifted a sword before. Still, she would have been more useful on the front lines. She was convinced that she could stop the Cyndinari from ever getting past the defenses and reaching the civilians in the first place.

Exhausted, Devlyn stepped forward again, holding the seven erendinth in a single, powerful wield. Whoever was inside the Shroud screamed and launched bolts of tenebrys at him. The bolts couldn't penetrate Devlyn's wield though, especially not since it was buffered and strengthened by his connection with Ellendren and Arlyn. The wield consumed the tenebrys bolts as they crashed against it.

"You will not take my cities from me," the woman in the Shroud screamed. "You will not take my empire—my reward!"

Devlyn's mind grew fuzzy. He began to think that this woman in the Shroud was right. He had been holding the wield for what had to be hours now, taking one slow and hard-won step at a time on the now-slick ground. It no longer crunched beneath his feet, and was slipperier, which forced him to also focus on balancing himself.

Pushing his wield against the Shroud, he took another step, and that's when he saw the gates of Eandyl solidify in front of him. The sturdy gates were sealed and Devlyn almost lost his breath at seeing them for the first time as they towered over him. Even without the sun shining on them, the pale amber color stone glowed and offered its own light into the dark mist surrounding the city. Devlyn could only imagine what this city would look like in the dawning sun.

With his interior senses open, he felt the city in its entirety. Eandyl was much smaller than Lucillia had been, and truly, there were many towns larger than Eandyl. Devlyn felt something here that other towns and cities did not have though. Something pulsed in the city of lumaryl, something very different from the Shroud. Even though the Shroud had engulfed all Krysenthiel, it had not been able to touch the city. The woman in the Shroud had not been able to go into the city. Eandyl had its own power, a power that lay dormant within it. That power felt familiar to Devlyn. It hadn't been able to stop the Shroud from poisoning the air and making Eandyl uninhabitable, but it had kept the mysterious woman out.

Reaching out, Devlyn placed his palm on the door, feeling some of the carvings. The entire surface was carved with elven figures and trees and flowering vines. He reached out with his senses for the power in the city, and as he did so, one of the of the sculptural reliefs yawned. The carving actually moved its hand to cover its mouth and made an audible sound.

"Is someone finally trying to wake us up?" another sculptural relief asked.

"It's certainly been long enough, hasn't it?"

"It's too cold to wake up. I'm not budging until I feel the sun again."

"That's not even our aryl."

The sculptural reliefs bickered among themselves. Devlyn didn't think they were aware of him yet. He didn't know how to ask for their help or even if they could help—they were carvings on a door! Instead, Devlyn reached further into the city and tapped the dormant yet incredibly strong power he had felt. Thinking back, he remembered the time he and Aliel had pierced through the Shroud. They hadn't wielded anything complicated to push the Shroud back then. He and Aliel couldn't even communicate then, but something had sprung from their connection—something possibly related to Devlyn being a descendant of Galithinol of the Gold Flight.

As he recalled that feeling, he wondered if the woman harassing him from inside the Shroud was right. What if he was going about this all wrong? While he could push the Shroud back from the city, its residue remained. The stormy clouds still covered the land that Devlyn had freed, unlike that time at Gwilnor, when he had pierced a hole all the way through from the clouds to the ground. That effort had let the sun reach the land that had been freed from the Shroud.

Connected to Aliel, Ellendren, Tariel, and Arlyn, as well as tapping Eandyl's own power, Devlyn reached further inward. He reached deep into the dark interior place where his spirit lay and he felt that pulse at his very core. The pulse quickened and blossomed in a dome of light around the city, then exploded upward and outward. The woman in the Shroud screamed and Devlyn sensed her retreat from the powerful pillar of light just as he felt himself collapsing.

Ellendren, Viren, and Arlyn rushed forward. His bond with Aliel slipped away, but before his eyes closed, sunlight spilled down through a large hole in the clouds and onto Eandyl. The city looked even more glorious than he'd imagined possible.

SECURED

Jaerol sat in the Ceurtriarch's overly crowded sitting room. Aaron was finally ready to share the plan he and the temple knights had devised to liberate Gwilnor from the Tenebrae School. The only person missing from the original group was Kevn, now that he had left the temple to travel to Septyl. Jaerol had no idea how Kevn planned to slip into Septyl while the Shroud still hung over the palace-city of the Ei'ana. That wasn't his concern though; the most important thing at the moment was that Liam was Razcul's prisoner and Jaerol intended to rescue him tonight.

Jaerol, Fiona, Danielle, Trethien, Renaud, Stephen, Bastien, and Daphnel all wore black outfits and expectant looks as they stared at Aaron who seemed to be waiting for someone. But Jaerol's patience was gone.

"So, care to elaborate more on this plan to liberate Gwilnor?" he asked.

"We're waiting for two others." Aaron looked at the door. "As I mentioned this morning, I intend to expand the temple's ward over the entire city. Since the Tenebrae do not have an army here—only wielders—it should be a simple matter of overpowering them and tossing them into the dungeons. Ultimately, the judgement of their actions rests with the Seven Chairs of Septyl, but we'll happily lock them away until Septyl is stable again."

"You just intend to march into the castle and take it by force?" Danielle asked, raising a skeptical eyebrow.

"There will, of course, be more finesse to it than that. I have the utmost faith in the temple knights and the others who've volunteered to help."

"And who are these other volunteers? Are they good with a sword?" Jaerol asked just as a knock came at the antechamber door.

"Your Holiness," a temple knight said as he bowed in the doorway. "The temple knights are moving into position and the city gates are sealed."

"Thank you, Ian," Aaron said. Jaerol impatiently thumbed the hilt of the skinny sword hanging from his hip. "We're almost ready, Jaerol, I promise. You'll rescue Liam tonight, I know it." Aaron placed a hand on Jaerol's shoulder to comfort and calm him.

"Thank you. You know what he means to me."

"You'd follow him into the Void to bring him back if you had to," Bastien said, as Daphnel, Renaud, and Stephen chuckled.

"So, what do you intend for our group?" Jaerol asked.

"While the temple knights storm the castle, you'll sneak into it through one of the secret tunnels and find Liam, Velaria, and the other prisoners," Aaron said.

"You know we'll likely cross paths with Razcul," Trethien said.

"I hope we do; he won't be able to wield tenebrys if everything goes according to plan." Jaerol grinned dangerously.

"What of us?" Fiona asked, glancing at Danielle.

"I know you're incredibly strong with the erendinth, but you won't be able to wield. The temple ward will indiscriminately sever your connection to the erendinth."

Fiona and Danielle both revealed the daggers they carried. "We're quite capable of defending ourselves without the erendinth, thank you."

"I don't recall either of you ever coming to the knight's courtyard to train, not that any of the knights would instruct their pupils how to fight with a dagger." Trethien eyed the daggers, impressed at Fiona and Danielle's handling of them.

"Do you think our families sent us to Gwilnor without training us to defend ourselves?" Danielle smiled flirtatiously at Trethien.

"Are we ready?" Jaerol growled, ready to get moving. The sun was already setting and the Arenthylean bells were ringing. The silver-like aldaryl bells announced the evening, and if everything went according to plan, the next set of bells to ring would also announce the liberation of Gwilnor Academy from the Tenebrae School.

Two loud thumps came from outside the sitting room on the balcony and as the curtains parted, Rusyl and Yelaris walked in, both of them quite naked.

"Forgive us for not being clothed," Yelaris said.

"We'll do no such thing," Jehn sprang out of a small door at the edge of the sitting room, apparently expecting the arrivals. He averted his eyes as he handed over two outfits to them.

"Thank you for coming, Yelaris and Rusyl," Aaron inclined his head in greeting.

Itching to get the rescue started, Jaerol tapped his foot impatiently. Once the dragons were suitably covered, he urged them to get moving. "It's time."

"May Anaweh bless you and keep you safe," Aaron said, gesturing a blessing on the group before they left the Ceurtriarch's quarters. "Remember, wait until full night before entering the castle. I don't know how long it will take to extend the temple's ward, but you'll know when it's done."

Jaerol led them along the perimeter of the Chamber of Light toward the cloistered portion of the temple, sparing a look toward the shaft of light before going into the corridor. They passed through the temple quickly, trying not to draw any attention to themselves, something made more difficult with Yelaris and Rusyl in their company.

Jaerol stopped in front of a plain door and knocked. Shuffling came from the other side and as the door swung inward, a broad grin greeted them. Therril ushered everyone inside his small office and it became extremely crowded, especially since the dragons' shoulder spans were easily double anyone else's.

"It's rare I get visits from the knights. You know, since you and Liam had your little adventure, I was asked to keep better watch of my window." The old elf had a mischievous glimmer in his eye that betrayed his words.

Therril took note of his former students. "I hope you three still have your theoretical books. If you're successful tonight, it won't be long until classes resume." Danielle, Fiona, and Trethien all mumbled excuses about not being able to take their school belongings out of the castle when they had fled.

Uninterested in anything that didn't directly affect their plans, Jaerol stepped onto the only window ledge.

"I see you don't need any instruction from me." Therril winked at Jaerol.

"So, this is the infamous window?" Renaud asked.

"I wonder what happened to those Dwonians who captured us, what, three years ago?" Jaerol asked.

"Weren't they defeated at Myrium?" Stephen asked.

"Most of the Dwonian warriors escaped being captured," Rusyl said.

"I didn't realize you and Liam had been captured by Dwonians. Does Devlyn know?" Danielle asked.

"Liam didn't want to bring it up—it wasn't a pleasant experience," Jaerol said as he stepped through and into the tunnel.

They walked quickly through the length of the dark tunnel. They had agreed that bringing a torch to light their path would have been too risky. There were too many people keeping a watch in the corridors of Gwilnor, even if this particular tunnel didn't let out in a public space. Jaerol knew the tunnel well enough to get them through without bumping into the walls too much. He felt his connection to the erendinth return once they had passed the temple ward. Still able to wield, they had no choice but to wait and hope that Aaron was able to do as he promised.

The dorthl ring that Velaria wore stabbed into her finger like a thousand tiny knives; she wondered if the pain would ever cease. She crouched in her cell, no one hovering outside the door since the ring kept her from wielding. She could still feel the erendinth, a painful reminder that she couldn't interact with them.

The door to her small cell opened and Hannah approached, knife in hand. She wielded a globe to light the space and Velaria thirsted to wield the erendinth again. She had grown numb to Hannah's abuse over the past months. Another leaf had sprouted and Hannah intended to cut this one off too. Velaria did her best to hide the newly grown leaves of her flowery garment, but Hannah always discovered the new sprouts, each one in a different location, and roughly sliced them off. Her cruelty extended to having Velaria's hair shaved regularly.

Hannah was only two steps away when the globe illuminating the cramped cell vanished, startling Velaria. Hannah's shocked gasp indicated that it was a surprise for her as well.

Miraculously, the ring fell from Velaria's finger, the stabbing pain gone, only its memory remaining. She reached out for the erendinth but couldn't feel them. The only time Velaria hadn't been able to feel the erendinth was when she visited the temple. *Had the temple's ward been extended beyond its previous limits? Was that even possible?* With her cell door open and Hannah still in shock, Velaria knew she wouldn't get this chance again. Leaping up, she crashed into the older woman, knocking her off her feet and into the wall.

Hannah screamed as Velaria wrestled the knife from her hand. Despite the threatening way Hannah had held that knife, she had no idea how to use it as a weapon. Grasping the knife, Velaria looked over the woman cowering on the floor. A fleeting thought of ending the vile woman's life crossed Velaria's mind. It went against everything she stood for, yet in that moment as she towered over the defenseless woman, she wanted nothing more than to execute her revenge against the women who had subdued Gwilnor and sought to destroy the Ei'ana of Septyl. She could not believe that this woman had called herself an Azurelle and had vied to become the next Chair of her School. Velaria shivered at the thought of her School under Hannah's direction. She had already seen the damage Hannah had caused Gwilnor while she had been chancellor, a Tenebrae even then.

Turning away, Velaria left the whimpering woman where she lay and locked the cell behind her. Aware of her cell's location between the North Tower and the dining hall, Velaria began to formulate a plan to finish what she had set in motion with the partly successful escape of the ei'ana and students. She would see those still loyal to Septyl free of the Tenebrae—not everyone had betrayed their oaths.

Gwilnor's male students were not the only residents of the North Tower. The Septyl knights were also quartered there and given the logistics of the limited and thwarted escape, many good knights had been left out of the plan. Velaria and the other Chairs had made the students their priority, which meant most of the knights and ei'ana had not been involved. They could now be useful. Clenching the knife in her hand, she made a run for the North Tower, hoping that whatever was preventing her and Hannah from wielding would last a while longer.

She paused when she reached the central stair of the North Tower, but only long enough to be certain no one was on the stair ahead of her. Taking the steps two at time, Velaria quickly reached the third level, and ran down the corridor, stopping at a door partway down and knocking discreetly.

While she waited anxiously, she kept an eye out for the patrols, and the moment the door opened, she shoved her way into Andrew's modest quarters. Andrew's oath to Septyl was still fresh. She hadn't wanted to present herself to a more seasoned knight. Even though she knew and trusted many of the knights from when she had studied at Gwilnor, she had also studied with many ei'ana and, until recently, never had had reason to doubt them. She did trust Andrew.

"Mother Velaria," Andrew stuttered, dressed only in his small clothes at the late hour and quite shocked at her sudden appearance. "How are you here? The Tenebrae…" His groggy mind tried to catch up with what was happening. Even with her shaved head and lack of proper attire, he recognized the Chair of Azurelle standing in front him.

Pushing him against the wall, she pressed the knife against his throat. "Are you still true or have you betrayed us too?" Despite her trust in him, she couldn't take any risk. She had once trusted Hannah and so many other ei'ana.

"I've done no such thing; I've been locked in my room more days than not. I wear my blue tunic proudly," Andrew said, startled and hurt by Velaria's reaction. "Mother, you need to cover yourself. I have some spare clothing, but they aren't proper for the Chair of Azurelle."

"They'll do for now. Quickly, we need to rouse the knights we can still trust. For reasons I cannot explain, I cannot wield." Velaria lowered the knife, looking Andrew directly in the eyes, making sure he understood her meaning. "None of us can." His eyes widened. "Are there still knights loyal to Septyl?"

"There might be some who've dishonored themselves, but I assure you that they are in the minority."

"Good. Let's organize the knights then. I want the exits covered; anyone who tries to escape is to be taken prisoner. If they fight back, do not hesitate to reciprocate—those women who have betrayed Septyl are no longer ei'ana. They are Tenebrae and dangerous. They are our enemies and seek to destroy Septyl. The same goes for anyone strolling freely about the castle. Knocking them unconscious would be best. I want as many as possible detained for questioning and justice." Velaria flinched at her words; she was starting to sound like a Vyoletryn with how much she wanted justice served.

"What if we harm one who hasn't betrayed us?" Andrew dug trousers and a shirt out of his wardrobe and gave them to Velaria before getting dressed himself.

"Have the knights declare that the orders come from me and those who are true to Septyl won't attack you but will follow my command. I want every resident in the castle confined in the dining hall. Separate those you believe are Tenebrae as best you can," Velaria said, and touched the small leaf sprouting from her side whole and intact under Andrew's spare shirt. Hannah hadn't had the chance to cut it off. "Now, let's move."

Rushing through the corridor, they woke everyone on the floor and gave instructions to alert the knights on the tower's upper floors to retake the castle. Moving down the stairwell, Velaria walked with a heightened confidence with Andrew at her side, knowing he would prove more lethal against a wielder incapable of wielding than herself with a dagger she'd never been trained to use.

Velaria and Andrew left the North Tower in the capable hands of the Septyl knights. She didn't think any of the students still in the castle had pledged themselves to the Tenebrae, but someone had betrayed her and the other Chairs. The Tenebrae had known they were planning an escape. They hadn't known precisely when—they couldn't have since Velaria had only signaled it an hour before it started. Still, even with her sacrifice, the Tenebrae had been prepared enough to thwart their plan and capture half the students and ei'ana who had tried to get away that night.

When yells began to echo through the corridors above, Velaria paused momentarily. She didn't think the knights could have outpaced her and Andrew. Surely, they weren't that efficient in rousing the North Tower? But she had other objectives and would leave the North Tower to the Septyl knights.

Velaria and Andrew continued through the corridors of the castle, the dining hall now far behind them, drawing near the main entryway. Velaria did not know who she was looking for specifically and lumping them all together as traitors seemed irrational, but she felt that she would know the difference between friend or foe once she saw them. She knew that thought was folly. So many of the women she had trusted had turned out to belong to the Tenebrae, a betrayal that stung her to the core.

"Young men—under whose authority are you outside your dormitory at this hour?" the demanding voice came from ahead, one Velaria did not recognize. She had forgotten for a moment that her head was shaved, her face dirty, and that she wore Andrew's clothing. She must have appeared to be the very image of a rebellious man.

"Swords are forbidden, young man," the woman hissed at Andrew. "And is that a knife in your hand? Under the chancellor's directive, all weapons are prohibited! Yes, I'm talking to you two!"

"If she runs, knock her out," Velaria said under her breath.

"What was that?" the woman asked. "Speak up!"

The moment the Tenebrae was close enough, Andrew pointed his sword at the woman, infuriating her even more.

"How *dare* you defy me! Chancellor Hannah will hear of this insubordination and you will be dealt with severely."

Velaria knew the woman was trying to embrace the erendinth— what ei'ana would not when threatened by a man with a sword? Smiling at the woman, Velaria said, "Last I checked, Hannah had been deposed by the Seven Chairs of Septyl."

"What have you done?" Realizing that she could not touch the erendinth and recognizing Velaria, the Tenebrae quivered and backed away.

"Bind her hands," Velaria said.

The Tenebrae stared daggers into Velaria's eyes. She didn't try to fight or flee; she knew she was defeated, at least for now.

Velaria tried to place the woman's face as Andrew wrapped a

leather cord around her wrists. "If you struggle, you will find yourself waking with a sore head or not at all."

The Tenebrae said nothing.

As Velaria and Andrew were about to continue through the corridors, several knights caught up with them.

"Mother," the one in the lead greeted her.

"Can two of you take this Tenebrae to the dining hall? The rest of you stay with me." Two of them stepped forward and took one of the woman's arms to escort her to the dining hall. The others followed Velaria toward a much larger group blocking the corridor ahead. Several women stood there, armed men standing protectively beside them. Velaria recognized Indryl.

"This is a fool's errand, Velaria. Submit while you still can," Indryl said.

"We trusted you to teach Devlyn how to wield—and you dare betray us!" Velaria couldn't hold back her fury. How many ei'ana had forsaken Septyl?

"Dear sister, you are the one who betrayed us. Kien wielders will destroy this world—Balance must never return!"

"You are a fool, Indryl."

"And yet you're the one who is outnumbered." Indryl laughed as she waved toward the two dozen knights who had betrayed Septyl, and now stood at her back.

UPRISING

Jaerol hurried through the castle, leading his small band up another stairwell. Whatever Aaron had planned had worked and even though they were no longer in the temple, he could not wield. Although the extended temple ward was proving useful, he hated being cut off from the erendinth, especially now that he could control his wielding. He hoped Aaron didn't intend to keep the wards over the entire city of Ceurenyl for long. Granted, Jaerol didn't know how much longer he would be in Ceurenyl after tonight.

Stopping at another landing, Jaerol threw his arm back to halt the others behind him. Someone was up ahead. Not just one person but an entire group and he thought he heard a brief conversation—well, it sounded like two women arguing—and then the sounds of swords clashing. Jaerol wondered if it was the temple knights. Had they already made it into the castle?

Whatever was happening, it was still further down an intersecting corridor and out of sight. Before Jaerol could determine what to do next, Yelaris pushed forward.

"Yelaris, wait," Rusyl called after her.

"Velaria's there—I will not wait!" Yelaris roared and sprinted on, Rusyl right behind her.

Jaerol saw the others looking at him, waiting for instruction. "Well, don't just stand there, you heard the dragon, Velaria's up there." They all rushed forward, swords at the ready. But the bodies that lay around the dragons who had run ahead showed that help wasn't needed. They had made quick work of the knights attacking Velaria and her defenders. Yelaris's arms were wrapped tightly about someone.

"Who's there?" Jaerol recognized the commanding voice hidden behind Yelaris' much larger figure. It was definitely the Chair of Azurelle, the Blue Dragon herself. How was Velaria free?

"Velaria?" Jaerol called back. He couldn't believe that she'd managed to escape. Then again, this *was* Velaria Treyven. If anyone could manage overcoming impossible odds, it was her.

"Jaerol? Oh, thank the Light, you're safe! They have Liam—of course you already know, don't you?" She disengaged from the hug she was giving Yelaris. "And Fiona, Danielle, and Trethien! What in the Light's name are you doing here? You should be with the Chairs and the others who escaped the castle, not sneaking back in."

"Supposedly saving you and the others," Trethien admitted. "But you clearly didn't need our help, did you?"

"Being severed from the erendinth gave me a slight advantage over Hannah who thought to pay me a visit at the wrong time. I trust you know what's happened to the erendinth?"

"Aaron and Kevn figured out a way to extend the temple ward over the entire city just as had been done during the Ceurendol War," Jaerol said.

"As I suspected, then. Is it permanent?" Velaria asked.

"Only as long as Aaron wants it to be. The temple knights will be storming the castle soon if they haven't already," Jaerol said.

"Good, I've already organized the Septyl knights. I've instructed them to round up everyone and take them to the dining hall. We'll sort them out later."

Jaerol couldn't believe how effective Velaria had been. She had been a prisoner less than an hour ago, had freed herself, *and* organized the castle's defenses to overthrow the Tenebrae. Apparently, all Aaron had to do was extend the temple's ward to cover the city and Velaria could have singlehandedly saved Gwilnor if left to her own devices. Jaerol had always known that Velaria was a formidable ei'ana, but what she was accomplishing this day would have legends and songs written about her in the years to come.

"What do you need from us?" Jaerol asked.

"Danielle, Fiona, and Trethien, come with us. Capable or not, I won't allow you students to confront a shadow elf with Jaerol. I need to get to the Chancellor's Tower and find out where everyone is hiding in the castle, friend and foe. Yelaris will of course come with us too." Danielle and Fiona flourished their daggers, ready to move.

Andrew eyed the daggers, impressed. "You handle those as though you were born in Sudern and have been carrying them from birth."

The two smiled at the compliment, but Bastien scratched his chin as he eyed Andrew up and down. "You're more than just Sudernese, aren't you? You don't carry yourself like the cutpurses there and I'd wager a month's salary that you didn't come from a family of merchants."

"You also bear a strong resemblance to a certain Sudernese family. My father and Duke Paolo Farneis are quite close," Renaud said.

"I take it my ruse is discovered?" He smirked and Jaerol looked at him differently, judging whether he could still trust him. "Well, my uncle didn't think my identity would remain a secret for half as long as it did." He took a step toward Velaria. "I suppose I should inform you, that my name is actually…"

"I know who you are, Andrea Farneis. You have a clever uncle, but do you really think he could dupe the Seven Chairs of Septyl?"

"Why did you never admit to knowing who I am? We've traveled together."

"I knew you would tell me eventually, and it was much easier to get the right sort of information to your uncle if he still thought us ignorant about your identity. Besides, there's another who will be less forgiving about your uncle's duplicity than I am." Velaria winked at him, referring to Abbie. "Jaerol, Razcul is keeping Liam in his private quarters, no doubt to taunt you specifically into rescuing him," Velaria said.

"Of course, he is," Jaerol shuddered at what Liam was going through.

"Be safe, Jaerol; we can't lose you," Velaria said, before leading her supporters toward the Chancellor's Tower.

Jaerol and Rusyl jogged away, trailed by Renaud, Stephen, Bastien, and Daphnel. The four of them wanted to see Liam rescued just as badly as Jaerol did. They couldn't know what was going through his mind right now, and he didn't trust himself enough to pay any attention to those thoughts either. He didn't have the time to reflect on what Razcul was likely doing to Liam. His focus was on saving Liam.

Jaerol rushed toward Razcul's apartment in the South Tower. Since the shadow elf was impersonating an Eldinari with the Emradiel School, he should have been staying with them in the Emradiel wing. Razcul wasn't that foolish though. The Eldinari would have easily seen through his disguise if he lived among them. So instead, Razcul had taken up residence in the South Tower where the guest suites were, the very place where Devlyn had lived before he had been abducted last year.

They were soon across the bridge to the southern wing of the castle. From the shouting he could hear at the far end of the corridor, the temple knights had arrived. *I'm coming for you, Liam.* He tried to send his thoughts out to Liam. He couldn't be sure that he'd been successful, so he turned it into a mantra, each repetition giving him strength and focus as they hurried through the castle and up the South Tower.

"And where do you think you're going?" asked a bulky man at the head of a group that seemed to include castle servants, a mix of cooks and cleaners, perhaps a dozen altogether.

"How does that concern you?" Jaerol asked.

"I don't think they're who they appear to be," Daphnel said.

"And what do we look like to you?" said another.

"They're servants of shadow all right. Jaerol, go on without us; you don't have time to wait for this lot to scatter," Bastien said.

"There's twice as many of them as you," Jaerol protested, even though he knew Bastien was right. His chances of successfully rescuing Liam would severely diminish once Razcul realized that the castle had been breached by those still loyal to Septyl.

"Go, we'll be fine. Save Liam. You two might've left the temple to become ei'ana, but you're still one of us," Daphnel said. "Besides, your former roommates could likely take on that group blindfolded, to say nothing of Rusyl, here."

Jaerol hesitated a moment longer, moving only when both Renaud and Stephen said, "Go." Rusyl cracked his fingers, practically looking forward to what was about to ensue.

Jaerol raced up the main stair of the South Tower. He knew exactly where Razcul's apartment was because Razcul had once tried to lure Jaerol over for a cup of tea with an old classmate. There had been nothing innocent about the invitation and if Jaerol had accepted, he likely wouldn't have woken up after.

Finally, Razcul's door stood before him. He felt a moment of panic as he considered his plan to rescue Liam, then turned the latch and pushed the door open, shocked that it wasn't locked. The shadow elf had likely placed a wield over the door, but that was now gone. The spacious sitting room was dark but Jaerol's eyes had already adjusted to the darkness since most of the castle was dimly lit at this time of night and any globes of wielded light had gone out with the temple ward. Only a few of the torches had been lit, supplemented by moon and starlight.

Various doors led out of the sitting room and Jaerol tried the closest. He peered into the lavatory, quickly and silently moving to the next where an empty bed filled the space. The door after that was locked with no key in sight. Liam had to be in that room. There was only one other door and it was slightly ajar. That had to be Razcul's room, and the key was likely in there.

Jaerol pressed his hand to Liam's door, drawing his fingers down against the wood. "I'll get you out."

"I know you will," Liam answered.

His heart leapt at hearing Liam's voice after two months apart. He wanted to free Liam and get him away to safety first, but that would have to wait.

"How touching," Razcul mocked from behind him. Jaerol's head snapped around and toward the now fully opened bedchamber door. Like the lock Razcul had likely placed on the door to his apartment, the shadow elf's disguise had vanished with his ability to interact with the erendinth. Razcul lazily clutched a sword, daring Jaerol to attack.

Jaerol paused for a moment as fear roiled in his gut. When Razcul had revealed his true self to Jaerol last year, nightmares from his past had resurfaced. Kiron's face floated in his mind again. The image was so clear that Jaerol felt as though he could speak to him again, like they used to—before Liam, before Gwilnor and Ceurenyl, before Gneal, and before he'd ended Kiron's life. Jaerol's heart still ached, those wounds freshly opened with Razcul's reappearance before him. Then it seemed as though Kiron was urging him to act—to rid the world of Razcul, free those captive spirits, and save Liam.

Jaerol shook himself and glared at the ugliness of Razcul's corrupted body; it looked as though he was decaying from the inside out. The shadow elf only wore a pair of trousers, leaving exposed the blisters and decay that marked his upper body.

"Are you going to be brave today? Interested in a rematch after our earlier duel?" Razcul pointed his sword at Jaerol. "Bow."

"Not today." Jaerol lifted his own sword, quickly scanning the dimly lit sitting room once again. The furniture was not going to make this easy. Jaerol locked his eyes on the elf who had caused him more pain than any other person. That he was also a shadow elf only added to Jaerol's hatred for him.

Razcul sprung at Jaerol in a fury, quickly putting Jaerol in a defensive stance. He fell into one of the jienzu forms. Not one that he had been taught at the Imperium, but one he had learned from Elayne, the Guardian knight. Jaerol maneuvered around the furniture, all the while trying not to trip over any of it.

Jaerol flicked his sword toward the hilt of Razcul's sword and managed to disarm the shadow elf. Furious, Razcul lunged at Jaerol. The immediate response caught Jaerol off guard and he tripped over a low table, falling backward, and dropping his sword. Razcul pushed the table aside and leapt onto Jaerol, straddling him, pinning him down, a knife clutched in one hand.

Jaerol grabbed Razcul's wrist to hold off the knife before the shadow elf could bury it into his chest. They grappled for control of the knife held horizontally between them as each fought to push it into the other's throat.

"Your spirit is mine, traitor," Razcul spat, his voice crisp and deadly.

"You're the traitor—forcing half our class to die at each other's hands, to prolong their cursed lives."

"How did that pathetic weakling Kiron let you kill him? Surely even one as pitiful as he could have destroyed you. You both shame the Cyndinari," Razcul spat.

Fingers wrestling for the knife, Jaerol could see the straining tendons and muscles layered beneath Razcul's decaying skin.

"Are you going to try to kill me too? Free the spirits I've captured? They could be yours. You could steal my strength for your own—knowing you chose to abandon your weak and soft skin would allow me to die proudly. Not that I would surrender to you." Razcul cackled a high-pitched laugh.

Jaerol could feel the spirits trapped inside Razcul, swarming, beating against the walls of their prison seeking release.

Razcul bared his teeth, his lips showing the faintest hint of a smile.

Remembering how defenseless he had always been against Razcul, not just once but in multiple encounters, Jaerol fantasized about possessing the strength that Razcul held. Staring into the shadow elf's eyes, eyes that dared him to accept the offer, he was tempted by the strength that Jaerol could use to see Erynor and his Deurghol destroyed.

"Jaerol!" Liam's yell reached him from behind the locked door and snapped Jaerol out of his trance. Things would change between himself and Liam if he became a shadow elf. Liam would never trust him again; their relationship would be destroyed. The temptation for that power vanished. Jaerol pushed hard, forcing all his strength against Razcul's hands, pushing the knife upward, away from himself, thoughts of Kiron and Liam uppermost, giving him extra strength. Then the high-pitched sound of Razcul's scream pierced Jaerol's ears before fading as a burst of light filled the room. Hundreds of souls rushed out of Razcul's body, his own wretched soul decaying as the spirits he had clung onto flew upward through the stone ceiling and toward Lumaeniel, the World-Beyond.

Razcul's crumbling body collapsed onto Jaerol. He shivered, the tension finally leaving him as he scrambled backward and away from the decaying corruption. Razcul's dagger lay buried beneath the mass of ashes on the floor, his body disintegrating without the great number of souls he had consumed over the past fourteen years holding it together. Jaerol let the moment wash over him. He had just killed Razcul, something that should not have been possible. He had complete confidence in his own strength, but Razcul had not been an ordinary shadow elf. Razcul had always been exceptional, even before he had been named the champion at the Grand Tourney when they had graduated from the Imperium. But Jaerol's love for both Kiron and Liam had given him the extra strength needed to defeat the shadow elf.

Jaerol ran to Razcul's bedchamber. The key to the door of Liam's bedchamber was on the table by the bed. He took it and rushed to the door, his hands fumbling until he finally managed to get it unlocked. Liam flung it open and hugged Jaerol tightly, squeezing the air out of his lungs even as they kissed. They parted and Jaerol scanned Liam's bruised body.

"Are you hurt?"

"I'm alive," Liam said. They held each other as though they were the only two people in the world, their heads touching.

The chancellor's office was blocked off, and not even Hannah or Yvonne had been able to penetrate the ancient wield that Velaria had enacted months ago. But intent on upholding appearances, Hannah had located her replacement office as near the official one as possible. Velaria hoped the wield on the original office still held, but she had her doubts. That wield was likely gone now with the temple's ward extended.

Candles lit the way, and more knights rushed up the stair hall. Grasping her knife, she walked the familiar way up to the chancellor's office, a path she had frequented often before Hannah's betrayal, when she had wanted to understand Hannah's reasoning for her actions as chancellor. Those actions were all too clear now.

Concerned about being ambushed from behind, Velaria had the knights search each floor of the Chancellor's Tower as they climbed toward the top. Fortunately, this tower was the castle's slenderest and didn't have any corridors to search through. Instead, only a few doors lined the interior walls of the stair hall. The knights signaled that this level was clear and they all moved up to the next, the last level before reaching the chancellor's office.

The knights gathered at the landing, forming a defensive barrier when they saw a door standing ajar. Wavering candlelight flickered onto the stone floor from inside. Velaria signaled Yelaris, Andrew, Danielle, Fiona, Trethien, and the other knights accompanying her. They edged toward the door, swords and daggers at the ready, more knights guarding the level below. She felt responsible for Gwilnor's students and wouldn't let them put themselves in harm's way. Andrew was a knight now, and more than capable of defending himself, and Danielle, Fiona, and Trethien thought they could too.

A shimmering blur shot out of the room and one of her knights crumpled, a dagger protruding from his chest.

Velaria watched the remaining knights rush into the room, swords ringing as they fought against their former fellow knights. Wishing she had enlisted more knights, Velaria rushed into the chaos, Trethien right behind her. Inside, Yelaris lifted men fully from the floor and launched them at their comrades.

Another knight fell.

Her knights were now equal in number to the men accompanying Yvonne. The fighting paused and Yvonne's defenders stood around her.

"I'll have them all killed," Yvonne said, her voice as cold as the ice retreating to the mountains' highest peaks.

"And you pretend that that wasn't your intent all along?"

"Well, of course." The woman's long silky black hair hung over her shoulder, and Yvonne deliberately tossed it behind her, staring at Velaria's shaved head. Velaria's useless verathn was clutched in one hand, a dagger in the other.

"This won't end well for you," Yvonne said, her lips curled into a sneer.

"You're hardly in a position to challenge me."

Shouts rose from below, signaling to Velaria that the combined efforts of the Septyl and temple knights had taken swift control of the castle. The dining hall had to be filled to the seams with residents, both true and false. Velaria didn't care, not trusting anyone at the moment. She would march every last one into the temple and let the Light determine whether they were Tenebrae or still loyal to Septyl.

Yelaris sent images to Velaria, asking her how she wanted this to end. Velaria shared a glimpse of Yvonne holding her captive the night she had been captured and the torture that had followed. The image sent Yelaris into a frenzy and she leapt across the room, blue scales rippling as she grew to her full size, crowding everyone in the room but pinning Yvonne to the ground under one of her claws, baring her razor-sharp teeth. Yvonne's defenders abandoned her and scurried away as best they could from the dragon.

"Thank you, Yelaris." Velaria allowed a small smile, then turned on the men who had betrayed Septyl. "Drop your swords." The metal clattered on the stone and the Septyl knights who had assisted her moved to detain them. Rough hands bound the rebel knights' hands behind their backs.

A Septyl knight rushed in, his eyes widening at the sight of the dragon pinning Yvonne. Remembering himself, he bowed to Velaria. "We've handled the last of the resistance. Anyone who can still walk is now held in the dining hall. The castle is secured, Mother Velaria."

Velaria's smile widened even as she kept her eyes on Yvonne; the woman was dangerous. Velaria still worried about what harm Yvonne might cause despite being pinned down in Yelaris' claws and unable to wield. But there was still one thing to do right now. She went over to the subdued woman and retrieved her wand. Even as she did, Yvonne tried to wrestle her dagger arm free but Yelaris' claws kept her from moving.

"Where is Nadia?" Velaria asked. She knew the snake had likely escaped, cowering back to Erynor in defeat.

"She will end you," Yvonne hissed. "And the Sons of Yanil will destroy this castle and everything it stands for."

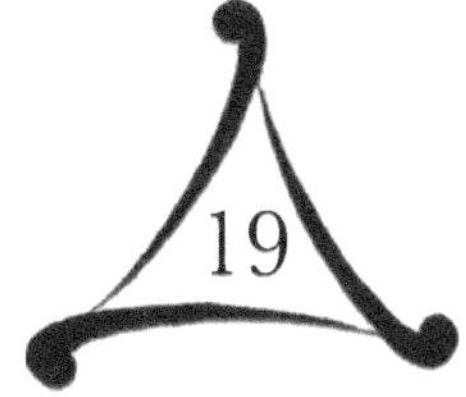

NEGLECTED DREAMS

A soft, warm breeze brushed Devlyn's skin as a bright light tried to filter through his eyelids. Fatigue kept him plastered to the bed—too
weak to even roll over onto his side away from the light. He had no idea
how long he had slept and neither did he know where he was. Again.
The blankets covering him were the finest he had ever felt and reminded
him of his lierathnil. He squinted, trying to remember the last time sunlight had woken him.

Golden light affronted his eyes when he finally forced them open.
Blinking against the brightness, he was surprised to see semi-opaque
walls glowing a brilliant amber, while sunlight spilled through a large
tracery window. Like in Lucillia, the windows were open to the elements
without any glass. Devlyn looked around the spacious room filled with
simple, elegant furnishings. A small fire crackled in the finely carved fireplace. The fireplace mantle was sculpted from lumaryl and it took on a
different glow as its inner light mixed with the fire.

You're awake! Aliel conveyed, unable to hide his excitement.

Yeah. Devlyn chuckled. Aliel's inner warmth mixed with Devlyn's,
rejuvenating him. *Where are you?*

*Would you like me to show you or would you like to wait and see with your own
eyes?*

*Your eyes are my eyes, just as mine are yours. Besides, I don't think I'll be al-
lowed out of this bed today,* Devlyn conveyed before lightly tapping his bond

with Aliel. His vision transformed and he was swept away in flight as he looked through Aliel's golden eyes. The phoenix flew past a spire that appeared woven of golden light made solid. Devlyn saw himself through a window in that spire before Aliel twirled up, away from the spire and around the palace to take in the entire city.

Devlyn couldn't believe what he was seeing. The entire city was built from lumaryl. He had been repeatedly told that that was the case, but seeing it took him to a different level. Harmonious forms rose and fell in the cityscape, plazas, and streets weaving through the mass of buildings. The whole city was a piece of art on display for its inhabitants to enjoy at their leisure. At least, when it last had inhabitants to enjoy it. But now, the elves were back. They weren't singing in the streets yet; they were still at war and fighting for their place in the world. Even as he took in the remarkable city with its too-delicate looking stonework of thin, sinuous lines, he also saw the Shroud to the north.

Devlyn was far too familiar with the diseased mist and clouds that were part of the Shroud blocking out the sun. He had forgotten what it was like to be so near to its perimeter with the advantage of sunlight. While the Shroud always looked ominous, seeing it next to a bright blue sky made its evil nature all the clearer. He was reminded of how foreign the Shroud was to Eklean. It belonged here no more than Erynor had a right to enslave the continent.

After the past months of living in the Shroud's shadow, Devlyn had grown far too accustomed to its weight on the world. Now that he could see one of Krysenthiel's cities freed of its long capture, he couldn't fathom how the Shroud had come to be. How could anything so terrible have been wrought to claim any parcel of Krysenthiel, let alone all of it?

As he took in the contrast between the incredible golden city and the surrounding Shroud, Devlyn felt someone nudge him, back where his body still lay in bed, as though to wake him. He pulled away from Aliel and returned to the room he still lay in to find Ellendren sitting on the edge of the bed with her hand on his chest, her fingers drawing swirling lines against his skin. He smiled at her and found that he liked her touching his chest. A tingling sensation went through his body and he pulled himself up to sit against the pillows. They had had so little time for themselves since they were married.

Ellendren blushed as she laughed. "Good morning." Her voice brightened the already luminous room.

"Good morning." Devlyn patted his hair down, knowing it was likely sticking up in every direction. "Did I pass out again?"

"You did."

"And did I dream it, or were the city gates talking to us?"

"That was no dream. They complained about being woken and would only open for the Aryl of Eandyl."

"They wouldn't open for Ei'terel Ellendren Lorenthien?" Devlyn smirked.

"Only after we become the Exalted Aryl, and not a moment sooner. We had to wait for Enithil and Binoral before the gates would let us in."

"Did everyone get into the city?"

"It's far too small for everyone, but we brought in those most at risk. The Guardians have set up their tents on the outer rim of our new camp outside the walls. They've already started seeing to the fortifications. You should know, Devlyn, that Cyndinari attacked the caravan."

"How serious was it?"

"They tried to divide our defenses before striking at the heart of the caravan on the open plain. Without defensive fortifications, it was good that Jeanne and the Guardians were prepared. They managed to push the enemy back, but we did suffer casualties."

"Were any civilians killed?"

"Thankfully, no. The Cyndinari couldn't get past our defenders. Jeanne will want to provide a full report later."

"How'd she take the attack?"

"I think she expected it. And honestly, I've never seen her in a better mood. There's a rekindled spark in her that I only glimpsed when we first met."

"She must have felt a great burden lifted. Elle, we might actually pull this off—we might actually reclaim Krysenthiel."

"Lucillia did foresee it."

"I suppose so." Devlyn thought back on Lucillia's annoying prophecy, a constant reminder that he was to pay an ultimate price for his people by giving of himself entirely. He still didn't know what that would entail, but it did make him relish Ellendren's company all the more in their moment of shared intimacy. Ellendren's palm still rested on his bare chest, her fingers spreading her inner warmth. His mind blanked. He massaged her hand and their eyes locked. She must have known what was driving him for she blushed.

His hands moved to her waist. If his intentions had ever been a secret before, there was no mistaking them now as his body betrayed him once the blanket slipped off when he leaned forward to hold her. She smiled and stood instead of leaning closer as he'd hoped. Devlyn's heart plummeted and he thought he would never be able to enjoy the sunshine again in that instant of rejection.

"Don't be dramatic." Ellendren knew his thoughts and Devlyn realized that she had only stood to kick off her shoes. His mind buzzed and the second she rejoined him, he had her in his arms again. They folded in on each other as they kissed. Devlyn shivered at how vulnerable and exposed he felt, but relaxed when Ellendren pulled him closer at the thought and his mind blanked again. Nothing else mattered in that moment.

Devlyn and Ellendren, shadowed by Viren, explored Eandyl for the first time the following afternoon. The aryls had wanted to summon a chamber meeting the moment Devlyn woke, but Ellendren had denied their request, pointing out that Devlyn needed his rest. He heard some of them grumble as they had left the palace that if he was well enough to explore the city, he should be rested enough for a chamber meeting.

Eandyl was remarkable and Devlyn was amazed at how well everything had been preserved. The entire city looked as though it had been abandoned no more than the day before they had arrived. All the furnishings were in perfect order, including the tapestries and portraits. There was something peculiar about the artwork though. He already knew about the talking carvings on the city gates and wondered if the same enchantments had also been sung into the tapestries and portraits and statues. All the paintings seemed to move or shift in their frames, if shyly. Devlyn even caught some of the statues fidgeting as he passed them.

He had discounted it as a trick of the eye. Surely those long-ago elves hadn't given life to everything they created. Or had they? Perhaps the art was already alive and the elves had only woken it with their songs and creative outlets. And if the art was alive, perhaps the buildings were too. Was all the art and architecture in Krysenthiel alive? He didn't want to think about that. Several portraits hung in his bedchamber after all.

As they continued their tour of the city, Devlyn marveled at how crowded the streets were. After fourteen hundred years, Eandyl was bursting at the seams with elves once again. Some of the wagons and carts lining the streets were being unloaded into the buildings. Treasured belongings from Lucillia that the elves had not been able to part with were now being carried into their new homes.

Devlyn wondered how the property was being allocated and whether it was being done fairly. The property couldn't necessarily be bought or sold, because the owners had all perished long ago. The thought had barely formed when Ellendren answered. "There are records in the archives here, showing whose property is whose."

"You have to stop doing that," Devlyn said.

"Sorry, it really isn't intentional. I simply know what you're thinking and not just because your thoughts are loud—that's different. We should ask Fendryl about our connection. I'm curious whether it was once common for elven spouses to share the mental intimacy that we do or if it's unique to us because we were declared married by the seraph in the Empyrean Sphere."

"I can't say. Alethea did encourage me to calm my thoughts though, but you said it's different."

"Your thoughts are still quite loud," inserted Viren from just behind them. "You should heed Alethea's wisdom. Not everyone should be aware of what goes through the Lorenthien aryl's minds, particularly as newlyweds."

Devlyn and Ellendren both blushed. "Is there any way to speed up that process?" Devlyn growled.

"Finding balance will always be the answer," Viren answered.

"And how are we supposed to find balance?" Devlyn asked, skeptically. How was he supposed to find balance in anything while Erynor was actively trying to enslave the world and release Ramiel back into Teraeniel?

"By not neglecting meditation and jienzu."

"Right." Devlyn kept from voicing his complaint that he wasn't neglecting either. "So, how are these records helping us track the owners of these homes? Do all the Luminari really know their ancestry that well?"

"Not quite. What we assume are the last owners and inhabitants of the properties are listed in the records. And beside those names are the current inheritor; not from fourteen hundred years ago when the Shroud doomed all Krysenthiel, but elves who are alive today."

"That's incredible," Devlyn said, relieved that he wouldn't have to be involved with distributing the property even as he ignored the fact that the records were somehow magically up-to-date. He didn't want to consider that the elves alive today simply shared the same name with a long-dead elf.

"There's more," Ellendren said, choosing her words carefully. "There are banks here that have been sealed since Krysenthiel fell and our people were enslaved. They have a similar ledger allotting wealth to various elves."

"That'll make the Goblin Guild's life easier," Devlyn said.

"That's part of the problem. Krysenthien banks were separate from the guild. Our ancestors had agreed to an exchange rate, but our coins were never part of the guild's bank."

"How is that a concern?"

"We're about to have a very complicated relationship with the guild as our coffers are filled with lumols, narols, and kenols. Our kingdom is about to saturate the market with a currency that hasn't been used in fourteen hundred years." Ellendren said.

Devlyn didn't know what to say about their future economic situation. He had had little training and education in regard to Eklean's economy. He had always assumed that the Goblin Guild would manage Krysenthiel's banks. Having little to contribute, his mind wandered to the engagement with the Cyndinari that Ellendren had mentioned earlier. "Do you think Jeanne will be ready to give a report on the Cyndinari attack soon?" Ellendren flushed at the change of topic and Devlyn could feel her frustration with him.

"I imagine so. Do you have enough strength for that today?" Viren asked.

"Waiting will likely be worse."

"Are you certain?" Ellendren asked.

"I'll be fine." Without further argument they made their way to the city gate and sought out the Guardians' camp. The elves who couldn't stay in the city were closest to the gate. They'd be able to squeeze into Eandyl in a hurry if the Cyndinari attacked again. They saw the First of the Guardians on the perimeter, supervising the raising of bulwarks for outer fortification. Before they reached her though, Liara, Prya on her back, swooped down and toward Jeanne. Concerned that it might relate to a potential ambush, Devlyn hurried over with Ellendren and Viren. They reached Jeanne as the red dragon thumped down.

"You have impeccable timing." Prya slid off Liara's back.

"How so?" Devlyn asked.

"We noted two riders heading this way. I believe they've come for you, Ei'denai," Prya said.

"Do you know who they are?" Devlyn asked.

"Hard to mistake that frizzy red hair, even from up in the clouds. They'll be here shortly."

"The only person I know with frizzy red hair is Abbie," Devlyn said. "Who's she with?"

"Another druid by the looks of him."

The only other druid that Devlyn knew was Eagan, Abbie's brother. Devlyn had thought that Eagan was still at Kweil Aitch with the other druids. What could have brought him away from there? Devlyn tried to remember the last time he had entered Somnaeniel and couldn't. He prepared himself for the scolding to come once Abbie and Eagan arrived. As he tried to come up with a defense, he could see the two horses trotting toward the camp. Knowing that he'd now have to wait for Jeanne's report, he waved at the approaching riders.

Abbie and Eagan were riding two of Perrien's coveted grey coursers. The horses stopped and the siblings dismounted, travelworn and exhausted, their expressions serious. Eagan looked at the gathered people, assessing whether they could be trusted.

"You've been avoiding the Dream." Eagan's eyes fell on Devlyn. As always, there were few pleasantries when Abbie and Eagan Wintyr were involved and they cut straight to the point.

A pang of guilt struck Devlyn, neither strong nor loud since his time and energy were pulled in dozens of directions. To him, entering the World-in-Between was the least significant and he began to mutter an excuse for not focusing on Somnaeniel. Eagan cut him off before it progressed past babbling.

"We don't have much time left. You are aware of what is happening there, yes?" Eagan pressed.

"Are the black puddles still there?"

Eagan took a step to close the distance between himself and Devlyn and placed his fingers on Devlyn's temple.

# 20

UNTARNISHED

Devlyn no longer stood on the outskirts of Eandyl, at least not fully. His body was still there, but Eagan had brought his spirit to Somnaeniel. Great lakes and oceans of the black ooze consumed vast swaths of the landscape, fading only with the horizon. Aggressive storm clouds warped the skies, and lightning without light thrashed violently in every direction, scarring the already black sky with darker voids. He searched for the Somnaeniel he remembered. Nothing of this place resonated with him.

"It's called dorthl." Eagan looked to the horizon, eyes set on an indistinguishable point.

"Do we know anything about it?" asked Devlyn, staring at the dark sludge.

"Only that to touch it, is to die. The Druids of Kweil Aitch have many theories, but none are proven."

"Can it really sever someone from the Light?" asked Devlyn, remembering Alethea's warning from so long ago. A sword separating an arm from a body flashed through Devlyn's mind.

"Alethea would have known more of it than we do. It is related to the Darkness—the Void—which consumed the Skylands, but it is stronger here."

Devlyn turned away from the dormant depthless ooze. "We shouldn't linger here."

"You are right, but we must," Eagan said and Devlyn looked at him in question. "You're aware that your ancestors distributed the lucilliae for different peoples to safeguard, yes?"

"I am." Devlyn didn't think that he had ever mentioned the lucilliae to Abbie or Eagan.

"One of them, the jewel of temperance, was entrusted to the druids. Ithendryl Lorenthien anticipated an attack on Arenthyl just before the Shroud came into existence and gave the lucilliae to us to secret away from Krysenthiel. Our people were transporting it to Kweil Aitch when they were killed."

"Did the druids ever try to retrieve it?" Devlyn asked, keeping his tone level.

"We could not."

"So, it was left discarded along the side of the road?" Devlyn bellowed, unable to control his tone any longer.

"I said nothing about a road." Eagan glared at him.

Devlyn looked from Eagan to Abbie, frightened by thoughts of where the lucilliae had been lost fourteen hundred years ago. "Where is it?" Devlyn took a hesitant glance toward the dorthl-consumed plains.

"While the lucilliae isn't the only reason you must learn to walk the Dream, its presence here *is* one of those reasons. We will not be able to enter the Dream once the Evil One claims this realm for himself. And as you can tell by the dorthl consuming nearly everything, we don't have much time."

"It's here in Somnaeniel—*physically*?" Devlyn pushed his hands through his hair, exasperated. "Where is it? We can't leave it here."

"You'll have to retrieve it in the flesh, but you cannot yet; to attempt so now would kill you. If you were able to enter bodily, I would have advised you to retrieve it years ago. But we must wait until you can enter without being killed in the process."

Eager to retrieve another lucilliae, Devlyn scanned the horizon, as though he might be able to see its light glimmer in the distance. Quieting his mind, he exerted his will outward, searching for that which his eyes could not see.

Eagan swung his hand up to Devlyn's temple, knocking him down. Devlyn felt the cold hard ground beneath him, and realized he was no longer in Somnaeniel, but back at the Luminari camp, surrounded by assorted people bearing concerned expressions. Eagan was sprawled on top of him. Devlyn's body ached. He wished Eagan could have waited to take Devlyn into Somnaeniel until reaching the privacy of a tent since having half of the Lorenthien aryl unconscious on the ground was not desirable for improving morale among the elves. Especially when that same person had been the one to promise to see them returned to Krysenthiel.

Ellendren, Abbie, Viren, Jeanne, and Prya surrounded Devlyn and Eagan but only Abbie understood why Eagan was upset.

Eagan pushed himself off Devlyn, his eyes narrowed. "Are you trying to get us killed?"

"What are you talking about?"

"You just revealed yourself to everything cognizant in the Dream. As though your thoughts weren't loud enough, you practically screamed at the top of your lungs for all to hear!"

"I'm sorry." Devlyn had never seen Eagan angry before, and this shift in his personality made him more terrifying than his sister.

Eagan glared at Devlyn, who was still on the ground but sitting up. "You've received countless lessons on stilling your mind, but your thoughts scream your presence. If you don't learn to control them, you will never be able to enter Somnaeniel in the flesh, and the lucilliae will remain there and will be consumed by the dorthl along with all the World-in-Between."

"Show me how."

"Alethea tried to teach you, but not even she was capable of the task! What makes you think someone with thousands of years less experience could show you the way?" Eagan fumed, his body shaking slightly.

Devlyn didn't have an answer.

Eagan paced, glancing at Devlyn with every turn. Devlyn's mind returned to the dorthl, its consuming depths overwhelming him as he recalled most of the World-in-Between blanketed in it.

Devlyn felt not just Eagan's glare, but his emotions as well. Most prevalent was his frustration, especially as his patience with Devlyn had worn thin. It was understandable, after all, if Devlyn had let everyone dwelling in Somnaeniel know their location.

"Do you think there are shadow elves there?" Devlyn wanted to know what had so terrified Eagan.

"Shadow elves are the least of your concerns." Eagan forced his eyes closed, irritated.

"What's there?"

"Not what but who." Egan opened his eyes, his frustration spilling through. "One of the Deathless for one. We do not know if he dwells there permanently, but we have felt him sporadically. If he does remain in Somnaeniel permanently, he's learning how to conceal himself from others. Which, might I remind you, is a very bad thing for us."

"So, the opposite of what I did," said Devlyn.

"Precisely; however, we're also relatively certain he is there in the flesh. How long he has been there is beyond the knowledge of the Druids of Kweil Aitch. It's possible he has only ventured into that realm with Erynor's recent return to power. Yet, it's also possible that he's been there since Erynor's fall."

"Is he responsible for the dorthl?"

Eagan's lips strained to a thin line. "In part. The Evil One is trying to turn Somnaeniel into his own domain; dorthl is only the beginning. Once the entirety of the World-in-Between is overcome by it, he will begin to wield it, reshaping the Dream in his own vision."

"I thought the Evil One was imprisoned, and incapable of escaping."

"His presence is too strong in Somnaeniel for us to have any confidence in the strength of the chains which hold him. He's either found a hole to exert his influence through, or someone from our side of his prison is weakening it, destroying it as we speak."

Looking from his lap to Eagan, Devlyn raised his head. "So, we just have to get the lucilliae out of there before he covers the entire place in dorthl."

"If the Evil One controls Somnaeniel, we will be his slaves in this life and the next."

Devlyn frowned, confused about where Eagan was going with his logic.

"Somnaeniel is named the World-in-Between because it is the threshold to Lumaeniel. If the Evil One becomes the master of that realm, all who die in Teraeniel won't be able to pass through and move onward to Lumaeniel. We will be severed from the blessed realm of Anaweh. Anadel will be restricted to Teraeniel or Lumaeniel, and any prayers to Anaweh seeking aid or comfort will remain unheard as our world is severed from the Creating Light's realm." Eagan paused, then spoke solemnly. "The Evil One will become Lord of the Dead if he conquers the Dream."

"Is there a way to stop him?" Devlyn hadn't put any thought into the Evil One recently. He knew that Erynor was only a servant of Ramiel, but how could Devlyn possibly devise a plan to deal with him while the Luminari were trying to reclaim their homeland?

"Stop him? We're far past that possibility. The Dream will soon be lost to us and the path for the dead to the World-Beyond will be shut when that happens. As serious as that is, there are other concerns that we must see to while there is still time." Eagan breathed heavily, noticeably trying to regain a sense of composure after their swift withdrawal from Somnaeniel. "There is another reason you must learn to enter the Dream physically and not only for the sake of retrieving the lucilliae. Another enemy is physically in the Dream. You cannot fight the Shroud from only the World-Below. Along with the Deurghol, Erynel is physically in the dream."

"Why do I know that name?" Devlyn shook his head, trying to place the name.

"She was and is one of the Sha'ghol. She died so that her son could be sired by a dragon of the Dark Flight. She *is* the Shroud."

"Erynel Meriden—Erynor's mother is the Shroud?" Devlyn's mind whirled at the revelation and he fretted over having to deal with yet another enemy. And if she was a Sha'ghol who had died and was somehow alive again, doubtless she would be incredibly powerful. "What of the lucilliae? Does Erynel know of it?"

"She is the one who killed the druids in the Dream. We believe she wears the jewel."

<hr>

Evellyn watched Erynor doze off on his throne. He had never fallen asleep in the throne room before, and she wondered whether she finally had an opportunity. She took a small step forward. She had no idea what she was thinking; it wasn't like she had a weapon to harm the Erynien Emperor. She considered throttling him but would she even be able to lay a hand on him before he woke or a guard stopped her? All the guards were at the other end of the throne room—they were far enough away. Would she have enough time to kill him before they pulled her off him? They would kill her the moment after she strangled their emperor. She made to step forward again, but Erynor's slumber was light and his eyes opened. She took the half-step back to her place. Anyone who noticed her movement would have assumed she was only shifting her weight.

Then she was thankful that she hadn't moved further, for as the emperor woke fully, a dark haze fell over the room, chilling the air and cutting off the sun. She could still see the sun shining outside the large windows, but whatever was happening, it could not penetrate this unnatural mist.

Erynor was just straightening himself up as a figure materialized before him. The woman did not appear solid and Evellyn wondered what sort of dark magic had brought her about.

"Bold of you to remain sitting in my presence." Her voice was sharp in tone but oddly muffled.

"I'm just waking, Mother." Erynor stood then, reached for his mother's hand and kissed it. Evellyn was stunned—this was Erynor's mother!

"You know I can't stay here like this for long but I must speak with you."

"Of course, Mother. What was so urgent that you had to come here to Broid?"

"You don't know?" She spun away from Erynor, practically shrieking as she did. "What have you been doing all this time? You should be closer to me and your son, not hiding away in your gilded palace."

"I have my instructions, just as you have yours."

"Do your instructions include allowing those children to reclaim Krysenthiel and destroy me in the process?" she screamed as she rounded on him, floating up a bit to come close to his face. She moved unnaturally, as though she were a phantom. Evellyn tried to keep her gaze focused on the floor but caught sight of a large yellow jewel swinging on a necklace around the woman's neck. Evellyn couldn't stop looking at it once she saw it; something stirred in her, not a warning, just a hint of cautious patience.

"What are you talking about?"

"I didn't bed Tolvenol and willingly die to give life to you for you to be held up here while children destroy my Shroud! They've already taken back Eandyl, you ignorant fool." The woman breathed heavily as she screamed at her son.

While his mother lashed out at Erynor, Evellyn couldn't be prouder of her own son. He had actually managed to somehow push back the Shroud and the Luminari had reclaimed one of their abandoned cities. Evellyn had never thought she would see the day. She was well aware of

Lucillia's prophecy, but she never wanted her son to have to sacrifice so much for their people.

"My advisors neglected to inform me." Evellyn recognized Erynor's dangerous tone. The next few days would not be enjoyable for anyone in the palace, least of all Evellyn. The bruises on her neck had only just started to fade from the last time.

"How long until your legions reach my borders? The meager force you have stationed there now is inadequate."

"They should be passing through Torsil now."

"What of the Dwonians? I have yet to see any of them around my Shroud."

"One of them is setting himself up as a king among their people and has taken one of Lawrence Maroven's daughters as his wife. He claims to be the new King of Mindale and Dwonia. He calls himself a chief-king."

"And the Mindalean king before him?"

"He was never useful to us and is likely dead or exiled."

LIBERATED

Alarm horns blew and bells rang to wake the newly arrived residents in the city of Eandyl. Despite signaling an attack, the sounds were quite beautiful—everything in Eandyl was beautiful. Devlyn didn't think he had been asleep for more than an hour when they started, but he could have just as easily been asleep for several. Ellendren sprang from their bed and was already slipping into her lierathnil in case she would have to bond fully with Tariel. Devlyn glanced at his own lierathnil and was grateful that Lyren had left a complete fresh set nearby. He pulled up the lierathnil trousers and slipped on a robe, not wanting to deal with laces, sashes, and clasps and he and Ellendren hurried out of their room and through the palace's corridors. Lyren trailed after Devlyn, carrying the clothing that Devlyn hadn't bothered to put on.

Knights, nobles, and servants were everywhere, some of them showing obvious signs of hasty dressing as they tried to figure out what was happening. Only Ellendren and the knights were properly dressed to confront whatever was coming. The knights hurried to their stations, some in the palace, others to join the defenses in the camps. Jeanne and the other Guardians would already be in the camp, preparing for whatever the threat they were about to face was.

Still having no idea what was going on, Devlyn grabbed a knight rushing past. "What's happening? Are we under attack?"

"I don't know, Ei'denai. There was talk of dragons," the knight said.

"Dragons?" Devlyn cursed under his breath. He knew he should have put on his full lierathnil. There wasn't any time for that now, even if Lyren was carrying it. He and Ellendren broke away from the chaotic corridors, looking for a likely balcony or window, Lyren doggedly following. The first room they went into had a balcony. Devlyn shrugged his robe off and handed it to Lyren. His transformation would destroy it. "You'd better hold this."

Ellendren had already transformed into her Phaedryn form. Shirtless, Devlyn transformed and followed Ellendren out to the balcony. Viren was likely searching for his griffin to fly after them. Devlyn knew that he would be furious once he found out that Devlyn and Ellendren had gone out to investigate a possible dragon attack on their own.

Flying off the palace's balcony and up above the city, they hung in the air scanning the horizon. Despite the late hour and lack of light, Devlyn and Ellendren in their transformed states could see Teraeniel as though it was the brightest of days. They could easily see the distant horizon but saw nothing of concern coming from the south. They assumed that the dragons would have come from the Cyndinari camp hiding in the Sorenth ruins. There was nothing moving on the southern horizon and the only stirring in that direction were the Luminari in the camps preparing for a dragon attack.

"There." Ellendren pointed east and Devlyn saw two dragons. They were too far away to see who they were or if they carried anyone. Devlyn tentatively reached out with his inner sense and could already hear Eagan yelling at him again for making a target of himself.

Too focused on the dragons in the distance, Devlyn wasn't prepared for the flash of ruby scales that swept about him and Ellendren. Devlyn glanced at the draelyn rider and dragon, Prya and Liara, and was grateful they weren't part of an attack. Neither draelyn nor dragon seemed concerned about the new arrivals. "Friend or foe," Devlyn yelled, hoping Prya could hear him over the rush of wind.

"It's Rusyl and Yelaris. I've informed Jeanne that we aren't under attack," Prya said, urging Liara forward and forcing Devlyn and Ellendren to fly faster. As they came closer to the incoming dragons, Devlyn's spirit lifted when he recognized one of the riders, Jaerol. Unless they brought harrowing news, Prya was right, there was no reason for the alarm. Devlyn looked toward the other rider, hoping it would be Liam or Velaria, but Ellendren identified him first.

"Is that Trethien?" she called.

Devlyn's thoughts turned to Gwilnor and he tried to keep them from souring. Had Jaerol and Trethien fled Ceurenyl with the dragons because the Tenebrae had control of the entire city now? Devlyn didn't think that Jaerol would leave Liam behind nor could he believe that Yelaris would abandon Velaria. What if they hadn't abandoned them; what if they didn't make it? Devlyn pushed that thought away and raced east toward the approaching dragons, Ellendren keeping pace beside him.

Rusyl and Yelaris must have seen them, for they paused and hung in the sky to wait for the Phaedryn to reach them. Images flooded into Devlyn's head, but he was too concerned about his brother and Velaria to decipher the meaning. He was even more concerned because of their arrival in the middle of the night. Surely something terrible had to have happened for them to come now.

"What's happened?" Devlyn called as soon as he was near enough.

Jaerol actually laughed in response—a giddy and relieved laugh. Devlyn hadn't thought the Cyndinari elf capable of it.

Worried that Jaerol had gone insane or had lost all his wits, Devlyn asked, "Where are Liam and Velaria?" He heard his frantic tone but didn't care. All he could think about just now was his brother. Liam had been captive to the Erynien Empire before. He had only recently gotten his older brother back and his mother was still the emperor's prisoner. Devlyn couldn't lose him again, especially as Alesei's threat against his mother's life hung about his neck like a weighted chain.

"They're free and safe at Gwilnor," Jaerol laughed again and Trethien grinned from Yelaris' back.

They hung in the air. "When was the last time anyone was safe at Gwilnor?" Ellendren asked.

"Since your brother, the Ceurtriarch, extended the temple ward to cover the entire city. He sent temple knights to liberate the castle, but Velaria had already single-handedly escaped her cell, roused the Septyl knights, and taken back a third of the castle before the temple knights even arrived," Trethien yelled as another laugh escaped Jaerol who was beyond delighted to be able to spread the news.

"Why isn't Liam here with you?" Devlyn asked.

"The flight would have been too much of a strain on him. He's resting and healing from his wounds. Razcul is finally dead and he can't hurt Liam or me ever again."

Devlyn felt his heart lighten at the news. He didn't realize how much the pressure had been weighing him down. He smiled and for a moment, it seemed like nothing else mattered. Gwilnor was free of Tenebrae control and Velaria and Liam were both alive and well.

"Jaerol, Trethien, why come now? It's the middle of the night and dawn is still a few hours off," Ellendren said.

"It was daylight when we left," Trethien said, shrugging.

"Velaria sent us. She wants the Chairs to return to Gwilnor as soon as possible to pass judgement on the captured members of the Tenebrae School."

"How many did you capture?" Ellendren asked.

"Far too many. It's a frightening number. Unfortunately, the Tenebrae Chair and most of their wise ones managed to escape. Hannah and Yvonne are both in custody though."

"I suppose it would have been too easy to cut the disease out entirely," Ellendren said. Devlyn could tell that her mind was spinning and he wondered what she was planning. "Follow us, we'll take you to where the ei'ana are camped."

Parts of the city were still likely under the impression that the dragons arriving in the middle of the night intended to attack. But the Guardians would have been aware that the approaching dragons were their allies thanks to Prya. Unable to reach out to most of the people in command, Devlyn sought out Viren's all too familiar consciousness. He knew Viren well enough to safely reach out to him telepathically. Jeanne would likely make it a priority that Devlyn hone that ability and learn to reach out to others without needing a personal connection to them. That ability would prove invaluable during a battle.

Viren was, as expected, displeased. How was he supposed to protect the Lorenthien aryl if they darted headfirst into danger without alerting him? Devlyn apologized and pointed out that there had been no danger as it was only Rusyl, Yelaris, Jaerol, and Trethien. Viren wasn't soothed, but neither did he push the issue.

Prya and Liara flew off before they reached the ei'ana's section of the camp, leaving them to land in a clearing large enough for the dragons, probably the training ground for the wielders and knights.

Wielded lights showed the ei'ana hurrying about the camp, preparing for an attack. They had heard the alarm and the entire camp seemed to be waiting outside their tents until they learned why they'd been roused. With the arrival of the dragons and Phaedryn, Gwilnor refugees crowded around the training ground, careful to give the dragons space. They recognized Yelaris—everyone in Ceurenyl knew Yelaris of the Blue Dragon Flight. The dragon was the principle reason Velaria had been elevated to the Chair of Azurelle. Whether they had agreed with the School of Azurelle's ancient custom didn't matter anymore and most ei'ana saw Velaria as the talented and capable Chair that she was. Her sacrifice was the reason the refugees had been able to escape in the first place. Devlyn smiled at how they would view Velaria the next time they saw her. If half of what Jaerol and Trethien had said was true, the people of Ceurenyl would be singing her name in every tavern for centuries to come.

Ellendren withdrew from Tariel first and Devlyn was grateful that he had at least put his lierathnil trousers on as he too withdrew. Even shirtless, he was cognizant of the ei'ana, knights, and students surrounding him.

Jaerol and Trethien leapt down and the two dragons took on their smaller forms. Apparently, the Blue Dragon Flight was no longer concerned about keeping their ability to change forms a secret. Jaerol handed them each a bundle of fabric that turned out to be tunics and they dressed in short order, taking no notice of the many eyes watching them in disbelief.

Mother Selenya walked out of the crowd, her expression severe. "What tidings do you bring from Gwilnor?"

"If we had the luxury of time, we would celebrate tonight and into the next." Jaerol smiled as he walked toward the White Owl. "Thank you for your clue. The Tenebrae have either been subdued or have fled."

"I'm happy to hear it. Is the temple ward still covering the entire city?"

"For now, Aaron thought it best to leave it in place, noting that it was the only reason the city had not fallen to Erynor during the Ceurendol War," Jaerol said.

"So, history is to repeat itself in the Second Ceurendol War. Let us hope the outcome is not the same." Despite the gravity of Selenya's tone, she smiled. "How is Liam?"

"Alive and resting, as is Velaria. Although I doubt resting will apply to Velaria anytime soon," Jaerol said.

"I believe you're right. If Cyrelle Azurelle had not already claimed you for his School, I would have tried to convince you to join the Albiens. It's clear what School you will join though; dragons don't ferry just anyone around."

Jaerol looked back at Rusyl, who just shrugged his shoulders. Devlyn wondered if they would have the same sort of bond Velaria and Yelaris had. Jaerol seemed to be digesting the possibility as Yelaris strode forward, her imposing figure towering over Selenya.

"Velaria has asked that you and the other Chairs return to Gwilnor to carry out judgement on the Tenebrae, as well as one of the Lorenthiens," Yelaris said.

"It's hard to believe any ei'ana would pledge themselves to that School." Selenya winced.

"They are ei'ana no longer. Cyrelle Azurelle spoke through Velaria. The Tenebrae are ei'ana no more."

"There are no records of one of the Founders speaking through a Chair since before Krysenthiel fell. We had believed the ability lost with Septyl," Selenya said, half stunned.

"Much is being remembered and much more will be once Septyl is reclaimed," Yelaris said.

"Of course, but how will we travel to Gwilnor? I would not presume that you will carry us there."

Yelaris didn't answer, but instead turned to Devlyn and he in turn looked to Ellendren. "Velaria is right; one of us should be there as they deal with the Tenebrae," she said.

"That should be you." Devlyn well knew that Ellendren was more attuned to the ei'ana than he was. While she wasn't an ei'ana, she had chosen Vyoletryn as her School following her novitiate with them.

"No, we'll manage without you here. Come, let's tell Viren and get a bag packed for you," Ellendren said. Devlyn wondered why she was being cryptic and so agreeable about him leaving the Luminari again. He also didn't understand why she wanted him to go. "Be ready to leave in an hour. Jaerol, you are returning to Gwilnor, yes?"

"Liam is there," he said, as though that was answer enough.

"Trethien? Are you returning to Gwilnor as well?" Ellendren asked.

"I believe my mother would skin me alive, child of hers or not, if I don't return to my family," he said.

"Should we come to the palace, or will you come back here?" Selenya asked Devlyn.

"It's less trouble for me to come back here." Devlyn and Ellendren returned to their Phaedryn forms and flew back to the palace. Dawn was still a few hours away but the entire city and the surrounding camp were now awake due to the alarm. Few of the elves would be able to go back to sleep after the excitement. Other than the Guardian knights, only Gwilnor's refugees would know that the potential attack was nothing of the sort. Devlyn wondered how many people had heard about the dragons and how many more were frantically running about, convinced they were about to die.

Devlyn and Ellendren's return to Eandyl's palace was met by several aryls in the entry hall demanding answers. They could barely get a word in as the worried aryls spoke over them, each expressing their concerns. Ellendren finally raised her voice enough to quiet them and managed to soothe the aryls and enlighten them about Devlyn traveling briefly to Ceurenyl. If not for Gwilnor's liberation and the late hour, the aryls would have likely demanded an immediate chamber meeting.

In their bedchamber, Lyren quietly handed Devlyn the other pieces of his lierathnil outfit. While he wasn't ashamed of how he looked—jienzu had filled out muscles he'd not known were there—he still felt awkward whenever he wasn't fully clothed. Lyren went about packing his bag while Devlyn slipped on the tunic shirt. He paused, glancing at the pouch with the lucilliae. Now that they were in the palace, a secure location, Devlyn considered leaving them behind. Ellendren was more than capable of keeping them safe. Truly, they were likely safer here in Eandyl's palace than on Devlyn's person. Even so, he had never intentionally left them behind since retrieving the two he had left secured by a wield in the drawer of the bedside table at Gwilnor. He had always carried them on his person, hidden away in his lierathnil's inner pocket, even as that pocket became bulkier from the four jewels now inside it.

"You could place a wield over the bedside drawer as you did before," Ellendren offered, hearing his concerns. "I agree, they're safer here in the palace."

"Do you think the Chairs would benefit from them?" Devlyn asked.

"You've already shown them the jewel of justice. I'm not saying that they won't benefit from the other three, but I worry as more people learn that you are collecting them. While I don't think anyone would be capable of stealing them from you, the risk is simply higher when you're in public. And there's no saying whether servants of shadow or Tenebrae remain in hiding at Gwilnor."

Devlyn placed the pouch in the drawer and wielded the same ward he had used at Gwilnor so long ago. The ward had been undisturbed for over a year and none of the Tenebrae had been able to unravel it. He finished dressing while Ellendren sat pensively, watching him, thinking something through, no longer concerned about the lucilliae. Devlyn recognized the distant and concentrated look in her eyes and knew not to bother her. He didn't have to hear her thoughts to know that she had another reason for wanting him to go to Gwilnor with the Chairs.

"Devlyn, Meridephaen is fast approaching. We've been so preoccupied with the Shroud, we haven't been able to devise a plan to rescue your mother. I don't know if Alesei's threat was empty or not, but we can't put it off any longer."

Devlyn felt his strength give out and his legs nearly buckled. No one in their camp knew anything about Broid and the little they did was from hearsay. Not even the Eldinari had visited Cynethol. The other elven kins had all distrusted the Cyndinari since the Skylands were lost, always blaming them for tampering with what they shouldn't have.

"Anyone we send to Broid will be sent to their death. I just don't see how anyone could infiltrate the Erynien Empire's capital, get into the palace, rescue my mother, and manage to escape as well," Devlyn said.

"I believe there is one who will have a chance. Curiously, Silvia gave me the idea. I'll never admit it to her, but she was right; we need access to someone inside the imperial capital. There will be danger and I am sure he won't go alone."

"That's why you want me to go to Gwilnor?"

"Yes. Jaerol is our only ally familiar with Broid. He likely still has contacts there, and better, he knows the city."

"Liam won't let him go without him," Devlyn said, thinking of his brother who had just been freed again.

"I think Rusyl might also go with them. You can shift them somewhere on Cynethol and Rusyl will be able to get them away when they rescue your mother."

SOPHILLIUM

Kevn looked into the Shroud from the ridge where he and Laureniel had landed. He couldn't say how he knew, but he would be looking directly at the palace-city of Septyl if not for the Shroud. He could feel it. The voice had asked him to come here and had somehow led him through safe paths to the city where Erynor had started the Ceurendol War by attacking the ei'ana at Septyl. The city had been abandoned since that catastrophe and the decimated ei'ana population had made Gwilnor Academy their home.

That choice had also led to the balance between kien and kiara wielders being forgotten. Kevn hoped history wouldn't repeat itself since the temple ward prevented anyone in Ceurenyl from wielding again. Balance was only now returning because Devlyn was born an elya and was capable of restoring balance between Eklean's kien and kiara wielders.

But now, Kevn intended to do what he had sworn he would never do—seek entrance to Septyl. He knew the catastrophic stories of ei'ana who had failed before. Few of the ei'ana who had attempted to enter the Shroud to reach Septyl had survived, and none of those survivors had returned with their minds intact. Whoever had reached out to Kevn had promised to bring him safely into the city. "Whoever you are, I hope you're still there." Had those past ei'ana also been contacted by a mysterious voice that led them to their doom?

Kevn patted Laureniel who shifted impatiently; she didn't like being this near to the Shroud and sensed that Kevn meant them to pass through that poisonous mist. It was something he had told himself time and time again that he would never attempt, not even for all the knowledge in Septyl's library, yet here he was. He nudged her forward and she extended her wings, leapt from the ridge, and dove into the Shroud. Kevn held his breath against the icy mist that now clung to his body. He couldn't see, in fact, he hadn't expected to, but he had imagined that the land would be bereft of life; nothing could survive inside the Shroud and certainly not for fourteen hundred years.

And he was indeed unable to see, so he opened his inner senses to his immediate surroundings. He couldn't quite believe what he perceived. The land that he expected would be desolate was actually encased in a thick sheet of ice. From the looks of it, even the tiniest flowers were preserved from the damaging effects of the Shroud's poison. Kevn wondered if the preserving ice was an effect of the Shroud or whether the Luminari elves had wielded it in place before they had been forced to abandon their home.

As they moved through the mist, his inner senses showed deep valleys, then a rolling hill that steepened before rising to an incredible height. The Shroud clung to the hill and greedily held on to the mountain's crest, unwilling to abandon its prize.

Kevn knew he had to be in the general vicinity of Septyl and every map and diagram he had studied pointed to that mountain, clutched tightly in the Shroud. Urging a still reluctant Laureniel closer and focusing his inner sense up that incline, he saw a crystalline wall of lumaryl shimmer. Even encased in the Shroud, it managed to shine through, its brightness at odds with the mist. Impatient, Kevn pressed forward. The closer he came to the city, the more lumaryl he saw. The Shroud kept him from seeing the entire city from one perspective, but through his inner senses, he had small glimpses of the once proud city of the Ei'ana, likely the first person to see the city in fourteen hundred years. "Now they'll have to let me become an ei'ana," Kevn said to Laureniel, hoping the alicorn didn't mind him talking to her.

Kevn viewed the palace-city in awe. Sweeping walls wove into grand towers and encompassed frozen courtyards, while curved rooflines fell and rose. Everything was wrought of lumaryl and the city sparkled in its own inner light, unhindered by the Shroud trying to suffocate it. The city reminded him of Gwilnor but with an order and symmetry that the castle lacked, and probably never intended. From the center of the palace-city rose a large dome.

Seven equal sides formed the dome's drum, peaked on every side with a pointed arch. Each side had a rose window depicting one of the emblems of the seven Schools of Septyl.

From his elevated angle, Kevn could see Albien's emblem best. Two naked elves, male and female, stood with their arms outstretched, each holding a scroll, a single white owl perched between them.

Transfixed by the stained-glass window, Kevn's head whipped painfully back when Laureniel dove steeply down to avoid a strike of tenebrys lightning. *Where had it come from?* Kevn tipped his head back to see a dozen dragons soaring toward him, each carrying a shadow elf. Scores of tenebrys streaked through the sky, Laureniel dodging them with one aerial maneuver after another so that Kevn had to hang on tightly.

Kevn knew he was no match for them, but he also knew he could not let them enter Septyl. The heptagonal palace-city of Septyl had seven clear entrances, one for each of the seven Schools. Sure that they were all barred, Kevn aimed Laureniel for the nearest entrance, which happened to belong to the Albiens.

In front of the gate, white flags and banners woven of lierathnil hung unfurled by a long-forgotten wind that had once blown them into their now-frozen and unresponsive forms despite the chilly easterly wind. A large, pointed arch formed the entry, a lighter stone indicating the molding, more silver than the typical golden lumaryl.

As they drew closer, Kevn saw a strong luminescent door shielding the entry. Another tenebrys wield rushed passed him, narrowly missing his left ear. *Open*, he thought, pleading that the ancient city hear him. His mind rushed through every language he knew, mentally screaming *open* in every tongue familiar to him.

High Aelish sprang forth as he came closer to the gate, while more bolts of tenebrys lightning exploded behind him. As the word formed, the gate finally peeled open, the doors angling inward just wide enough to allow Kevn and Laureniel through.

They flew into a large atrium, surrounded on every side with arcades emanating light; banners of the Albien emblem hung from balconies. "Shut the gates," he yelled in High Aelish, relieved to find the gate already slamming shut as tenebrys crashed against them. The fully opened gate would easily allow entry to a dragon.

In the center of the atrium rose a statue of a tall woman with an owl perched on her shoulder. Saeryn Albien, in the form of a lumaryl statue, glared at every being who crossed the entrance, her eyes weighing their worthiness to enter her School. She shone in her own brightness and Kevn could only imagine what this atrium would look like with the morning sun pouring through the lofty windows. Even with the golden lumaryl, the atrium and statue possessed a hint of the white color of the School they belonged to.

Kevn's heart raced as he stared into the founder of the Albien School's still eyes, aware that tenebrys lightning continued to pound against the palace-city, fearful that the gates would not stand against the force. He looked around again, marveling at the scale and ornamentation still present.

Three pointed arched corridors branched from the atrium. From their proportions they were more akin to roads than interior corridors; each could fit eight horse drawn carts abreast or even a dragon. This was a city after all. A silvery figure stood in the central corridor. It looked like a woman, but before Kevn could focus on her, she was gone.

Follow.

The command filled his mind and he dismounted. Laureniel

nudged him toward the central corridor. She was safe here in Septyl. For some reason the Shroud could not pass through the gates; its poisonous mist would not breach the city.

Leaving Laureniel behind, Kevn walked into what should be a sun-filled corridor. It looked like a glass ceiling covered the walkway. It would have once allowed sunlight to pour into the causeway. Kevn knew from his research that the ceiling was not glass, but a thinner form of lumaryl, just as translucent as glass, and clearly capable of withstanding tenebrys.

The corridor opened to a large space, a second atrium with ceilings just as high as the first. This one had three distinct statues of the same lumaryl stone at the center. A male and female elf with scrolls tucked under their arms stood on either side of an owl perched between them. Kevn instantly recognized the emblem of the Albien School in statue form rather than the flatter relief version he had always seen before.

More causeways branched off from the atrium. Counting a total of six, he looked around, trying to decide if there was an obvious choice. On the far side of the room, Kevn glimpsed the remnants of the silvery wisp.

Follow.

The order rang clear in his mind again, but as he walked past the statues, the more uncertain he grew. He was undoubtedly the first person to enter Septyl since before the palace-city had been abandoned. The ei'ana who had remained behind had likely set traps for when it was again accessed, fearful that it might fall into the Tenebrae School's control.

Kevn was barely considered a student at Gwilnor Academy, let alone a professed ei'ana belonging to one of the Seven Schools. There was no doubt in his mind which School he would choose, but that was a thought for a later day.

"Please don't spring any of your ancient traps on me," he said in High Aelish, convinced that it would be the only language understood by whatever magic drove Septyl.

Reaching the corridor where the wisp had appeared, Kevn warily continued his trek through, searching for vents or obvious signs that there could be a deadly mist flowing through a crack in the floor.

A third atrium opened at the end of the causeway. The statue here was surprisingly of someone he knew. The likeness of Mother Selenya, the current Chair of Albien, gazed down on him, her expression just as he remembered. Kevn wondered how that was possible; no one had entered Septyl to change the statue from whoever had been the Chair at the time Septyl was abandoned. Dozens of other statues sat in niches around the atrium. None were as large as the central figure, but they were clearly the previous Chairs of Albien.

Kevn felt the statuary appraise him from their vacant eyes, eyes that showed none of the intellect of the women and men they represented. Still, even though they did not move, he was sure they were observing him. They seemed so lifelike, as though they could easily step forward to attack Kevn if they wished.

A pointed, arched opening stood at the far end, beyond Mother Selenya's representation, and in the center of that opening stood the silvery wisp. She remained in place this time and held Kevn's eyes in her own, weighing him as did Saeryn, Selenya, and the other statues, but she was no statue. She beckoned Kevn forward, her transparent hand extending to him as he neared her.

Kevn looked at her and imagined that she wanted him to hold her hand. Allowing the nameless wisp to close her fingers around his own, a chilly sensation rushed through him, yet oddly, it was accompanied by a warmth he had not expected, nor could he make sense of.

Sophie.

Her name was Sophie. Kevn couldn't tell if it was that he recognized her or whether the wisp had spoken her name to him in the same way she asked him to follow.

Hands clasped, they walked through the wide corridor, only his feet on the lumaryl floor making a sound, echoing lightly as they walked along. A broad stair rose at the end of the corridor, a door at the highest landing. Curling script in High Aelish engraved in the stone framed the pointed archway, bearing a light of its own, wholly different than the lumaryl's luminosity.

Feeling Sophie nudge him forward as she let go of his hand, Kevn took each wide tread slowly. A weight fell on his shoulders, growing heavier with every step he took. Unsure why this was so, or of its origin or purpose, he turned to look down at Sophie on the bottom tread, only to discover she had disappeared again.

Heavy doors without handles guarded the sanctum beyond. These doors seemed more protective than even the lumaryl gate at the entrance to the palace-city. With a shaky hand, Kevn placed his fingers against the smooth wooden surface, surprised to discover how little wear it had.

An awareness filled his mind—a consciousness that was not his own. Kevn tried to pull his fingers away, startled and terrified by the feeling, but couldn't. His fingers were rooted against the wooden doors and his feet planted at the threshold.

Something searched his mind and heart as he was frozen in place, probing through his inner depths. Defenseless, he waited as all his secrets were exposed to this nameless presence. He blushed as thoughts he had never spoken aloud came to the surface. Time lost meaning in those moments, and his heart leapt when the door slowly swung inward, permitting him entrance.

Unlike the rest of the palace-city of Septyl, the chamber beyond was cast in long shadows, created by the opened door he stood at. He watched his own shadow disappear into the depths, merging with the others in the dim light.

Follow. Sophie penetrated his mind again, but he saw no trace of her.

With a hesitant step, he crossed the threshold. He considered wielding a globe of light but found it oddly irreverent in this place. Still cast in shadows, Kevn moved forward, and as he did, the door behind him squealed shut.

Darkness bathed the entire space. *And now you're locked in some room in a city in the Shroud, a pawn of some ancient trap against intruders.* His heart raced and he told himself how foolish this was. His instincts told him to stay put, yet he took another step, expecting a trapdoor to drop him into a dungeon where he would lie forgotten.

Follow. The gentle message was soothing, but his anxiety stayed with him as he moved blindly forward.

After a great many paces, a cloudy light in the form of a small orb appeared. It was clear that a statue held the orb aloft, but the light was too dim to discern any of its features. Drawn to the cloudy orb, Kevn hoped it was not a trap. His every instinct screamed at him to leave the orb alone, to wield a globe of his own light, force his way out of this place and return to Ceurenyl to help Aaron however he could.

Against his better judgement, his fingers extended toward the cloudy, incandescent orb. It felt like glass beneath his touch.

Transported, Kevn was lost for words. Thousands of small cloudy orbs floated about, held aloft as if strings of varying lengths suspended them from the domed ceiling above. Bobbing up and down, Kevn observed them with interest, eager to learn more about the curious orbs.

The same cloudy light he could see in the first orb seemed to surround him in this place—wherever this place was. He was sure he no longer stood in the chamber inside the vacant palace-city of Septyl, and his inner senses told him he no longer stood in Eklean. An excited thought leapt to one of the Skylands, perhaps Luminare.

"For one as curious as yourself, I imagine you have many questions," a woman said.

Kevn turned to find an elf with golden brown hair and silver eyes gazing upon him. A simple white garment covered her, bound at her right shoulder with a golden pin that bore an inscription he was unfamiliar with. Kevn recognized the silky cloth as lierathnil. It fell in elegant waves, resting in a puddle on the floor.

"My name is Sophie, and you are inside my sophilliae, one specially made for those who would don my mantle. Only those who the Sophillium deigns worthy can access this sophilliae."

With every word, Kevn found himself astonished. She spoke in High Aelish but the language had become so familiar to him that he no longer needed to translate it in his mind.

"I place it under your care; I entrust my life's work, and the work of countless others who were here before you, to your charge. Know that under no circumstances is a sophilliae to pass the Sophillium's threshold. The wealth inside the Sophillium is a comprehensive whole, each dependent on another, constantly expanding. Each sophilliae contains a certain knowledge, available to any desiring it. As their guardian, you are entrusted with sharing the sophilliae here, opening our doors to any who wish to learn.

"Take this understanding and continue our craft as the Sophillian. Bring my nomination to the Seven Chairs of Septyl and the Exalted Aryl."

The cloudy light dispersed, Sophie was gone, and Kevn stood in the vacant room he'd first entered, the room cast again in a heavy darkness. He didn't quite understand what had just transpired, but he willed a brightness and was surrounded by innumerable orbs glowing, each with its own soft cloudy light. There was nothing remarkable about the light, for the lights in the corridors beyond were much brighter, but this ethereal light felt right to Kevn. The corners of the heptagonal room faded into obscurity, a fitting representation. The only way to discover the secrets of each was to explore them, just as one would explore any form of knowledge.

Kevn had long fantasized over what Septyl's library would contain. He had imagined thousands of shelves lining the library, weighed down by books and tomes too heavy to comfortably hold while reading. But this, this was something more. There wasn't a book in the entire library—only orbs.

Standing tall was a statue of Sophie, creator of the sophilliae, founder of the Sophillium, and the first Sophillian to protect and gather knowledge. She stood just as he had seen her inside the sophilliae. Beside her was a table, a folded garment with a pin resting on it. Lifting the golden pin from the white lierathnil, Kevn examined it. The edges were smooth and the surface bowed outward. Several small jewels floated within, each of a different color, connected by swirling lines creating a geometric pattern. Bringing the pin closer to his eyes, he noticed the lines were flowing script in High Aelish.

He also noticed the dirt and grime covering his fingers and quickly returned the pin to the lierathnil garment. "I'll have to take a bath before putting that on," he said aloud, considering the difficulties associated with cleaning lierathnil.

Turning away from the garment and pin, he saw a sophilliae bobbing before his eyes, its cloudy light calling to him. He knew he should remove his dirty clothes and clean the dirt of travel away but decided that could wait for later.

Pressing his dirty fingers against the smooth, cloudy surface, Kevn was again transported.

DAER

Alex frowned at the Daer fortifications—a wooden palisade rein-forced by mounds of dirt cresting a low hillock along the Skrein Sea—disgruntled that he had not dealt with the invaders sooner. While he stood by his choice to defend Everin from giants, shadow elves, Dwonians, and a renegade Perrien militia led by his own uncle, that choice had given the Daer more time to strengthen their position here. Setting up a Daer colony in Thellion was one thing, but the Daer had also seized the locals along the Skrein Sea and used them as forced labor. Alex would be damned if his rule as the first Thellish king in several ages was marred by his own people being enslaved by a foreign invader.

Sanjin had told Alex that the Daer had once had colonies all over Ogren and were only forced off the continent after the other kingdoms had fallen victim to the ogres in that land. Supporting colonies in a continent largely populated by ogres had proven unprofitable and the Daer focused their colony building in Ja'horan after that. Now it seemed that Eklean was next.

Alex nudged Dennion forward. He could be flying above it all, but the winged horse trotted on the ground with the rest of the army march-ing north to the Daer colony. Everyone who had received the winged horses were on the ground, riding as his entourage. When the column reached an area that was a safe distance from the Daer colony, the troops immediately began setting up camp. Alex had wanted their siege of the

Daer colony to begin that same day, but he understood that was impossible. Military campaigns were never short nor quick endeavors. Still, the sooner he forced the Daer out of Thellion, the better. Diana and his mother had likely already reached Elothkar and were setting about making wedding plans. Alex had only glimpsed the large caravan of artisans traveling from Everin to prepare for the wedding and he already felt the drain on Thellion's coffers their wages and his generous patronage would bring. He knew his mother would clash with the Evellion artisans every step of the way, insisting that Perrien had the superior culture. Curiously though, the only difference Alex had noticed between the two Thellish provinces and their cultures during his time in Everin was that the mountain city was much colder.

Alex was the first to see a rider holding a white flag aloft trot out of the Daer palisade toward the Thellish army. Oliver and Karl, standing by him awaiting orders, eyed the approaching messenger with suspicion.

"How far can we go out to meet him before we're within range of their archers?" Alex asked, squinting as he did. Something about the rider didn't seem right.

"He's already out of their range. Do you want to meet him in the field?" Oliver asked.

"Better than waiting for our camp to be set up to receive him. We can't do much else while we wait." Alex nudged Dennion forward and Oliver and Karl followed, the three of them stopping beyond the area where the camp was setting up to await the envoy.

Alex watched the curious looking Daer approach on an animal he had never seen before. It had much of the appearance of a horse, but with elongated limbs, and its knees were higher off the ground than any horse Alex knew of. The Daer himself was quite long and spare with a taut, lean face, wiry muscles, and an ebony complexion that was in contrast to his long white hair. More striking than his snow white hair were his purple eyes which could be readily seen even at a distance. None of it seemed human or eleven and Alex shifted uncomfortably as the Daer stopped his too tall mount just speaking distance away, the odd animal now towering over him, Oliver, and Karl. The Daer wore a bright coat over an otherwise plain ensemble that did nothing to conceal the extraordinary length of his limbs.

"I am Jenyd of House Tarneth, advisor to Senator Koth and humble servant to the Daer Empire, requesting that you cease setting up your military encampment and return from whence you came," the rider addressed them haughtily.

"Could say the same to you," Karl growled quietly from beside Alex, eyeing the Daer's lanky, stretched out figure.

"And I am Alexander of House Vaerin, King of Thellion—the king of this land." Alex was already tired of this man. "Tell your senator and empire that they are not welcome to establish a colony here in my kingdom nor are they permitted to enslave Thellish citizens."

"We heard that a new king had taken up the old crown of Thellion. If your ancestors had not allowed their kingdom to fall all those ages ago, you would share in the longevity and splendor of the Daer. Eklean's short lived kingdoms have proved they would not last the test of time and neither will this new one. The Daer Empire extends a hand in friendship to barbarians of lesser developed lands. Embrace the Daer Empire in peace and friendship before we withdraw our gesture."

Alex blinked in response. He couldn't believe the gall of this man. Did Jenyd actually think that his little speech would incline Alex to hand over Thellion to the Daer on a silver platter? He couldn't tell how many soldiers were behind the Daer's palisades, but surely, they didn't outnumber Alex's army. "Thellion will not be joining any Daer Empire. Your presence here, your unlawful colony, and the abduction of Thellish citizens is an act of aggression that will not be ignored."

"So quick to confrontation. Has this continent truly not progressed past primitive barbaric tendencies? I really must urge you to reconsider your position. Your people will flourish and evolve in ways you could never imagine under the grace of the empire."

Alex just managed to not roll his eyes. "Our terms are that you vacate your illegal colony and free our citizens."

"You are offered the opportunity to embrace the Daer Empire and you deny us? The last time a Thellish king ruled this land, terms were met and our colony grew to a thriving city that remains to this very day. Eklean was made the richer by our presence."

"There aren't any Daer colonies on Eklean and there certainly aren't any Daer. Your people haven't been seen here since the Guardian Senate disbanded," Karl said.

"Are you so sure?"

"The only city I can think of that might have begun as one of your colonies is Daerinth and that's only because of the name," Oliver said, scratching his chin.

"Yes. The inhabitants hardly resemble Daer today. But that colony began in the days when we had kings. Now we are all each other's kings. We've changed since those days—we've become more than human." Jenyd looked down his long nose at Alex, Karl, and Oliver.

"Daerinth has also pledged itself to another empire. Did you know that?" Karl asked.

"They must have been greatly impoverished to choose another as their rightful liege and return to an imperial rule. Mistakes can be corrected."

"You should focus on that colony rather than establishing a new one. It seems your colonies care little for their imperial origins," Alex said.

"I would not be so sure of that if I were you. Still, you make a convincing point. Terms will be drawn up. In six days, a tent shall stand here and Senator Koth and his representatives will meet with you. Pray don't do anything foolish before then." Jenyd spun his unfamiliar mount around and trotted back to the palisaded colony.

"Are they all like that?" Alex asked as Jenyd rode away.

"It's as though he didn't hear anything we said," Oliver said.

"Insufferable ingrate," Karl spat.

"We should head back and consult with Sanjin about this. He's had more experience with Daer," Alex said. They turned back toward camp to find that the tents were mostly pitched by the time they returned. It never ceased to amaze Alex how proficient soldiers were in getting things done. He didn't want to be the one to tell them that they'd be sitting idle for the next week. And he feared whatever mischief their idle hands and minds would get into to occupy that time. He had intended to make this a quick campaign—push the Daer out of Thellion and rescue the captives turned slaves. They now had to wait for a meeting with the senator before they could even consider assaulting the colony. The Daer didn't actually think that he was going to change his position, did they? Surely, they weren't that foolish and so self-absorbed to think that Alex would concede on either of his demands.

Alex handed Dennion over to a stable hand and headed to the large command tent. Its roof canopy had been lifted but only one of the canvas walls had been hung. Men bustled about, preparing to raise the rest. Aen busied himself about as he organized the space, unrolling maps of Perrien in a logical manner on the recently set up tables. Their available maps weren't the best representations of the area though and it seemed that the only thing accurately depicted was the coastline. These maps didn't show a single landmark, cave, or pass. For all Alex knew, the Daer were more familiar with the area than he was.

"Have you seen Prince Sanjin, Aen?" Alex asked.

"He stopped by earlier but went to see to the Charrenese tents. Shall I find him?"

"That won't be necessary." Sanjin came into the tent, followed by Reia and Sara just as another canvas wall fell into place. "Have the illustrious Daer chiseled away part of Thellion to shine its civilization down upon it?"

"We're having a meeting with one of their senators in six days. The scoundrel representative wants to draw up terms," Alex said.

"Terms already? They typically make you wait a month for that, all the while claiming your uncivilized violent tendencies are further reason for their occupation of your land." Sanjin glanced at the map, then grabbed some objects sitting at one end of the table and started arranging them in an order Alex couldn't determine.

"I promised Diana that I wouldn't be long—we don't have a month."

"Don't let them find out about the wedding if you can avoid it. They'll delay the talks even further because of the happy occasion," Sanjin said, moving the tools about on the table, until Alex realized that they represented buildings arranged in a small town.

"If they're not fighters, why aren't we marching toward those palisade walls sooner and sending these Daer away on their ships?" Karl asked.

"Our first contact with the Daer in over fourteen hundred years and you want to refuse their meeting and rush in wagging your swords about?" Reia held Karl in one of her unrelenting glares.

"The Daer love diplomacy and while the outcome might very well end with, how did you say it, *wagging* our swords about, but shirking their invitation to negotiate would be unforgivable. This colony is led by only one senator. If you deny him his chance at terms, he'll return to Daereneth with news of the barbarous Thellish king and the entire empire will make it their goal to establish themselves here in hopes of civilizing this country through conquest."

"What are their military capabilities?" Oliver asked.

"Not to be underestimated. The only reason Charren hasn't been swallowed by the Daer Empire is because Karithel floats in the sky above the channel between Daereneth and Ogren. Fortunately for you, the senators rarely work together. They prefer that their accomplishments are exclusively their own." Sanjin positioned the last pieces of what was now clearly a collection of buildings arranged in a particular order and pointed to one. "Senator Koth will be staying here; naturally it will be the largest building in the colony and positioned near the center. Jenyd is likely staying with him until his own manor is built. Since he's not a senator, he'll have to wait until the colony can dedicate its resources to something other than fortifications. That one will complain the entire time; House Tarneth is a well-respected family in the empire and has had its fair share of senators throughout the ages. Young Jenyd intends to see his house return to the senate."

"If he's so important, why isn't he already a senator?" Reia asked.

"Openings rarely occur in the senate since the upper tier of the senate hold their positions for life. Technically, he could contest for a lower tier seat, but he would never stoop to that."

"If altercations are unavoidable, do the Daer have any wielders or mages that we should be concerned about?" Oliver asked.

"They've had both in the past, but they haven't sent anyone to study with the Kilnae Del in centuries and I doubt they had sufficient knowledge to teach the arcane. The same is likely true in regard to their wielders."

"That's a relief," Alex said.

"He wasn't finished," Reia stared at Sanjin, unflinching.

"The Sorcery. They use a dark magic bent on manipulation and control. As far as I can tell, it's the next closest thing to tenebrys, if not worse," Sanjin said.

"Worse? How could it possibly be worse than lightning that negates existence?" Alex asked.

"The Daer have always had a strong relationship with anadel. The Kilnae Del posit that that relationship possibly accounts for how they've evolved from human to what they currently are." After seeing Jenyd, Alex couldn't imagine him ever being human. "There are two branches of the Sorcery. One, which the Kilnae Del believe came first, came about at the same time the Daer ceased to be human and became the Daer we know today. Their magic is based on the anadel lending them their strength, and as far as I can tell, it's similar to how Devlyn and Ellendren Lorenthien interact with their phoenix, only it was never a permanent bond with the Sorcery. The second branch took advantage of the anadel, and instead of harnessing their power, they seized anadel in talismans, to be used as permanent weapons."

"We thought they had stopped doing that." Reia looked down toward the table.

"It's possible that they had when the Guardian Senate last breathed, but they would have had little reason to continue abstaining without that international body overseeing them."

"Is there any way to know which branch of the Sorcery is here?" Sara asked.

"Afraid not. The Daer senators have not voiced any public opinions on the Sorcery, making it impossible to know if any one senator condemns the more sinister of the two branches. That being said, it's largely speculated that the higher tier of the senate belongs to the Sorcery and continues to trap anadel in talismans."

THE VEIL

A strong wind howled through the large courtyard that had once housed the only entrance to Gwilnor. It had long been viewed as the most secure of the castle's entrances, and even though the castle was no longer sealed, Devlyn could think of no better location to shift to with six of the Seven Chairs of Septyl. The seventh, Velaria Treyven, stood at the top of the stair leading into the castle. A score of Septyl knights surrounded her. Her hair was gone and her scalp shone in the courtyard's torchlight. She showed no sign of weariness, not on her face nor in her bearing. She stood just as proud and confident as the first day Devlyn had met her in Cor'lera. He could already hear her reprimanding him for slouching, and for once, that made him smile. Aside from clearly having been abused and ill fed, Velaria was alive.

Despite everything that she had so recently accomplished and every level of abuse she had undergone before that, her small smile greeted Devlyn still bonded with Aliel, Viren, Jaerol, Rusyl, Yelaris, and the other Chairs. The Septyl knights parted, allowing the new arrivals to be greeted and welcomed back to Gwilnor by the woman who had saved it.

Tears brimmed in Devlyn's eyes at seeing Velaria alive. His dreams had been plagued with images of her as the Tenebrae's prisoner. He had received no news from the castle after his escape and Velaria taken captive and his imagination had assumed the worst. Devlyn lingered behind the Chairs while Paurel, crying with relief, already had Velaria's hands in her own. The Seven Chairs exchanged brief accounts, matters too important to wait for the privacy of their chamber. Devlyn expected Velaria to follow the other Chairs into the castle, but she remained where she stood on the stair, holding Devlyn's gaze even as he withdrew from Aliel.

"Thank you for going to them, Jaerol. I know you had more important matters to see to," Velaria said.

"That stubborn lethien wouldn't lie down to rest until I left." Jaerol let out an exaggerated sigh. "Is he well?"

"A Crimsyn I've never had reason to doubt did not leave his side in the infirmary. Your friends from the temple are also with him. Renaud and Stephen kindly rejected any offers to be relieved of their watch in lieu of other knights guarding Liam. They said they had no interest in dealing with a Cyndinari's wrath if anything happened to him." Velaria, a Cyndinari herself, laughed at the last part.

"They're both dramatic. Still, if you don't mind, I would like to go see him now."

"Of course; you have done more than enough. Go be with him." Velaria smiled as Jaerol and Rusyl followed after the Chairs, leaving only Velaria, Devlyn, Viren, Yelaris, Aliel, and the remaining Septyl knights in the courtyard. A number of the knights had followed the Chairs inside as escorts and protectors. "You look well," Velaria said.

"Thank you," Devlyn replied, unable to peel his sight from her shaved scalp and leafless body. "I'm sorry for what they did to you. I still feel guilty for leaving you behind."

"There was no choice in the matter. Much more would have been lost if they had taken you as well. Erynor would have ensured you would not escape," Velaria said. Her words did little to ease him. The last time he had seen her, Yvonne had a knife to her throat. "Will you walk with me?"

"Of course."

Velaria didn't turn to go into the castle, but rather walked toward the courtyard's great arch. It spanned over two stories and was large enough for a dragon to fly through. Velaria stopped before reaching the bridge that led to the castle grounds, staying on the terrace instead.

"I remember the first time I saw Gwilnor," Velaria said, thoughtful and reminiscent. "An ei'ana named Nadia had brought me here when I was a child. That first glimpse from the mountain pass had left me speechless. Nadia had told me the castle had that effect on many upon seeing it for the first time. She had recruited me as a child, and she told me I had the capacity to be a gifted ei'ana. My parents had wanted to make the trip with me but couldn't afford it."

"Were your parents ever able to make the journey?" Devlyn asked. Aliel had nestled on the balustrade and Viren and Yelaris hung back, both keeping watch on the nearby bridge for any uninvited guests.

"Nadia killed them after I began my studies here."

Devlyn's eyes flared wide. "Why?" was all he could ask.

"Nadia, like many of the ei'ana we had trusted, belongs to the Tenebrae School. She had hoped that I would seek revenge at the news of my parents' death, that I would bend my attention and will on power. I grieved at their deaths, but I did not respond as Nadia anticipated a Cyndinari would. I did not become what she wanted me to become. Nadia is more than just a Tenebrae though; she is also their Chair."

"Were you able to capture her when you liberated the castle?"

"She slipped away like the snake that she is. She must have noticed when the temple ward was extended and fled through one of the castle's secret passages. She likely used the same one the Tenebrae used to smuggle you out for Alesei."

Devlyn went to the edge of the terrace; Ceurenyl unfolded before him and he wondered if there was some way to find Nadia. He had no idea what she looked like or whether she was an elf or a human. "Is there any way to track her down?"

"She likely fled the city with a small contingent of Tenebrae and servants of shadow. Finding her and uprooting others like her is not why I asked you or Ellendren to come back to Ceurenyl. I hope to keep you here for only a week, but in that time the Seven Chairs will pass judgement on the Tenebrae, both communally and individually. Hannah and Yvonne will receive the harshest sentences, but many more will live out their lives in a prison."

"I don't understand; why bring me here for their trials? Surely you don't expect me to devise the punishment for an ei'ana," Devlyn stammered. He might be an aryl, but what right did he have to overstep the Seven Chairs of Septyl?

"These women might have spoken our counsels but they are no longer ei'ana. The authority of the Seven Chairs is limited to Septyl. Since they are technically not under our jurisdiction any longer, as the apparent heir of the position of the Exalted Aryl of Krysenthiel, we require you or Ellendren to sanction our judgement on the Tenebrae."

Devlyn's skin crawled as he walked through Gwilnor's corridors, despite Aliel's bright light and Viren's armed company. Viren had insisted on joining him in Gwilnor, claiming that his presence was all the more pivotal since Devlyn wouldn't be able to wield. It would only take a dagger in the back from a Tenebrae who had not yet been identified or a servant of shadow lurking in the dark to alter their plans. Still, leaving Ellendren without Viren's protection bothered Devlyn. He knew she was safe in Eandyl, but he couldn't stop worrying about her. That was a minor worry though compared to what really nagged at him. Time spent away from the Luminari would only prolong the removal of the Shroud. And now that he understood that it wasn't simply a matter of removing it from Krysenthiel, that he also had to remove it from Somnaeniel, and according to Eagan, very soon, he felt more pressure. Ignoring the Shroud's presence in Somnaeniel would all but guarantee its return.

Devlyn had no choice but to return to the World-in-Between. Erynel wasn't only the source of the Shroud, she also wore one of the seven lucilliae about her neck. Time was limited though—Ramiel's influence in Somnaeniel grew every day. Devlyn had wanted to avoid returning to that increasingly dangerous realm, especially as dorthl would soon consume every aspect of it. Despite the dire news from Eagan and Abbie, they had yet to pull him back into the Dream.

A dizzy spell washed over Devlyn as he turned down another corridor. He reached out to the wall to brace himself, expecting his legs to give out, but they didn't. At least, he thought they hadn't. The air felt different though. He turned to ask Viren if he had noticed anything, but the Guardian knight was gone. Devlyn spun around to take in his surroundings. *Where'd Viren go?* he conveyed to Aliel.

"He didn't go anywhere and technically neither did you," Eagan seemed to appear out of nowhere.

"A little warning would have been nice before drawing me into Somnaeniel," Devlyn said.

"I tried. Why do you think your mind was so occupied with the Dream moments ago?"

Devlyn looked anew at the corridor. It was a perfect mirror of the corridor where his body still was, likely being supported by Viren. Then he realized something was very different here. "How is there no dorthl here?" The lack of the dark ooze was a comfort, yet it stirred more questions.

"The Evil One cannot infect this city. The Light in the temple keeps it back just as it does the Shroud. That corruption cannot come near Anaweh's Light."

"So, that means Gwilnor is the perfect place to teach me more about this place, right?"

"That's one of the reasons. The other is that Erynel will think you are still in Eandyl. She knows of you now and will not underestimate you again. If she senses your presence here, she will try to destroy you."

"What about Aliel?" Devlyn turned to the phoenix who was hovering over his shoulder.

"Forgive me, Aliel, but your being is like a beacon here."

Don't hesitate to reach out if anything happens, Aliel conveyed before vanishing.

Devlyn immediately felt the phoenix's absence and wanted to follow him back into Teraeniel and reunite with his body. "What now?"

Eagan extended his hand and Devlyn flinched at the touch. It felt odd. He had touched people here in the Dream before, but this time it felt as though his hand would pass right through Eagan's.

"Are you here physically?"

Eagan didn't answer as the two of them shifted to the uppermost balcony of the Dragon Tower. Unlike Teraeniel, Somnaeniel did not have a sun and telling the time of day was impossible here. While the everlasting twilight of this realm would have typically rolled over everything, dark storm clouds now tainted the sky. Devlyn recognized those storm clouds—they were the same that had swallowed Alethea. Devlyn wondered if this was where she had been stolen away to. Was she trapped somewhere in this realm? He knew the Eldinari in Stellantis were investigating her disappearance, but he felt responsible. Those clouds would not have taken her if she had not gone with him into the Illumined Wood. She had taught him so much over the past few years and all she had received in return was a likely gruesome death.

Devlyn took in the misty view from the balcony's vantage point. Somnaeniel had an ethereal quality to it and even though he knew that nothing in this realm was solid, it still felt odd to see a different version of Teraeniel. Most out of place was the East Tower.

"How is it still whole?" Devlyn had seen the damage done to the Vyoletryn's wing by the fire started by the rogue kien wielders who had pledged their allegiance to the Erynien Empire.

"Gwilnor has been here for thousands of years; it is older even than Krysenthiel. The Dream requires more time for a monument such as this castle to alter here. The East Tower will likely be repaired before any change is reflected here." Eagan looked away from the East Tower and into the Shroud. "I trust you know you will need more allies in the battles ahead."

Caught off guard by the comment, Devlyn replied, "I'm confident with our allies." He listed off the races and nations who had already pledged themselves to fighting the Erynien Empire.

"For fighting Erynor, the people of Eklean might be able to overthrow him. But Eklean, especially a divided Eklean, cannot defeat the Evil One alone. The King of Thellion has made more advances to strengthen intercontinental alliances than the Lorenthien aryl who would be the Prefect of the Senate. Provinces of the Daer Empire are already lost to us, as are some tribes of Ja'horan. The Qien Dynasty is unified in name, but the empress holds the diverse people and kingdoms there together by a thread. Ogren is largely overrun by ogres now, and Charren is the last bastion for humanity on that continent; the other kingdoms, all brought low by the ogres, splintered into tribes and now hide in the forests. The Meridean Conclave is still ongoing and will remain until the Prefect of the Guardian Senate interjects—you can't hope to succeed without the merpeople."

A bubble of rage boiled inside Devlyn's chest. "Of course, we plan to bring back the Guardian Senate. But how many nations do you think will send ambassadors to Eklean while the Shroud still stands and the Erynien Empire controls southern Eklean? They can't exactly sail here and hope to pass unscathed through the southern Eklean."

Eagan smacked his head. "The longer you view this conflict consecutively, the less chance we'll have at actually defeating the Evil One. Everything will be lost to the Void if Teraeniel doesn't unite against this threat. Why do you think the Guardian Senate was created in the first place? Your ancestors lived on Eklean for thousands of years before they took an interest in the affairs of the other races. Do you think they did it for power or because they cared about the well-being of everyone? Have you considered that they knew the Evil One would be freed and started taking the first steps to stop him?"

Devlyn stepped cautiously away from Eagan. It bothered him how much the druid knew about the past for someone so young. "How do you know all this?"

"The Druids of Kweil Aitch have not forgotten what Eklean was like before the Luminari elves arrived. The fact that your people remember nothing from before makes us wonder why we're trying to help you in the first place."

"That's not what I asked." Devlyn tried to keep his anger under control. Eagan looked no older than twenty-five, yet he seemed intimately familiar with historical events, as though he had lived them or experienced them in some manner.

Eagan glared back at Devlyn, seeming to compose himself as well. "I would not speak of this here. Perhaps you will learn if your people reclaim their lost wisdom."

"Fine. Now, I assume you didn't bring me here just to scold me about the current status of the Guardian Senate."

"It was only one of the reasons. There is another. You need to learn to enter the Dream physically. Erynel cannot be defeated in Teraeniel alone and neither can you retrieve the lucilliae if you are not physically here."

"Is Gwilnor really the safest place to practice?"

"No. Our options are limited though. There are a few havens in the Dream that dorthl cannot touch; Ceurenyl and Kweil Aitch are such places. I believe there are sites in Ja'horan as well, but I have not found them yet. The druid elders think they might be caves."

"What about the other continents?" Devlyn asked.

"Qien's centralized monasteries are still free, but I cannot say for Charren or Daereneth. A dark cloud has fallen over those continents and I believe they are lost to us in the Dream."

"How do you mean?"

"It would be easier to show you." Eagan extended his hand and they shifted.

Dorthl surrounded them in wide patches and Devlyn looked out across a body of water to where the dark clouds seemed to touch a land-mass. While the clouds hung over the rest of Somnaeniel, threatening to consume everything, the threat to that landmass or continent had been realized.

"The Void is strongest in Daereneth. The druid elders have forbidden me to step foot on that continent. We believe it completely covered in dorthl. And considering what we can see from here, that seems likely."

"Where are we now then?"

"Where you should not be."

Devlyn and Eagan turned to find an old woman with ebony skin and hair black as a moonless night. Her clouded eyes looked past them and into the nebulous clouds behind them. Looking again, Devlyn thought he had met the woman once before. "I remember you," he said.

"Yet you do not remember or take heed of my warning." She turned on Eagan, scowling. "You are a fool to come here as you are. We once thought the druidic clan in Eklean wise. It appears the clans are more different than we thought."

"Unprecedented times call for exceptional measures." Eagan bowed his head in deference to the old woman.

"Who are you?" Devlyn asked.

"An elder among the druids in Ja'horan. Our clans long ago settled in places here where the veil between the Dream and the waking world are thin. Only one such place exists in Eklean, but Ja'horan has many—more than any other continent. You may call me Izara, child of the stars."

Devlyn had not realized that there were druids outside Eklean. "A pleasure to meet you again, Izara."

"There is no pleasure left to the Dream. You take too great a risk coming here. The Dream will soon be lost—you know this, young druid," Izara said, looking at Eagan.

"He must learn to walk the Dream, Elder, before the Dream is lost to us."

"So that is why you risk so much." Izara looked back into the dark turbulent clouds. "The flower petals have never been given to anyone who was not a druid."

"He intends to destroy the Sha'ghol who taints the Dream and the waking world with the Shroud," Eagan said.

"The Dream would be richer if Erynel Meriden was banished from it. Even if you succeed in defeating her, that will not save this realm—she is but a pawn, as is her son."

"I know," Devlyn said. He wanted to avoid another lecture about how he was not doing enough to save all creation from the Evil One. "If we don't defeat her though, my people will never reclaim our homeland."

"The Skylands are forever lost to the Void," Izara said.

"Not Krysenthiel, though. Verakryl still lives beneath Erynel's Shroud," Devlyn said.

"Teraeniel has indeed been dimmer without the Tree of Life to brighten it. As though the Void's strengthening presence hasn't darkened the Dream and waking world enough, we have been denied the Light from the Tree there and Anaweh's Breath has been stifled here. The Void is trying to suffocate the Breath—soon there will be no space for the Breath here. This realm will return to the Void. The Evil One will swallow the Dream and the waking world. He does not want to escape his prison—the Void is no prison to him. No, he wants to expand and reclaim all that it once claimed and more. But you already know this, don't you, child of the stars?"

Devlyn nodded. He remembered Fendryl's warning well. The draelyn had also cautioned him about the Evil One's schemes to return creation to the Void. "What must I do?"

"When the time comes, drink the tea of the flower that Eagan offers. The flower only blooms twice a year. She will next open her petals on the shortest night."

"Meridephaen—the summer solstice." Devlyn winced. Without

warning, his surroundings shifted again and Devlyn found himself on the stone floor of the corridor in Gwilnor. Neither Izara nor Eagan had given him any warning that they were sending him back. He simply woke up in the castle. Viren had waited there the entire time with his back to Devlyn, standing guard with Aliel, only turning when Devlyn pushed himself to his feet. "That was unexpected," Devlyn said.

"I could say the same. Eagan or Abbie, I presume?" Viren asked.

"Eagan. Did you know there are druids on other continents?"

"The druids have always been secretive. They never sought a place among the Guardian Senate, like the ei'ana and ei'ceuril had, but they would arrive unannounced at times, always accompanied by the centaurs. It's still a mystery how closely related the druids and centaurs are."

"Does that mean there are centaurs on the other continents?" Devlyn asked.

"Wherever there's a miervae and a great forest, you'll find centaurs and fauns. Come, the Seven Chairs have been in deliberations all day."

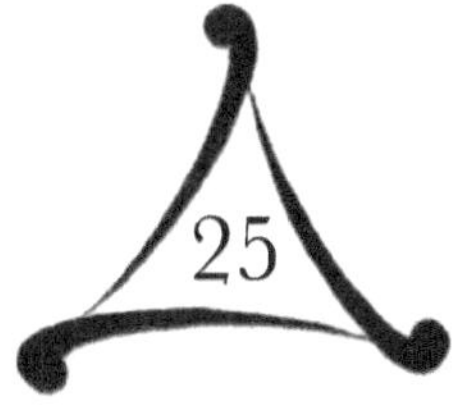

ENCOURAGED

Ellendren took a sip of her tea. There were stores of kryseniel tea that had miraculously survived the Shroud and Ellendren had never tasted anything so delicious. The amber liquid swirled in her cup, and she allowed the aroma to fill her nostrils before taking another sip. She looked across the small table in Kaela's parlor at her sister who was sipping at her own cup of tea, also savoring the taste. Kaela's lodging in Eandyl's palace was an apartment on the same floor as Devlyn and Ellendren but further down the corridor. The space was smaller than theirs, and had fewer rooms in general, but the accommodations were still extravagant. The lumaryl walls glowed in the evening light, complimenting the color of their tea.

"I've been putting off speaking with you about our—my House. I do not wish to see it fade into history." Kaela took another sip of the fragrant tea.

Ellendren had been dreading this conversation. She wanted her family's legacy to continue just as much as her sister did. Did she and Devlyn have the authority to recognize new aryldoms and bring them into court? "I just don't know the procedures to implement our family into Krysenthien court."

"The Roendryns have served the Luminari for twelve hundred years. There is nothing to implement. The bigger question is why do I not have a seat at the chamber meetings? A Roendryn belongs there just as much as anyone else."

"Kaela, you and I both know that is not the only issue. You are unwed. You know just as well as I do that there is little we can do until that changes."

"And if I were to be married?"

"Then we would have a better chance of raising the issue with the other aryls. Our family has served in the Lorenthiens' place since Erynor was last defeated; we were essentially a house of stewards keeping the throne warm, believing the Lorenthiens had perished."

Kaela paused and looked up from her tea. "What was that you said?"

"About you being married? Kaela, I know you've been distracted, but surely you haven't forgotten the simple requirement before an aryl can be an aryl."

"No, about our family. About the Roendryns being a house of stewards." Kaela's eyes lit up. "What if you and Devlyn officially recognized our family's role to the Luminari for the past twelve hundred years? In so doing, not only would you legitimize our family's leadership role and acknowledge Lucillia's particular role in our people's pilgrimage, but you would pave the way for our family to continue in that same position. In case something dire were to happen and the Lorenthien aryl can't perform their role as the Exalted Aryl, the Roendryn aryl could step in and return to the role that we've had since our House was born."

"The Roendryn aryl would be set apart from the other minor aryls, but still remain among them and not upset the balance of the high aryls." Ellendren looked down into her tea, running through countless scenarios of how the high aryls would react—how Silvia would react. Kaela was right though; their family had faithfully served the Luminari for twelve hundred years and were the foundation of their liberation from the Erynien Empire. It was only right that the Roendryn aryl continued in that capacity. Essentially, nothing would change, only there would be an acknowledgement of the Roendryn aryl's role as stewards.

Kaela leapt up and spun about, her skirts twirling as she did. "Well, I should be off."

"To where?" Ellendren turned to watch her sister reach for the door. "Surely you don't intend to run off to Stellantis and propose to Wyn without an invitation."

"And leave the excitement here? I wouldn't dream of it! He'll have to come to me. But until then, I'm going to continue to allow our eligible bachelors the honor of courting me in the hopes of becoming an aryl."

"I thought you said the Luminari nobles were, how did you say, dull?"

"And that they certainly are; now if you'll excuse me, I have an aryldom and stewardship to secure."

Shaking her head, Ellendren followed her sister out of her parlor and into the palace corridor. She didn't bother trying to keep up with her sister or try to figure out what political game she was playing today. And neither did she spare a moment for the poor lords whose parents had made every chamber meeting resemble a battle. Instead, she made her way back to her own chambers, losing herself in thoughts of the politicking that would be required to return the Roendryn aryl to their place. Fortunately, Kaela was a talented politician and quite capable.

Without paying attention to where she was going, she bumped into someone and immediately apologized, blushing in the process.

"Oh, hi, Elle." Trethien smiled at her. Her time with Trethien flooded to the front of her mind. So much had happened since the last time that Ellendren and Trethien had spoken over two years ago. It had been a bit embarrassing when he had made a scene over their broken betrothal. She of course understood why her parents had agreed to the betrothal with the Narielles. Trethien was one of the few Luminari lords near her own age. The next eligible lord was either a decade older or younger. There were other lords closer in age, but they were the youngest of their line and heirs, just as Ellendren had been. For the Narielles, joining with House Roendryn was an elevation in political status that they had greatly desired, and without sacrificing their heir.

"Hi, Trethien," she replied after a shocked pause.

"Congratulations on your marriage. I didn't realize you and Devlyn were to be wed so soon."

"Neither did we, to be honest. I'm sure you've heard by now, but the seraph declared us married while we were in the Empyrean Sphere." Ellendren chose her words carefully; she still felt a kinship with Trethien after all. They had grown up and attended Gwilnor together.

"I'm sure my mother has been easier to deal with since the marriage. I can only imagine how difficult she's been."

"You have no idea." Ellendren laughed.

"What? You think I'm blind to my mother's scheming? I've only been back for a day and it's already apparent. She was likely more unwilling to accept the ending of our betrothal than I was…um, sorry about the scene I made, by the way. My actions were unforgivable and beneath me. You didn't deserve that…and neither did Devlyn."

"You're forgiven, Trethien. I have missed your friendship and if it's any consolation, I know firsthand that Danielle fancies you. She was quite awful at disguising how she felt about our betrothal."

"Truly? She is stunning and from a respectable House. She's not betrothed to anyone?"

"Not the last I heard. Although it has been a while since I saw her. Weren't you with her in the temple?"

Trethien scratched his head, seeming to think about the past months he'd spent around Danielle. Ellendren decided to drop that line of conversation.

"How are Danielle and Fiona?" Ellendren asked.

"Quite well. If only I knew about Danielle sooner."

"Will you be staying with your parents?" she asked.

"That's the plan for now. I was never intended to become a Septyl knight after all. Although, if what you say about Danielle is true, perhaps I'll follow her to Septyl."

They continued to talk and Ellendren learned of his involvement with the liberation of Gwilnor. For the first time in a very long time, Ellendren saw Trethien quite differently. He wasn't the spoiled and entitled noble he had been when she had last seen him. He had changed—well, so had she. As Kaela would say, he certainly wasn't a boring noble who'd spent his entire life being pampered. And then an idea struck Ellendren.

"Trethien," she asked, "would you ever consider publicly courting my sister?"

"I never had the opportunity to get to know her. It would certainly please my mother but why mention Danielle if you also think I should court Kaela instead?"

Ellendren looked over her shoulder and lowered her voice. "Only temporarily; she's quite taken with Wyn."

"Devlyn's cousin—the Eldinari?" Trethien crossed his arms, clearly expressing his doubt about whatever Ellendren was suggesting, even if he wasn't quite grasping her meaning yet.

"That's him. If your parents were to see you and Kaela together, they would likely lend their support to officially recognizing my former house as a house of stewardship."

"You are scheming against my mother—the queen of scheming? She'll see right through it."

"But what if she didn't? What if the desire to have you still belong to House Roendryn won out?"

Trethien stepped back and scratched his chin until he came to a decision. "Will you explain everything to Danielle for me? I doubt she would forgive me for courting another Roendryn."

"I'll tell her personally." Ellendren smiled broadly and hurried off.

Stellantis was abuzz with the news of the Luminari elves retaking Eandyl. Other than Ceurenyl, Eandyl was now the only other Krysenthien city no longer suffocated by the Shroud, and it was the first to have been freed from the poisonous mist. Lucillia had prophesied that defeating the Shroud was possible and that the Luminari would in fact return to Krysenthiel. Still, the Eldinari had all but thought that would never happen, even with a Lorenthien aryl, both of them Phaedryn, leading the Luminari again.

Wyn was planning to rejoin Devlyn and Ellendren and help them in any way possible, but he couldn't leave Stellantis just yet. He had consulted with the Eldinari aryls still here about his dream in the Void. They had wasted little time on shock at his revelation and had begun devising a plan to rescue Alethea. The aryls were quick to ignore Alethea's own instructions of forgetting about her. The only problem they couldn't figure out was how to cross into the Void without dying.

The most startling news that Wyn had brought to the aryls was how many mortals had passed into the Void instead of choosing to go to Lumaeniel. How had the Evil One lured them away from Anaweh's Light? What lies had they been told that would lead to choosing a near non-existence in the Darkness? Wyn had sensed tens of thousands in Tosk alone and Jaris had said there were many more cities in the Void.

While Wyn was concerned about the number of souls there, he was more worried about finding a way there himself and living to tell the tale. He joined the aryls in fretting over how to rescue Alethea despite her directive to not do so. The more they tried to figure out a solution, the more Wyn was convinced that he had only one option. He'd only met one person who had gone to the Void and returned, Yloran Eth Gnashar. The Sha'ghol's last known location was Lankor although she had assured Devlyn and Wyn that they would not find her at her pretend orphanage again.

Surely, she wouldn't have stayed in Lankor nor in Yanil at all. Wherever she had ended up, it would be where the other Sha'ghol would not find her. Unfortunately, that list was very long and Wyn didn't know where to start.

As he thought on where a Sha'ghol might go to hide, he remembered that Yloran had insinuated to Devlyn that she expected him to provide her with proper accommodations when the time came. Perhaps Wyn didn't have to scour the world for Yloran; perhaps all he had to do was return to Devlyn and wait for her to come to them. Wyn wondered how viable that option was. Could Alethea wait that long? How long could she realistically survive in the Void? Another mystery that no one in Stellantis had an answer for.

Now that the Luminari had retaken Eandyl, Wyn wondered when the aryls would permit him to leave Stellantis. They had his account of Alethea's demise and supported his intent to enter the Void. How long would they hold him here to prepare for something that none of the Eldinari knew how to prepare for? They had never experimented with the Void before. Only the Cyndinari had been foolish enough to dabble with it, and that interaction had proven disastrous, resulting in the loss of the Skylands.

Wyn walked through the tree canopy city, nodding at but not stopping to chat with the various elves he passed. He had agreed to meet Dalenya as the stars shone that night. The Eldinari cherished the quiet lights of the night. Once he reached the Lierafen's dwelling, he climbed the many steps to the viewing terrace. Dalenya and a number of other elves were already there. A cluster of elves sang a hymn, praising Boriel for leading a group of elves to Eldinare in the Elder Days. Despite the elves' long lives and even longer memories, those stories were fading to myths and legends. Boriel might have led them to their Skyland, but did dragons of the Blue Flight really carry them to Eldinare as the song being sung held?

Wyn made his way to Dalenya. She smiled affectionately before stepping away from the elves gathered around her. Wyn followed her to the terrace's edge to better take in the stars above. They twinkled softly, telling a story of their own.

"Alethea taught me how to listen to the stars. She'd been teaching me how for a long time, but I only finally heard them when we stayed at the Abbey of Kyrendal."

"I'm sure you would have preferred to have gone with Devlyn to Tenethyl," Dalenya said.

"I did when he left. But after Borephaen…" Wyn choked at the image of Alethea being taken by the Void.

Dalenya placed her hand over Wyn's. The gentle touch warmed him. "She has taught our people much. She was—is—a living vessel of our history and culture."

"I'm going to find her and I'm going to bring her back to us."

"Be careful. Alethea would not want you risking everything for her sake. She did not train you for you to lose yourself in rescuing her. She would not want you to suffer the same fate as the Sha'ghol, Deurghol, or shadow elves. We do not know how the Void will mark you."

His heart ached, as though a heavy weight had been added to it. "I'll be careful; I promise."

"I know you will be." Dalenya smiled.

"When will I be able to leave Stellantis?"

"Not tonight. Tonight, we must listen to the stars and hear what guidance they might offer. The stars have never guided us wrong. If you listen closely enough, you might even hear Boriel offering you her wisdom."

They stood there in silence. Wyn wanted to discuss his plans for leaving. He wanted to see to any preparations that would allow him to better rescue his mentor and relative. He knew he should quiet his mind and open his heart to the stars to allow those anadel to commune with him.

"Your thoughts are troubled," Dalenya said, aware of his tumultuous mind. "Remember what she taught you."

Wyn tried not to growl as he forced his active mind to still. There would be time enough to plan; he knew that. But right now, thinking of anything else was proving difficult. Thinking of anything that Alethea had taught him made his heart ache. He could still hear her gentle urging and instructions as though she had just led him through a mental exercise.

"Are you certain you are up to this, Wyn?" Dalenya asked.

He nodded and breathed intentionally to calm his mind. Dalenya was right. He had to listen before acting. Alethea didn't have the luxury of Wyn being smothered by his grief. His anxiety melted away with each intentional breath, the rhythm of his heart humming in his chest as he lost himself between his heartbeats and breathing. Those were soon joined by a gentle song. He knew this song. He had learned it when he had first grown aware of his spirit—the song was his and it belonged only to him. There was no other song like it, for every anacordel had their own unique song resting in their heart. His song was a rush of wind through the trees rustling the leaves and birds singing in response. The tune rose and fell and grew bolder and softer and more harmonious with everything it grazed.

As the tune continued its ascent and descent through the various recesses of his being, it suddenly and unexpectedly hushed. Wyn wasn't prepared for that—he wasn't ready to end his contemplative moment.

He hadn't realized that his eyes had been closed, but when he opened them, he saw that he had somehow left Stellantis behind. This didn't feel like a dream, but neither had his recent excursion to the Void. He was not in the Void this time though, but he didn't think he was still in Teraeniel either as his eyes adjusted to the all-encompassing light around him.

Dazed, Wyn looked around for something—anything he could latch his mind onto.

"Young Lierafen," a mighty voiced said.

"Who's there? Where am I?" Wyn's voice sounded like a squeak next to whoever addressed him.

"I am a seraph. The guardian of your people brought you here. I heard your song; the song of your being says much of who you are."

"Is this the Empyrean Sphere?" Wyn asked.

"It is," another said. Wyn spun to find Boriel, the enthiel and guardian of the Eldinari, behind him. She did not look like an elf here, but rather appeared as an incorporeal being of light. "You've set yourself on a dangerous path. Ramiel is not keen on allowing people to escape his Void."

"I can't abandon Alethea," Wyn protested, uneasy about hearing the Evil One's name spoken.

"Nor would I ask it of you. But you have come to it of your own will so I do not need to inspire another elf to rescue Alethea. One like her does not deserve the fate Ramiel intends for her. It is a fate no anacordel deserves," Boriel said.

Wyn flinched at her use of the name again.

"The Betrayer has no power here." The seraph's voice thundered. "He has forgotten where he came from—that he exists is only because the Creating Light wills it."

"Does that mean Anaweh can snuff him out and save Alethea?" Wyn asked, hopeful.

"It is not Anaweh's way. The Creating Light is in a constant state of creation and would never unmake a creation, even if that creation is tarnishing the fabric of creation," Boriel said, not once implying that she wished Anaweh would undo Ramiel.

Wyn didn't think he could hold that same position. Ramiel was intent on swallowing all that existed into the Void. If Ramiel succeeded, all Anaweh's creation in Teraeniel and Somnaeniel would cease to exist. But Wyn was not an anadel and whatever wisdom they held was beyond him.

"No, Anaweh would never unmake a creature, even if that being is Ramiel. It is not in the Creating Light's nature to destroy or devour," said the seraph.

Wyn nodded. He couldn't imagine the Creating Light destroying anything or anyone either, not even Ramiel. "Why was I brought here?" he asked.

"I do not desire an elf in my care, a child of Eldinare, to venture to the Void without sufficient protection," Boriel said, her voice was more songlike than speech.

"And I find you worthy," added the seraph. A fiery wing extended toward Wyn's chest and he felt his entire being catch flame—his body, soul, and spirit were engulfed in that incredible inferno of pure light—lumenys. Its nature was not soft and quiet and sublime as he had always imagined it. Lumenys was all those but more.

"The Void will try to consume you. But remember, before Teraeniel and Somnaeniel came to be, the Void was everything that Lumaeniel was not. The seven irythil brought the seven erendinth from Lumaeniel and created Teraeniel and Somnaeniel, pushing back the Void in the process. If Ramiel had not sequestered a piece of the Void, it would too have been filled with creation," said the seraph.

"You are not powerful enough to dispel the Void that Ramiel has preserved, but the erendinth will protect you from being swallowed by it," Boriel said.

"How am I to enter the Void and escape? Jaris implied that the only entrance is through death," Wyn said.

"I believe you have already figured that out," Boriel said, looking past Wyn's thoughts and into his memories.

"Yloran Eth Gnashar," Wyn breathed, barely audible.

"She will not help you without cost," said the seraph.

"I don't understand."

"The Luminari are prepared to bring down the Shroud. If you fly there quickly, you may reach them in their greatest hour of need," said the seraph. Boriel smiled faintly and began to fade with the rest of the Empyrean Sphere.

Blinking, Wyn came back to himself to see Dalenya sitting opposite him. She hadn't moved. He readjusted to his surroundings, taking in the dimmer and more subtle light of Stellantis. Dalenya also opened her eyes.

"Tell me where you went," she said.

"I was with a seraph and Boriel in the Empyrean Sphere."

"You can wield lumenys now."

Wyn felt that transcendental erendinth all around him; even at night when the only lights were from the stars. Reaching into himself, he embraced lumenys and washed the terrace in light.

"Give Fendryl my affection when you see him." Dalenya said.

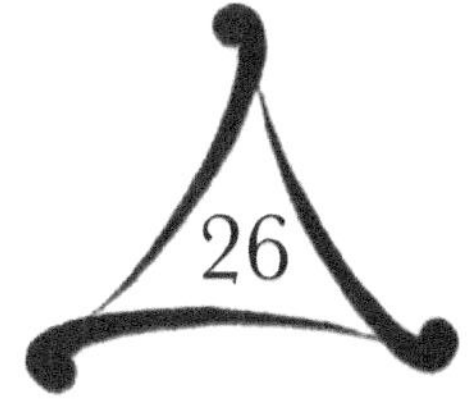

RETICENT HOPE

Devlyn passed through the dark tunnel connecting Gwilnor to the Temple of Ceur. He'd considered walking through the city, but Viren had insisted that he would have had to enlist at least ten additional knights. Having no desire to cause a spectacle or lead a parade, Devlyn had chosen to take the not so secret passage, with only Viren and Aliel for company.

The Seven Chairs had rarely called on him and when they did it was merely for him, as the Lorenthien aryl, to witness their rulings. Truly, despite their brief conversation when he had first arrived, he was beginning to wonder why Velaria had asked either him or Ellendren to be present. The Seven Chairs were more than capable of deciding the Tenebrae's sentence without his input or witness. And to make matters worse, their proceedings were being delayed for some reason.

With his unexpected lack of commitments, he figured he might as well visit the temple. He didn't want to spend the entire time he would be at Gwilnor stolen away to Somnaeniel. He didn't care if Ceurenyl was free of dorthl in the World-in-Between; he only had so much endurance to be in that place at a time and even less to be schooled by Eagan and Abbie.

He tapped on the window that was not a window when he reached the end of the long tunnel. Therril answered happily and Devlyn, Aliel, and Viren passed into the surprisingly bright room to find Therril and

Aaron drinking tea.

"You do realize that I have a real door, yes?" Therril beamed, with a mischievous twinkle in his eye.

"That would have required a military parade through the city," Devlyn said as he hugged Therril.

"Well, you are an aryl now and are to become the Exalted Aryl of Krysenthiel. You'll have to get accustomed to those," Aaron said as he too embraced Devlyn. Viren hung back as much as the small room allowed, and simply nodded to Therril and Aaron as Aliel found the back of a chair suitable for a perch.

"Doesn't mean I can't avoid spectacles like that when I'm able to," Devlyn said, not looking forward riding in a carriage through cities to wave and smile. He truly hoped his future held more than that.

Therril's responding laugh somehow indicated that Devlyn was being foolish for holding such a hope nor would he be successful in avoiding being a spectacle. "So, what brings you here to this humble ei'ceuril's office?"

"Depends; are you going to ask about theoreticals?" Devlyn hadn't touched any of his old schoolbooks since the last time he had seen Therril and had had to apologize for it then.

"I have a hunch that your mind is too preoccupied for the noble art of theoreticals. A clear and leisurely mind is needed for such an august study," Therril said.

"I've never known you to be at leisure," Devlyn replied.

"I've had nothing but leisure and idle time since those terrible Tenebrae took over Gwilnor and refused to allow me back into the castle. Granted, I could have snuck in if I wanted to, but Fyreh and Myrah seemed to be taking care of the students well enough without my help. Still, I'll have to start my classes from scratch when studies resume. But only if whoever is named as the new chancellor deems me fit to teach again." Therril winked.

"I've heard that you're in consideration for the next chancellor,"

Aaron said.

"Wouldn't that be a mistake!" Therril bellowed. "I'm too absent minded for that post. Nothing would get done and I'd have no time to devote to my own studies."

"What more is there to learn of theoreticals?" Devlyn asked, knowing he would regret the question.

"Ho-oh! We've barely scraped the surface. But I'll spare you that; you'll have to at least learn the basics before we have that discussion." Therril laughed and his infectious joy swept the others into a jovial laughing fit. Once they had calmed, Therril said, "As for chancellor, I think Myrah will get the job. Her brother, Fyreh, is of course another contender but Eklean isn't ready for a kien wielder to be chancellor; him teaching their children how to wield is enough for now."

"Even though he's an Eldinari and never lost Balance?" Devlyn asked.

"Those words mean little to those who cannot wield. Besides, Fyreh seems occupied enough with his classes. He'll likely become the new wielding magister, and who knows, the chancellor might have need to recruit more instructors for wielders in the coming months. Our students have a lot to catch up on after the years under Yvonne's, um, tutelage," Therril said, relieved that Gwilnor could resume teaching Eklean's children.

They chatted on and Aaron told Devlyn that Kevn had indeed left the city, intent to reach Septyl. When Devlyn had pressed for specifics, Aaron couldn't give any, only that Kevn felt something, or someone, calling him to Septyl. Devlyn worried it might be a trap, but there was little he could do now. The Luminari would not entertain him leaving them once more to go off on another adventure, unless that adventure led to the Shroud being destroyed and everyone safely returned to Krysenthiel's cities.

"Now tell us, have you truly managed to push back the Shroud—how?" Aaron asked, all too familiar with the Shroud's ugly presence at

Ceurenyl's western edge, ever threatening to push into the city.

"We have." Devlyn smiled as he said it, as though it was too incredible to be more than a dream. "Ellendren and Arlyn were part of the wield as we pushed it back."

"Is being a Phaedryn required?" Aaron asked.

Devlyn scratched his chin and thought about it. Aliel and Tariel were certainly instrumental in pushing back the Shroud, but he didn't know if they were any more necessary than himself or Ellendren. "I honestly don't know. Why do you ask?"

"Because there is a temple filled with ei'ceuril, some of us capable of wielding lumenys, and all of us wanting to see the Shroud banished, if not pushed as far back from Ceurenyl as possible," Aaron said.

"Of course!" Devlyn smacked his head for not considering it sooner. The ei'ceuril and the Temple of Ceur had made Ceurenyl a bastion of protection, not just from the Erynien Empire, but also from the Shroud. And there were hundreds of ei'ceuril here. Perhaps their special connection to the Creating Light would supersede the necessity for them all to know how to wield lumenys. Arlyn had told Ellendren and him, that as an ei'ceuril, he could always call on Anaweh's Light. "How much time do you need to prepare?"

A score of temple knights marched toward the city gates, with Devlyn and Aaron under heavy guard as forty ei'ceuril processed with them to the edge of the Shroud, beyond the temple ward. They went out of the city and down the winding path and then along the river back until it fell away and they stopped as near the Shroud they dared approach. No one wanted to be swallowed by it.

Devlyn had told Aaron what to expect from the endeavor, but he wondered how beneficial his input actually was. After all, he'd fallen unconscious each time he had tried to push the Shroud back. Whether or not Aaron could replicate the wield mattered little right now. Devlyn had only had the opportunity to confront the Shroud in one location and it stretched over vast swaths of land—an entire kingdom had to be freed of it, not just one city. Clara and Therril were among the forty white robed ei'ceuril. And Devlyn knew that Clara was likely the strongest and most skilled wielder in the temple.

Eager to push back the Shroud with the ei'ceuril's help, Devlyn and Aliel bonded, and their light thrummed in the gathering, illuminating the ei'ceuril and knights.

As Devlyn embraced lumenys, he felt his wield join with the ei'ceuril. Most notable of them was Clara and how she interacted with lumenys. She had learned to wield that transcendental erendinth long ago and her abbey in the Ashton Wood had ever sung to the Light. Clara's touch was gentle and powerful, quiet and sonorous. She wanted the land cleansed of the Shroud so it might finally heal.

Building up his wield, Devlyn wove the wields of all the ei'ceuril together, channeling through him, as though he was a conduit. A wave of light rushed toward the Shroud as he released it and it crashed against the Shroud, like water against a cliff. The forces pushed against each other and Devlyn could sense Aaron drawing strength from the temple.

The Shroud felt immovable and Erynel screeched from inside it. "You will not take my empire! I will destroy everything and everyone you hold dear, little Lorenthien."

Devlyn refused to engage verbally with her. He didn't care to play her mind games and instead pushed harder against her Shroud. Erynel cackled in delight at the clash. Clara wove more force in her wield, enough for Erynel to decipher her identity through Devlyn.

"So, the little flower hasn't wilted yet." Erynel's full attention fell on Clara. "How does it feel to have lost everything? Do you miss your precious Aldinare—your sisters and brothers? Do you think they survived the Master's gift? Do you think them wise enough to have accepted it?"

"They'll find their way home to Anaweh's Light," Clara said, having long made peace with the loss of Aldinare.

"None in the Master's realm can escape," Erynel said, then laughed wickedly. "They will be forever trapped, cut off from the lie you believe. There is no mercy in death, only power for those strong enough to seize it."

"Ramiel will not share his power with you. You will wander lost all the days of your afterlife, and even when this world no longer resembles what you knew, still will you wander lost, dwindling, growing smaller and weaker and insignificant, until not even by the standards of the Void will you exist," Clara said, her voice prophetic.

Enraged, Erynel lashed out anew, both in word and in her wield. "You will regret ever drawing breath, slave! The Master will see you reduced and abased, the same as those left behind in your wretched Skyland. Your mind will dull, taking your memories of who you once were, like the rest who belong to the Master's realm. Anaweh will not save you—cannot save you—just as your revered Creating Light didn't save those still on Aldinare."

"Ramiel does not care for you, Erynel. I'm sorry you cannot see that." Clara looked up to the sky, seeking Vespiel, the evening star. Devlyn heard the quiet prayer and recognized that she spoke in High Aelish but could not decipher her words. A surge of strength flowed from Clara and then through Devlyn. Whatever she had done had apparently worked.

Erynel screamed and fled the pulsing light; the Shroud singed at its edges as it too was pushed back. When Devlyn released his wield, Clara went to Therril. They held hands, tears rolling down their cheeks. "They're alive," they said simultaneously, not allowing themselves the hope that anyone could survive the Darkness that had consumed Aldinare.

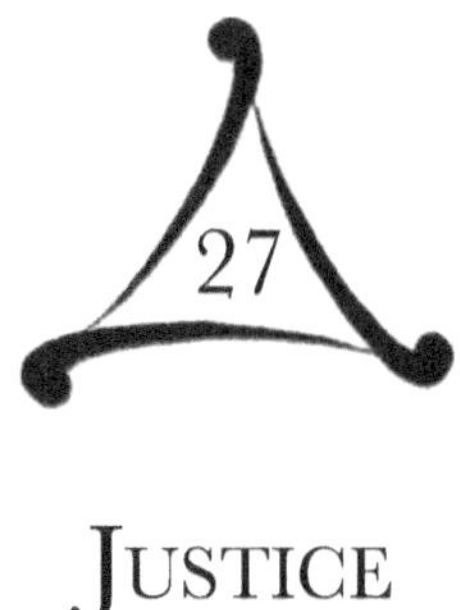

JUSTICE

Velaria sat alone with her thoughts in an unused room near the holding cells where the Tenebrae were being confined. Two weeks had passed since Ceurtriarch Aaron Roendryn had expanded the temple ward to the entire city, giving Velaria and the other ei'ana and knights still faithful to Septyl the edge they had needed to overthrow the Tenebrae and their unrefined kien wielders.

The kien wielders had been returned to the lower levels of the temple, to their previous accommodations, but they were now criminals and not just pampered residents. Velaria was uncertain about what their fate would be and she had discussed it with the other Chairs without reaching a decision. After all, given their forced confinement, Velaria had some sympathy for their wanting freedom, regardless of the cost.

The Tenebrae who had poisoned Gwilnor were a completely different matter. While the men who had spent the majority of their lives locked away in the Temple of Ceur because they could not control the erendinth might have options, these women had not only carried out a successful coup but had allied themselves with Erynor and had forsaken Anaweh, the Creating Light, for the Evil One and his promises of power.

Velaria held no compassion for those women.

She sat at a small table, a simple chair opposite her, identical to the one she sat in. She and the other Chairs of Septyl had spent the past two weeks conducting private interviews with each of the suspected Tenebrae. It had been a lengthy process as a staggering number of women had been isolated in the dining hall the night Aaron had extended the temple ward. Velaria had had her suspicions about which women were still true to Septyl and which were false, but every resident who had not been immediately imprisoned was to be interviewed by each of the Chairs. The women sent to Gwilnor's prisons were known Tenebrae, stripped from their status as ei'ana. Most of those women would not be interviewed. Their guilt was unquestionable.

After Gwilnor's liberation, every day had been the same. Velaria would wake at an early hour, walk through the castle to sit in this small room, listening to the women she had once believed were her sisters defend themselves. Each interview didn't last more than an hour and most of the women spoke freely as they tried to defend their actions and connection to the Tenebrae. Some spoke of coercion and deceit, while others focused on the apparent deterioration and decline of Septyl. One woman even tried to bribe her with a thousand crowns. Velaria wondered whether the woman had offered the same bribe to each of the other Chairs.

Velaria had wanted to speak with Hannah before her trial later that day, but every time she had visited the deposed chancellor, Hannah had kept her lips shut tight and her eyes focused on the door behind Velaria. She had been kept in the Cells of Justice in the Temple of Ceur, where only the innocent were capable of walking across the barrier of light. Jaerol was the only person Velaria had ever witnessed to cross that barrier.

Exhausted, Velaria brushed the red stubble growing on her head. She missed her long hair—it had never been cut so short—but she missed the vines and leaves and flowers that grew from her skin even more. There were many more sprouts now that they weren't being clipped on discovery, but they were too small yet to act as a proper dress, so she wore a regal blue gown, befitting the Chair of Azurelle. She rose to make her way to the Chamber of the Seven Chairs of Septyl. She passed through the castle quickly and descended the stairs that led down to the most secure location in the castle, directly beneath the Chancellor's Tower. Her wise ones awaited her arrival in the Azurelle salon, an anteroom to the Chamber of the Seven Chairs which was beyond the portal at the far side of the salon. Each Chair had a private office here, but they were rarely used as the Chairs also had other offices in their School wings, offices that had windows.

Before Gwilnor had been liberated, each of the Chairs had been assisted by seven wise ones, but now, each School except for Arantiulyn—a thought that brought a slight sense of unease every time it occurred—had several vacancies to fill. Velaria felt sick that she had trusted some of those women in her School's leadership. Even though she had not been the Chair of Azurelle long enough to have selected a wise one yet, she still blamed herself. She should have been able to see through the duplicity.

Velaria nodded at the five wise ones in the salon, then at the two knights pledged to Azurelle when they pulled away the drapery over the portal leading to the Azurelle balcony for her and she went through to the chamber balcony.

Heavy blue drapes hung behind her seat, and the large golden emblem of Azurelle—two naked elves wielding, a dragon behind them—was suspended above it. Seeing the emblem behind the Chair of Azurelle always gave her courage. The motto of the Azurelles came to her mind: *the zealous soul must be temperate.*

She found it appropriate for today. *I wonder what would have happened to these women if they had stayed true to their own School mottos,* she thought.

An empty platform lay in the center of the seven-sided chamber. To have every Tenebrae defend themselves in this chamber would have required an entire year, a year they did not have. Septyl could not waste her resources on these women who had picked away at her foundations. That was the point of the individual interviews. Each Chair met with the various women, each conducting their own judgement, concurring after each day's meetings.

The purpose of this formal meeting was to carry out their judgements and consequent sentences, beginning with Hannah.

"Is this really necessary?" Melanie asked, stirring the weighty silence in the still chamber.

"If you had agreed to holding the interrogations in the temple, this meeting could have happened last week, and we'd be all done," Loretta said.

"I too have voiced my unease about using the temple as such and Phendien has agreed and supported it," Agnelle said.

"The Temple of Ceur ought not to be so abused. Besides, whoever we walk through the Chamber of Light could be guilty of various transgressions, and belonging to the Tenebrae isn't necessarily one of them," Phendien said.

"They're all guilty, and we have better things to do than determine *how* guilty these women are, which, mind you, marching them through the Chamber of Light would not tell us. Our defenses are in shambles and our knights have been busy repairing them. Their work would go much swifter with assistance from all of us and not just the Arantiulyns," Melanie said.

"We've already had this discussion; now can we please move on to carrying out our judgement. The sooner we do, the sooner we can turn to more pressing matters," Paurel said.

A Septyl knight of Azurelle entered the lower level of the hall. "The deposed Chancellor of Gwilnor, Hannah Torin," he announced.

"Bring her forth," Paurel said.

The knight exited, returning moments later with a heavily chained woman. If the knight had not identified her, Velaria would not have known who the woman was without tapping her interior sense. Hannah seemed shrunken somehow, yet defiance screamed on her face. Her kind grandmotherly facade was gone.

Hannah was escorted to the platform at the center of the room, forced to stand throughout the proceedings. Velaria had always thought the custom of having people stand cruel, especially for children seeking admission to Gwilnor, but she felt no remorse now as this woman was forced to stand under the heavy burden of her chains.

"Hannah Torin, you have disgraced yourself, the office of chancellor, Gwilnor Academy, and all Septyl." Paurel paused, allowing her disgust to weigh on Hannah. "Have you anything to say for yourself?"

Velaria had never heard the Chair of Vyoletryn speak with such abhorrence. However, looking down at Hannah, she knew that she would have spoken in the same manner.

Every Chair held their gaze on the woman standing in the center of the chamber, waiting to hear her defense. Velaria did not care what the woman said; her crimes were evident and judgement had already been passed in Velaria's mind.

"I'm told," Hannah started, her voice as soft and grandmotherly as ever, "that you've rounded up every suspected Tenebrae at Gwilnor."

None of the Chairs responded.

"Have you grown so foolish to believe that you could eradicate Septyl's true power? Your Seven Schools and seven erendinth are child's play next to Tenebrae and tenebrys; not even lumenys can stand a chance against the dominant power! Hear me, you Seven Chairs of Septyl—Septyl will always be weak without the unity Erynor provides! And if you believe you have purged Septyl of my sisters, I hope you're prepared to…"

"Get her out of our sight," Paurel said, refusing to allow Hannah to speak another word. The knight returned to escort Hannah back to the temple.

"Hannah is right," Velaria said, breaking the brief silence that followed in Hannah's wake. "We have to be prepared for more Tenebrae living among us. I hate to say it, but we cannot assume anyone is innocent."

"Is that not extreme? We cannot survive if we don't trust each other," Agnelle said.

"After what has just happened, I don't think we can afford to take anything for granted," Velaria said.

"I agree with Velaria," Paurel said, her voice weary.

"What of the other Tenebrae who are currently our prisoners? Following Hannah's performance, does anyone here still believe we need to hold individual trials?" Melanie asked.

"Mother Melanie does have a point," Phendien said. "We simple don't have the time to invest in individual judgements like this; even our individual meetings are wasting precious time that we do not have."

"What of Hannah and Yvonne? They single-handedly did more damage than the rest. To say nothing of them being Tenebrae wise ones." Velaria heard her voice rising, still disgusted with Melanie for refusing to go to the temple and thereby prolonging the judgement and the sentencing. But Velaria could do nothing about that, since Agnelle and Phendien had sided with Melanie for various reasons.

"And how much more severely do we wish to punish them?" Agnelle asked.

"Surely you don't expect them to receive the same punishment as the other Tenebrae," Velaria said, still uncertain about what punishment they might deserve. "They undermined the education of young wielders. And Hannah was surely the one who killed the previous chancellor."

"Poor Oranna." Paurel sighed, sounding just as tired as Velaria felt. "What do you suggest for them that the others would not receive?"

"I think we ought to provide the majority of the Tenebrae with a program that might see them function as ei'ana again one day, allowing them to return to the world and not simply languish in a dark cell forever. To put it plainly, we need them." Velaria hated to admit that last part, but it was true. They would need as many wielders as possible if the Evil One broke free of his prison. And there was a chance some of the Tenebrae did not understand who they were truly aligned with.

"As for Hannah and Yvonne?" Paurel asked.

"I do not think they deserve such concession." *Nor would I trust them,* Velaria thought privately. "I think their crimes deserve a life sentence."

"I tend to agree with your sentence for the broader majority, but what if Hannah and Yvonne are repentant in the future?" Agnelle asked. "Surely, you would not recommend keeping them confined even then."

Agnelle had always had a merciful heart, and for the most part, Velaria admired it, however, it currently appeared unreasonable. She certainly did not want to revisit the Tenebrae once again taking control of Gwilnor Academy. Even though she was willing to be more lenient toward the other Tenebrae, she could not find it in her heart to have any mercy for Hannah and Yvonne.

"Would it be prudent to hold off our formal condemnations until this whole mess is over? This war with the Erynien Empire that is," Melanie said.

"Would that not be irresponsible?" Loretta asked. "We can't simply lock people up without a trial, especially ei'ana."

"The Tenebrae are no longer ei'ana and they tried to destroy Septyl from the inside out," Velaria said, losing patience with the other Chairs. "We cannot wait for a more convenient time."

"What blanket sentence would we assign? Do we lock all the Tenebrae up with Hannah and Yvonne?" Loretta asked.

"They should spend the rest of their days in the darkest and deepest cells we can find," Melanie said.

"As beneficial as the temple ward is, we cannot endorse its continued presence. Our students have been without proper training for over a year," said Paurel. "We will have to either place Yvonne and Hannah under constant supervision, or come up with an agreement with the Ceurtriarch, and have them reside in the temple."

"Is no one else unsettled by turning the Temple of Ceur into a prison?" Agnelle asked.

"I too am bothered, but what alternatives do we have?" Selenya asked. "The temple is the securest location in all Eklean but transforming it into a prison is troubling."

"We've always made it one," Loretta said, almost regretfully. "How many kien wielders have we gathered and put there, never to return to their families? I don't see an alternative."

"What if we established a prison of our own?" Melanie asked.

"That's a possibility, but we do not have the resources to begin such a project, nor to sustain it," Paurel said. "We'll have to arrange something with the Ceurtriarch. I move to inform Ei'denai Devlyn Lorenthien of our decisions here today and hear whether he has any objections to our proposals. Until then, this chamber is adjourned."

Velaria rose and went through the blue drapery and into the concealed passageway that linked her balcony to the salon. Her wise ones looked up expectantly, wanting to hear the final judgement, but Velaria simply pursed her lips and left. She passed through a series of private passages to the Azurelle wing in the Dragon Tower.

Usually, Velaria would wield a globe of light to illumine the darkened passages, but now she was forced to carry a torch, lit by hand. As she walked alone, Hannah's voice echoed in her mind, reminding her that there were more Tenebrae.

Vowing to herself that she would never allow anyone to abuse Gwilnor or Septyl again, she began to consider a new chancellor. Whoever she and the other Chairs selected would have to be beyond reproach, and unfortunately, that number was miniscule. Therril, Fyreh, and Myrah seemed the only likely candidates.

IMPERIAL REQUESTS

Devlyn paced the small room in the North Tower, home to Gwilnor's male dormitory and the knights of Septyl. He had something to ask Liam and Jaerol, who watched him curiously from their seat on one of the beds in the room, while Viren waited outside in the corridor. They knew he wanted something; that much Devlyn had unintentionally gleaned from their thoughts. But neither of them had any idea what Ellendren had suggested and wanted him to ask of Jaerol. And Devlyn was sure that Liam and Rusyl would likely insist they join the dangerous mission as well.

Gwilnor had only just been liberated from the Tenebrae and Devlyn didn't want to place them in harm's way again. Over the two weeks he'd been in Ceurenyl, he had gone through dozens of scenarios, looking for the best way to ask them to do something impossible. He still didn't know how to broach the subject and today was the last day he could ask them.

He couldn't be away from the Luminari any longer—he had to finish removing the Shroud. He'd spoken with Velaria last night and she had reasserted the ei'ana's intent to reclaim Septyl, and that meant that he had to push himself to his limits to free all Krysenthiel's southern territory. As eager as he was to free another city and the Delmira Wood, he knew that Septyl would be given the most attention. The Seven Chairs were ready to return with him to Eandyl today.

But Evellyn was running out of time. As much as Devlyn wanted to prolong putting his brother in a dangerous situation again, something had to be done, and soon. He stopped pacing and looked at Liam who returned the look with a raised eyebrow, as though saying *just ask, already!* Just as he found the courage to speak, Rusyl flung the door open and strode in without knocking.

"That's really not advisable," Jaerol said.

"Your mind is open to mine; I know when to knock, or better, stay away." Rusyl winked.

"No one ever mentions that if you ride a dragon once that it's like a contract with them, allowing them intimate access to your mind," Jaerol said, noticeably trying to lighten the mood.

"I could find someone else to bond with. It doesn't have to be permanent," Rusyl said.

"I wasn't suggesting that. But not even Liam is aware of my every thought like you are."

"For now." Liam smiled. Even after everything he had gone through, he still smiled. Devlyn's guilt flared. If he could arrange it so that only Jaerol could go on this quest, he would. That would be impossible though and Devlyn knew it.

As he drew yet another deep breath and tried to broach the topic, Rusyl said, "Oh, just ask them already. And of course, we'll all go."

"Ask us what?" Liam held Devlyn's gaze.

"It seems that I'm not the only one whose thoughts you listen in on," Jaerol said. "Is that common with all dragons?"

"It was once common among the elves too, but you've all grown young and forgotten yourselves," Rusyl said.

"Sounds dreadful. I would have lost my sanity if I had to listen in on the thoughts of my classmates at the Imperium."

"Devlyn, what did you want to ask of us?" Liam repeated himself.

"It's more of a favor, actually." Jaerol, Liam, and Rusyl listened attentively as Devlyn told them about Alesei visiting the Luminari camp and threatening them, telling them to halt their advances against the Shroud or else she couldn't promise Evellyn's safety in Broid. Even as he talked, he could see them all trying to figure out the best rescue plan.

"After all this time, Alesei is still trying to catch you in a trap so she might present you as a gift to Erynor," Jaerol said.

"Ellendren and Arlyn thought so too, and the high aryls are in rare agreement; I cannot rescue her," Devlyn said.

"So, it's confirmed—she's been in Broid all this time?" Liam had been quiet, but Devlyn could feel his brother's anxiety. Liam's would have been one of the last friendly faces Evellyn had seen before being taken to Broid. At least, the last friendly face still alive. Aside from Liam, none of her family had survived Gneal's dungeons. "What does Erynor want with her? Surely, he doesn't still think there's some sort of weapon hidden in Cor'lera, does he?"

"She is a trophy to him—the same as he would make of Devlyn and Ellendren if he could capture them; just as he did with the Lorenthiens before. A mentor of mine from long ago told me how he likes to collect people, especially powerful people, and degrade them as his slaves. My mentor told me that he feels more powerful with them—they are a reminder of his conquests," Jaerol said.

"This mentor of yours," Devlyn paused as the face of a beautiful woman bloomed in his mind. She had told him that she had known Jaerol and his past lover. "Is her name Yloran?"

"Yloran Eth Gnashar. How do you know one of the Sha'ghol?"

"She nursed me back to health in Lankor."

"Truly? Who would have thought the once terrifying and powerful Sha'ghol would have made a good Crimsyn healer?"

"Even more of a miracle considering she wasn't able to wield in Lankor because of whatever that stone the city floats on is," Devlyn said.

"Be happy it was never placed on your finger as a ring." Liam absently brushed his finger, seeming to check for something that wasn't there.

"A ring?" Devlyn asked.

"A dwarf of Zorik Schtam came here offering *gifts* for Razcul and the Tenebrae. Velaria and I were both forced to wear one of those dorthl rings. While they negated our access to the erendinth, they strengthened Razcul's grasp over tenebrys."

He had only learned that name—dorthl—as the black ooze in Somnaeniel that promised death. How was it here in Teraeniel and how was it a physical substance that could be mined? "Is it the same dorthl as in Somnaeniel?"

Liam and Jaerol shrugged; they knew little of World-in-Between and had never gone there themselves. "That evil substance manifests differently in the different realms. It would be a completely different substance in the Void, and even in Lumaeniel if the Evil One could pry his way into there," Rusyl supplied.

Devlyn worried. Dorthl had only recently started to manifest in the World-in-Between as Ramiel's prison weakened. And if the entire city of Lankor was built on top of dorthl, exactly how long had it been in Teraeniel? Did the Evil One intend to cover the entire world with it as he was currently doing in Somnaeniel? "Has it been here all along?" he asked at last.

"At least in the Shadow Mountains, beneath Mount Cyngol where the Evil One had built his fortress before he was banished," Rusyl said.

"And the enemy can turn dorthl into a weapon, like a verathn to magnify their strength?" Devlyn asked.

"It would seem so. I did not learn of the dorthl rings at the Imperium, but I doubt they are a new creation," Jaerol said.

"As though Razcul wasn't already strong enough before." Devlyn remembered how he had just barely escaped his fight with Razcul.

"He would have been near invincible if Aaron hadn't extended the temple's ward. He died by a blade in the end," Jaerol said.

"And you saved me by doing it." Liam smiled again and Jaerol took his hand.

"I suppose I owed you for saving mine first."

"Should we leave?" Rusyl asked, lightening the mood. Jaerol growled at the dragon in his smaller form, while Liam laughed.

"There's still more to talk of, I think. But, thanks for the offer, Rusyl." Liam turned back to Devlyn. "Have you devised a plan to rescue our mother? I know you want to rescue her yourself, but surely you know it's a trap."

"I do—I know I can't go to Broid. Besides, the Luminari need me here. The longer the Shroud stands, the longer we are vulnerable to Erynor." Devlyn looked up at Jaerol. You're the only one who knows Broid. None of our allies, even those who lived before the Ceurendol War, are familiar with the imperial capital."

"I haven't been home in fourteen years," Jaerol said, crestfallen and clasping his hands together. "I wouldn't exactly be welcomed there either."

"That might be true, but we wouldn't want to be recognized in the first place," Liam said.

"*We?* Me going to Broid is dangerous enough, but Liam, you were just a shadow elf's captive. You're not seriously considering joining me, are you?" Jaerol sprang from his seat, apparently forgetting what Rusyl had already said that they'd all go.

"She might not be my birth mother, but Evellyn treated me as though she was. She doesn't deserve to be Erynor's slave—to be anyone's slave. Devlyn might not be able to go, but I can."

"I've told you what Broid is like. You know how terrible it is there," Jaerol said.

"Which means I'm more prepared than most."

"What if they capture you again? I can't lose you."

"I could not sleep knowing that you were there without me."

Jaerol now paced back and forth before letting out a frustrated breath. "Fine. Will you be joining us too, Rusyl?"

"I don't know a free dragon who has willingly flown toward

Cynethol in the past two millennia."

"You'll only have to fly away from the island," Devlyn said, receiving three very curious expressions. "Queen Alesei only gave us until Meridephaen."

"Of course, she did. Still, that might work in our advantage. The final rounds of the Grand Tourney take place on Meridephaen and Erynor always attends. I doubt he'll take his prized slaves to the Coliseum. We won't get a better opportunity to sneak into the palace," Jaerol said.

"You do realize that Meridephaen is in two weeks, yes?" Rusyl raised a questioning eyebrow.

"Yes, and that's why you will only need to fly away from the imperial capital—I'll take the three of you there and shift back after. How much time do you need to prepare?"

Devlyn hugged Liam again. He had thought Lankor had been hot, but Cynethol in the summer was a whole different level of heat. His feet sank in the sandy beach as the waves lapped against the shore. Stepping away from Jaerol, Liam, and Rusyl, Devlyn shifted back to Gwilnor with Viren. He still had one more meeting before he had to return to Eandyl. He hadn't bothered shifting back to the bedchamber in the North Tower of the castle but shifted to the main courtyard overlooked by most of the classrooms.

Devlyn passed though the arcade, Viren trailing behind him and Aliel hovering over his shoulder. Classes had been suspended for the past two weeks and this area of the castle was practically deserted. Classes would restart soon enough and the students would bring life back into the desolate shell that the Tenebrae had been cultivating.

He paused in front of a familiar door and knocked. "Come in," Kai called from inside. Devlyn pushed the door open to find Kai at her desk.

"Magister."

"Ei'denai." Kai looked up from her neat stack of parchment. "To what do I owe the pleasure? Have you come to enroll in my class for the new term or perhaps explain why you have missed so many of my lessons over the past few years?"

"Um, no, um, sorry about that. I could use more of your classes though, especially now."

Kai offered a tight-lipped smile and her eyes crinkled. Devlyn let out a sigh of relief. He'd thought that perhaps no one had told Kai that he had been kidnapped and everything else that had been happening. "I'm not sure how much more you could learn from my classes. I'll soon be using your negotiations with the Schtamite as one of the most consequential political achievements in the last millennia. To say nothing of the rebirth of Thellion. I suppose young Alexander Vaerin wasn't sleeping through all my classes after all."

"I suppose not." Devlyn laughed as he took a seat near Kai's desk. "I don't feel like I did much with the dwarves though. All we did was talk and remind each other of old promises."

"Do you intend to write the next tome for my class to study too?"

"I don't understand."

"Dialogue and loyalty are possibly the most apt words to use when defining politics, certainly the most practical ones. Well, honest politics that is. There's too much deceit and betrayal in the world these days."

"Well, I still feel the novice when speaking in front of the Luminari aryls. Most of the time I'd rather let Ellendren handle everything."

"She did have the benefit of learning from the last Aryl of Lucillia, as well as living in the center of the Lucillian court before beginning her studies with us here. I hear her sister is just as skilled."

"I still haven't heard her deny anyone anything and that certainly doesn't mean she's agreed to any of it!"

"I should have her in as a guest lecturer someday." Kai folded her hands on her desk. "Is there something you came here to ask of me?"

Kai cut straight to the point. He had no idea how she knew. Hopefully this request would not be as dangerous to fulfill as the earlier one he'd made today.

"Yes." Devlyn shifted in his chair. "I'm sorry to ask this and I don't quite know how to broach the subject."

"Say it plainly and I'll let you know how offensive it is."

"Right…um…you're not from Eklean, are you?"

"Perhaps you do need to return to my classroom more regularly." She held him in her cold gaze anew. "Why do you ask?"

"It's about the Guardian Senate. We're running out of time to reassemble it. The Evil One is growing stronger—we fear it is only a matter of time before he is free of his prison. I'm not familiar with the other continents. I don't know their peoples, customs, histories, or languages. I have no idea if they'll want to rejoin the Guardian Senate or if they've already aligned themselves with Erynor and Ramiel." Devlyn felt himself rush through everything, trying to cover up his poorly phrased question of Kai's origins.

"You shouldn't use the Evil One's name, even if Ceurenyl is warded." Kai stood and crossed her arms behind her back. "Suppose you are right; suppose I was born somewhere other than Eklean and came of my own volition, rather than my ancestors traveling here from a different continent long ago. What is your intent? Do you want a tutor to educate you in the other civilizations across Teraeniel?"

"We must reconnect with the other continents and soon. I'm afraid we're already too late with the Daer Empire. They're setting up colonies in Eklean and enslaving people here. Their arrival is the first contact we've had since before the Ceurendol War. We've had no interaction with Ja'horan or Qien. I have no idea if they'll treat us the same as the Daer have. Will they be enemies to fight off or allies to embrace?"

"I cannot help you with Ja'horan, Daereneth, and certainly not Ogren. I would recommend a visit to the Seafarers of the Jahro Islands if you want to establish a connection with Ja'horan. Just don't accuse them of being pirates. As for the Qien Dynasty, the Misty Sea separates our two continents and those waters are filled with sea dragons at Erynor's command. Those monsters of the deep have kept Qien and Eklean divided for two thousand years now."

Devlyn caught a few key words that increased his excitement at the possibility of Kai going to Qien to bring a message to the Qien Empress. He had no idea how he would deal with sea dragons but imagined a visit to the merpeople was in order. "Will you go?"

"You do realize that most people who have left their homeland have left for a reason, yes?" All the excitement that had been building up deflated. He had not considered that. He understood Jaerol's hesitancy to return to Cynethol, but he had never heard of a reason to avoid Qien. "You also assume, that if I am from Qien, I'd have access to the Qien Empress or to Her Radiance's imperial court," Kai continued.

"Would you?" Devlyn didn't know how else to phrase the question. He now saw the many flaws in his thinking and was suddenly relieved that Ellendren wasn't here to witness this interaction.

"There is another aspect of politics that can never be overlooked." Kai turned away to look out the window.

"What's that?"

"Luck. The empress' name is Qien Wei. The imperial dynasty took its name from the once-divided continent. The first empress did not name her dynasty after herself but took the name of her land as her own. It just so happens that I am the current empress' cousin. I am Qien Kai. As a wielder, I would have been sent to a monastery, one of the central monasteries given my familial tie to the empress. I would never have been permitted to leave after that. My life would have been one of ultimate sacrifice to the Qien Dynasty."

"They kill their wielders?" Devlyn blurted.

"No. But wielders are expected to forfeit everything for the glory and unity of the dynasty." She sighed and looked about her classroom. "Myrah won't be pleased to learn that I'll be leaving."

"Why?" Devlyn asked, barely containing his excitement now that she had agreed.

"She's been named the new chancellor and I am sure that looking for a new politics magister was not on her agenda for getting Gwilnor back in order. I trust you have a way to get me to Zhongshi, the imperial capital. I had to evade giants and sea dragons, cross the Frozen Mountains, the Misty Sea, and then the Purged Desert of Dwonia when I left Qien. That dangerous path is likely the only reason I was never followed. And so, I would sooner not have to repeat that journey again—I am not as young as I was when I first came here."

29

TERMS

A rectangular tent with vertical purple, black, and white stripes waited just ahead, equally distanced between the Daer colony and the Thellish military camp. Alex's usual advisors—Karl, Oliver, Reia, Sara, and Sanjin—accompanied him, but Sanjin had advised that Aen should also join them. It seemed that the Daer held more respect for their adversaries when they were accompanied by their slaves. While Aen was certainly not a slave, nor even an attendant, Sanjin had insisted that the Daer would not see a difference. As Alex's squire and occasional page, they would view Aen as a subservient servant.

Daer in military garb greeted them when they reached the tent. Their lanky elongated bodies were all the more unsettling when they stood rather than sat on their even odder mounts. They didn't smile at their visitors but let a shallow look in their eyes show their contempt. Only Sanjin knew their language; they had exchanged brief words before the guards showed them inside the tent.

Aside from a long table in the center, the tent was sparsely furnished. Alex had difficultly focusing on the furnishings though, distracted by the sight of six slaves waiting by a serving table laden with refreshments. He barely had the chance to pick a seat where he wouldn't see the slaves before they had left their stations to offer wine and meats to the visitors. Fortunately, they weren't captured Thellish citizens and they didn't seem to speak the Common Tongue. As one of them offered a glass of wine to Alex, who was about to shoo the slave away, Sanjin stopped him.

"Let's not end our talks before they start. Denying service from a Daer, a senator no less, is an unforgivable affront," he said.

"What about them insulting me by establishing a colony in my kingdom and enslaving Thellish citizens?" Alex grumbled.

"Just take the wine." Sanjin accepted his own glass and Alex forced a smile of his own and sat with a glass of wine.

Despite having deliberately arrived late, the Thellish party waited without their Daer hosts. While it was annoying, it was not long. The Daer dignitaries arrived, accompanied by yet more human slaves. None of them appeared to be Thellish either, which Alex was grateful for. As the Daer entered the tent, their long limbs moving too lithely for Alex's liking, he wondered which of them was the senator. They were all dressed extravagantly and Alex expected that any one of them could be Senator Koth. Then the gathered Daer parted for a slave-borne palanquin bearing an opulently dressed Daer adorned with many jewels. Layers of silk formed his outfit, knit together with gold chains.

Senator Koth was an older man, much older than the other Daer in attendance. Rather than take a seat, the slaves positioned the palanquin at an empty space at the center of the table, which made it seem more like a throne.

His own slaves attended to him and they were quick about seeing his unspoken desires met. A glass of wine was quickly put in the senator's hand. Senator Koth took a small sip as though to soothe his throat before speaking.

"You must be the young Thellish king I've heard about."

Alex inclined his head, hiding his irritation that the senator had not introduced himself. "Senator Koth, I am Alexander of House Vaerin, King of Thellion."

"Enchanting." Senator Koth's gaze moved to Sanjin. "Prince Sanjin al'Sanhir."

"Senator." Sanjin tipped his head.

"Please accept my condolences on behalf of the Daer Empire, Charren's neighbor and dearest friend."

"Condolences, Senator?" Sanjin blinked.

"Have none of your bejeweled baubles lit up with a message from Karithel? How curious."

"What's happened?"

Senator Koth leaned forward. "Your father, the king, has died. I haven't received any detailed reports myself, but a missive bearing the news did find me in this remote location. Curious indeed that you haven't been summoned home."

Sanjin fidgeted next to Alex and swallowed whatever he'd wanted to say at first, simply saying, "Thank you for the information, Senator Koth." Sanjin had had a lifetime of experience with the Daer and was one of the few people in Eklean who had dealt with them before. Sanjin knew the Daer senators and their noble houses by name. Reia seemed familiar enough with the Sorcery, but Alex didn't think that would be much help in the negotiations. Still, he hoped he wouldn't have to deal with whatever magic the Daer had today.

"Jenyd delivered a troubling report," Senator Koth turned his attention back to Alex. "Threats made to a civilization that extends its hand out in friendship is most troubling to us."

"Establishing a colony in another kingdom's territory without sanction and enslaving its citizens is hardly a display of friendship," Alex said.

"Their lives are improved by our presence. In fact, the people you refer to don't seem to know who you are. They don't identify as Thellish, but rather Perrien."

"Perrien is now a Thellish province."

"So, you acknowledge that it once was not? The people we brought into our empire never knew you as their king. If given the choice, they would not return to you. No one would spurn the opportunity to join our empire."

"I doubt they enjoy being slaves," Karl said.

Senator Koth turned on Karl, his too-long neck extenuating the eerie movement. "Those people lived in shacks on a frozen ocean. Their assemblage of huts was hardly an excuse for a village. They are better served now as part of our colony, graced by our civilization. Their labor will pave the way for their children's children who might one day be Daer citizens."

"Under the Lucillian Concord of 32.4A, slavery in any form is prohibited in Eklean. The concord was necessary following the collapse of the Erynien Empire after they willfully ignored the Exalted Aryl, the High King and High Queen's edict to abolish slavery in Eklean in 1081.2A. The same edict was extended to any nation wishing to join the Guardian Senate," Sara said.

"Daer colonies only answer to the Daer Empire," Jenyd said.

"If that is your position, then you give us no option." Alex ground his teeth. After only two interactions with the Daer, he was finding them utterly intolerable. "You are not welcome in Thellion and your actions are considered ones of aggression. We will have no choice but to respond in like manner if you hold to them. If you do not peacefully vacate Thellion, then we will attack your unsanctioned settlement."

"Quite the reactionary sort, aren't you? Engaging us in battle will only prove the need for our continued presence. Even barbarians can be civilized." The other Daer around the senator snickered. "Our terms, should you deign to accept them and embrace our friendship is that we maintain our colony, establish an embassy in your capital, and in exchange for denying your citizens a path to enlightenment, you will permit us to reclaim our previous colony in Eklean, Daerinth."

"I have no authority over Daerinth. It was a Sorenth city that has pledged itself to the Erynien Empire." Alex considered the other terms. He knew the Daer weren't to be trusted; everything Sanjin had told him about the Daer made him want to push the Daer out of Thellion entirely. Still, if he did, Senator Koth had promised that the Daer would return in larger numbers. Alex didn't have the resources to renew a war in Thellion and also join forces with Devlyn to fight the Erynien Empire. Thellion had to remain stable when he turned his attention to the south again. "Release our citizens, promise to never abduct or engage in slavery here again, and I will permit you to remain in your colony. In exchange for an embassy in Elothkar, a Thellish embassy will also be instituted in the Daer capital."

"So those are your terms?" The senator clasped his hands in front of his chest and leaned forward. The movement made Alex think of a snake—too sinuous for his liking.

"Those are my terms. Slavery, in any form, will not be tolerated here. I don't want to start a war, but if you farm our people for forced labor, we will have no alternative."

"This might be agreeable. We will draw up new terms in your Common Tongue and we shall return to this tent in a week. As a token of our good will and sincerity, we will give your citizens the option to leave us and return to you as Thellish citizens."

"If they choose to stay and remain as laborers for you, you will pay them a fair wage. Let me repeat myself, slavery will not be entertained here, nor is holding innocent and free people against their will."

"It shall be done."

Sanjin's pacing in the command tent back at the Thellish camp worried Alex. The Charrenese prince had yet to say anything and Alex had no idea if his apparent anxiety was in relation to the news of his father's passing or the tentative terms with the Daer Senator.

Aen was the only other person present as Sanjin had asked to speak with Alex privately and didn't mind Aen's perpetual presence around Alex. The squire watched Sanjin as intently as Alex did. While Aen was still young, he was almost a teenager now and was already starting to grow out of his childish appearance. Before long, Aen would be one of Alex's most trusted advisors.

Alex and Aen waited for Sanjin to start the conversation, still having no idea what he wanted to discuss. Pressing his fingers to the bridge of his nose, Sanjin finally stopped pacing. "To start, that meeting could not have gone better. A single colony is a small exchange for war with the Daer. That might still occur in time, but at least for now you will remain in their good graces."

"I'm not sure if I want to be in their good graces. That colony is going to be a thorn in my side."

"I'm sure it will be," Sanjin said.

"You don't want to discuss Senator Koth and his terms though, do you?"

"I do not. I will say that if the terms are drawn up as discussed today, then you should accept them and hurry back to your betrothed."

"You won't be joining us, will you?" Alex noted that Sanjin had removed himself from their plans.

"My father is dead and for reasons unknown, I was not informed. King Sanhir al'Gahnir might have passed his prime in life, but he was by no means elderly. I fear he was assassinated, and whether it was done by the Daer or some other agent, I cannot say. I am the crowned prince though, and upon my return to Karithel I will assume my father's role and receive his crown."

"Is it safe to return to Charren if your father was killed?"

"No, but it is my duty to return."

"How can I help? You've done so much for Thellion."

"I came here with the goal of establishing an alliance. For reasons that we still do not understand, the once peaceful ogres have become aggressive and whoever leads them has near complete control of Ogren. Charren is the last human kingdom with a presence still in Ogren. Our people cannot live on the continent if the ogres continue their raids. As it is, we are having difficulty maintaining our farms. We have stores enough, but I do not know how long they will last. My people will starve if we do not push the ogres back. I know that you will not be able to fulfill our bargain yet, but I'm afraid Charren cannot wait for the conclusion of Eklean's conflict with the Erynien Empire."

It was Alex's turn to pace. His military had grown from a small band of would-be rebels into an army of a kingdom encompassing three provinces that had once been separate countries in their own right. Alex had yet to divide his forces, and truly, by eliminating the renegade Perrien threat led by his uncle, he had hoped to avoid doing just that. Even if he had not come to an earlier agreement with Sanjin, after spending so much time and forging the new Thellion kingdom together, Alex couldn't consider abandoning him.

"We should call a meeting." Alex turned to Aen who immediately understood the unspoken instructions and hurried out of the tent.

"For what? You don't need to bring them in to tell them that I'll be leaving," Sanjin said.

"Well, they'd certainly be upset if you left without saying farewell, but no, that's not why I'm asking them to join us. I want their opinion on how many troops we can send with you to Charren."

"But what about Erynor? Now is hardly the time for you to be sending any part of your army away from Eklean."

Aen returned impossibly quickly with Karl, Oliver, Reia, and Sara. "One of these days your page and squire will have to learn proper manners in respect to ei'ana." Reia glared at an all-too-pleased Aen as she strode in.

"I didn't want to miss anything," Aen said.

"Miss what? Have you come to a decision about the Daer?" Karl asked.

"I already told him he'd be a fool to reject their proposal," Sanjin said.

"I suppose there isn't much more we could get out of it without engaging ourselves in another war." Oliver scratched his chin.

"Agreed, but that's not why I've asked you here," Alex said. "After learning the news of his father's passing, Sanjin can no longer remain with us here in Eklean." Condolences that had been offered earlier were repeated and Sanjin gratefully received them. "With Sanjin returning to Charren, he will be entering a likely hostile environment, to say nothing of the ogre aggression in Ogren. I would like to commit troops to Sanjin for his return to Karithel to help alleviate the pressure his kingdom is experiencing."

They quieted after that. No one outright said that doing so was a mistake, but no one spoke either, hinting at their perceived disapproval.

"I told you, it is not the right time," Sanjin said. "Your full military is needed here."

"You have proven yourself an incredible ally time and time again. It speaks to the merit of your kingdom. To forsake you in your kingdom's time of need would be unforgivable of us," Reia said, turning to Alex. "I regret to inform you, Your Majesty, that I will no longer be able to fulfill my duties as your advisor. I have full confidence that Sara will continue in her capacity and serve Thellion well."

"This is hardly the time to leave," Alex said, taken aback by Reia's resignation.

"My loyalty belongs first and foremost to Septyl. The ei'ana have been sequestered on this continent for too long. I will write to Mother Velaria and the Chair of Arantiulyn, informing them of my change in responsibilities. Doubtless, they will send another ei'ana to replace me," Reia said.

"Forgive me, Reia, but you are wrong in your assumption. I cannot permit you to travel to Charren, at least not without another ei'ana—I too will join you, Prince Sanjin," Sara said.

Alex turned to Oliver, the last of the original group that Alex had traveled with from Ceurenyl. "Do you intend to join them too?"

"Would you have someone else lead your troops to a foreign land and speak and act in your stead?"

"How many troops would you recommend sending?" Alex asked.

Karl chewed on his cheek as he thought. "I reckon the force we have stationed here is prepared for another excursion. They already said their goodbyes to their loved ones. It's also the only company we have stationed this far north."

Empire

Crisp white sand met the gentle roll of the waves. The water was never rough here; children could swim in the sea without supervision, which Jaerol had certainly done when he was a child. He didn't know how often he had run off with Kiron to go swimming. That had continued while they had studied at the Imperium. Kiron had dreamt of leaving Cynethol to travel the world with Jaerol. But Kiron had transitioned to whatever awaited in the World-Beyond and Jaerol had left the island home of the Cyndinari elves. And now, Jaerol was home—a home he never wanted to see again. A home that had had so many happy memories, memories that had soured with Kiron's death.

When Devlyn had asked where he should take them on Cynethol, only one place came to mind—only one place was safe. Teran was the only person on the entire island that Jaerol felt safe to approach. Teran's estate was his first thought, but he knew couldn't openly go there. Jaerol was a fugitive traveling with a lethien and a dragon. His uncle's bought-off staff would sell the information about Jaerol's return and whereabouts before Teran could even pour them a glass of his celebrated wine. Jaerol never understood why his uncle, a vintner, had to worry himself over his competition. Surely wineries weren't that competitive. Instead, Jaerol shared a memory of the beach near his uncle's estate with Devlyn, and without any further preparation, Devlyn had transported Jaerol, Liam, and Rusyl from their tower room at Gwilnor to Cynethol then swiftly returned to Ceurenyl with Viren.

The sand dunes were the same, but storm clouds hung in the sky here too. The storm threatening all Eklean had also looked down on the Cyndinari, cutting them off from the sun. As Jaerol, Liam, and Rusyl waited, listening to the water gently lapping back and forth, Jaerol wondered if his uncle still lived at this estate. Jaerol had left Cynethol fourteen years ago and hadn't had any form of communication with his family since. It wasn't that he had wanted to cut them out of his life; it was to protect them. He had left Cynethol with his ruse intact but he had known that it would not last forever. While the classmates who had become shadow elves decayed and turned fouler with time, deteriorating from the inside out, Jaerol's appearance remained untarnished. He had wanted to protect his family from any association with him when he eventually became a known traitor.

Despite growing up on Cynethol and having once thrived in the island's climate, his years away from home now left him unadjusted to the hotter, humid weather. It was uncomfortable, too hot for the attire he'd worn at Gwilnor. Meridephaen, the peak of summer was only two weeks away. Jaerol had already shed his outer garment and untied the top of his shirt to breathe some. He couldn't remember the last time the weather had been warm enough for him to wear the silks that were common in Cynethol. Liam and Rusyl had also shed and loosened clothing to get more comfortable, and for a brief moment, Jaerol wished that the blue dragon had not joined them. How many times had he whispered into Liam's ear about taking him to a real beach and letting the sun warm their skin? It was hard to do that when there was a third person along, even if it was Rusyl. And on top of that, the storm clouds hid the sun today.

While Jaerol was admittedly happy to finally be in weather warm enough to wear his light silks again, he also wished that it wasn't in the heart of the Erynien Empire. The dangers of being recognized and subsequently turned over to the authorities would easily result in no possibility of ever seeing the sun again. He would never again feel Liam's embrace or the soft touch of silk.

Peeking up the path toward the estate, Jaerol wondered if he could sneak up without any of his uncle's staff recognizing him. Teran likely still had the same staff as when Jaerol had regularly visited. Fourteen years or not, they wouldn't have forgotten him. Better wait until his uncle came to the beach as was his habit. Teran loved taking solace in walking by the water. Just as Jaerol's patience was wearing thin, he heard the approaching swish of footsteps in the sand.

Jaerol signaled the others and they made for the dune grass, hoping it would hide them well enough in case someone other than Teran had come down to the beach. For a fleeting moment, Jaerol fretted over whether his uncle still owned the estate.

The shuffling sounds came closer and Jaerol chanced a look through the tall grass.

"Who's down here? I can see your footprints—I know you're here." Jaerol smiled as he recognized the voice.

"Uncle!" He stood and took in an older version of the uncle he remembered from long ago. His cinnamon hair had faded and his skin, while still the typical Cyndinari bronze, seemed less warm than Jaerol had remembered, to say nothing of the wrinkles lining his face.

"Jaerol?" His voice was thin, mixed with disbelief at the sight of his nephew.

"Uncle," Jaerol repeated and moved to hug Teran.

Teran embraced him in return, kissing Jaerol on the cheeks and holding on to him as though he couldn't quite believe that he was real. "They told us you were dead and a traitor."

"I suppose I am, in their eyes."

Teran squeezed him all the harder. Liam and Rusyl came out from the grass and Teran's mood shifted, somewhat defensive now. "Who are they?"

"This is Liam, uncle. We've been in a relationship for a few years now. He brought me out of the darkness following Kiron's death and my part in it."

"You beautiful boy." Teran pulled Liam into a hug, as though welcoming him into their family.

"And this is Rusyl. We've sort of bonded."

"How does that work with Liam here?" Teran asked, taking a step back in surprise at Rusyl's size.

"Not romantically," Rusyl interjected, towering over the others.

"Well, let's get you three up to the house; you must be exhausted after your journey," Teran said.

"Less than you'd think," Jaerol said. "Is the house safe? I thought your staff reported back to your competitors."

"That hasn't been an issue for a while now, as you'll see." Teran led the way back to the manor. Jaerol had loved coming here as a child and teenager. Not being able to return to Cynethol to visit his uncle and his home had been one of the more difficult parts about his first assignment in Gneal. He had been convinced that he would never be able to visit the estate again. He had assumed that he would have to live as an exile from his people when they learned that he had not become a shadow elf. No one fooled the Erynien Empire and lived to tell the tale.

They passed the vineyard before reaching the manor house. The endless long rows of trellises were still there, but few were properly tended. They seemed to have grown wild and were in desperate need of pruning. The manor house appeared the same from the outside, but something was different. Jaerol had never considered his uncle's home to be dingy before, but it looked as though the entire estate was in desperate need of attention.

"Uncle, what's happened here?"

Teran plucked at a grape that should have been harvested weeks ago. "It's been this way for a few years now. No one will work for me. I'm keeping up with one of the older vines, but maintaining the entire vineyard is too much for just me—I'm also not as young as I once was." Teran offered a weak smile.

"Is it because of me?" Jaerol had feared this. He had distanced himself from his family after he had left for Gneal. No one had known what he and Kiron had done at the Grand Tourney, but Jaerol had always known that it was only a matter of time before the Erynien Empire discovered his duplicity. He had so worried about his family suffering on his behalf.

"Don't blame yourself. I'm proud of you and what you've done, or rather, what you haven't done. I thank Anaweh every day knowing that you did not become a shadow elf. And to see you alive and not dead as we were told…" Teran choked up and Jaerol hugged him.

They resumed their walk and reached the manor house. If the outside looked grimy, the interior was also in a desperate need of a good cleaning. Cobwebs clung to the corners and thick dust lined every surface. Jaerol had always viewed his uncle as a motivated and confident elf; to see the state he had allowed his home to fall into was alarming. Had his uncle truly been this dependent on his staff? Jaerol suddenly worried about how Teran was eating if his chef had also left. Teran did look thinner, nearly gaunt.

Liam reached out for Jaerol's hand. He didn't have to say anything, Jaerol knew what he was thinking just by the touch. Devising a plan to sneak into the imperial palace and rescue Evellyn wasn't going to take a full two weeks. They couldn't do anything to save Evellyn until Meridephaen when they knew that Erynor would leave the palace for the final rounds of the Grand Tourney. Much of the time before then would have been spent somewhat in leisure, devising different plans on how to best sneak into the palace. That wasn't entirely necessary though. Jaerol already had the plan worked out. The best way to get into the palace was through the sewers. While the palace was secure and under heavy guard, no one in Cynethol was stupid enough to break into the imperial palace. Which meant that in the meantime, he could help tidy his uncle's manor.

The image Kai had shared with Devlyn had transported them to a warm oasis. Waterfalls trickled over short ledges into an otherwise still pond. The lily pads had stood out most in Kai's memory, as though they were the most peculiar and interesting feature in the garden. Yet the courtyard was unlike any Devlyn had ever stepped foot in. Two forces dictated the space: nature and order. They weren't necessarily opposing forces here, but neither did they seem in balance.

The courtyard walls formed a perfect square and each wall had a round portal at its center. Everything about the architecture was symmetrical, yet the built environment stopped at the perimeter walls. There wasn't even a path through the seemingly natural garden. An oblong pond filled a third of the courtyard and a shallow waterfall filled whatever silence there would otherwise be here.

"Where are we?" Devlyn asked, startled by the change of scenery from Gwilnor to wherever Kai had envisioned. All he could surmise was that they were in Qien.

"Her Radiance's Palace of Celestial Bells; one of her thousand palaces," Kai said.

"A thousand?" Devlyn coughed. What sort of empress needed a thousand luxurious palaces?

"The Qien Dynasty is quite large and has stretched well over a thousand generations and each empress longs to build her own palace."

"A thousand still sounds like a lot."

"It's also a symbol of unending."

"Are there always a thousand? Exactly a thousand?"

Kai glared at Devlyn, who had only just withdrawn from Aliel. "With each additional palace that is built, one is released from the imperial household. The empress visits all her palaces during her coronation, visiting each of the one hundred kingdoms that form the Qien Dynasty. Each kingdom has ten palaces."

"And where is this Palace of the Celestial Bells?" Devlyn asked.

"It is the empress' least favorite."

"To avoid being caught?" Devlyn surmised. Perhaps Kai didn't want anyone to know she had returned yet.

"Because she knew We would be here."

Devlyn spun about, but Kai already faced the speaker. A red and gold gown unlike any fashion he was familiar with clung to the woman's form. Her eyes were the same as Kai's, a startling icy blue, and she carried herself in the same manner as Kai did, or rather, as Devlyn had always known Kai to. But now, Kai knelt before the opulently clad woman who could be none other than Empress Qien Wei.

"Foolish of you to not kneel." Qien Wei stared at Devlyn. In her eyes, he was but a teenager who had snuck into her palace without her authority.

Swept away by the empress' inherent authority, Devlyn moved to kneel, but Kai stopped him. "It is not proper for you." She kept her eyes on the ground, not daring to look at her empress.

"It is proper for all who step foot on this land, and in Our own palace no less."

"Forgive me, Your Radiance, cherished hope of the hundred kingdoms, this is no ordinary elf I bring before you."

"And what sort of elf is it that We speak with?" Aliel flew down from his perch, unseen until now, and shifted the light in the courtyard as he hovered by Devlyn's head.

"Ei'denai Devlyn Lorenthien," Kai said.

Reflecting on meeting the Qien Empress, Devlyn could only scratch his head at the all too brief encounter. Upon hearing his name, Qien Wei had vanished in a whirlwind of fabric out the portal, although a different portal from the one she had used to enter, for she had to cross the entire courtyard to do so. Eight robed men and women had come in after the empress had gone, all wearing what appeared to be ceremonial attire, the men in orange and the women in red. Their hair was all shaved to the scalp and Devlyn had almost missed that the ones in red were women. The four women had taken Kai through one portal while the four men had escorted Devlyn through another. Curiously, Aliel had chosen to remain in the courtyard garden.

The men had led Devlyn to a quiet chamber that felt very much like a chapel, only he didn't think the Creating Light was worshipped here. While it was different from any chapel he was familiar with, it shared the stillness he had learned to associate with holy places. Before they had been separated, Kai had told him he could the trust the monks.

Only one of them stayed in the room with him, standing with his back toward the exit and staring at the round sand pit in the room's center. Unlike the garden he had been brought from, this space had no distinction between nature and order. The pit of sand, while natural, was in a perfectly round circle, and not a grain of that pristine sand was out of place. The surface appeared as though it could be solid stone.

Tired of waiting and feeling like he'd introspected enough, Devlyn moved toward the round doorway. The monk shifted his weight and placed himself between Devlyn and the exit.

"I would like to leave," Devlyn said.

The monk replied, but not in any language that Devlyn recognized. His body language communicated his reply well enough though. Another man entered behind the monk, this one obviously not a monk as he had a head of thick black hair and his outfit was quite different.

"You should not have been in the water garden—men are not permitted."

"And who are you?" Devlyn was grateful that he spoke the Common Tongue.

"That is not important. What is important is why you have returned after your people abandoned us for fifteen hundred years."

"Abandoned?"

"Do not think our memories are short because we are mortal, elf."

"Why would I think that? You realize that I'm also mortal, yes?"

"Curious." The man drew near. "Is this the case for every elf?"

"Only the Luminari and Cyndinari elves are mortal now. The Jewel of Life is inaccessible; Erynor ensured that."

"Ah, the promise of immortality. Did you know that some of the Cyndinari also came here, promising just the same? Apparently, it's a pastime for you elves. Funny though, neither you nor the Cyndinari have that which you seek to barter with."

"Barter? I didn't come here to barter."

"Are you so sure? You return Her Radiance's favored cousin and you have no intent to barter? Curious indeed."

"I didn't realize their relation until this very day."

"If not to barter, why then did you come all this way to Zhongshi?"

"My people are trying to reclaim Krysenthiel, even as the Erynien Empire thwarts our every step. I didn't intend to remain here after bringing Kai—I cannot. I have to return to my people. I asked Kai if she would return to her homeland and approach her empress on our behalf. We hope to reestablish the Guardian Senate and we'll need the world's leaders to come together to fight the growing threat of the Evil One before everything turns to shadow."

"I would not presume to speak on Her Radiance's behalf, but Qien is not in the position to look outward. We have our own problems to see to at present. The hundred kingdoms and their kings squabble among themselves. Some fight for more territory, others for wealth, and still others seek power. But a troubling thread knits them together, an increasing disdain for Empress Qien Wei and the Qien Dynasty. There is even a rumor of one of those kings calling himself an emperor with a mandate from the living gods." The official turned and left Devlyn with the younger monk.

Devlyn could already hear Kai reprimanding him for not knowing how to properly communicate with the Qien Dynasty. Speaking another nation's language was a sign of respect. Unfortunately, Devlyn had never learned this foreign tongue. He wondered if he would have learned it at Gwilnor if he had stayed longer—would he have received a full education if Alesei had not kidnapped him? Alesei might not have set the current events in motion, but they were irreversible and right now, the Luminari needed him. They needed to reclaim Krysenthiel. He had to get back to them. He had spent enough time away.

As he tapped that place deep within his heart, he felt Aliel, still perched in the water garden. *We should return to Eklean*, Devlyn conveyed.

Not yet. I think the empress intends to meet with you.

How are you so certain? She vanished the moment she realized who I was.

You and Kai startled her. She was not prepared to receive the Lorenthien aryl.

Withdrawing from their connection, Devlyn walked toward the round sand pit in the room's center. He crouched at the edge and examined the smooth surface. The sand was so fine and perfectly still that it looked like a solid stone slab. As he reached out to touch it, the monk said, "Don't," in the Common Tongue.

"You speak the Common Tongue?" Devlyn had assumed that the younger monk didn't speak the Common Tongue used in Eklean.

"I'm gifted with languages. Not that I have the opportunity to use them often."

"Why didn't you speak to me earlier then?"

"Talking is only one part of communication. Listening and watching are undervalued."

"You sound like someone I used to know, well, two people, I suppose." The memory of Alethea disappearing into that storm cloud flashed through his mind like lightning. "Will you tell me your name? I'm Devlyn Lorenthien."

"Qien Di."

"So you are related to the empress?"

"I am Her Radiance's son. You should not have been in the water garden; it was not proper."

"That other man said the same, the one who refused to tell me his name. Why is it not proper?"

"That was Bon Li, the prime minister." Qien Di bowed his head in respect, as though simply speaking someone's name warranted reverence. "Water is proper to women, as is air. Stone and fire are proper to men. Our world exists in harmony, a series of polarizations existing in balance. The heavens and the world are separate, their perfect symmetry allows the harmony of creation. Life and death, nature and built, water and fire, women and men. We all come together at the moment of celestial unity, but otherwise, we must exist separately to maintain harmony."

Devlyn puzzled over what Qien Di saw as juxtapositions. It made little sense to him. Creation didn't exist in balance by having things separated. "Is the water garden reserved for women or kiara wielders?"

"As monks, we are confined to our monasteries. A group of us are selected to attend the empress, though not as servants for she has plenty of those, but as spiritual guards and guides. I was only just brought to Zhongshi. As Bon Li mentioned, the Qien Dynasty is threatened. The empress has already suppressed one rueful king bent on war. He's been exiled and his oldest son and heir, only a child mind you, has assumed his place. A regent who supports the Qien Dynasty is effectively running that kingdom."

"Where were you before coming to Zhongshi?" Devlyn asked.

"Beishi Monastery. It's one of the four central monasteries. Each of the auxiliary capitals has one, well, one nearby. Monasteries wouldn't be effective if they were in built in cities."

"Are there only four?"

"Far from it. Those four maintain harmony for the whole dynasty. Each kingdom has two smaller monasteries, one for women and one for men."

"Your kien and kiara wielders are separated? How do you learn to wield in balance if separated?" Devlyn frowned, suddenly worried.

"We are not wielders. We are simple monks preserving harmony in the Qien Dynasty," Qien Di said.

Devlyn was about to object; Kai had told him that the monks were selected solely based on their ability to wield. She would not have been given a choice about joining a monastery if she had stayed. Instead, he asked, "What made you want to become a monk then?"

"We do not choose to become monks ourselves. Monks are able to see who the heavens have selected to enter the monasteries and maintain harmony. It is a great honor to be told you have been chosen."

Devlyn again considered telling Qien Di that he was a wielder. The monks were able to sense those like themselves because they too were wielders. Devlyn paused for a moment. Qien Di had just told him that there were two hundred monasteries scattered across Qien, not including the larger four central monasteries, and they were all filled with wielders, whether they knew it or not. "Exactly how large are those monasteries?"

"The central monasteries are quite large; my community at Beishi was around four hundred. The smaller monasteries average around thirty monks."

Devlyn stifled his gasp. The Qien Dynasty had an incredibly high number of wielders who could potentially help sway the direction of Erynor's war or even thwart the Evil One.

"You should meditate and prepare to meet Her Radiance. Talking with me will do little to prepare you to meet my mother."

"Will she see me?"

"Her Radiance would not have had you brought to this chamber otherwise. Granted, you've spent most of your time here talking and not meditating. Quite the opposite of what this chamber is intended for."

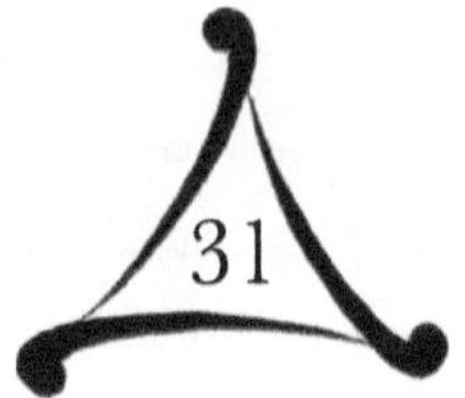

HARMONY AND POWER

Without any warning, Qien Di had told Devlyn that it was time and together they had come to wait before these great red lacquered doors. The doors were inlaid with intricate gold channels, and led to the imperial throne room, but they had remained closed.

Devlyn couldn't help but be impressed by everything he had seen as they had walked through the Palace of Celestial Bells to the doors. The architecture was entirely different from any he had seen before. Unlike many of the human castles and palaces in Eklean, there was nothing cold or chilling about this palace. While the structure was still built of stone, it was softened and warmed by paper screens, red lacquered wood, and thousands of tiny bells hung on strings that rang gently with the wind.

Qien Di waited beside Devlyn, wearing his orange robe. The tiny bells continued to chime just as a much larger bell bonged from above. Devlyn hadn't noticed, but a massive bronze bell hung directly above the great doors to the imperial throne room. Eight resounding bongs echoed before the doors slowly swept open. They scraped across the stone floor, an indent in the floor showing where they had swung for thousands of years. They stepped forward into the room and Devlyn saw the imperial throne a great distance away. Red lacquered columns supported the high vaulted ceiling. All the columns had jade statues twirling up their shafts; as they walked past them toward the throne, it took Devlyn only a moment to realize that the jade statues were carved as dragons. They were very different from the dragons Devlyn knew. These looked like serpents with long whiskers and manes that made their head look twice as large. But there was no mistaking that they were dragons.

The throne was carved of the same jade and it too took on the resemblance of a sinuous dragon. It filled the entire width of the far wall and it looked as though the empress sat on a living dragon and not a carved seat. When Devlyn had first met Empress Qien Wei, she had been wearing a scarlet outfit accented with gold. Now, she wore the opposite. It reminded him of Ellendren when she wore her gold lierathnil, only Empress Qien Wei's gown was accented with red scrollwork. The empress shone just as brightly as any Phaedryn would when adorned in gold.

Devlyn almost missed Kai kneeling at the clawed foot of the Dragon Throne. She too had changed and her head was now cleanly shaved, the same as Qien Di's, and where Qien Di wore the orange monk robe, Qien Kai wore red.

"Come forward." Qien Wei's voice resonated with power, filling the massive throne room.

Devlyn and Qien Di approached the Dragon Throne. When Devlyn stopped in front of the empress, Qien Di knelt by another clawed dragon foot, mirroring Kai with the empress between them.

"Qien Kai has told us much of you, Ei'denai Devlyn Lorenthien. While it would delight us if you knelt in our presence, We would not demand it a second time. Know that you are the first to receive such an exception since *I* first sat on the Jade Dragon, Guanxi. It is not to your title or future throne that We grant this exception, but rather because the heavens have blessed you with a phoenix. A living god has not been seen awake in a very long time."

"A living god?" Devlyn was confused. Aliel was an anadel, not a god.

"A difference of language. We have never fully understood how the elves' relationship with the gods work. We at first thought it a lack of reverence, but our gods have told us otherwise. We were told that the elves were selected long ago because of a choice they made in the Dawn Age, a choice which blessed them." The empress paused, waiting for Devlyn to acknowledge her statement.

"You refer to the elves' choice to remain in the Valley of Saeryndol and to remain unchanged from Anaweh's original design?"

"As you know it, yes. Qien Kai has told us that you have come here knowing little of the Qien Dynasty. She has already apologized profusely for your lack of understanding our language."

"That is true. Qien Di, your son, has shared some of this great dynasty's long history and current challenges with me."

"And what part of our history has Qien Di shared with you? How Qien Ji stood up to the hundred kings, started the Women's Revolt, and united the hundred kingdoms as she founded the Qien Dynasty? How the jade dragons have been frozen in jade since the betrayal, depriving much of the continent of rain since? Or how your ancestors once came to us regularly as friends?"

"Again, I know too little of your dynasty and its rich history. I must admit though, your monasteries are intriguing. Can all the monks wield the erendinth?

"Our monks are not ei'ana. They ensure harmony," Qien Wei said.

"But they could be." Devlyn glanced at Kai.

"Long ago, when the elves still lived among the heavens, and before our dynasty dawned, a terrible beast ruled the continent, a dragon unlike our living gods. The jade dragons fought daily against the great dragon; every night, they subdued him to keep the continent from shattering, but every dawn, the fight resumed. The incredible energy pouring off the jade dragons was on constant display. A child who lived near the great volcano that was the great dragon's lair watched the jade dragons fight the beast every day, striving to heal the continent and saw that the beast was subdued every night. The child learned harmony by imitating the jade dragons and so, the first monk was born.

"One day, the child followed the jade dragons up the volcano's slopes, carefully avoiding the lava flow, for the child could not fly as they did over the molten rock. The child witnessed the unending struggle firsthand. Replicating the actions of the jade dragons, the child joined them and the great dragon was subdued earlier than on any other day. Until the moment the child joined them, there had been no change.

"The jade dragons took note of the child monk and in the extra time they had gained, they taught the monk more of their ways. Other humans soon flocked to the monk and dragons to also learn. The great dragon was subdued earlier and earlier every day as more monks joined the battle. In an effort to seal the great dragon away, four of the jade dragons bonded with four monks, and from four points they struck the beast. They did not stop their assault that night but continued for a whole year. Other monks and jade dragons joined to supplement the paired monks and dragons. Four monasteries were built at those locations, each housing one of those four jade dragons, still waging their silent war with the great dragon."

"This dragon—" Devlyn started, thinking of what sort of beast could rule a continent and resist what seemed to be a dragon flight he was unaware of. "Who else knows this story?"

"Every child in the Qien Dynasty knows this story. The hundred kingdoms were only formed following the beast's demise. And it's for that reason alone that the kingdoms do not interfere with the monks and the monasteries. Not even We, as empress, would impose on them."

"Has this dragon ever woken?" Devlyn asked, fearing the answer.

"Only once, and that is a dark day in our history." Qien Wei seemed to gather herself, her voice not as strong. "A woman came to Xishi Monastery. She knew enough of our customs to go to a monastery that only had women monks, where men were not permitted. Our monks knew of the elves at that time, but few had met them. A red dragon had carried the woman to the monastery. Unlike the jade dragons that we knew, this one had wings and was not as long. Given that a living god had allowed her to fly on her back, the monks welcomed the elf into Xishi Monastery. The monks have never made that mistake again—not in any monastery. The elf attacked the monks, disintegrating them with her foul lightning. She left Xishi to burn to ash as she flew on her dragon to the volcano's summit. All Qien quaked as the great beast roared once more. We feared the monasteries had failed and we would return to those dark days as fire fell from the sky as would rain. Monks flocked to Xishi from the surrounding monasteries. The beast was again subdued and we never heard of that woman on the red dragon again. Some legends to the south hold that she was seen flying away on her dragon."

"Erynel Meriden." Devlyn breathed deeply.

"The mother of the Erynien Emperor?" Qien Wei asked.

"She mated with that beast and delivered his son, bringing forth a draelyn born of the Dark Flight, into the world. Like every other woman, Erynel died as she gave birth to a dragon's child. The dragon the monks have been holding back is not just a dragon of the Dark Flight; it is Tolvenol, Primus of the Dark Flight, and Erynor's father." Devlyn no longer had any desire to ask the monks to join Eklean in their war. The monks were already engaged in their own fight. And if they failed and Tolvenol was freed, the Evil One's escape from the Void would be all but guaranteed.

"She is dead then," Qien Wei said.

"That's complicated. Erynel Meriden was—is a Sha'ghol. The Evil One has held on to her soul in the Void and released it back in Teraeniel as the Shroud," Devlyn said.

"A fitting guise for one as evil as she. Qien Kai has shared that you came here with a request for Us. She said that you had intended that she ask in your stead, but she knew that would sour any future friendship. So now, We ask you, Ei'denai Devlyn Lorenthien, what do you request of the Qien Dynasty?"

Devlyn had been thinking of how he was going to ask this from the moment he had first met Empress Qien Wei. It had been rolling through his mind, even as he spoke with the prime minister and then Qien Di in the meditation chamber. He had thought of little else as he had walked from that chamber to the great red lacquered doors.

"The Luminari elves strive to reclaim Krysenthiel. We intend to recover all that we have lost, what was stolen from us, including our Life immortal. While the Erynien Empire is a very real threat, the Evil One has all but dominated the World-in-Between. We fear it will not be long until he escapes the Void. Teraeniel's only hope of surviving his return is if we come together to stand against him, the same way that your continent came together to subdue the Dark Primus."

"What do you request of the Qien Dynasty?" she asked again.

"Rejoin the Guardian Senate when it is reestablished."

"We remind you that we never withdrew. Sea dragons severed us from Eklean and they remain in the Misty Sea to this very day."

Perhaps the merpeople can help, Aliel conveyed.

I don't know how Alethea contacted them before. And neither has there been any news of Ferinn and the Meridean Conclave, Devlyn conveyed back.

"Ei'denai?" the empress interrupted his private communication with Aliel.

"We'll have to devise a way to deal with the sea dragons. Exactly how closely related are they to your jade dragons?" Devlyn asked.

"They once thought of each other as kin. We do not delight in the idea of slaughtering living gods. We might be in in the midst of a drought, but We would never suggest pouring forth a new river with the death of a sea dragon. Still, they were the ones to betray the jade dragons. It is they who are the reason our living gods have turned entirely to jade."

Devlyn finally understood. The jade sculptures in the throne room were not carved, but frozen. There had to be over fifty dragons twined around the columns, and then there was the massive dragon that Qien

Wei sat on—Guanxi. Devlyn's eyes widened in understanding as he looked about the imperial throne room once more. "How?"

"Betrayal. Make no mistakes, We know Erynor was involved. To learn that he is the spawn of the great dragon who has plagued our continent for as long as our memories stretch is discouraging. We have no idea what he promised the sea dragons, but they have ensured we never set sail from Qien."

A renewed sense of urgency sprang in Devlyn. He had to reach out to the merpeople, but he would have to deal with Erynel and dispel the Shroud first. Time was running out. "Before I leave, do I have your assurance that you'll rejoin the Guardian Senate?" he asked, more desperate then he intended.

"As *I* already said," Empress Qien Wei rose to her feet from her Dragon Throne—not a throne, but the jade dragon, Guanxi, "We have never withdrawn our support. Rebellion and civil war might be imminent here, but we will not forsake that august body."

———————————————

Jaerol had left his uncle's estate well before dawn to reach Broid before anyone could notice him sneaking into the city—but more importantly, before the others at the estate could stop him. He walked down a familiar street. He tried to avoid these. Anything which was familiar to Jaerol was also dangerous. This was not the street he had grown up on, but it was the street Kiron had. Even as he tried to avoid looking at the house he knew too well, Jaerol found himself stopping in front of it.

Burnt yellow stone with a hint of red marbling formed the building, the curvilinear lines vastly different from the architecture of the Luminari elves. He had a passing thought that the Eldinari elves' architecture was probably unique in its own way as well, but he hadn't visited the Eldin Wood to judge for himself. Proud columns and luscious arches formed the building, similarly to the others around it, crafting a single city in an artistic manner. There was a beauty to the city of Broid, but the entire place was tainted, corrupted. The lavish architecture was empty to him now.

An overwhelming urge to destroy the entire city came over him. He recognized the all too familiar feeling boiling in his chest as he remembered the dreadful day he had been forced to murder Kiron. He'd refused to steal his spirit though and become a shadow elf but had made everyone believe that he had. If he had not, they would have immediately killed him and Kiron would have died for nothing. Jaerol had once wished they had.

Suppressing his emotions, Jaerol pushed past the house, and followed the curve of another familiar street he should avoid. Years had passed since Jaerol had lived here, more than a decade, but he still feared being recognized so he kept his hood up, despite the humid temperature.

The street opened onto one of Broid's main thoroughfares, a broad boulevard with trees of red and orange flowers along the edges. The grilae trees still bloomed, marking Broid as a Cyndinari city. Jaerol always found it odd how the ancient Cyndinari—the elves responsible for the loss of the Skylands—had brought the grilae trees to the land below. Jaerol had not tasted the fruit of the grilae trees in over a decade; none had been shipped to his post in Gneal and getting any in Ceurenyl was a preposterous idea. His mouth watered as he remembered the taste.

"Go on, grab one," said an older elf who had stopped beside him.

Jaerol had not realized that he'd paused to gawk at the tree. "Perhaps another time." He turned to walk away, not looking at the other elf.

"I remember you."

Jaerol froze.

"You might be taller now, but who could forget that happy child? You and Kiron were always together; don't think we didn't know what you two were to each other."

Jaerol turned to the elf and recognized one of Kiron's old neighbors. "We used to call you old Zara."

"Oh, yes, you both thought I had lost my hearing and my wits."

Zara smiled warmly at Jaerol. "Come with me; I would like to make you breakfast."

"I really can't," Jaerol said, even though he was hungry. He had spent the past week cleaning his uncle's manor house, but every morning before the others woke, he had snuck into Broid. The city was just as he remembered it. Liam, Rusyl, and Teran were going to be furious with him when they discovered what he had been doing every morning. Only Teran would have been able to walk freely in Broid, but he would have drawn too much attention. Everyone knew Teran and his connection to Jaerol had made him all the more notorious. Jaerol had hoped his hood and fourteen years away would have been enough to let him go about in secret. That was clearly not the case though. Zara knew exactly who he was.

"I won't accept no for an answer. And it's best an unfamiliar elf is not seen prowling the streets before the sun rises."

He thought about running. He could easily outrun Zara, but that would be more suspicious than a hooded elf in the middle of summer walking through Broid before dawn. Without much choice, he nodded his consent and followed Zara back to Kiron's street. Zara's home was several buildings over and on the opposite side of the street from Kiron's old home.

Closing the door behind them, Zara invited him deeper into her home. The entry led to a small parlor, and a long corridor led from the parlor to the rest of the house. Zara turned into the dining room, with warm colors on the walls and furniture embellished with ornate carvings.

"Please, have a seat," she said, leaving Jaerol alone while she went into another room.

"Can I help you with anything?" Jaerol asked.

"Not at all," she replied before the door swung closed, allowing a glimpse of the kitchen behind her.

Jaerol chided himself for his stupidity in acknowledging who he was. Now he was alone with another Cyndinari elf in her home. There was no telling who else was here in this house. For all Jaerol knew, Zara could be sending messages to the authorities as he sat at her table. He didn't know if they would drag him to the Imperium or the palace to be dealt with. The chance of anyone in Broid showing any manner of kindness was laughable.

Memories of the crowd cheering when he'd killed Kiron at the Coliseum flooded his mind. Those same cheers kept him up some nights, and Liam would rub his back or chest to help him fall back to sleep.

Allowing Liam to follow him to Cynethol was a mistake. The last time Jaerol had been here with someone he cared for had ended terribly. The thought of any harm coming to Liam consumed him with dread. The only positive side was that Jaerol could not be forced to kill Liam in the Grand Tourney.

Zara returned with a platter of fruit, bread, and jam.

Jaerol's mouth watered at the grilae fruit, mashed into the recognizable jam he had loved so much as a child. Smiling at Zara, he blushed when his empty stomach rumbled.

Zara smiled, wrinkles creasing her face as she gestured at Jaerol to eat.

Grasping the red-orange fruit, Jaerol took a mouthful and the juicy fruit dripped down the corner of his mouth. His taste buds exploded. He had never forgotten the taste of the grilae fruit, but he had not realized how much he had missed it.

"Not everything of Cyndinare is evil," Zara said, her smile weak now.

Jaerol looked uneasily at Zara as she frowned.

"I know what they did to you—what they made you do. I don't expect you to ever forgive us for our twisted traditions, but Cyndinare will ever be part of who you are. You've learned the best of who we are and left the majority of our sins on this island with us. There are few among our kin who can claim to have done so."

Jaerol had moved on to the bread and jam. He chewed slowly as he listened but remained leery of Zara's next actions.

"You must wonder why I invited you in. Surely if anyone else recognized you, I would be placing myself in remarkable danger."

Jaerol's mouth was full so he nodded instead of speaking.

"When I was young and beautiful, I was a serving girl at the palace. Erynor only permitted those who met his physical standards, and were a pleasure to his sight, as palace servants. I still have contacts with some of the palace's personnel. I've watched your movements over the past week, and your gaze is always set on the palace. I know who Erynor holds inside."

Jaerol had stopped chewing. Holding the half-eaten bread, he looked at Zara, worried about how much she had gleaned from his actions. How careless had he been? His worry about Zara betraying him grew. But she had welcomed him into her home and fed him breakfast. He had begun to trust her during their brief encounter, and he had known her when he had been a child. Still, if she had noticed him this past week, surely there were others in Broid who had as well. Were they waiting for something? Did they know why he had come back to Broid?

"To my knowledge, she is safe."

"How can I get her out?" Jaerol was less concerned with others recognizing him than he was with accomplishing his mission. They could leave the island after rescuing Evellyn.

"You cannot when Erynor is in the palace. Such an attempt is a death sentence." Zara took a bite of the grilae fruit herself. "But you already know when he'll be out, don't you?"

Jaerol nodded, worried about confirming his plans to this elf. "How can I get in? Where is she kept?"

"I will help you, for a price." Jaerol felt his muscles tense. There always was a price. Cyndinari did nothing if they did not directly benefit, even a sweet old woman. "How many will need to get into the castle?"

"Only me," Jaerol lied. He would not let anyone know that Liam was here.

"You do look handsome enough to be one of Erynor's personal servants. Fortunate that you never stole Kiron's spirit, for if you had become a shadow elf, your looks would have faded long ago. Perhaps I could arrange a meeting with my contacts in the palace. Like I said, not everything of Cyndinare is evil."

"What if someone recognizes me?"

"Few see a servant's face in the palace and not because they are veiled. Those in the Erynien court do not care about servants. And while Erynor knows your name, he would not remember your face."

"When will you try to get me in?"

"Come back tomorrow. I'll have everything arranged."

"But how will you manage this?"

"You think no one has ever smuggled anything in or out of the palace before? Palace servants have little love for their cruel master. We know better than most what evils he has tied us to. The whispers leaving the castle terrify me. After all my long years of listening, I have never been so scared as a I am now."

"Your price?" He hadn't forgotten.

"When you return home again, do not bring fire down on us all. Broid is a city of pride, and we are lost in our vices."

TROUBLED DREAMS

Devlyn slept deeply that night. He was exhausted. In a single day, he had gone from Ceurenyl to a Cyndinari beach outside Broid, back to Ceurenyl and then to Zhongshi, another imperial capital on a different continent, met with Empress Qien Wei, then back to Ceurenyl only to return to Eandyl with the Seven Chairs. A number of others had also journeyed back to Eandyl with him, Andrew among them. He had returned late last night and was relieved when he woke that even Eagan had allowed him to sleep undisturbed.

Once he woke, he soon learned that the Luminari had not sat idle over the two weeks he had been in Ceurenyl. Ellendren sat at the vanity brushing her hair in the morning light while Lyren drew a bath for him. Devlyn waved groggily at Ellendren's back and pulled the blankets over his face to hide from the sunlight spilling into the bedchamber.

"I'm afraid there isn't time for that today," she said.

"Why not?"

"A group of elves are starting their journey west for Verenthyl to-day. Only Eandyl's citizens and those destined for Tenyl, Winstyl, Reinyl, and Arenthyl are to remain here."

"When was that decided?"

"While you were gone, I'm afraid. Our scouts have been seeing increased movement by the Cyndinari; they are no longer limiting them-selves to the Sorenth ruins. Jeanne fears that they intend to trap us here with a siege if we stay much longer. She also believes that they've been reinforced by one or more of the Erynien Empire's legions."

Devlyn allowed Lyren to guide him out of bed and toward his bath. As he sank into the water, he reached out to Aliel, flying somewhere over the city, and peeked through the phoenix's sight. The first train of carts, horses, and elves was disappearing into the horizon. *They're moving fast, aren't they?*

It's a long journey to Verenthyl and not everyone can shift through space like we do, Aliel conveyed.

When will they reach the Shroud's edge and when will we be needed?

From the looks of it, Ellendren and Arlyn have spent the past weeks pushing the Shroud back in that direction. We might not be needed for a few days.

"You've been pushing the Shroud back?" Devlyn asked, surprised at Aliel's revelation.

"Arlyn and I had bonded with you often enough to figure out the mechanics. Don't worry, we kept our distance from Erynel and didn't push the Shroud back enough to catch her attention. The sun won't shine on that reclaimed land until it is pierced properly or wholly gotten rid of."

"That's brilliant. Pushing it back requires less energy anyway. We might be able to cover more ground if we continue with that method and only pierce the Shroud at cities." Devlyn dipped his head under the warm water, wielding ignys into it to keep it warm.

Don't spend all day in the tub, Ellendren sent. She had likely said it verbally after Devlyn had submerged into the water.

"But the water feels so nice," he said as he breached the surface for air.

"Because you made it that way." She spun around, smiling. Devlyn couldn't ignore the urge to pull her into the water with him. She likely wouldn't speak to him for a week—she'd just finished getting ready for the day. And Lyren and Pevrel were currently attending their bedchamber. Devlyn still hadn't figured out a polite way to ask them to leave. "Are you listening?"

"Sorry; did you say something?"

"We have a chamber meeting today. It will be the last full chamber meeting for quite some time. Ciraenth and Aegian Ginielle will be heading for the Delmira Wood, Kyiel and Fyona Lauriel will go to Verenthyl, and Naesiv and Valerie Aerquin will stay in Verenthyl with their people until the way is open to Ostyl."

"Maybe we should figure out a way to clear a path to Winstyl or Tenyl first."

"Being rid of the Narielles and Taeriniors won't come that easy. And even when Krysenthiel is completely rid of the Shroud, full chamber meetings will resume more regularly."

"How will that happen? The aryls can't travel to Arenthyl and return to their own cities every week." Even as he asked it, he was reminded that Krysenthiel didn't have any roads connecting her cities—they weren't needed. The only roads connected Eandyl and Verenthyl to human cities beyond Krysenthiel's borders. As he continued to soak, his mind drifted to the Delmira Wood and the elves who would live there and what that settlement would look like. He hadn't seen any reference to a city being hidden away in the trees. Perhaps they resided in the treetops like the Eldinari elves, or maybe their home resembled Lucillia. If so, why wasn't there a city with a name there? Assuming that he would one day visit the Aryl of the Delmira Wood, he pushed that curiosity aside.

Once bathed and dressed, he and Ellendren made their way to the chamber hall. Devlyn felt less reluctant about this one since there would soon be a gap in full chamber meetings. He knew they were required, but the meetings usually felt more like adults bickering than doing something productive. A full chamber meeting likely would not occur again until they reached Arenthyl. Devlyn had to stop himself from fantasizing about that day; his mind would be useless for the upcoming deliberations if he started picturing himself in Arenthyl.

They walked into the chamber hall and even though it was a full chamber meeting, many of the minor aryls had decided to skip out on this meeting, especially those who would be traveling today. Just as Naesiv cleared his throat to begin, Devlyn inwardly groaned when he caught sight of the Narielle and Taerinior aryls who were remaining in Eandyl, providing them the opportunity to dictate the meetings.

"It is with a happy heart that we mark this occasion as the next and necessary step in reclaiming Krysenthiel." Naesiv extended his hand and a group of children came into the chamber hall, all wearing crowns of flowers. They pranced to the center of the room and performed a recital for the aryls.

Devlyn looked closer at their crowns and wondered if the golden petals were indeed the fabled kryseniel flowers of Krysenthiel, brought down from Luminare before the Skyland was lost to the Darkness. Even though it was now summer, he had assumed that the thick sheet of ice layering Krysenthiel would take months, perhaps even years to melt away from the delicate flora.

The children bowed as they finished and each child presented two flowers to each aryl. Devlyn and Ellendren happily accepted the kryseniel with thanks.

"Our friends from the Eldin Wood went to great lengths to quicken the melting process in one of Eandyl's meadows to give us hope in the days to come. These are the first kryseniels, the namesake and emblem of our lost kingdom, to have been seen and smelled since before that fateful day when the Shroud claimed Krysenthiel," Naesiv said as the children left the chamber hall. "Seeing as this will be our last gathering for some time, I have left the agenda open for discussion."

Devlyn groaned inwardly again as Ellendren pinched him under the table. He knew he couldn't express how he felt about this but pretending he would enjoy the next few hours would be near impossible. What was the point of a chamber meeting if their plan was already established?

"I move we return to the placement of the Guardians. They are our best defenders and we simply cannot keep them in one location," Toral said, speaking above the others once the meeting started. "Every Krysenthien city must be defended."

"Our numbers are too diminished to offer a suitable defense of every city. And as we've already discussed and have shown you all here, every city has its own defenses. Krysenthiel's cities will not fall with Luminari stationed inside," Jeanne said.

Devlyn thought he caught sadness in her voice about admitting the Guardians' current status. "How is the recruitment process going?" Devlyn asked, hoping that at least their numbers were increasing.

"We've received requests to join from Eldinari and some humans, as well as many Luminari. Those already present have been added to our list. They're more than welcome to fight along our side, but they will not receive a formal training until after the Erynien Empire is subdued. Our current Guardians all have more squires than they can properly train, to say nothing of our other responsibilities."

"We still anticipate adequate protection of Winstyl when we reach the city," Sylvia said.

"Every city will be protected, but the Guardians can only be divided by three, one group to Verenthyl, another to Eandyl, and a third to Arenthyl. Dividing them any further, as the First of the Guardians has already made clear, will weaken us all. And Prya and Liara will be accompanying the caravan to Verenthyl today," Devlyn said, already exhausted by the meeting. This issue had been decided over a month ago and Devlyn cursed Naesiv for not setting an agenda. To his surprise, Sylvia melted into her chair, and did not rebuke him. He wondered how long that would last when the attendance at these meetings shrank.

"Is there any chance that the Shroud can be removed entirely at once?" Kyiel asked.

"Each attempt to push the Shroud back has been incredibly strenuous. It would likely require an incredible amount of power to remove it completely," Ellendren said.

"If it is possible, is there a plan in place?" Kyiel asked. "Will we all rush in as though we were playing a running game or has a more dignified approach been considered?"

"If the Lorenthien aryl figures out a way to remove the entire Shroud in a single blow, then we will have to anticipate an open attack," Jeanne said. "As it stands, we are incredibly vulnerable outside our cities and until the seguian arches are opened and connected, we will have to journey there by foot. We will be attacked. We'll have to be prepared for shadow elves, dragons, Deurghol, legionnaires, and any other number of soldiers that Erynor will launch at us."

"They wouldn't dare. Do they not have any decency?" Valerie asked.

"I can't speak to their decency," Jeanne said. "But they will launch their entire might against us. They have an advantage over us while we are out in the field, and they know that will change once we reclaim all our fortified cities. After all, if it was not for the Shroud, we would have never lost Krysenthiel."

The meeting continued in that manner. The aryls were terrified to be out in the open again and they all wanted the full protection of the Guardians, even in their diminished numbers. Plans were made, others were solidified and the entire meeting lasted three hours. Devlyn left it exhausted.

He had mixed emotions as he bade farewell to the Aerquin, Ginielle, and Lauriel aryls who were headed west. Their caravan included the Seven Chairs and most of the ei'ana.

———————

Abbie tapped her foot. She'd already had this argument with her brother and as the solstice drew closer, she was beginning to think that he would remain stubbornly unmoved from the position he'd taken. Andrew looked from Abbie to Eagan, uncertain whose side to take. The fool boy thought he had a say. Men, especially rich ones who had a duke for an uncle, always thought their opinion was needed and mattered. If Andrew, Andrea, had been a duke's nephew from any other kingdom, Abbie wouldn't have spared him a moment of her time. But Andrea Farneis was Sudernese and slept with a dagger under his pillow and Abbie liked that. He was also good with his sword. Still, that didn't mean it was okay for him to stick his nose in druid affairs.

Abbie shot him a pointed look as he cleared his throat, making him reconsider what he thought would be important to say.

"The solstice will be here soon and you've said it yourself, he's not ready. You'll need all the help you can get," Abbie repeated her position. A position her brother likely knew every word of by now and how each point could be twisted to her advantage.

"I have no say in that decision. Just because I've drunk both the moonshade tea and the starshade tea doesn't make me an elder," Eagan said.

"He won't be ready. You'll need all the help we can muster if he steps into the Dream without being fully trained. Every servant of shadow and half-life in the Dream will be drawn to him. You'll be overwhelmed if he's not ready," Abbie said.

"Like a bug to a flame." Eagan sighed. He hadn't moved; not even when Abbie and Andrew had found him meditating in one of Eandyl's palace gardens. "You're right. We'll be overrun. The elders know this. They know he's not ready nor will he be. We had four years to prepare him, to train him to walk into the Dream physically to defeat Erynel and reclaim the lucilliae before the Dream is lost to the Void. But those four years were broken and parceled. Perhaps if we'd had a full uninterrupted four years with him and were able to dedicate every day to training him, he would be ready."

"We could not train him as we were. He is not a druid; he's never stepped into Kweil Aitch's catacombs," Abbie said.

"And the elders rejected the idea of bringing him to Kweil Aitch.

He was so close to our emerald isle. If only the elders could have seen the wisdom of letting him interact with and learn from our ancestors," Eagan said.

"Your ancestors?" Andrew asked.

"When a druid dies, a piece of them is left behind in this world, or rather a connection to them. The catacombs of Kweil Aitch stretch far beneath the island's surface. There are many places across the waking world like Kweil Aitch, but our home is the largest. The veil between our waking world and the Dream is thinnest there. Truly, it's difficult to determine whether you're in the Dream or the waking world. Ja'horan has many such places and their druid clans are scattered like sand across their boundless continent, while Eklean's druid clans share Kweil Aitch," Eagan explained.

"I don't understand," Andrew said.

"In those places where the veil is thin, our ancestors can be reached. We don't learn how to become druids from the living, but from our ancestors. The elders have set Abbie and me on the impossible task of teaching an elf how to walk the Dream as a druid would, but without the benefit of how we druids actually become druids."

"So, what's going to happen when Devlyn drinks this moon-something tea and isn't ready?" Andrew asked.

"When I enter the Dream, I slip into it. No one notices when a druid enters the Dream physically. Because we are born and live where the veil is thinnest, we belong equally to the Dream and the waking world. But for others, especially those who have not had sufficient training, they stomp around as they physically step into the Dream. Every druid will feel Devlyn enter the Dream and so will every foe who wishes him harm. The Evil One has all but claimed the Dream. While his fiercest beasts cannot escape the Void, there are smaller ones that prowl the Dream. To say nothing of his servants of shadow. We can only hope that Erynel is the only Sha'ghol that we will face after the solstice."

"We?" Abbie caught her brother.

"Not you." Eagan growled. "The elders know Devlyn won't be ready. And neither do they intend to leave him stranded. Druids of every clan will come to his defense."

"Why wasn't I told?" Abbie asked, furious.

"Because you cannot enter the Dream physically. You haven't completed your training."

"Only because I was asked to leave Kweil Aitch and go to Gwilnor to watch for the Lorenthien's arrival," Abbie yelled.

ENSNARED

Devlyn had tossed and turned, his fitful sleep stoked by the departure of some of the elves from Eandyl for Verenthyl. He knew the caravan was protected by both Guardian knights and Prya and Liara, but the Cyndinari forces were being too accommodating. They were planning something big. While he was focusing on the Shroud, the Cyndinari were likely devising a way to take advantage of his distraction. Rolling over again, Kyiel's question about removing the Shroud all at once played through his mind. What if he could disperse the Shroud entirely just by defeating Erynel?

Facing Erynel and soon was unavoidable. Not only did she have the lucilliae of temperance, but the Shroud would always be a threat as long as she continued living her half-life. Meridephaen, the Cyndinari's high feast day was quickly approaching, and Eagan would soon have the required flower for the tea that would let Devlyn enter Somnaeniel in the flesh. He had no idea if the druids' flower would only allow him to enter that realm once, or if it would keep that door open indefinitely. The latter mattered less since Somnaeniel would soon be impossible to cross into. Navigating around the pools of dorthl became more dangerous every time Devlyn visited while he slept. Even if he could return physically after Meridephaen, he doubted that he would. Entering Somnaeniel while he slept was dangerous enough.

Rolling over again, Devlyn moved to get out of bed, waking Ellendren in the process. "What's wrong?" she asked, her voice groggy.

"Nothing. I'm having trouble sleeping is all. Go back to sleep." Devlyn left their bed chamber and went into the salon. Pushing his fingers though his hair as he sat on the couch, he exhaled, frustrated at not knowing Erynor's next move. He knew this war was bigger than the Erynien Empire; he hoped he was making the right moves to get the rest of Teraeniel engaged. Eklean could not defeat Ramiel alone. He remembered the beasts that had attacked Tenethyl when he had glimpsed Thien's past. They were unlike anything he had ever seen. Some of those monsters were larger than dragons! Even if he and the Luminari reclaimed every Krysenthien city, what good would those lumaryl walls be against monsters twisted by the Void? While Krysenthiel's cities had an advantage for withstanding such an attack, most cities did not—every other city Devlyn had ever visited only had stone walls for protection. Stone would not save the inhabitants from Ramiel.

Eagan was right—Devlyn had been wasting time, distracted by Erynor's war of conquest. A war that Erynor was currently losing but whoever won this petty war mattered little if Ramiel escaped the Void. The Shroud, while a significant barrier for the Luminari, was a distraction. Erynor wanted to wipe out the Luminari resistance and cast them back into chains. While Devlyn could not shirk his responsibilities to his people, neither could he allow his energy to be entirely consumed by Erynor and the Shroud. He had to do both. He felt the crushing weight of his duties weigh him down and he slumped.

As he sat there with his thoughts, he knew he did not have the luxury of removing the entire Shroud as he, Ellendren, and Arlyn were currently going about it. At their current pace, it would require years, possibly decades, to free all Krysenthiel from it. Their lost kingdom was simply too vast to continue removing the Shroud in this manner. While they had certainly made significant progress, they had only reached one city and weren't even a quarter of the distance to the next city. They hadn't even started to press inward toward the cities bordering the lake.

At this rate they might never live to reach Arenthyl.

Closing his eyes, he reached out to Aliel who was perpetually watching Krysenthiel's borders. *Anything new?* Devlyn conveyed.

They're planning an attack. It seems that they're waiting for something though.

Reinforcements?

Possibly. Or for the next caravan leaving Eandyl.

They hope to trap us between their forces and the Shroud. They don't think we can remove all the Shroud before they engage us in battle. The weight of that truth pressed down.

What are you planning? I know your mind and heart, but something is unresolved.

Could we defeat Erynel in Somnaeniel and thereby remove the Shroud entirely?

It sounds possible. We'd be doing two things at once. It would require an incredible amount of concentration. I would recommend focusing on the jienzu forms before Eagan offers you the druid's tea.

Devlyn nodded and went out onto the balcony. The air was crisp in the predawn hours. He gazed across Eandyl's golden domes and spires. Bridges arched between buildings and the sinuous forms gave the city a unique flow. It appeared to be a pattern of some sort, but he couldn't recognize it. Eandyl glowed softly in the dark, the lumaryl allowing the inhabitants to sleep.

Taking a step away from the balustrade, Devlyn positioned his feet, rooting them into the stone, making his posture steady, yet bendable. Time passed as he moved from one form to the next. Morning twilight faded as the sun crested in the east, illuminating Eandyl in a wondrous display of color and the Arenthylean bells began to chime to welcome the dawn.

Ellendren came out to the balcony in her nightgown to find Devlyn dripping in sweat, holding a particularly difficult jienzu form. His body ached, but nowhere near as badly as it once had when Viren had first taught him this form. Aliel was right, his mind had to be capable of destroying the Shroud and Erynel in the same breath, all the while avoiding the dorthl consuming Somnaeniel. He had no idea how he was going to manage that, but he would prepare himself as best as he could.

"You've decided something." Ellendren plucked a cherry from the bowl of fruit that Lyren had brought out while Devlyn practiced.

Devlyn eased out of the form, careful not to hurt himself or strain a muscle. Just because it didn't hurt as much as it once had, didn't mean he could speak while holding that position. "We can't continue removing the Shroud as we currently are. We're running out of time."

"I agree, but how do you recommend removing it all at once? It's not like we are intentionally choosing the slower option over a more expeditious path."

"Erynel is the key. I have to defeat her and figure out a way to banish her and the Shroud simultaneously."

"Erynel Meriden is a Sha'ghol, capable of immense power. You have my complete confidence, my love, but how will *we* manage such?"

"I don't know how we'll manage it." He smiled, admitting that doing so on his own was impossible. "But I don't think you can come to Somnaeniel with me." Devlyn saw the flash in her eyes and quickly explained himself. "The Shroud is in both realms, Teraeniel and Somnaeniel. While Erynel is the source, I don't think we can banish the Shroud from only one realm. We are one—we are the Lorenthien aryl and will be the Exalted Aryl of Krysenthiel—one of us has to be here and the other there."

"So, you've decided that you are more fit for the more dangerous of the two tasks?" Ellendren crossed her arms and pivoted one leg, her stance assertive.

"I don't think either of us will be safe. Erynor has been holding himself back. I don't think he expected us to break through the Shroud; he wasn't prepared for that. But once we make our move—once we no longer have Eandyl's walls to protect us, I'm afraid we will see what the Erynien Empire is truly capable of. We'll both be in grave danger, Elle."

"Do you believe it's possible to actually remove the Shroud entirely in one pass?"

"We have to. We don't have a choice."

"If we fail, we will be trapped between Erynor's forces and the Shroud."

"I think that is what they are planning for. They're waiting for us to leave Eandyl—they know we won't stay here, it's only a matter of when. The only reason they haven't attacked the caravan heading west is because most of our population is still here."

"Did Eagan say when the tea will be ready?" Ellendren turned to look over the city.

"No, only that the flower would bloom on Meridephaen."

"Right. Then we have a week to plan. We'll have to meet with Jeanne first thing this morning to discuss the change in plans. Our forces will be less concentrated after we leave Eandyl and each group strikes out for a different city. We'll also have to send a message to the caravan heading for Verenthyl—they'll have to plan to split up."

Jaerol waited at the servant's entrance, dressed in near transparent silken garments, leaving nothing of what garments were supposed to hide to the imagination. Liam, Rusyl, and Teran had all told him that he was a fool to trust Zara—Cyndinari were not to be trusted, especially in Broid. The worst part about revealing Zara's plan, was that he'd had to confess to the others that he'd been sneaking into Broid without their knowledge. Liam had been the most upset about that. Jaerol still didn't see an alternative. Liam and Rusyl would have noticeably stuck out in the crowd. Only Cyndinari elves inhabited Broid—there was no one else. After they had agreed to the new plan, Jaerol had left them again, only not in secret this time.

Zara had given him instructions of where to go and which boulevards and streets to avoid. She didn't have to tell him, but he also stayed clear of the Coliseum; he didn't need Kiron's ghost to visit him as he tried to focus on rescuing Evellyn while blending in as a palace servant.

Another patrol of guards passed by, making Jaerol's heart race. He had told himself before even reaching Cynethol that he would have to stay away from the guards to avoid being recognized. Still, no one in the palace should know him. They might know him by his reputation of disgracing the Erynien Empire, but that didn't mean they would know what he looked like. There was one possible flaw in his thinking though. One of his old magisters or classmates could be visiting the palace while he was there; shadow elves were hardly strangers to Erynor's court. Some of them could have risen through the ranks since his graduation and be a constant presence in the palace for all Jaerol knew.

Despite his worry, this was his best chance to get into the palace and blend in with the servants. As a servant, he'd be able to move about freely. He let out the breath he hadn't realized he was holding when the guards didn't stop to question him. Oddly enough, they paid him little mind and barely glanced his way. Either Zara had convincingly disguised him as a palace servant or the guards were in on the plot. The latter was impossible. Coordinating duplicity among the palace guards would have been too messy. Only one guard would have to turn in the others for their plan to fail. Even as he thought it, Jaerol wondered if the palace guard and servants were of the same mind. Neither group were shadow elves—they were regular citizens hoping to earn a decent wage to support their families. Zara had said that there was still good to be found among the Cyndinari. While Jaerol had thought that was once true, he also assumed that he had killed the only good Cyndinari to draw breath in Broid.

The servant's entrance door finally opened and an old woman looked Jaerol up and down, her eyes lingering a moment too long. Jaerol had never been a shy or modest elf, but neither did he walk around practically naked in public for someone to appraise him as though his body was nothing more than a bauble to be bought and sold and put on display. This woman's silk was noticeably opaque and did not reveal her body as his own outfit did. "Yes, you'll do. Zara still has an eye for those His Imperial Majesty will find pleasing."

"And what is that?" His skin crawled at the suggestion.

"You will learn to never ask questions. Follow me."

Jaerol passed the threshold and into the palace's underbelly. He knew that this part of the palace would not be as extravagant as the levels above, but he had expected it to be brighter. Only torches lit the dungeon-like, windowless space. The woman listed servant protocols as they moved through the corridors. It was endless and Jaerol wasn't surprised to learn that he wasn't permitted to speak or even make eye contact with anyone who wasn't also a servant, unless asked to.

The woman took him to a room filled with bright pillows. He had never seen so many pillows in one place before. Water splashed in a central fountain as Cyndinari elves, all men, lounged about. Their outfits were similar to his own and if Jaerol had not kissed Liam that very morning, he might have forgotten that he was in a relationship. Tempting thoughts were already seeping into the corners of his mind. He was suddenly and surprisingly grateful that he'd only be here for a week.

"We cycle through His Imperial Majesty's personal servants, so that he does not grow bored. You will wait here with the others until summoned. Don't expect that to happen any time soon." The older elf left and Jaerol took in what he felt had to be a fantasy or perhaps Yloran's private salon. He would never forget the handsome elves attending her when he and Kiron had visited the Sha'ghol's mansion.

Jaerol chose a spot by the fountain and reclined there. He didn't want to talk to any of the servants here. He worried whether he had enough self-control in a setting like this, and also didn't want to accidentally reveal his mission or his identity. He had no idea if every servant here despised the empire nor did he feel inclined to find out the hard way.

He felt the other servants staring at him. None of them drew near at first, simply watching from a distance. He tried not to worry about them and instead swirled his finger in the fountain. The water twirled pleasantly about his finger and he had to suppress the urge to wield aquaeys. Any one of these servants could also be a kien wielder, and if they were, trained or not, they would know if he pressed into the elemental erendinth. They would also notice that Jaerol could wield with control. While kien wielders were becoming more accepted now that Balance was returning between kien and kiara, that likely was not the case here at the heart of the Erynien Empire. The Cyndinari wielders he had known thrived on the imbalance and encouraged kien wielders to lose control of their abilities, wreaking havoc wherever they went.

Restraining himself, he looked away from the water and one of the servants made eye contact with him. He smirked and walked over. Jaerol tried not to stare but found it impossible. This elf was gorgeous and his strut only added to the allure.

"Tieran." He extended his hand in greeting.

"Kiron." Jaerol had chosen to use Kiron's name. Using his own would have been disastrous.

"You're older than new servants typically are. It's clear why you were chosen, an elf as handsome as you, but it's curious that you weren't brought here at a younger age. Someone here will think you're trying to replace them." Tieran smiled.

"I'm not replacing anyone."

"You're not familiar with how this works, are you? Don't expect to make friends here. For every servant that comes in, one leaves. We're either moved to a less desirable position, such as the kitchens, or we disappear."

"What do you mean by disappear?"

"None of us will ever leave the palace." Tieran chuckled. "Once we enter, there is no leaving. Erynor's secrets can't be released outside the palace. Only death will take us away from this place."

Jaerol's heart stopped. Zara had said that she was a former servant. She had said there was a league of servants that wanted to see the empire collapse just as badly as the rest of the continent. Even as Tieran spoke, Jaerol knew what he said to be true. It had been too easy to get into the palace. Not a single guard had stopped him to ask for his credentials, not that he would have any as a servant, but they would have at least confirmed his identity before granting him entrance into the palace. How could he have been so foolish? He knew better than to trust a Cyndinari. He had wanted to believe Zara—she remembered him and Kiron together all those years ago. He had wanted to believe that there was still hope for his people.

34

Cor'lera's Secret

Devlyn and Ellendren watched the next train of wagons leave Eandyl from their balcony at the palace. Two lines crawled in separate directions, although both were heading more-or-less north. The largest caravan was destined first for Tenyl; a small portion would remain in the coastal city, while the rest would continue on to Arenthyl. Everyone assumed that Lake Saeryndol was frozen, which would allow them to easily cross it. By having the largest caravan travel for Tenyl instead of Winstyl, they hoped to fool the enemy into thinking that the Luminari did not intend to remove the entire Shroud at once and reclaim all Krysenthiel.

Winstyl was far closer to Arenthyl than Tenyl and would have made their intentions clear to the Cyndinari. The larger caravan would also attract the enemy and keep them away from the smaller and less defended caravans. Jeanne had offered another, strong, reason to take the northwestern route. If they failed to remove the Shroud, they would be able to retreat to the east. Devlyn did not want to consider that option, but nor could he lead the Luminari to certain death if he and Ellendren failed their people.

Meridephaen had finally come and Eagan had already gone. He had not left as the others had but had stepped physically into the Dream. Devlyn had only seen Abbie once since her brother had disappeared and from past experience, knew to avoid asking how she was holding up. Today was stressful enough without Abbie Wintyr lashing out at him. Even so, their brief encounter had been tense.

By the time Eagan returned, the wagons would have gone as far as they could that day and would have stopped for the night. They would not pitch tents, limiting themselves to sleeping on the ground or in their wagons or carriages and picketing the animals. That would enable them to be back on the road quickly the following morning. Waiting to leave until after the Shroud was destroyed was not an option.

If they didn't start out before the Shroud was dispersed to get as close to their destinations as possible, the Erynien Empire's forces would attack them in the open even before Eandyl's walls were out of sight once the Shroud was gone. With any luck, it would be gone by dawn tomorrow and the elves would be able to continue their race to their cities before the Erynien Empire caught on. Devlyn knew the gamble they were taking if they failed to destroy the Shroud. His caravan would be forced to retreat west out of Krysenthiel and outrun their pursuers.

The Luminari needed the head start. They had to fool the Cyndinari into thinking that they could be trapped against the Shroud and would have no place to go to avoid the ensuing fight out in the open. Unfortunately, that was a very likely situation if Devlyn failed to defeat Erynel. If the Shroud remained in place, there would be little hope for the Luminari elves' future. Ramiel was scheming something beyond Erynor's plots. Devlyn didn't have time to waste another day on the Shroud. Whatever battle the Erynien Empire was about to launch against the Luminari in their vulnerable state would look like child's play compared to what would happen if Ramiel escaped his prison. Not so much if, but when.

Devlyn turned to Ellendren and kissed her, his tension eased by her agreement to spend most of the day with him in Eandyl. He knew that she had only done so to ensure that he rested, but it was now time for her to go too. They held on to each other, neither wanting to part. If everything went according to plan, they would reunite in the morning. He worried about how much could go wrong tonight though. While he would continue to wait in Eandyl for Eagan to return, Ellendren would fly to the group heading toward Tenyl. Tariel would survey the horizon, just as Aliel would keep his vigil here at Eandyl. If the Erynien Empire moved against them, they would know. The Empire doubtless already knew that the Luminari were migrating *en masse* and Devlyn was determined to be prepared when the Cyndinari began their strike against the Luminari. He hoped they would wait until tomorrow—that they would try to give the Luminari a sense of security. Erynor did enjoy toying with his enemies.

"I'll see you tomorrow." Ellendren kissed him again.

"I look forward to it." He smiled as she bonded fully with Tariel, her yellow and white lierathnil shimmering in her golden light. Viren and Arlyn were already with the caravan destined for Tenyl and then Arenthyl, and anxiously awaited Ellendren. With a final kiss, she turned, leapt from the balcony, and flew north.

He kept his eyes on her until she disappeared into the horizon. Eandyl felt empty now that only its permanent residents had stayed behind. Because the Luminari elves were no longer immortal, there were fewer of them in the city that had been built and designed for a much larger population. He wondered if the Luminari would ever return to their original numbers.

Waiting behind with nothing to do felt foolish and cowardly. The rooms he and Ellendren had shared here no longer had any of their belongings and he already missed her constant, calming presence. Even Lyren had gone with the Arenthyl caravan, leaving behind only what Devlyn currently wore , the four lucilliae and two coins in the pouch in his secret pocket. Ellendren and he had agreed that it was best if he held on to them once again. He had carried them this far and it felt right that he be the one to deliver them back to Arenthyl.

He was almost alone and right now, would even welcome Trethien back if it meant having someone to keep him company. Andrew was somewhere in the palace, but he had only remained because of Abbie and Devlyn did not want to experience another encounter with a druid today.

He considered practicing the jienzu forms again, but that would end with him getting sweaty and possibly exhausted. He needed to preserve his strength. The leisure he currently had didn't seem appropriate. The majority of the Luminari elves were out in the open again, vulnerable to attack, while Devlyn waited in a palace protected by Eandyl's defensive lumaryl walls. It just didn't seem right.

For the plan to succeed, Jaerol had to be called to attend the emperor and his court. Unfortunately, he was biding his time in the male servants' luxurious pillowed salon. Servants came and went, pleased that they had been selected to attend their emperor while Jaerol was not. The more they were called upon, the more they were seen as pleasing to their emperor—their status at court was secured while Jaerol had none. With every day that passed, the servants swaggered and smiled smugly around Jaerol, confident that he would soon be sent to the kitchens. He'd heard their mean comments and their cocksure laughter; he was too old to be pleasing to their emperor.

Little did they know, Jaerol had no intention of wasting away in the palace waiting to please Erynor. Getting into Erynor's good graces was the last thing he wanted. Not only had Jaerol deceived the empire for ten years about his status as a shadow elf, but he had recently killed one of their high-ranking members and helped liberate Gwilnor in the process. One way or another, Jaerol was leaving today. Staying in the palace—staying in Broid—was too risky. It was Meridephaen and the emperor would be away from the palace for most of the day, watching the Grand Tourney in the Coliseum with the rest of Broid.

After the brief chat with Tieran the week before, when he realized he'd fallen into a trap, he'd frantically reached out to Rusyl, casting images to the blue dragon. Rusyl had responded, sparing the energy only to tell Jaerol that he was a fool and that he couldn't believe that Jaerol had trusted Zara in the first place. Rusyl had agreed to revert to their original plan and enter the palace through the sewers with Liam. For all that Jaerol knew, they could already be in the palace. But reaching out to Rusyl required too much concentration and he couldn't spare any of it just now. And there was the great risk of one of Erynor's dragons perceiving the images.

Today's batch of servants to attend the throne room were called and as they began to leave the salon, Jaerol cast two tricky wields. The first concealed his wielding; although he'd only had to do that one a few times before, it was simple in execution. The second was more complicated as he had to place it over everyone in the salon, and then maintain it. There were easily forty elves there and Jaerol had to make them all think that he had disappeared without causing alarm.

If anyone became aware of his second wield, they could easily undo it and find Jaerol, disguised as a servant, standing in plain sight. He'd either be killed for trying to escape, or worse, he'd be recognized as himself. Either way, being discovered meant death. Pressed into the erendinth, he slipped out the door and followed the last servant called to attend the throne room.

The servants walked up and through the palace; the corridors became more ornate the further they went from the servants' quarters. Glowing red stone dominated the main level. Jaerol easily recognized it as cyndaryl, the very substance of the Skyland the Cyndinari had left. Large robust red columns lined the corridor, supporting a barrel vault that arched over them. A majestic portal of the same cyndaryl stood at the end of the corridor lined with sculpted dragons. Jaerol gulped, staying near the group of men walking toward the throne room.

They passed through the grand portal and Jaerol noted that the sculptural dragons were an onyx color rather than the ruby cyndaryl used in the rest of the portal and grand corridor. Jaerol prepared his wield for whoever else might be in the throne room. Surely, there would be just as many female servants as male. Jaerol didn't allow himself to consider Evellyn not being here. She was Erynor's greatest trophy and he delighted in showing off his trophies. If she wasn't here, Jaerol would have to search the entire palace to find her, something he knew he didn't have enough time for. He had no idea if Erynor would have placed her among the other servants or assigned rooms to her. He cursed himself as he followed the others; he should have found a way to inquire about her whereabouts.

As the male servants fanned out, Jaerol saw the female servants waiting behind the blessedly empty throne. A quick scan revealed the one slave who stood out among the others. Only one elf here was not Cyndinari. Instead of cinnamon hair and bronzed skin, her hair was spun of silver and gold; her skin glowed softly in the morning light. She stood slightly away from the other, younger servants. Erynor did not display Evellyn Lorenthien here for her youthful appearance, though her beauty was immeasurable, especially when standing next to the vain young elves. Her kind and gentle eyes radiated something these other women lacked. But there was more in those eyes—recognition. She could see him. The onyx statues! They had to be dorthl—his wields had been severed as he passed through them. *Idiot.* He was still behind the rest of the male servants and they didn't seem to care; it wasn't their place to say whether Jaerol should be here or not. He wrought his wields anew, although sloppier than before, allowing only Evellyn to see him.

She glanced at him, acting uninterested as though he was just another Cyndinari eager to serve his emperor. Jaerol went over to her, carefully maintaining his wields.

"You break protocol and they seem not to care," Evellyn said, her voice low.

"They cannot see me," he whispered. He might be invisible to the other servants and attendants who remained in court, but they would hear him if he spoke too loudly.

"Yet you are dressed as a servant."

"Only as a ruse; we need to get you away from here before Erynor returns."

"You cannot. I am always watched, even when the emperor is not sitting on his throne. Besides, who would send you to my rescue?"

"Your son."

Evellyn's eyes widened and she struggled not to appear as taken aback as she felt. "He's not here, is he? Please say he hasn't come to this place."

"No, but Liam is here."

"Where?" Evellyn carefully looked about the throne room, dampening the effect of a mother dragon ready to pounce on anyone threatening her hatchling in case it was noticed.

"I dare not speak it here."

Her eyes narrowed. "You are a Cyndinari; why should I trust you? What trap are you laying before me?"

"You trusted Mother Velaria Treyven."

"She is a Chair now?"

Jaerol nodded. "I'm sorry, but we must leave."

"I told you, I cannot. They are always watching—you should not have come here."

"They won't be able to see you, I promise."

"Bold for one who sees so little," came a slithering voice, followed by the throne room doors slamming shut.

Jaerol spun around to see shadows spilling into the space around a central figure, standing at the balcony above the only entrance. Jaerol cursed under his breath—how had he missed a bloody Deurghol! The other servants whispered among themselves and Jaerol released his wields to prepare a defense. Even as he did, he knew he could not stand against one of the Deurghol. Jaerol had only seen a Deurghol from a distance before and that wasn't when he was targeted as its prey. He'd never witnessed their destructive power and had never intended to. The Deurghol's skeletal form in deathless existence clung to this realm, unwilling or unable to pass into the next. Jaerol had never understood how the Deurghol had come to be, only that they were involved with the bringing about of the Shroud.

"You wish to fight me? Do you think you can defeat me?" The Deurghol unsheathed the sword that drank in and tainted the light it touched, warping it when it came too close to the corrupted verathn. A single cut would immediately kill Jaerol.

As the servants scattered to the corners of the throne room, Evellyn said, "I trust you have a way to get us off this island."

"A blue dragon, if we can get past this Deurghol."

"That'll do. Erynor wasn't wrong to fear that a weapon was hiding in Cor'lera, one that could destroy his renewed empire." Evellyn began to glow a brilliant gold and for a moment, Jaerol thought that she too was a Phaedryn. He had no idea how that was possible. How could another phoenix be kept hidden all these years, in the Erynien court of all places?

Tenebrys streaked down from the balcony. Jaerol leapt away from Evellyn, hoping to draw the Deurghol's attention away from her, but as he looked back, he realized that Evellyn needed no protection. She wielded all seven erendinth unlike anyone he had ever met before. Even as he tried to follow what she was doing, he couldn't—her wields were far more sophisticated than anything he had seen.

Realizing that Evellyn was more dangerous than she had ever let the Erynien court know, the Deurghol launched more tenebrys bolts, some of them hitting the servants. They didn't even have a chance to scream before they crumbled into nothingness. Light wrapped around Evellyn as a negating and electrifying darkness swarmed about the Deurghol. The throne room flashed between light and dark as the Deurghol exploded more tenebrys lightning outward, but Evellyn's light swallowed them all. Something—someone—seemed to come out of her, someone terrifying to behold. The being of light rushed toward the Deurghol, grabbing and squeezing him until his mortal shell started to crack under the radiant fist.

The Deurghol screamed and something broke through him. "Please, just kill me," he pleaded, whimpering. "Free me from him."

"You're mine, slave!" screamed another voice from the Deurghol's lips.

"Begone—return to the emptiness from which you came," a voice said from Evellyn's mouth.

"Ramiel will be freed soon. You cannot stop his return. Everything will be his! The Void will swallow all and even your precious Light won't escape it. You can't…" the Deurghol's deeper voice screamed even as his host did. Jaerol covered his ears to muffle the screeching of the two and the air rippled before it exploded outward, causing every window to shatter in a vibrant burst of colorful glass.

The servants who still drew breath huddled, crouched in the corners, covering their ears. Jaerol thought some of them might be blind or deaf now. He turned back to Evellyn, terrified of the power she had just unleashed. She was not a Phaedryn; no wings had come forth. "What—who was that?" he asked, shocked to hear he could still speak.

"Not here. You said you can get us off this island."

"Right." Jaerol reached out to Rusyl and exerted a gentle reach for Liam. He felt them both in the bowels of the palace, hiding in the sewers as originally planned. Jaerol extended his hand to Evellyn and they hurried out of the throne room and down the first flight of stairs they came to. Jaerol had resumed his earlier wields, making Evellyn and himself invisible to anyone who might see them. The deeper into the palace they went, the less stressed Jaerol felt. They might actually get away from this place.

Deep in the cellars, Jaerol felt Liam nearby and before he had the chance to embrace him, Liam lunged at Evellyn, immediately wrapping her in his arms and weeping into her shoulder as she wept on his. They clung to each other, the agony and trauma of the past fourteen years— Dolan's murder by his own brother, their abduction from Cor'lera, and all the tragic events in Gneal's dungeon—coming to the surface.

Jaerol had been there the day Liam and Evellyn had been separated—he had just arrived in Gneal as an Erynien emissary and Evellyn was to be taken to Broid by the same caravan that had brought him north. Liam and Evellyn cried quietly together and just as Jaerol grew anxious, Rusyl coughed, reminding them that they were all still in danger. They left the corridor and passed into the room Liam and Rusyl had been hiding in and went into the palace's sewers beyond it. The stench immediately affronted Jaerol's nose. He knew where the sewers let out, aware that they had to pass under the Coliseum, beneath Kiron's ashes, cold and alone in an urn before they reached the bay.

They hurried along through the nastiness until sunlight poured into the opening at the end and as Jaerol squinted into the sunlight, he saw shadows flickering somewhere above. Then he heard the roars.

"We can't go out there," Rusyl backed into the tunnel.

"What's out there—who's out there?" Liam asked.

"The Dark Flight; there has to be at least a hundred of them." Rusyl backed further away from the opening, petrified of the dark dragons outside.

"They've never come out during Meridephaen," Jaerol said.

"They won't be here long," Evellyn said.

"Do you know where they're going?" Jaerol asked.

"To stop my son from reclaiming Arenthyl. Let us pray they are too late."

STEPPING BETWEEN

Devlyn sat with his legs crossed in his chamber after eating a bit, eyes closed, but open to Aliel. He could see more than he had ever been able to with regular eyes. The more time he and Aliel spent bonded together, the more his eyes took on the qualities of the phoenix's.

As he sat in the still quiet of the empty room, his thoughts shifted to Ellendren. She would be doing something similar, likely in the safety of a carriage or wagon instead of the palace. With any luck, their days of caravans and tents would soon be over. Arenthyl called out to him; he could feel the ancient Luminari city beckon him as though it too was alive. He had felt something similar here in Eandyl, but since he was neither the aryl of this city, nor the Exalted Aryl yet, Eandyl had not quickened to him. He hadn't mentioned the feeling to Ellendren—the thought was absurd, cities weren't alive, they didn't have a consciousness like a person. Or did they?

"It's good that you're using your time wisely."

Devlyn was jolted out of his introspection by the unannounced visitor, spinning to find Eagan holding a pouch. "You could have knocked first."

"From the Dream? I did not come through any other part of the palace but shifted directly here from the sanctuary where the moonshade flower grows in Ja'horan. Why would I go somewhere else first, just to come here?"

"Entering someone's room without notice isn't advisable."

"We don't have the time for formalities tonight." Eagan moved further into the salon. "I trust you have a kettle to prepare tea, yes?"

"Of course." Devlyn went to a cupboard and grabbed a tea set from it. Before he even had the chance to fill the tea pot and warm the water, a heated discussion spilled through the door to the corridor outside his chambers.

"My sister and Andrew are here."

Devlyn left Eagan to make the tea while he went to open the door. The commotion outside was putting the knights standing guard outside his room in a difficult situation. If only someone had told them not to stand in Abbie's path. "Ei'denai," the two knights intoned when he opened the door, looking apologetic for the disturbance.

"It's fine, they can come in. I should have told you to expect them."

Abbie brushed past the two knights, Andrew on her heels. He smiled warmly at Devlyn; they had spent so little time together since Devlyn had been abducted from Gwilnor. It felt like Devlyn had only learned yesterday that his real name was Andrea Farneis, nephew to Duke Paolo Farneis of Sudern.

"Hello, Abbie," Eagan greeted her and nodded at Andrew as he prepared the tea.

"You weren't going to tell me that you had returned—you were going to offer only Devlyn the moonshade tea and try to keep it from me!"

"The decision is not mine to make. I have no authority to offer it to you; you know this."

"Devlyn isn't even a druid and you offer it freely to him."

"You know that is unavoidable. Besides, the moonshade flowers that bloom on Meridephaen are not potent enough for the drinker to enter more than once."

"I know that teas from both solstices are required for permanence—the moonshade and the starshade. But I will not wait another year while our people fight and leave me behind." Abbie planted her hands on her hips.

"Then you'll have to answer to the elders after. They will sanction you for this."

"They've sat idle long enough, Eagan."

"The sword is not how we fight the Void." Eagan shook his head.

"Our *strength* will see our throats slit as we sleep to walk the Dream turned nightmare," Abbie said.

Eagan held two glass cups. The length of the argument had provided the proper amount of time for the moonshade flowers to steep, turning the water a deep purple. Devlyn and Abbie each took a cup. "You must step into the Dream the moment it passes your lips."

"And how do we do that?" Devlyn looked into the cup of the steaming purple liquid.

"You'll feel a pull and a light-headed sensation as though you will pass out. Don't resist it," Eagan said.

"I'm going to be dizzy moments before fighting a Sha'ghol?" Devlyn looked uncertainly at the purple liquid.

"It fades quickly. Now drink," Eagan urged.

The moonshade tea was unlike anything Devlyn had ever tasted before and as the dizzy spell came over him, he had to force himself to not fight it. And just as he was about to lose consciousness, he felt a jerk. Everything shifted and he expected to see pools of dorthl everywhere. But they were still inside the palace so he could not see the pools or the storm clouds roiling above.

"Are all Krysenthiel's cities protected from the dorthl?" Abbie asked, making the connection quicker than Devlyn could.

"We'll soon find out. A pleasant surprise if so," Eagan said.

The dizziness wore off and Devlyn's mind settled. The three of them shifted to the edge of the Shroud, nearest the location where the caravan set for Arenthyl waited in Teraeniel. Reaching out to Aliel, he felt the phoenix thrum inside his being and in the innermost place of their hearts, they fully embraced. A burst of light followed and the two stood as one, fully bonded. His vision should have bloomed, as though everything he saw appeared spun of golden light on the brightest of days. But here in the Dream, Devlyn saw little light as he stood beside the Shroud; dark clouds stormed above and large oily puddles of dorthl reaching the size of lakes covered the land in every direction.

"What will you two do while I confront Erynel?"

"Do you truly believe the Sha'ghol is our only threat here?" Abbie didn't bother hiding the disdain from her voice.

"The Evil One has near complete control of the Dream; he'll know we're here. He might not be able to attack us directly, but he'll send those who can. We'll ensure that no one tries to surprise you," Eagan said.

"There's only the two of you." Devlyn looked toward the horizon, worried about what else was coming for them.

"We are not alone. The druids have not forgotten our failure to Ithendryl and we will remedy it." As Eagan spoke, figures began to materialize around them. The druids from Eagan and Abbie's clan were easily identifiable with their frizzy red hair, but other druids also appeared, and, by their looks, they were from every continent. What dangers were they anticipating that had not been shared with Devlyn? Who had the Evil One sent to hold this place?

Devlyn couldn't focus on who the druids would be fighting or how they would go about it. He had his own work to do. He turned and looked at the Shroud, its diseased tendrils hungrily reaching out to take back the land it had recently lost, to grow as it poisoned the rest of the world.

Ellendren stepped out of her carriage. The moon was full above and Devlyn had vanished out of her awareness and crossed over into Somnaeniel. She would have fretted if she had not been prepared for it; he was simply gone. He was not just miles away, but in a wholly different realm. Around her, a few tents had been put up, but no one seemed capable of sleeping and many wandered about.

Arlyn, Jeanne, Byron, Toryn, and Viren greeted her before she could move away from the carriage. "You would have made your ancestors very proud," Jeanne said. "The last woman to sit on the Crystal Throne, Ei'terel Ithendryl Lorenthien, insisted that I endure in safety while my sister and brother Guardians perished at Erynor's hands. My heart ached for centuries. But now, I understand her foresight and wisdom in her choice—she saw you and Devlyn as our promised hope."

"You honor me, Jeanne," Ellendren said, wrapping her arms around the First of the Guardians. Astonishingly, Jeanne returned the embrace.

"You remind me very much of Ithendryl. Perhaps some of her golden blood runs through your veins as well."

"If not hers, Lucillia's House has proven to be just as noble."

"I do wish I had known this Lucillia and from whence she came. Her line will see the Shroud destroyed this night."

They all knew Lucillia's prophecy and the promise that they would return to Arenthyl. They had already come so far from Lucillia, the place where the woman had died and where the city named after her eventually followed her back into the woods. All that remained was the statue and small pool around it, in the forest where their city once stood.

"Has there been any hint of an attack?" Ellendren asked.

"Our scouts have been vigilant. We would have had some warning if the enemy intended to attack tonight. They cannot sneak up on us so easily." Jeanne turned to look toward the Shroud. "Are you ready?

"It's time."

"We'll keep you safe while you destroy the Shroud," Jeanne said, turning to Byron, Toryn, and Viren. "Stay with them, they'll need as much protection as you can give."

"My sword already belongs to you." Viren bowed to Ellendren.

Committing herself, Ellendren put an arm through Arlyn's and they began walking through the encampment toward the edge nearest the Shroud, Tariel zooming down from above. Ellendren remembered the first time she had seen the Shroud. Just a child, she had been terrified by it. She had always thought that if she studied hard enough, if she practiced wielding enough, she could heal the land of its taint—its poison.

Before completely leaving the camp, she bonded fully with Tariel and the night seemed to explode as light and color filled her vision. This was how the world was meant to be seen. She had no idea why she could only see the world this way when bonded with Tariel, but she knew it was not an issue with creation. It was how creatures saw the world. What had caused anacordel's eyes to grow dim to the radiance of the created world? Even with her thoughts so occupied, she noticed that the temperature dropped the closer they drew to the Shroud. She would have been shivering if not for her connection with Tariel.

"Focus on your task and only your task; no one will get anywhere near you to interfere," Byron promised, his sword unsheathed and ready.

Ellendren nodded and smiled at her uncle before turning back to the Shroud. Emptying herself, she allowed the quiet and stillness inside her to reach out and press into lumenys. The feel was familiar now, yet it always felt new and wonderful, especially when standing beside the diseased Shroud that greedily reached out.

She felt a disturbance already inflicting the Shroud. It was acting differently and as she pressed into lumenys, she felt her connection to Devlyn fully return—she sensed what he was doing in the World-in-Between and with a steadied stance, she joined her wield with his. She had no idea how she was able to connect with him, but if she squinted, she thought she could see him beside her. Did he stand there beside her in Somnaeniel? She reached out a hand to where she thought he stood. Before the doubt could cross her mind, she felt his hand grasp hers.

<hr>

Ellendren stood beside him. Devlyn somehow saw her even though she was not here in Somnaeniel—she couldn't be. He didn't understand how this was possible, but he didn't care. He was already wielding lumenys and when he squeezed her hand, he felt Ellendren pressed into lumenys as well. As a kiara wielder, she had to embrace the elemental erendinth and press into the transcendental erendinth, a process that was opposite to kien wielders. *Give to receive, receive to give.* The simple mantra flowed through his mind and he lost track of the order. He let go of her hand and stepped forward. Erynel would know he was here in the flesh.

Embracing lumenys always brought a different scent to the Shroud, and it was even stronger here in Somnaeniel. The poisonous quality multiplied and convulsed, yet it also shuddered from lumenys wielded jointly by himself, Ellendren, and Arlyn. Devlyn had not felt Arlyn as he had Ellendren, but knew that he was there, just as he knew Viren and others were also there to protect the two wielders standing in the face of the Shroud.

Filled with lumenys, Devlyn wielded it and stepped forward, creating a pocket of light as he walked into the Shroud. His wield flowed gently from him, confronting the Shroud. The Shroud repulsed the contact.

"Foolish child." Erynel stepped forward, and the Shroud condensed around her, hanging from her body like a gown. "Do you truly desire death in this realm? I will not give it quickly. My son wants to keep you alive; he likes his pets far too much."

"Your son is a murderer."

"My son is not here nor is he *my* Master. Ramiel cares little if you live or die. Of course, he'd rather your phoenix be contained like the others in Ythinor's belly." Devlyn drank in more of the erendinth, filling himself with lumenys as Erynel began to wield tenebrys. "You cannot stand against the true power, child. The seven erendinth might have brought about creation, but they are also limited to creation. The Void is older than Teraeniel and Somnaeniel—that primal force has no beginning and has endured. Anaweh's Light was limited to Lumaeniel for eons, a span of time that not even we elves can fathom, before the other two realms were created, carving away the Void's dominance, diminishing it to the realm that Ramiel now dwells in. All that is now will be swallowed by the Void and there will be no recourse for the Light!" Erynel shrieked as though she was experiencing a euphoric ecstasy of some sort. Devlyn could feel the near-electric tenebrys consuming her as she drank more of it in.

***

For the first time, Abbie was solid here in the Dream. She'd trained her entire life for this—every druid did. In ordinary circumstances, she would have drunk the moonshade or starshade tea as part of an ancient druidic ritual, deep in the catacombs beneath Kweil Aitch. But these were not ordinary times.

Instead of receiving the tea from her elders, she was receiving their disapproving looks. But they had not condemned her for drinking the moonshade tea without their blessing, not yet at least. Just now, they could spare few words as they readied themselves to stop the creatures crawling out of the dorthl puddles.

Ramiel and his fiercest monsters might still be trapped in the Void, but smaller creatures in his service could slip through the cracks made by the dorthl, the Void made manifest in the other realms. It existed in both and acted as portals between the realms. If the barrier between the Void, and Teraeniel and Somnaeniel was destroyed, the three realms would merge into one and there would only be the Void.

Gripping her sword, Abbie took a steadying breath and appraised her situation. Several Void creatures were moving straight for her. They looked as though they were formed entirely of dorthl. Or were they simply covered by the residue of the dorthl they had passed through? Their bodies moved oddly, as though they had never experienced gravity. Were they physical beings? Could they be killed? She couldn't pose her questions to any of the elders—they were all busily dealing with the creatures themselves. Launching herself toward the nearest hound-like creature, Abbie intended to find out whether they could bleed.

The vicious hound was slick, mirroring the oily dorthl puddles. Its teeth were sharp and it snarled as Abbie leapt toward it. She was immediately swatted aside by a swipe of a paw, its powerful muscles outlined in the oily slick residue as it sought Devlyn. It hadn't been sent here to kill the druids, but to stop him from destroying the Shroud.

She felt a bruise already forming on her hip and snarled back at the Void beast. For half a breath, she considered charging the creature again. Then she remembered that she was in the Dream; her body wasn't bound by the same laws that governed the waking world. She didn't have to fight it here as she would there.

Smirking, Abbie moved toward the creature again, close enough to get its attention before shifting. She'd never considered shifting as a battle tactic before; it wasn't something she could do outside of the Dream, at least, she didn't think so. And the only time she had ever shifted so short a distance was when she first learned how to shift.

The transition was immediate, and the beast's confusion evident as it swung its head around looking for Abbie. Instead of staring at the beast head on, she now looked at it from behind and darted forward with her sword raised. She cut down and it caught on flesh causing the beast to howl in pain. Abbie couldn't tell if it bled but knowing that she had hurt it was enough for now. The beast snapped its fangs, but Abbie shifted before they could close on her. Now on the beast's opposite side, she thrust her sword into its chest, hoping to pierce its heart and end its miserable life. The beast howled anew but did not fall. It smashed its large head against Abbie, throwing her back, her sword still in its chest.

Abbie tried to stand but the Void hound was too quick and was on top of her, its sharp claws digging into her shoulders and arms as she struggled against it. Dark poisonous blood spilled from the wound where her sword was still lodged. Frozen in fear, Abbie couldn't shift away. Her mind was too troubled and terrified, and just as she thought the beast would snap its jaws around her neck, a sword lopped off its head, severing it cleanly from its neck. Its body stood there, unwilling to die, blood pouring from it onto Abbie, stinging as it did.

The stinging sensation brought her out of shock, and Abbie pulled herself out from under the creature. She looked up and saw an old woman standing beside the beast. Abbie recognized Izara, the druid elder from Ja'horan. "You should not be here," Izara said.

Abbie tried not to scowl at her as Izara helped her stand. "You know why I'm here—we're here."

"You still have much to learn, young druid. These beasts might be ferocious but they are not our betters and neither are they the Dream's masters."

Abbie wanted to argue with the Ja'horan elder. She wanted to tell her how her training had been cut short to help Devlyn. But instead she pulled her sword out of the beast's side. "I won't leave this fight," she said, defiant.

"Then stay at my side and learn."

The battle pressed in on them, ending the conversation. Druids from every clan had come to fight the beasts sent from the Void. Abbie stayed with Izara and was amazed, for despite the elder's advanced age, she used her sword as though she was still in her prime. Not only did she readily shift as she fought, Izara also seemed to have a power over the Dream. Somehow, the ground that was free of dorthl would stir and twirl, winding around void-beasts' legs to hold on to them, trapping them and giving Izara and Abbie precious moments to kill the beasts.

HUBRIS

Feeling the violence surge within Erynel, Devlyn also heard the distant sound of screaming. He had no idea what the druids were fighting, but their battle had already begun. He couldn't turn back now; he couldn't even look over his shoulder to see how the druids were faring.

"They will all die with you and my Shroud will blanket all! My empire will have no end!"

Devlyn further embraced lumenys. He knew wielding only lumenys, a single erendinth, wasn't going to be enough to defeat Erynel, but he had to start somewhere and launched a beam of pure light at the Sha'ghol. She cackled as she flicked the beam away with a burst of tenebrys before directing her wield at Devlyn. The tenebrys lightning lashed dangerously and intensified the closer it came.

Even as he continued wielding, Devlyn felt that his strength and Ellendren's was too little. Arlyn was assisting her in Teraeniel, but the immensity of Erynel's strength and the Shroud mocked them, as though they were children in the face of a much older power. Even as Devlyn tried to defend himself, he felt the Shroud unaffected.

A child's cry reached his ears. How were there children here in Somnaeniel?

"Children easily slip into this realm more frequently than most. Ramiel feeds off them and now that this realm is nearly his, their accidental dreams here will find them waking to an empty shell. Only nightmares will they dream as they are lost forever—fodder for Ramiel and his servants." Erynel screamed again in delight as she blasted more bolts of tenebrys, not just at Devlyn, but in a show of the enormous power she had, recklessly launching the bolts in any direction without the slightest hint of fatigue.

Devlyn could now hear more children whimpering; the cries were more devastating than the Shroud and Erynel.

Submitting once again to lumenys, Devlyn felt it flow into him. Holding it inside, he crafted his wield anew, and linked with Ellendren in Teraeniel, and through her with Arlyn, he drew as much lumenys as he dared to hold without overwhelming himself. He used his arms to direct his wield, and it barreled outward, straight to Erynel, piercing her like a lance and passing through her into the Shroud to disappear leagues beyond.

Erynel shrieked in agony. "How dare you!"

Devlyn looked past her and into the barrel-shaped opening behind her where the frozen, ethereal ground was free of the Shroud for the first time in fourteen hundred years. The wield had occurred in both realms; he had felt Ellendren release the same wield and knew that she saw the same barrel-shaped opening and frozen ground. There was no snow, only grass and flowers encased in ice. It was only a single piercing through the malevolent Shroud, but he knew it was permanent—the Shroud would never be able to reclaim it.

He wanted to fall to his knees to catch his breath but could not. Doing so would have meant defeat. The effort required to pierce that hole, a leagues-long hole, into the Shroud had depleted him.

Grasping his knees, Devlyn took a gasping breath, then another. He felt a comforting hand on his back. He didn't have the energy to think of how that was possible, but he knew it was Ellendren's. He didn't understand it any more than how he had held her hand before confronting Erynel.

"I can't do that same wield a thousand times," Devlyn said through gasps, having no idea if she could hear him. "I don't think I could manage it a second time."

"We'll figure it out," Ellendren said.

Devlyn felt Erynel unleash another explosion of lightning, the tenebrys bolts streaking and branching haphazardly. Something about her seemed off now—unhinged. Had his last attack managed to harm her? It had pierced her after all. If so, it had only enraged her. Even as he focused on Erynel, he could not ignore the druids in their fight behind him. They were too far back for him to know what was happening and he didn't have the energy to reach out to them. Even if they did need his help, there was little he could do. Erynel laughed again as she rose above the ground, power humming off her in electric, thin branches of tenebrys, there one moment and gone the next.

"You cannot win, child. Krysenthiel is mine. Ramiel gave it to me and I will not release it nor can you hope to defeat me to take it back."

She began to form another wield, her power seemingly unconstrained. Her shadowed garment rippled as she constructed her wield and Devlyn saw the yellow lucilliae, one of the virtues prized by his ancestors, hanging around her neck. He didn't understand how she managed to wear it. The lucilliae of temperance seemed to have no effect on her. Was she so consumed by vice that she could not experience what the jewel offered? Was its presence there, and its influence over her corrupted heart, closer to a negation of the virtue and did it fuel its vicious extreme? For someone such as Erynel, did the jewel inspire the opposite of temperance when she beheld it?

Devlyn would have to make use of that line of reasoning; it offered possibilities, perhaps not beneficial in any way, but it did seem that the more power Erynel pulled in, the more threatened she felt, and the more she seemed to crack. He had yet to witness anyone consume so much of the erendinth that it destroyed them, but he had felt that possibility. Knowing when to stop pulling power into himself had always been a concern.

"Your Master can't help you here—not yet. He didn't give you enough strength." Devlyn risked the jibe, terrified about how it might end.

"*I* created the Shroud, you fool! A pinch point between the realms, allowing the Deurghol to pass through to claim their offered hosts." The electricity buzzing off her intensified; Devlyn could feel how much tenebrys she already held in her person and felt it increasing. He couldn't imagine how one person could hold so much raw power and not be destroyed. Holding that much lumenys would have likely left him incapacitated, but tenebrys—Devlyn couldn't finish his thought as he flung himself into the sky to avoid her lightning. The ground exploded behind him.

"Ramiel left you here alone. He offered you a stolen kingdom with no subjects. Your son stole us all away in chains and he too lost us when he vanished to lick his wounds for twelve hundred years. Your Master gave you nothing in return to be his pet—his slave." Devlyn zipped away again, now forming his own wield. He still maintained his shield of lumenys, but he also pressed into the elemental erendinth and embraced the other two transcendental erendinth. Wielding all seven erendinth at once, he formed a wield unlike anything he had configured before. It didn't have the electrifying feel of what Erynel wielded, but it touched something else. He felt something deep within himself as he interacted with all seven of the erendinth now.

Tenebrys exploded toward him again, and he lost his concentration to dodge the blast. Whatever he had felt deep inside had disappeared. He couldn't focus on that right now. Instead, his instincts driving him as he wielded, he formed a wield he had only imagined before; each erendinth was like a thread that he wove together in a braid. His wield sprang from him as Erynel again attacked. The wields collided in an explosion of light and dark, but neither stopped. Ears numb from the blast, Devlyn continued his wield, pushing it against Erynel's. The unleashed torrent continued where the two wields met, the outward explosion nonstop. Where Erynel's tenebrys wield tried to consume, corrupt, and destroy all that it touched, Devlyn's wield felt like it wanted to nourish and create and repair all that the tenebrys had poisoned—all that the Shroud had touched.

Devlyn stepped forward while Erynel drank in more tenebrys. She screeched and cackled. "Ramiel would never desert me like your Uriel and Auriel have! They have abandoned this realm and the light Uriel brought will soon be gone."

Stepping forward again, Devlyn knew he didn't match Erynel's wield, but he didn't have to. He maintained his strength and pushed forward, and like a balloon with too much air, Erynel and the awful amount of tenebrys she held exploded. Devlyn's wield, no longer fighting against something, launched forward and past where Erynel had been. Destroying her had not swept away the Shroud as he had hoped, but Erynel was gone and the yellow jewel fell from her neck, dropping at an incredibly swift rate.

Flinging himself toward the lucilliae, Devlyn caught it before it fell to the ground, miraculously uncorrupted by Erynel's possession. While she had worn the jewel, he had feared that its effect on her wasn't so much of a repulsion of the actual virtue, but rather that she had managed to alter the lucilliae to echo her own vice. Instead of her overabundance and lust for power consuming him, Devlyn felt the balance within the lucilliae. Moderation and complete control over himself answered his touch. Still hanging in the air, Devlyn took out the pouch with the other lucilliae and placed the fifth one inside. Violet, indigo, blue, green, and now yellow lights filled and wove together in the pouch. Devlyn's two lumols dimmed beneath the five lucilliae. He returned the bulging pouch to his inner pocket.

He could hear the druids still fighting somewhere, but knew he couldn't stay to fight, Teraeniel urgently calling him. He felt Ellendren reaching out to him. Searching out Abbie and Eagan, he said, *Erynel is dead. I have to get back to Teraeniel.*

Go, we felt her defeat. We are already retreating, Eagan replied.

The militarized grouping and readiness immediately caught Devlyn's attention as soon as he stepped out of Somnaeniel. Ellendren still stood beside the Shroud with the caravan close behind her and Arlyn, Viren, Byron, and Toryn standing by. If any tents had been pitched overnight, they were now down and packed; all that remained were animal-drawn wagons and carriages surrounded by thousands of armored elves.

Landing beside Ellendren, both still in their Phaedryn forms, he hugged her tightly. Fendryl must have felt Devlyn's return, for his griffin carried him toward the small group. Jeanne, Viren, Byron, and Toryn fell to one knee, their hands covering their hearts, and Fendryl inclined his head in a sign of respect.

"Please hold the formalities; I don't think we can afford them at present," Devlyn said.

"We can't," Jeanne said, rising from her knee, her eyes still downcast and her hand covering her heart. "We've received messages that the caravans nearest Verenthyl are already under attack and Eandyl is under siege. We've managed to maintain communication, but shadow elves are involved, and there is at least one report of a dragon."

"Any indication of the enemy's numbers? Are we holding them off?" Devlyn asked. He didn't know how to help them—he couldn't go back. He was needed here.

"The ei'ana have held their ground, and our forces are holding them off, but it's uncertain how long the other caravans can maintain that without any proper defenses. I'm not worried about Eandyl, the city will protect its people. We can also assume that a Deurghol is riding that dragon and Aren is likely searching for you."

Looking from one face to the next, Devlyn tried to think of something to ease the pressure on the other caravans. Their strength was terribly divided. Any one of their caravans could fall if he shifted his full strength against one caravan's defense. "How far are they from here? I might have defeated Erynel, but the Shroud still stands."

"She is gone then?" Fendryl asked.

"She is and the lucilliae of temperance is returned to us," Devlyn said.

"Thank the Light." Fendryl sounded relieved.

"My scouts spotted Erynor's forces. They'll reach us within the hour if we don't start moving. The wagons and elves unable to fight are closest to the Shroud and are ready to move forward the moment the Shroud is gone. I must return to the front. Destroy this blight on our home. We all have faith in you, Ei'denai, Ei'terel." Jeanne bowed and left to deal with the defense.

"Right, shall we?" Devlyn planted his feet and linked his wield with Ellendren and Arlyn. They formed the wield he'd used against Erynel, and as he felt the sensation deep within his being that appeared when he was wielding all seven of the erendinth, the sky darkened more than it already was. Dawn was still over an hour away but whatever light there had been, had vanished.

"I don't think my sword will fend this one off," Byron said, loud enough to draw Devlyn's attention.

Scanning the field for shadow elves, Devlyn saw only the docile Luminari elves, either too ill or too old or too young to fight.

"Devlyn…" Ellendren said, barely a whisper. She covered her mouth as she looked up.

Following her gaze, Devlyn swallowed hard then expanded his wings to launch himself into the air. He heard Ellendren scream No! after him as he flung himself up, Byron and Viren urging her to stay on the ground.

Shadows clung to the creature hovering in the sky. He hadn't descended toward the Luminari elves, only waited above as if assessing how best to deal with them. Menacing lightning crackled around Aren, threatening to lash out in any direction.

Tears formed in Devlyn's eyes from the wind whipping past his face. Even as he raced up, he pressed into the elemental erendinth before submitting and embracing the transcendental erendinth. The erendinth intermingled to create a beam of proportions he could scarce imagine.

Even as he unleashed his wield, black lightning rocketed through the sky, crisscrossing haphazardly. The energy flowed from Devlyn in a burst, noticeably different here than in Somnaeniel. Devlyn could feel that it had the same effect, but it had a physicality here that it had not had in the World-in-Between. As the two wields collided, Devlyn was pushed back by the blast and dark residue filled the sky.

Already exhausted after his battle with Erynel, Devlyn wielded aerys, forming a cyclone to throw Aren off course, to distract him while Devlyn caught his breath.

He had almost completed the wield when a flash of light spun through the air. Dazedly searching for the source, Devlyn saw Ellendren nearby, hurling dozens of miniature bolts through the sky. She had ignored the others and joined him to fight Aren. She wielded with a finesse that Devlyn could only envy. The light of the tiny bolts stung his eyes and they pierced into the shadows clinging to Aren.

Devlyn was both relieved and conflicted by her presence. Should anything happen to her while fighting this battle, he would never forgive himself.

This battle does not belong to you alone, Aliel conveyed to Devlyn, reminding him that Ellendren was more than capable. Devlyn agreed with the phoenix but was not enthused about it.

The Dark Phaedryn launched more tenebrys lightning in an extending arc. Seeing Aren here sickened Devlyn; Aren was impeding the Luminari elves—elves he had once led as their Exalted Aryl. Aren had not only betrayed his people, but for five and a half thousand years, he had allowed Eklean to remember him as a hero. Memories of the dream Devlyn had had of the Queen of Sorenthil's murder at Aren's hand bored into his mind. Aren had pulled Karina into the sky, then held her suspended while he sent tenebrys piercing into her before killing her. This elf had also corrupted one of the miervae in the Illumined Wood, forcing Devlyn to kill the great tree to prevent her from becoming a wraith.

Filled with haunted thoughts, Devlyn unleashed a second wield. He felt it surge from his being, arrowing toward Aren as an execution. As he watched his wield approach the Dark Phaedryn, pain erupted in his own chest, pain beyond anything he had ever felt or could imagine, searing right through him like a lance, rekindling the old wound on his back caused by Aren and the Deurghol's attack in Lankor.

Unable to breathe, Devlyn gaped in midair while an eternity seemed to pass. Paralyzed, he felt wind against his body and a scream reached his ears, a scream more painful than the actual wound.

Time no longer existed as he plummeted. There was a faint hope that someone might catch him as he faded in and out of consciousness.

An elated Ellendren saw the unbelievable wield Devlyn had just launched at Aren, proud of her husband and what he was capable of. Just as she thought the battle over—no one could survive that wield—she saw the tenebrys lightning leave Aren to twirl past and around Devlyn's wield.

It moved at a pace she had never dreamed possible, lashing though the sky and dividing as it went, seeking its target.

Tears formed when she felt the blast hit Devlyn. She felt it strike through her own chest, peeling through her insides, missing the heart, before passing out through her back.

She screamed as it exploded through Devlyn, unable to say whether it was more painful that she felt it herself, or that she knew the pain he suffered.

Thoughts had ceased.

With her golden wings folded flat against her body, Ellendren plummeted after Devlyn, streaming through the air faster then she had ever flown before. Wind tore at her face as she lunged after him and away from Aren, neglecting to protect herself from another attack. Whatever that monster did now no longer mattered. All that mattered was saving Devlyn.

37

Encased in Ice

Watching the scene through his grey, shadowed vision, Aren looked unbelievingly at the girl who flew after the boy without any chance of saving him. The two reminded him of someone. A husband and wife from a past memory, shielded deep in his mind, inaccessible. Something about the sight stirred him to reach back into that memory, but an even stronger and violent force barred him from it.

That particular sensation was not new; it was one of his earliest memories after the others had faded—the memories he could no longer access. Whenever he'd tried to access old memories from a time before the pain, that ferocious barrier tore at his mind before he could reach them.

Still, he felt something different just now. It too reminded him of something, but any attempt to remember never ended well for him. The pain associated with the one called Erynor was only a thimble of suffering compared to the suffering engendered by his Master. Aren knew he was the way he was because of his Master.

The greyed-out scene below continued, the boy falling at a great speed as the girl, arms outstretched and wings flat, tried to save him. *Fool girl.*

In that greyness, color and light began to flow from the boy. Color? Light? The world was only grey—what was happening? Had he once seen the world in color and light? Had his Master also blocked them as he'd blocked Aren's memories?

Eyes wide, Aren lost himself in that brilliance. *I know those colors.* Five different colors wove together with golden light that came from the boy and girl. A memory pushed through the haze of his mind. Those colors had once meant something to him—the virtues of his people—the people he had left behind somewhere. Vast valleys of luscious grass and golden canopies of flowered trees bloomed in his mind. Deep inside, Aren felt a terrible pain, that dreadful agony that was his first memory—but he felt more memories cloaked behind it. Pulling his gaze away from the five lucilliae, he tried to forget the colors. Blinking, he hoped the greyness would return and bury the pain associated with its memory.

Chancing a second glimpse, Aren again saw the five lucilliae. *How do I know what they are called?* Allowing his vision to linger, he felt something else push its way into him.

A tear rolled from his eye.

A dream long forgotten had come to pass. His descendants had done what he had once hoped for. Surrendering to some of the virtues of his people, the virtues contained in the jewels, broke through his interior, touching a place long frozen and forgotten.

The melting and breaking ice felt to Aren as though his entire body would shatter. It was just as painful, if not more so than that first memory when he had woken in darkness. He looked around at the whiteness that covered the ground below. Only the clouds above and the fog before him were the grey he knew so well. Neither belonged to this world.

Echoing deep inside him came a song, a beauty he had once regularly enjoyed and that had been hidden away. *Aren—I implore you, destroy this shell. Free us both.*

Yeniel? The name was as familiar as his own, as much a part of him as his wife—Jaequlyn. He did not feel her presence. She had transitioned to Lumaeniel. How and when he had no idea. Why was he here and she not?

Thick sheets of ice encased his heart; he remembered creating them to protect himself from the despair he'd felt at what he was forced to watch. Hundreds of thousands of Aldinari elves, tortured and corrupted, unable to escape the hell that was once the beautiful and tranquil Aldinare. Aren remembered enduring through thousands of years watching them suffer and becoming something different as he watched. They had started to worship him as though he were a god. He had endured through it all. His own people had accomplished their dreams in creating Ceurendol, only to have Erynor cut them off from their Life immortal and the virtues, unknowingly condemning himself and the Cyndinari. Erynor's own mother had returned and brought about the Shroud to cover Krysenthiel, a name Aren only knew from Erynor. And now, the Sha'ghol, Erynel Meriden was gone again.

He then relived a different memory. His youngest son, Theilyn, murdered by Erynor, during what was supposed to have been a peace talk with his great-grandson, Faerndryn. Aren only remembered Faerndryn as a youth when they lived on Luminare. After that, Aren had begun to suppress everything that he was and allowed the ice to lock everything away. That pain. That had been his first memory before his tortured past and the love that came before it had returned just now. *Theilyn. My son.*

Cold hands hugged Devlyn against a colder body. Squinting through wounded eyes, he thought death itself was greeting him. The creature holding him had no hair, but the eyes did not belong to the shell that held them, for a light poured through the once-dead grey eyes.

Realizing who held him, Devlyn started to press into the erendinth to renew his attack. How was he on the ground and his body not broken? Devlyn felt another hand on his shoulder, a warm hand. Turning his head, he saw a terrified Ellendren looking down at him. His wield dissolved before it gained any substance.

Too many questions assaulted Devlyn as he tried to reconcile Aren holding him like a child, and Ellendren standing beside the creature that just tried to kill him. *Did he save me?*

Devlyn remembered falling. He remembered that last moment when his vision darkened and his memories stopped, a kindness before what should have been the end.

"There's little time. Erynor is sending his legions. If we can't reach our cities, Erynor will destroy us all," Aren said.

"But…how?"

"You freed me—the virtues of our people, placed in the lucilliae, freed me." A distressed look overwhelmed Aren as he spoke. "I don't deserve forgiveness; my crimes are too heavy to bear."

"What are you saying?" Ellendren asked.

"Only that I want that Shroud destroyed."

"We have already tried; it's too much. Erynel is gone and yet it remains. Even if you added your own strength, what more can we possibly do to it?" Devlyn asked.

"It's not my strength that you need. Only the Luminari can reclaim their home."

"Are you suggesting…" Devlyn shook his head. "But that's impossible."

"How do you think Ceurendol was crafted?"

"But that was after your time," Ellendren said. "How could you possibly know about Ceurendol?"

"I was forced to watch; I saw everything, then forgot everything." Aren turned his gaze northwest toward Arenthyl. "There isn't the time to tell you all."

Devlyn recalled when the Illumined Wood had lent him strength to banish the shade that had been forming from the miervae's corpse. Could it be the same? Could he connect with all the Luminari? Did he even have the strength to do so? Quieting his heart, he searched. And as he expanded his awareness, he realized that he wasn't—they weren't—alone. It had started with him bonding with Ellendren and Arlyn, but it didn't end there.

In great swaths, he felt pulses cross the land, tiny lights huddled across Krysenthiel's outer rim. With Arlyn's smiling approval and Ellendren's joyous support, Devlyn started connecting with startled individuals who were unaccustomed to another bonding with them in such an intimate manner. Memories and thoughts collided with his own, senses of invasion and insistence for privacy rebelled against him. Spreading ever outward, hundreds of Luminari became thousands, evolving into tens of thousands and more. The entirety of the Luminari opened up to him, not just in Krysenthiel, but in Cor'lera and other villages where some were still in exile.

Devlyn had never imagined there were so many Luminari. As shocking as the number was, the distances he crossed to reach them was even more startling. He was sensing them as far south as Sudern and even in Broid.

There was only one Luminari in Broid—his mother. An inner light bloomed from her being. The connection brought conflicted emotions. Here he was trying to reclaim Krysenthiel, while his own mother was still Erynor's slave in Broid. Jaerol, Liam, and Rusyl came to mind. Had they succeeded in rescuing her? He knew she was still in Broid and it worried him.

Still supported by Aren, a wondrous glow grew within Devlyn, emanating from his heart, now connected with every Luminari elf. He pushed himself to his feet as the incredible power joining them hummed in the air, radiating off Devlyn in powerful waves. Rather than forming a single beam to pierce into the Shroud, Devlyn wielded a wave of lumenys and felt a calling from within the Shroud. It was not the Shroud, but something—someone else. Whoever it was, was locked within it, frozen in Lake Saeryndol.

Bound to the Luminari elves, their very essences connected to his own, Devlyn reached out through the Shroud to the creature, delving into the ice, trying to call it forth. And then, he felt yet another presence.

He felt his mother, felt her heart filled with a radiant light that wasn't her own. It poured forth from wherever she was in Broid and tore across Eklean at an incredible speed until a terrifying fire, reminiscent of the seraph, fell from the darkened sky. Within his heart of hearts, Devlyn recognized this being, and knew it as the enthiel Auriel, Guardian of the Luminari. Realization swept over Devlyn—his mother had been holding Auriel all this time. The Lorenthien heirs had, in turn over the years, kept Auriel safe and hidden from Ramiel and Erynor.

Unable to pull himself from his wield, he joined his essence, and that of all the Luminari, to their enthiel, just as Auriel's astonishing power broke into the Shroud. Devlyn felt the enthiel collide with the solid ice that was Lake Saeryndol and connecting with yet another presence—a greater presence—that was somehow frozen in the waters.

The long-quiet Uriel, Lord of the Stars, stirred inside his glacial prison, adding his own power to Devlyn's. Rapt, Devlyn felt as though he should fall prostrate in the presence of one so near Anaweh's own likeness.

As incredible as connecting with the entirety of the Luminari elves had been and still was, bonding with Uriel and Auriel left Devlyn in a euphoria he could not contain. He unleashed his wield and a giant wave of light washed over the Shroud. Devlyn felt it stretch across every length of Krysenthiel, penetrating through and even into Somnaeniel, from a meadow of golden flowers to the highest peak of Mount Verinien, and on to the deepest depths of Lake Saeryndol.

Yet the Shroud did not disappear and Devlyn's heart plummeted even as he maintained the wield. From behind him, a sickening laugh filled his ears. High above soared one of the Deurghol on a dragon. Was it the same one that had attacked him in Lankor?

Nearly overwhelmed with grief at his failure, he knew that if the combined efforts of the Luminari and two anadel could not destroy the Shroud, nothing could.

Yet he did not release the wield, too reluctant to admit defeat.

From the corner of his eye, he saw a flash of shining metal. He tried to reach out for Toryn as she sprinted past them, racing into the Shroud, her sword held aloft. The determination he felt through their shared connection amazed him. There was no saying what had overcome her, but she was ignoring all the calls to stop. She was jeopardizing her life for nothing.

Toryn didn't know what had come over her. She was already exhausted and her part in the battle hadn't even begun, a battle she knew was only just beginning. But she had felt the incredible amount of energy that had passed through her. She had never felt so connected to her people before. It felt like golden threads of light linked every Luminari elf together. As though the Lorenthien aryl had sought out each and every one of them and had pulled the individual threads back toward them so the aryl could act as a conduit.

When the incredible wave poured over the Shroud, Toryn, like every other Luminari, held her breath. Lucillia's prophecy was well-known to them all, and Devlyn had reaffirmed it by promising he could destroy the Shroud. Yet it remained. The powerful wield that had just been unleashed had set it humming but it was still there. The aryl's wield didn't seem to have affected it.

A ball of anger rose in her throat and she heard herself growl, "No." She refused to believe that after everything they had gone through and with the complete and combined strength of her people, the Shroud was still there, the grey mist still visible.

Toryn didn't know how to wield. She didn't even know if she had the ability to learn. She didn't want to know. All Toryn had ever wanted was a good sword, and to become a Guardian knight. She would have to survive today. She would have to survive this foolish motion her body was making. She knew that the Erynien legions weren't her only enemies. She had long viewed the Shroud as her enemy too. Toryn would fight that ethereal beast, incorporeal mist or not.

She did not hear the aryl and the others screaming at her to stop, nor did she look back. Still connected to every Luminari elf through the Lorenthien aryl, Toryn charged into the Shroud with her sword held high, yelling, "For Lucillia! For Arenthyl! For Krysenthiel! For Luminare!"

Her sword felt charged somehow, as though she had somehow managed to channel her spirit into it, linked to every Luminari elf. Toryn didn't understand what exactly was happening, nor did she want to. She did want to use whatever this sudden power was though and she swung her sword at the poisonous mist.

As her sword slashed through the air, she thought it would be an empty and meaningless act and braced for the weight of the sword not connecting with anything, but to her surprise and relief, her sword caught. It tugged through the Shroud somehow and seemed to pierce it.

———

Flying through the outer reaches of the Shroud, Devlyn felt Toryn's luminous spirit sharpening around her sword. Devlyn's wield drew strength from her, his own resolve hardening when tremors shook through the Shroud. What had Toryn and her sword done?

Wave after wave of all seven erendinth rolled over and through the Shroud, Toryn still sprinting deeper into it and slashing at it as though it was a physical beast. Devlyn held his breath as his wield impossibly covered the entirety of Krysenthiel.

There was no explosion, only a shudder then mist and darkness vanishing into nothingness, leaving only starlight to fall once more on Krysenthiel.

38

GOLDEN LANDS

The Shroud was gone. Impossibly and wondrously gone. Devlyn closed his eyes, then opened them again to see if it was just a trick, to see if the Shroud would return to plague the land as it had done for fourteen hundred years. But only frozen, golden-hued flowers remained where it had stood moments before the sun dawned. The sun rose and rays of light spilled across the frozen land of Krysenthiel. Sparkling, ice-encrusted petals began to glint in the golden lights of the morning sun, a quiet stir from a slumber long overdone.

The turbulent clouds that had been threatening Teraeniel, warning of Ramiel's return and that had somehow been interlaced with the Shroud, had been banished with it. Those clouds would be back—Ramiel was not finished nor would he give up because Erynel had lost her Shroud. Their absence was enough for now though; not even Ramiel's threat could dampen the Luminari elves' ecstatic joy at returning to Krysenthiel. Devlyn felt the atmosphere warm with every moment as he flew higher, Ellendren and Aren on either side of him.

The caravan that had been stopped just beyond the Shroud was once again underway. Arenthyl was a long way off and Krysenthiel had no roads to quicken the journey. Wanting nothing more than to celebrate the defeat of Erynel and the Shroud, the very real threat of Erynien legions marching to battle loomed over everyone. They only had a small window to complete the journey across Krysenthiel to reach the island city resting on the slopes of Mount Verinien. While the entirety of Lake Saeryndol was frozen through, Uriel's resurfacing had likely quickened the melting. The entire lake wouldn't return to its natural state immediately, but the uppermost layer could melt, making the water too deep to wade through.

"You might have destroyed the Shroud, but you cannot escape! The chains of slavery are your only future." Devlyn felt the Deurghol's presence before its voice reached his ears, squealing in his mind. It would not let Krysenthiel thaw and return to a land of flowers but would see it scorched, sending unrelenting fires toward the slowly defrosting ground, determined to leave nothing but smoke and ashes. Ellendren and Aren were also aware of the Deurghol and its dragon, and the three of them headed off in different directions. They had to stop it.

Twirling in the air, Devlyn wielded ignys, pressing himself into the fiery power to redirect the dragon's flames back into its belly. Sending the blast in any other direction might allow it to fall on the Luminari elves below.

Through his bond with Ellendren, he could feel her below him, unperturbed. She was seeing to the safety of the caravan and would ensure that no harm reached those in her charge.

Bolts of tenebrys lightning flew from the Deurghol's palms, streaking over his dragon's head and thundering toward Devlyn.

Already embracing lumenys, Devlyn wrought a wield against the tenebrys bolts. Light and darkness danced in the sky as the two wields fought each other, casting shadows across the land below. Devlyn had always thought that tenebrys was the antithesis to lumenys, but after destroying the Shroud and Erynel, he had realized that lumenys was only part of the equation. The seven erendinth of creation were what had first scattered the Void when the seven irythil had come to create Teraeniel and Somnaeniel.

Holding the Deurghol's attention, Devlyn signaled Aren.

A wield Devlyn had never seen flew toward the Deurghol. Aerys was the dominant erendinth, intertwined with animys and lumenys, the slightest hint of umbrys woven in as well. The wield was near invisible to Devlyn as it rushed from above. He expected the wield to strike the Deurghol, but instead it spun about the dark dragon like thread, clamping its wings against its sides.

With a sickening scream, the Deurghol fought against the constricting wield on the dragon, clearly not anticipating that Aren would have turned sides. It was still an amazing turn of events to Devlyn.

He watched as the dragon and Deurghol fell at a dizzying speed. Expecting them to crash on the ground, Devlyn held his breath thinking them done with, when at the last moment the dragon's enormous wings unfurled. Wary of facing Devlyn and Aren alone, the dragon and Deurghol flew back south to their allies. "So, death is what you choose," the Deurghol hissed, his voice barely reaching Devlyn's sensitive ears.

"He'll be back," Aren said, hovering next to Devlyn. "He won't come alone either."

Flying beside Aren felt odd. This elf—this corrupted Phaedryn—had tried to kill him time and time again, nearly succeeding in Lankor. Aren changing sides was unthinkable. Perhaps the stories told to children about Aren were true, and that he truly had not been himself since returning from what many believed was beyond the grave. Devlyn wanted to trust him and given that there were limited options, he found himself leaning toward it. Still, he was uncomfortable.

"How far to Tenyl?" Devlyn asked, his gaze still on the dragon's large body, growing smaller as the distance increased.

"By wing, only a couple hours, but those on foot won't make it until tomorrow morning, assuming they do not stop to rest tonight," Aren said.

"We can't afford to stop," Devlyn said, watching the slow pace of the tens of thousands below, trudging through mud mixed among the thawing greenery. Krysenthiel had no roads—it had never needed them. But now, wagons and carriages rolled slowly through the trampled terrain with their wheels regularly getting stuck. They pushed on though, wheels laboriously freed from the sticky muck and the caravan crawled on at its impossibly slow pace.

Sounds of another battle reached Devlyn's ears. *So soon?* The Deurghol he and Aren had fought had retreated only far enough to return with a larger force, charging toward the Luminari with an additional three dragons. These dragons were not as large as the one the Deurghol flew on, but they were still dragons, and capable of horrendous destruction. Knowing that each one carried a shadow elf fully capable of wielding tenebrys didn't ease his unsettled stomach either.

The great shadows accompanying the dragons fell on the Erynien legions below.

Waiting for the dragons to divide and fly past the Luminari defenses and toward him and Aren, Devlyn's heart dropped as he watched the dragons pour down flames on the rearguard. Someone in those ranks wielded ignys to push the fires away, but Devlyn had no idea if that same wielder was capable of warding off tenebrys-laced fire.

Launching himself toward the beleaguered defenses, Devlyn filled himself with all three of the transcendental erendinth, while pressing into the elemental erendinth. He remembered all too well how to deal with shadow elves. He could rid them from the World-Below.

Maniacal laughter amid horrendous screams filled the air as he rushed toward the nearest shadow elf, staying clear of the Deurghol.

His wield was nowhere near as clean and refined as Aren's had been, more brute force than anything else. Devlyn launched it at the nearest shadow elf. The first notes of tenebrys flicked into the sky, but his wield consumed the shadow elf before she could give form to her negating lightning. Tearing into her core, Devlyn felt the dozens of spirits caught within her, extending her wretched life, corrupting her further with every addition.

She screeched horrendously and a burst of lights swept out of the decaying body, no longer kept whole by their sustaining qualities. Each spirit lingered for a moment, swirling liberally before fading as it passed to the World-in-Between to find the World-Beyond. Devlyn wondered if the shadow elf would pass to Lumaeniel or if Ramiel would pull her into the Void to serve again in some other capacity.

Pleased with the demise of the first shadow elf, Devlyn sought another, leaving the dragon crashing to the ground, caught in the same binding wield that Aren had wielded on the Deurghol's dragon. The fall wouldn't kill the beast, but it would at least remove it from this battle.

Devlyn's golden form did not remain unnoticed; destroying the shadow elf called forth the attention of the other two, as well as the Deurghol. Bolts of tenebrys shot from below, amid the Erynien forces.

Great, they're down there too. He should have expected there would be more shadow elves than just the three on the dragons.

He knew he could not destroy them all, let alone hold them off. But looking down, Devlyn watched as the Luminari and Eldinari elves took the upper hand in the battle, shattering the Erynien offensive.

"Don't expect you'll reach any city for protection," said the Deurghol, his words slithering into Devlyn's heart. "You know with just as much certainty as I do, that force after force will crash against your so-called Guardians, breaking them as was done long ago. This battle has been fought before, and the full force of the Guardian knights could not withstand us then."

Each word cut into Devlyn's heart, as though the Deurghol voiced each of his fears aloud.

"Twisted words will never substitute truth," said Aren, suddenly appearing beside Devlyn.

"Was it painful?" A sinister smile showed behind the Deurghol's shadowed veil. "Regaining those memories you once held so dear? Our Master will not be pleased—you were one of his favorite pets."

"I am no one's pet; least of all Ramiel's!"

Hearing the name aloud sent a shiver down Devlyn's spine. He had learned to avoid using that name, lest he call forth the attention of those seeking him. What harm could the name be now though? The enemy knew precisely where he was and what the Luminari were hoping to achieve.

"You dare speak the Master's name? You will not live to repent your sins."

Devlyn heard the fury in Aren's mind. He had not meant to hear Aren's thoughts, but they thrashed there, screaming for anyone to hear. Devlyn wanted to return the threat, but nothing came to mind that would defend Aren. Turning in midair, the Deurghol again promised to return even as he called a retreat for the dragons while the legions continued their battle below. Certain that every dragon was at a safe distance away, Devlyn followed Aren to the ground and sought out Jeanne.

Aware of Aren's conversion, if not the whole story, Jeanne eyed him carefully. Devlyn knew that Jeanne cherished the memory of Aren, holding every tale of him made legend dear to her heart. Her breath was quick, and her face glistened with sweat. "Of the three caravans, this one has the furthest distance to travel, and the largest number to move." Despite her exhaustion, her back was straight and her shoulders set back. "These fields were never meant for travel."

Devlyn turned to Aren, and asked, "I know the Time Key was after your time but, as Phaedryns, could we open a seguian to Tenyl?"

"I don't see how. We can pass through space and time on our own, due to the phoenix's nature, but I can't imagine us capable of forming a seguian, let alone one large enough for everyone to pass through."

"You can't," a squeaky voice said. "But *we* can."

Standing beside him and coming to just above Devlyn's knees, impossibly, was Skimp. The minum bowed his head to the elves present. The last time Devlyn had seen Skimp was when he had taken him, Velaria, and Alex from Everin to Gwilnor.

"How did you…" Devlyn began, remembering the Time Wardens had an uncanny sense of foreknowledge, but also wondering if the Luminari elves' time of need is what had brought the minums out of hiding. They had vanished from their home in the Freiton Wood just as Erynor had been desperately seeking to control their power by gaining the Time Key for himself.

"If you'll beg my pardon," Skimp said, his head tilted back to look up at Aren. "It was your wife, Ei'terel Jaequlyn, who encouraged your grandson and his wife, Desmyn and Valeriel Lorenthien, to create and bestow the Time Key to us, permitting us to shape our own future, free of threats from the taller races, free from chains and forced servitude. She gave us more than anyone could give anyone."

"She was always my better," Aren said.

"She spoke otherwise." Skimp grinned, showing no issue with Aren. "Should we unlock Tenyl's gates and get us all to safety?"

"How do you anticipate getting everyone there?" Devlyn asked.

"Tiny seguians are the least of what we can do," Skimp said, still grinning ear to ear. "Aren, go with the first group, just to make certain it's safe on the other side."

Jeanne motioned twenty knights under her command forward as Skimp formed a seguian between his palms. It was the minute size Devlyn was accustomed to, and Aren with twenty other armed elves crossed before the seguian closed.

"Now, you'll want to fly up there and get a better view." Skimp formed another seguian, disappearing in the globe.

Devlyn cast Jeanne a shocked look.

"I'll keep anyone from reaching the Time Wardens. The Guardians will be the last to cross, Ei'denai."

"Thank you, Jeanne. I'll see you behind Tenyl's walls," he said and leaped into the sky.

Devlyn first looked south for the Erynien legions, still engaged with the Luminari defenders but the dragons were nowhere along the visible horizon yet, still regrouping, he assumed. Shifting his sight to the enormous number of elves and wagons and animals below, Devlyn saw nine large spheres appear along the edges of those still trekking through the mud. Recognizing the giant orbs as the largest seguians he had ever seen, Devlyn was awed at the size, each one large enough for eight horses abreast to pass through comfortably. The seguians formed a large horseshoe around the elves.

After a moment of confusion, the first wagon went through, quickly followed by the masses. Devlyn watched the numbers slowly dwindle. There was no way of knowing whether they were crossing into conflict, but Devlyn hoped for the best, terrified that some sort of trap awaited them.

One column ended and the first seguian closed, only to reopen at a more congested node. Devlyn watched in awe as those gathered below dwindled in number, saving themselves a potentially perilous journey, with shadow elves and a Deurghol nipping at their heels.

As the gathering decreased with every moment, Devlyn was prepared to allow himself a sigh of relief when a rumbling sound came from the south. He quickly spun about and squinted to get a better view. To no surprise, an incredible force of legionnaires—was it Erynor's entire army?—charged against the remaining Luminari, creating a second battle front. It would take the better part of an hour to reach them but glancing down at those who had not yet crossed the seguians, Devlyn feared that it was an hour they did not have.

Diving down to Jeanne whose eyes were trained on the southern horizon, he spoke quickly.

"We have to slow them," Devlyn said, panic cresting his voice. "We'll never be able to stop them before we all reach Tenyl."

"I would suggest ordering anyone who does not require the seguians to leave now, particularly the Eldinari elves and their griffins. Have them double up, the griffins are strong enough. That will at least alleviate some of the congestion for the seguians."

Devlyn reached out to Fendryl, who was near the frontline, armed and ready. *Fly for Tenyl, take as many as you can on the griffins.*

Even as he wondered whether Fendryl would oppose the idea of abandoning the fight, Devlyn watched hundreds of griffins tear into the sky, each carrying two elves, some three.

Give Jeanne my regards. Fendryl, among the last to leave, accompanied the words with a wave.

Returning to the sky, Devlyn worried, caught between the diminishing numbers and the advancing Erynien legion. A dark cloud hung over the legion, keeping the sun's rays off their numbers and announcing their nearness.

Two more columns ended and two more seguians closed, forming again at other points. With every Luminari that disappeared through a seguian, Devlyn felt his tension ease, only to increase when he looked on the enemy advance. With the Eldinari elves flying to Tenyl, the Time Wardens had a better chance of saving them all, but their method still required time. The painstakingly slow process had left Devlyn nearly biting his nails.

He returned to Jeanne. "There's too many of us."

"Then we need to slow the enemy."

"At what risk? I won't let our soldiers sacrifice themselves."

"The sacrifice is ours to give."

"Forgive me Jeanne, but you are needed for the coming battles."

"I will not desert this field while one elf remains."

"Then you'll have to protect me yourself, because I'm not going without you!" Devlyn did not realize he was yelling, nor did he notice how closely he and Jeanne were standing.

Devlyn watched her struggle with her own fury, knowing perfectly well that it was directed at him, and not the Erynien legion.

"If you take one step in front of me, I will incapacitate you, Ei'denai, and will personally toss you through a seguian."

Nodding his consent, Devlyn pressed into terys and aquaeys, thinking the muddied ground required some maneuvering. The sun hung in the sky as it reached its midday zenith, impassively watching the impending battle. Carefully crafting his wield so it wouldn't be seen by shadow elves or enemy wielders, Devlyn laced it into the mud, freezing it to form a seamless sheet of muddy ice. Stretching his wield across the entirety of the Erynien legion, Devlyn expanded the sheet of ice twenty soldiers back.

The Erynien legion was still a ways off, but Devlyn intensified the ice, readying it for their arrival.

"Ei'denai," came a squeaky voice below his waist.

Looking down, Devlyn found Skimp. "What are you doing here?"

"This is the next group."

"You've gotten everyone else out?"

"Nearly. By the time this group passes to Tenyl, no one but the Erynien legion will be here."

"You'll have to start at a different point," Devlyn said, throwing a final imploring look at Jeanne.

Understanding, Skimp disappeared.

"Good thing he didn't argue," Devlyn said.

"Never forget who you are." Jeanne did not turn to Devlyn as she spoke, but kept her gaze south, vigilant as though she stood on a watchtower.

Livid screams echoed from the south. Devlyn couldn't hear them slip and tumble all over themselves but could imagine it and smiled.

"Any more tricks?" Jeanne asked.

"I doubt they'll fall for that a second time."

"You only know a single trick?" Her eyes had narrowed with the taunt.

Narrowing his eyes in return, Devlyn pressed himself into aerys. Sensing the nearness of the legion on the air, he unleashed his wield as he looked behind himself to see how many still had to cross the seguians. Skimp had assured them that they were nearly finished, but the mass of bodies told him otherwise.

Aerys rushed south in a strengthening gale that threw soldiers and shadow elves backward. It seemed to further enrage the legionnaires and

Devlyn saw them rushing toward him and Jeanne, screeching and cackling as they ran. Pressing into terys, Devlyn dug into the ground, heaving dense boulders from below the surface, hurling one after the other against the enemy, doing everything he could to buy the Time Wardens more time.

Jeanne unsheathed her slender verathn, a beautiful and unmatched sword. Much like Jeanne, the opaque crystal surface had a light of its own, daring any to challenge her. Jeanne cleaved her sword vertically, slicing the first enemy fool enough to come at her.

Wielding ignys and terys, Devlyn now launched exploding stones at the Erynien legion, interlacing his wields with animys and umbrys against the shadow elves. Sweat glistened on his brow, and a semicircle of defeated Cyndinari elves began to form around Jeanne and himself.

Chancing a glance backward, he saw that only he and Jeanne remained. Another wave of legionnaires pushed forward. Pressing deeper into aerys, Devlyn wielded a globe of air about himself and Jeanne, keeping the attackers back. He grabbed Jeanne's wrist and for a moment Devlyn thought she would sever his own hand from his wrist.

Eyes closed, Devlyn imagined the place he had never visited, and willed himself to Tenyl.

CITIES OF LUMARYL

Vaulted ceilings and soaring towers defined the Taerinior aryl's palace of Tenyl. Devlyn recognized some architectural elements he'd seen in Gwilnor, and in Eandyl; lofty pointed arches forming the rooflines greeted him as he took in the city, the whimsical touch of each building playing off the other, as though the whole city harmonized. As impressive as the palatial forms were, lumaryl gave Tenyl a dimension of liveliness that felt unprecedented and wholly unique. Even after experiencing Eandyl, Tenyl felt wholly new and wonderfully different. A constant glow thrummed through the lumaryl, and Devlyn thought that the stone from Luminare could perhaps lift on its own accord to do what it pleased.

Devlyn had apologized to Jeanne the moment they had appeared outside Tenyl's illustrious gate lest she chop his hand off for daring to remove her from the battle before she was ready to go. Then he had hugged Ellendren who had been waiting for him there.

Reaching Tenyl had left everyone in heightened spirits, including the reinstalled Aryl of Tenyl. Ei'denai Iridil and Ei'terel Enoria Taerinior, had personally welcomed Devlyn and Ellendren to their ancestral home, offering them the finest rooms they could find. Rooms they would undoubtedly claim as their own once Devlyn and Ellendren went the rest of the way to Arenthyl. Still, the thought was nice and Ellendren made sure Devlyn acknowledged the Aryl of Tenyl's generosity.

Devlyn passed Enoria again as he walked through the palace. She was beside herself in excitement, and for a moment, Devlyn thought she was just as likely of floating as the lumaryl was.

"Hello there, Devlyn. Is the suite acceptable? I see you took advantage of the bath hall."

"It was very refreshing and I feel much better for it."

"I am delighted to hear that. You would not believe the state of the furniture here in the palace," Enoria said, keeping step with Devlyn.

"Is some of it damaged? The furnishings in the suite you offered to Ellendren and me seem to be in pristine condition," Devlyn said.

"Yes, exactly! Our attendants have spent the day reporting to me on the palace's state, and the vast majority of the furniture surprisingly shows no signs of deterioration. Remarkable, isn't it?" Enoria beamed.

"Truly. Eandyl was in much the same condition," Devlyn said, caring little about the state of the furniture here in Tenyl's palace. The Luminari might have a brief respite from the Erynien legions, but they still had to reach Arenthyl before there was another assault. Hopefully, they could maintain the distance currently between them. Erynor would not permit his army to rest, and every legionnaire likely now made for Arenthyl, hoping to thwart the Luminari from claiming their greatest prize.

"Yes, but this is not Eandyl, now is it?" Enoria flung her arm outward as though Tenyl was the most spectacular city in the world. Enoria and the elves who had been headed to Tenyl did not have to risk another journey but Devlyn was already thinking of the next move for so many more elves who needed to get to Arenthyl. Tenyl's lumaryl walls would keep Enoria and the others here safe from the Erynien legions for the time being.

"Forgive me, could you direct me to your husband? We have to arrange our next move," Devlyn said.

She flushed momentarily, realizing that she had been too focused on her city. "Would you listen to me go on about the palace's furnishings while we still have to reclaim the rest of our kingdom! You must think the worst of me. I believe he's digging through the old records, searching for family names associated with property, like they found at Eandyl."

"Thank you, Ei'terel."

"Of course. You're not thinking of leaving the city today, are you? You only just arrived!"

"I'm afraid we have little choice in the matter. To wait would put us in further peril." Devlyn placed his hand across his heart, bowed to Enoria and left her as she was returning the bow.

He continued his search for Iridil, relieved to not have a shadow elf or Deurghol launching tenebrys at him presently, although the battle for Krysenthiel was far from over. They had yet to receive any news from the other caravans. He hoped they had reached their destinations. Were Ostyl, Verenthyl, and Winstyl unsealed and occupied once more? The only consolation was that the largest Erynien legion had done what was expected of them and had followed them to Tenyl and away from the other caravans, knowing that Devlyn and Ellendren were with them. He hoped the ei'ana heading toward Septyl had managed to repel whatever Erynor had thrown at them. If they could deal with the Tenebrae School infiltrating Gwilnor, then surely they could fight off an attack by shadow elves and soldiers.

His feet echoed along the long corridors of the palace, his eyes moving from one expansive window to another, enjoying the remarkable views of Tenyl's gardens, bridges, and towers. Every wall offered its own ornamentation, sung from the lumaryl stone into beautiful scrollwork and busts set in niches in the walls. Sections of lumaryl stone formed vast paneled frames, where whimsical tapestries hung, untouched by time or deterioration. Devlyn recognized the lierathnil tapestries instantly, each just as wondrous and mysterious as the next. They presented beautiful and whimsical landscapes, most likely depicting Luminare. Despite the urgency he felt about finding Iridil, Devlyn did stop a few times to take in the individual threads, for he swore he could see movement in the images, either a small animal or a leaf blowing on an unseen breeze.

Finally reaching the old archives, Devlyn found Iridil immersed in piles of books taken from the vast shelves lining the large room. Ten other elves were tending their own piles of books when Devlyn came in.

"Ah, Ei'denai," an elated Iridil greeted him. "You won't believe this. We of course expected to find the records of Tenyl, showing family names and their property, but look at this." Iridil shoved a hefty book into Devlyn's hands.

At the top of the page was a single line in Aelish, but beneath, listed in columns were family names and their property. Not all that surprising, but as Devlyn followed the column down, dozens of names appeared, accompanied with dates and their rightful property.

Turning a page, Devlyn's eyes nearly popped from his head. Words and numbers on the page were changing as he read them. "How is this possible?" Devlyn could barely speak, he was so shocked.

"I was surprised too! But come, look at the Taerinior records." Grabbing a second book, Iridil flipped through the pages before landing on a specific page.

Devlyn followed his finger until it landed on Iridil and Enoria Taerinior. Next to their names was a vast sum of lumols, narols, and ke-nols, still unaccounted for, but in golden ink Devlyn read, PALACE OF THE ARYL OF TENYL: REDEEMED.

Amazed by the discovery, Devlyn rubbed his eyes just to be certain. He had seen how the Luminari records worked in Eandyl, but he hadn't yet seen the scrollwork immediately update.

"I dreaded the process of assigning or selling off property in the city, but now I can't help but look forward to it," Iridil said, turning the page to another listing. "You'll have to forgive me, here I am scouring through ancient, yet magically updated records, and you most likely need to speak to me about something urgent."

"Actually, I'm quite relieved about this discovery. I was worried they might be unique to Eandyl. Ellendren might have figured it out, but I would not have walked into the archives on my own." Devlyn took another look about the room. "But yes, I did come here on a different matter."

Iridil placed the heavy book atop the pile nearest him, turning his full attention to Devlyn.

"As you know, Arenthyl is still vacant, well, for the most part," Devlyn said, remembering the small contingent of Aldinari elves inside a protective barrier of their making in the city. "As it stands, we cannot stay in Tenyl. Even with every available space taken for sleeping, Tenyl is about to burst at its seams and we still couldn't squeeze everyone into the city if we were attacked."

"You're completely right; if it wasn't for the resources we brought with us, this city would be depleted of its natural fruits by the end of the week. Miraculous that after all these years, the trees still bear those golden fruit."

"It really is a miracle. I never imagined that the fruit of the kirenae trees survived," Devlyn said, just as mystified by their healthy appearance after fourteen hundred years frozen beneath the Shroud, without so much of a hint of deterioration. "Considering Tenyl's location, Jeanne does not believe Erynor will attempt a siege here, but we cannot say the same for Verenthyl and Eandyl. That being the case, as we already discussed, Jeanne is leaving only eight Guardians here. They'll continue their training and recruitment, bolstering their numbers while leading the defense of Tenyl."

"Of course," Iridil said.

"For reasons we still don't fully understand, you and Enoria, as Aryl of Tenyl, have a special link to the very stones of this city. As you've discovered, lumaryl has unique properties, but most importantly, if the Aryl of Tenyl decides to deny entrance, no one can come in."

"Quite right; Enoria and I have already lifted the ward, if that's even the correct wording. I feel absolutely at a disadvantage with all this terminology so familiar to the ei'ana. For the first time in my life, I wish I had left Lucillia in my youth to study at Gwilnor."

"Believe me, you're not the only one feeling disadvantaged." Devlyn laughed, the truth in the matter more disturbing than he cared to admit.

"Fortunately, there are some from that time to educate us," Iridil said. "Will the minums create seguians again?"

"They've attempted to create a seguian into Arenthyl, only to discover that doing so is impossible. Lake Saeryndol is still frozen solid, and they've chosen three points where they can take us, each a two-hour march from the city."

"I wish you well, Ei'denai."

"Thank you, Iridil. Once we reach Arenthyl," said Devlyn, careful not to say *if*, "and settle in, we'll reestablish lines of communication." Devlyn bowed and said farewell to Iridil, off to meet Ellendren. She was already waiting at the docks with other Luminari destined for Arenthyl.

He quickly reached the docks, where he saw thousands of Luminari elves there, waiting with their belongings. Lake Saeryndol loomed as far as the eye could see beyond the city's edge; even Devlyn's lighted vision could see nothing but the frozen lake in the distance.

Ellendren's luminous form immediately caught not only his attention but nearly everyone else's eye. She had always been beautiful, but when bonded with Tariel, Devlyn found it all but impossible to look away; she was a bright star.

Making his way through the crowds—it wasn't too difficult as people parted to let him by—Devlyn reached Ellendren and kissed her on the cheek. She blushed instantly, making him smile.

"Are you ready to go home?" he asked, his nose against her forehead.

"More than ready. I've read countless books on Arenthyl, and I've even spoken with Jeanne about what to expect, but every time I mention it, she tells me, words could never do it justice."

"She must miss it."

"Could you imagine? Fourteen hundred years locked away in a mountain fortress."

"Jeanne would have died before betraying Ithendryl and leaving the Guardians' fortress before it was time. Besides, it was only their connection with Aliel's egg that kept them from aging all those years."

"Very true. Well, I think the Time Wardens are ready," Ellendren said, noticing the crowds shifting. "They've already sent three groups of knights through to secure the locations."

"That's good to hear," Devlyn said, a longing look in his eyes. "Are you sure you're all right with this, Elle?"

Turning him a hard look, Ellendren held Devlyn in her gaze. "We've been through this. There are three Phaedryn and three different locations. I love you, Devlyn Lorenthien, but I'll see you in Arenthyl when we get there." Holding his hand for comfort, Ellendren wrapped her arms around Devlyn's neck a final time before joining her group.

Searching for his own group, Devlyn saw Skimp, three orderly rows of elves, soldiers and Guardians in the front, unarmed Luminari in the middle and winding through Tenyl's streets and out of sight, and the Eldinari would be at the end of the column, covering the rear.

Reaching the front of the column, Devlyn found Skimp and Viren waiting for him.

"We're ready, if you are," Skimp said.

"No trouble on the other side?" Devlyn asked.

"None yet," Viren said, an unprecedented smile on his face.

"You've gone through?" Devlyn said, envious that Viren had already seen Arenthyl.

"It's just as I remember, if you don't include the frozen lake that is."

Yearning to see the city he had heard so much of, Devlyn looked at Skimp. "Let's get these seguians opened and put a resounding end to the Luminari pilgrimage."

A large mirror-like sphere appeared in front of Skimp, the same size as before, but the image Devlyn saw in the globe was unlike anything he had ever beheld. Placing one foot in front the other, Devlyn walked into the seguian, his front foot stepping on ice.

He paused and found himself unable—unwilling—to move. He could hardly breathe. Before him was a seven-tiered city rising from a rocky peninsula off Mount Verinien. Massive, yet fluid walls terraced every level. The entire city was woven of lumaryl, salvaged from Luminare. Golden light reflected through the stone, making the city radiate against the southern slopes of Mount Verinien, the peak of which rose to a height that Devlyn could not fathom. Its girth was three times the size of any other mountain he had ever seen and he imagined that it would take an entire day to fly around its circumference, an entire year without wings, perhaps more.

Battle for Arenthyl

Arenthyl rose out of Verinien's roots, a peninsula jutting into Lake Saeryndol. The sun had long since risen to its zenith, making the city shine and reflecting the sun's glorious light. The city itself had the appearance of a golden hill; lumaryl turrets were interspaced between fluid walls and domes and bridges and great citadels and spires leapt upward from behind them.

Catching his breath, Devlyn felt Viren's hand clamp his shoulder. "Poets of every nation and race had once sought Arenthyl for inspiration, her glistening walls in the morning sun, complimented by her palaces and towers; not even Mar'anathyl stood her equal. There's a reason your throne is named the Crystal Throne."

"You were born here?"

"My family, the Dekenurels, mostly lived in the fifth tier. Few remained there though as most of my family joined the Guardians, leaving property and family behind."

"I never knew you had to sacrifice so much to become a Guardian knight."

"After a certain tenure, many retire, and return to their families, starting their own family as well. I don't imagine any of us Guardian knights remaining will dream of that though."

"Not even when this is all over?"

"With Ceurendol restored, we can hope for such one day, but that will have to wait."

Thousands more elves poured through the seguians near Devlyn, as they began their final march on the frozen lake toward Arenthyl. The soldiers formed a protective barrier for those unable to fight, keeping a diligent eye over the ice. Staying near the seguians, Devlyn watched as the last of the Eldinari elves passed through, with the seguians closing and only Skimp remaining where his had stood open a moment before.

"You understand that we cannot remain here, yes? Erynor still hunts us." Skimp looked up at Devlyn, his expression serious.

"I do. Good luck," Devlyn said.

"And to you, Ei'denai Lorenthien." A small seguian appeared between his palms, taking Skimp away to some unknown place and time. Somewhere he and the other minums were safe from Erynor.

Relieved, Devlyn leapt into the sky to get a better view of his group. Hovering above the crowd, Devlyn watched as the front of the column breached the crescent port that was protected by watchtowers on either end. Towering walls shadowed the southern docks, rising at a slight angle to meet at a single point in the center. From his view, five separate gates opened into the city from the docks, divided between three different levels. The lower gates led to the lowest and first tier of the city, while the central gate appeared to open onto the second tier, cutting through the terraced wall of that level.

Devlyn was just able to identify the other two groups in the distance heading for the two other docks. Aren protected the eastern group, while Ellendren guided the western group. Scanning the frozen lake, Devlyn looked south over the vast distance between himself and the coast. Straining his eyes, he thought he saw a growing figure solidify on the horizon.

Whatever it was, it was moving at an incredible speed. There was no need to tap his inner sense; the corrupted scent of tenebrys oozed from the figure. Devlyn realized that the blot on the horizon was not a lone figure, but a large company of dragons flying north. "DRAGONS!" he yelled. How could they have possibly reached Arenthyl already? These were many more than the few he had fought before reaching Tenyl. And then Devlyn thought, what if they had already been in the Shroud? And if not, they must have flown directly to Arenthyl, ignoring the other battles and hoping to prevent the Luminari elves from reaching their final goal.

Knowing how quickly they could cover the distance between them, Devlyn dove for the nearest Eldinari. The star warden wore the customary black leathers, her ebony hair pulled back in a tight cord.

"Carry as many unarmed elves as possible to Arenthyl, starting with those furthest back," he said. "I want every armed elf protecting the port; they're not to enter Arenthyl until the last civilian passes through her gates."

The Eldinari nodded and headed to the nearest unarmed elf she saw. She had instantly passed the message to the other Eldinari who immediately began helping elves to their griffins.

The griffins would speed the process of getting elves to safety, but they would not save enough time. Already, what had been a blotch on the horizon became easily identified to everyone. Devlyn's heart sank as he counted dozens of dragons soaring toward them.

There was no saying how many shadow elves were among them, but he knew there was at least one Deurghol who flew at the front, leading his wretched kin forward.

We need you at the port. Fendryl's words echoed in his mind.

Unhappy about abandoning the rearguard, Devlyn soared over the vast number of elves below, Arenthyl growing in size with every flap of his wings. He quickly reached the crescent port, where he ignored the glowing iridescent lumaryl to search for Fendryl.

He stood with Ellendren at a sealed gate lined with sculptural reliefs of elves, trees, and flowers.

"What's the matter?" Devlyn asked in a panic. "Why aren't you with your group?"

"We need to unseal Arenthyl." Ellendren spoke with an air of calm that ignored the dozens of dragons descending on them while more and more elves filled the port, crowding into the immense crescent space.

"What, do we just command it to open?" Devlyn asked, puzzled. Neither he or Ellendren had been involved with opening Eandyl or Tenyl's gates.

"We have to declare ourselves as the Aryl of Arenthyl, together," she said as the great many figures on the gate slowly woke and recognized the visitors crowding the docks.

Devlyn spared a final look south and saw the ei'ana in the rear wielding against the dragons and diverting tenebrys bolts shot by shadow elves. It was too soon; the shadow elves should not have reached them that quickly, even with the dragons flying at dizzying speeds.

Turning back to Ellendren, he took her hand in his, and together, they both delved into that quiet place in their hearts. They did not have the time to figure out a puzzle, so he did what he did with Aliel, imagining that it was the best way he could possibly declare himself.

Ellendren felt what he did through their bond and duplicated it.

They each touched the sealed gate with their free hand. Warm stone greeted Devlyn's flesh; it felt alive. It was imploring him and Ellendren to break the seal so the city could bring within her vacant walls her rightful inhabitants.

"We, the Aryl of Arenthyl," Devlyn and Ellendren said in unison, "lift this seal. May your walls once again protect and nurture the Luminari elves and any who come in peace."

At first, nothing happened.

Devlyn felt the sleepy stone recognize him and Ellendren as Lorenthiens. An acceptance of sorts followed before the gate lurched open. Unlike any other gate Devlyn had seen, it didn't open inward as a door or even lift as a portcullis, but rather, the stone wove into itself, creating an entry within the deep portal. It seemed that every sculptural relief worked itself into a new position inside the portal. A sense of welcome greeted Devlyn, oddly enough, coming from the stone itself.

Sensing that every other gate opened in a similar manner, Devlyn mentally shared a kiss with Ellendren before each returned to the air. She had to return to her own group as well, for their safety was in just as much jeopardy as his own group.

Panicked shouts and screams rose from the crowd below him, now pushing their way through Arenthyl's opened gates.

He quickly joined the rearguard of the moving column. The Eldinari had carried as many elves to the ports as they dared but now shifted their focus to the dragons and shadow elves wreaking havoc.

Tenebrys crashed on the frozen lake, sending pillars of steam and chunks of ice in every direction. Devlyn worried about the stability of the frozen waters.

Geysers shot upward with every bolt of tenebrys that struck the ice, searing into its icy depths. Submitting to embrace lumenys, Devlyn intercepted the sinister wields, each one adding to the threat of drowning the Luminari elves still far from the safety of Arenthyl. With every bolt that Devlyn nullified, ten more blasted from above.

Devlyn had not discovered how many ei'ana were among the Luminari elves, and even though every Eldinari was a capable wielder, ei'ana or not, he worried that halting the dragons and shadow elves to get everyone safely behind Arenthyl's wall would prove an impossible task.

Among a flurry of griffins and Eldinari, Devlyn rushed into the midst of five dragons. Burning heat singed his skin as he entered the fray. Recalling the wield Aren had used earlier against the Deurghol's enormous dragon, Devlyn pressed into aerys, while also embracing the transcendental erendinth. Forming lace-like threads of the erendinth in delicate rings, he wrought his wield around the nearest dragon.

Its black scaly wings were immediately clamped to the beast's sides, and the shadow elf atop, too weak to undo Devlyn's wield sat helpless as they plummeted. Maintaining his wield, Devlyn watched the dragon crash on the ice in a burst of steam as chunks flew upward. Hot mist funneled up from where the dragon had struck, melting further and deeper into the ice, creating a pool of hot water in the frozen lake.

Diving after the dragon, Devlyn embraced lumenys more fully, wielding a beam of incredible light against the shadow elf, who was still trying to free his dragon from Devlyn's wield. Devlyn ushered the imprisoned spirits once bound by the shadow elf free of their captor, allowing them to flow away from the decaying remains of their tormentor.

Turning back to the masses above, Devlyn started another wield, momentarily jerking back when a tenebrys wield struck toward him. Following its path back to the wielder, Devlyn was horrified to see the largest of the dragons just above him, ridden by the Deurghol that Devlyn had been dreading ever crossing again. Eyes leveled on the dragon's belly, its head snarling at him, Devlyn pulled himself upward, maneuvering himself around and over the dragon.

Wispy black tendrils covered the Deurghol, a darkness that swallowed all light near it. The Deurghol held Devlyn in his trance, his shadowy presence hungrily expanding ever outward as it drank in the light.

Suspended alone in a globe of his own light, Devlyn felt the world grow dark as the Deurghol's shadows encased him, only the creature's eyes visible. Devlyn felt as though he was suspended in nothingness or had passed from the World-Below to the Void. But those pitiless eyes held him in place.

Closing himself off from the constricting shadows that surrounded him, Devlyn isolated himself to keep the Deurghol's influence at bay. Nestled in his interior self as the darkness continued to expand and press against his defenses, Devlyn held on to that quiet light. Aware that his time grew short with every breath, he wielded a sphere of lumenys about himself, expanding it like an air bubble in a deep sea, desperate to not drown. Instead of simply pushing the darkness off, his wield encompassed the suffocating shadows, pulling tenebrys into the wield's brightness, denying it any chance to scatter to resurface.

With the Deurghol now at his mercy and his own wield drawing the darkness away, Devlyn pulled the nothingness and corruption from the Deurghol's corpse, like a vacuum at its chest.

Horrendous shrieks spewed from the Deurghol as its very being was singed in the purgative light. Lost in the battle, the Deurghol shriek-laughed as it paled from the world of the living.

Temptations washed across Devlyn's mind with the passing.

An image presented itself to Devlyn. He could take up the forsaken black mantle that the near-dead Cyndinari was too weak to maintain. That elf might have borne the mantle since the Shroud was brought about, but he was too weak now to continue in his Master's service. The temptation nagged at Devlyn—a confidence hummed in his chest. He could be strong enough to challenge Erynor as both a Phaedryn and a Deurghol. He was a Phaedryn and he could resist the evil of that mantle and become so much more. He reached for the black mantle.

His hand trembled forward, the inherent wrongness of the act trying to break through his silent conscience.

Devlyn screamed a familiar voice in his mind. The distant feminine voice reminded him of someone. Lost in the darkness of temptation, he still knew that voice. Yet in his isolation, he could not touch the memory associated with her. His mind was blank and all he could see was the dark mantle.

Other voices broke through the solitude. They too were familiar, yet so distant that he could not see their faces.

Devlyn thundered a voice Devlyn had never heard before, pulling him from the emptiness. *You are needed as you are. Do not abandon the Luminari elves for the desolating Void. Let the Light of Anaweh guide you back to my care.*

Auriel? Devlyn's inner thoughts sounded like a squeak next to the greater voice.

Come back to me, Child of Luminare.

INACCESSIBLE

With a great effort of will, Devlyn forced his eyes open and saw the shadowy mantle of the decaying, no longer deathless Deurghol, wavering about him, its tempting power still trying to pull Devlyn into itself, lest it too fade with its dying host and return to the Void.

Yielding to the voices in his mind, Ellendren's face bloomed foremost, followed by a face of brilliant light.

The enthiel Auriel, the Morning Star and Shepherd of the Luminari elves, held Devlyn in his brilliant and burning eyes, two living stars settled beneath his brow. "Look upon me, Child of Luminare. Do not let this one fail you."

Mesmerized by Auriel's eyes, Devlyn allowed the pristine light to wash over his own vision, his eyes tearing as he felt the burning light flood into his being: body, soul, and spirit. Transfixed, Devlyn lost himself. His body felt weightless and his senses were no longer as he remembered them. A dream of colors and light coursed through his mind, reality no longer holding him, confusing what he had accepted as real or possible, with the dust of dreams.

Devlyn opened his eyes again.

A comfortable mattress supported his weight, and dozens of people surrounded him. Not remembering withdrawing from the phoenix, Devlyn was surprised when Aliel nudged his head. He looked around the room of lumaryl, the sun bursting through and causing the room to glow in a wondrous golden light. Ellendren was near him as well, Tariel just behind her.

In the mix of faces, one beckoned immediacy.

"You've returned to us," Auriel said. The anadel did not scream within Devlyn's mind this time, nor thunder with the powerful voice Devlyn had heard before but spoke at a dignified level.

"What happened?" Devlyn asked, trying to make sense of how he now rested in the most comfortable bed he had ever slept in. What had happened to the battle?

"We thought you were gone," Ellendren said, wiping a tear from her cheek. "The light from the sky vanished as the Deurghol held you in a wield of tenebrys; I saw it from the west as it expanded and darkened with every moment. And when I thought I had seen the darkest shade possible, it became even darker. It looked as though the Void had broken free and started to claim Teraeniel."

"Among the fighting, this Child of Luminare implored Anaweh, the Creating Light. Hearing her prayer, Uriel agreed to my intervention."

"You should have seen it," Wyn said, seeming to appear out of nowhere. "Songs and ballads about the enthiel are still performed in Stellantis, but to see Auriel act was something else entirely."

Not having noted his cousin at first, Devlyn blinked. "Wyn? When did you get here?"

"I made it to Tenyl just as the last Luminari were passing through the seguians and followed," he said, grinning. "Once my account of Alethea was recorded and verified, I was free to return to help, which I almost missed."

"Forgive me, Auriel, but what did you do?" Devlyn asked, apologetic about asking something of an enthiel—the guardian of his people.

Auriel looked to Wyn, who was barely containing himself.

"He appeared in an eruption of light, right in the middle of all those dragons and shadow elves. Dozens vaporized with a single swath of his hand, while those far enough away retreated, likely all the way to the Shadow Mountains or Cynethol to hide," Wyn said, practically bouncing on his feet. "Then, he grew to a size larger than a giant, holding you and the Deurghol in the cup of his hands, the dragon long gone at that point."

"You saved me?" Devlyn asked.

"The choice to take the mantle or deny it was yours alone," Auriel said.

"But how did I get here? What of that dream?"

"Suffice it to say, after you made your choice, you had not a hint of strength left and if I had not already been holding you, you would have surely fallen."

"And the visions?"

"I took you within myself. You experienced what only a few have or ever will."

Lifting his hands, Devlyn examined himself. "Am I changed?"

A jubilant laugh escaped Auriel. "As close to anacordel as I claim myself to be, I'll never understand the constant desire to become something other than who you already are."

Taken aback by the truth which struck too close to Devlyn's heart, his chin dipped, and he was crestfallen to realize that he was blushing with a little bit of shame.

"I've come to believe it part of Anaweh's design, sanctifying the very act of discovering one's true self," Auriel said, his smile now gentle, if gentle could ever be applied to this creature, even when he stood in the form of an elf at a normal height.

"How long have I been sleeping? I was sleeping, yes?"

"Eight days," Ellendren said, letting Devlyn know through their bond how painful each of those days had been for her.

Shocked by the revelation, Devlyn wanted nothing more than to rise, get out of bed to test his strength, looking imploringly at Auriel and the others surrounding him, only too aware of his nakedness beneath the too thin sheet.

The room quickly emptied, Ellendren taking her leave as well, leaving Aliel behind. Only then did he take in how magnificent the room was. It was an enormous size; all the furniture was woven of an intricate wood, and not a single wall was unadorned. Lumaryl sculptures and colorful lierathnil tapestries lined the room. An opened door allowed a breeze from a spacious balcony. Lyren came into the room, an outfit neatly folded in his arms.

"My savior," Devlyn said, twisting his body off the bed, and reaching for his small clothes.

Lyren blushed as he bowed and diverted his eyes as Devlyn dressed. "I believe that term is reserved for you, Ei'denai. You had us worried; all of us." Lyren offered the trousers next.

"Thank you." Devlyn pulled them on then walked onto the balcony to overlook a mass of spires surrounding a central dome. Luscious gardens spilled over the courtyard, surprisingly well kept and ordered. A gentle wind brushed across his bare chest, and despite the summer heat, the morning wind off the frozen lake chilled him.

He took a final look over the city, alluring enough to keep him on the balcony staring at it all for hours. Returning to his bedchamber, Devlyn shoved his arms through a simple shirt that Lyren held for him, lacing up the front before tucking the bottom into his trousers. Devlyn next accepted the lierathnil outer garment, woven in an emerald green, reminding him of the color his eyes had once been. Lyren had likely had the outfit selected and ready days ago, not expecting Devlyn to require so much rest.

As he walked about the royal apartments, he instantly wished he had been conscious when he had been brought into them, as he now found it all but impossible to find the exit. Lyren nodded toward one of the doors just as intricate as the others in the spacious apartment and as Devlyn approached, he heard voices filter from the opposite side. He pushed the door open onto a spiraled stair, finding Ellendren, Wyn and

Viren waiting for him.

"Certainly took your time," Wyn said with an accusatory wink.

"Nonsense," Devlyn replied, feeling rested and excited to see the rest of the palace and city.

"Boys," Ellendren chided. "Come, there's one room we haven't been able to get into yet."

"You've explored the entire palace already?" Devlyn asked, more impressed than shocked, but still a little jealous.

"You were dreaming for a full eight days, what else was I going to do? Swim through a frozen lake?"

"It'll be nice when we can. I wonder what else is down there?"

"How do you mean?"

"Well, there was already an irythil trapped in the ice and it's a big lake," Devlyn said.

"We'll just have to wait for it to melt and invite the merpeople to explore it." Ellendren took his hand in hers. "Now come on, I've been waiting for you to wake up for this last room."

Pulled down the spiraling staircase, his arm yanked ever downward, he meekly followed while Ellendren glided down the stairs, Wyn and Viren keeping pace with them. Several floors below, Ellendren directed him through a corridor, unceremoniously leading the way through the long-vacant palace.

"Which room didn't you go into, and why?" Devlyn asked, his curiosity piqued.

"You'll see."

"The throne room? Did you want to wait to see the Crystal Throne together?"

From behind them, Wyn snickered.

"Oh. No, that was one of the first rooms I sought out once I knew you were resting peacefully," Ellendren said, admitting that she did not even consider holding off that room.

Ellendren kept him in the corridor, and he noted how it curved ever so slightly, opening onto a larger, drummed room with a crystal-line dome above. A throne with two seats was situated on a lucid dais, wrought from either a thousand diamonds, or considering its seamless nature, a single diamond-like stone larger than imaginable. The throne rose twice his height beneath an intricately sculpted baldachin supported by four winding columns, all crafted from the same material.

"The Crystal Throne," Devlyn said, his voice hushed as he saw what he and Ellendren were expected to sit on, lost in its effortless gleam.

Ellendren led him widely around the Crystal Throne, clearly already accustomed to its magnificence.

Three large doors were nestled into the back of the curvilinear throne room. Both outer doors were ajar, and as Ellendren pulled Devlyn past the first, he saw a faint violet light emanate from within. It was only as he saw the light that he considered the lucilliae.

"We've already returned the five we have to their proper shrines," Ellendren said, aware of Devlyn's concern. He hadn't even thought to check on them after waking. They stopped in front of the sealed central doors directly behind the Crystal Throne. "I haven't been able to open them. Not even Auriel was able to manage it."

"And you think I can?"

"I thought *we* could," Ellendren said, tucking a loose strand of hair behind her ear. "As we did with unsealing the city."

"It's worth a try." Devlyn's grip on Ellendren's hand tightened. "Do we think…that is, is the central jewel of Ceurendol behind these doors?"

A shy smile broke across Ellendren's face, a feature Devlyn had not seen in a very long time. Seeing it resurface actually caught him off guard, reminding him of forgotten insecurities.

Devlyn closed his eyes and rested the hand that wasn't holding Ellendren's on the door. He felt her move to do the same.

Reaching into the quiet place within his heart, he embraced his most inner and true self, declaring himself, not only to his wife, but to all Arenthyl, and particularly to this door which might hold the pivotal lucilliae of the Jewel of Life behind it.

Soft steps fell on the tiled floor behind them.

Taking no notice, Devlyn opened his eyes, assuming he and Ellendren had done everything needed. With a quick glance at each other, they nudged their weight against the door.

Nothing happened.

"Why didn't it work?" he asked, sizing up the doors once again.

"It's not you, if that's what you're worried about." They turned to look at the silver-pale stranger who had come up behind them.

"I don't understand."

"My name is Etrien Fernoril, and I have been here for many autumns."

"I'm Devlyn Lorenthien, and this is…"

"I know who you are; all of you. Your presence has returned much to this place," Etrien said, his piercing silver eyes passing over the small gathering. "The doors won't open until Ceurendol senses that which might cleanse it of its taint."

"Ceurendol is tainted?"

"How did you imagine Erynel returned from beyond the grave, bringing the Shroud?"

Here ends the Fifth Part of

The Jewel of Life:

Spires of Arenthyl

LOOK FOR THE SIXTH PART OF

THE JEWEL OF LIFE

Appendix A
Glossary of Terms

Abbey School

The preferred system of education for children throughout Eklean. Those deemed capable are sent to higher studies, preferably at Gwilnor Academy.

Aelish

Native language of the elves. Largely forgotten, only used in academic circles.

Aerys

An elemental erendinth. The essence of air.

Albien

One of the seven Schools of Septyl. Albiens focus on truth and care for many of Eklean's libraries. Motto: Truth is discoverable. Emblem: A naked male and female elf holding unraveled scrolls with an owl perched behind, cast in gold on a white field. The chair of Albien is known as the Seeker.

Aldarch

Deific rulers of Aldinare who reigned from their sanctums.

Aldinare

Western Skyland of the Aldinari, one of the four elven kindreds. Lost to the Darkness. Only a hundred Aldinari escaped the Skyland with their lives.

Alicorn

A legendary beast native to the Skyland of Aldinare. A winged unicorn.

Anadel

Spiritual creatures that predate Teraeniel and Somnaeniel. Their native home is Lumaeniel. There are four known classifications of anadel: irythil, enthiel, lorendil, and naril.

Anacordel

Creatures of body, soul, and spirit.

Anaweh

The Creating Light.

Animys

A transcendental erendinth. The essence of spirit.

Aquaeys

An elemental erendinth. The essence of water.

ARANTIULYN

One of the seven Schools of Septyl. Arantiulyns focus on strength and protection and oversee the Knights of Septyl. Motto: With fortitude, we will protect. Emblem: A naked male and female elf in a fighting stance with swords in hand with a lion prowling cast in gold on an orange field. The Chair of Arantiulyn is known as the General.

ARCANE GEMS

Sources of magic used by the Mages of the Kilnae Del.

ARCHSTEWARD

Part of the Ei'ceuril hierarchy, they are elevated wise ones. Before kien wielders were restricted to the Temple of Ceur, archstewards lived in every major city of Eklean tending to those faithful to Anaweh, the Creating Light.

ARENTHYLEAN BELLS

Twenty-four bells composed of four materials that ring every hour.

ARYL

The united head of an elven house composed of a king and queen or lord and lady.

AUBURNIS

One of the seven Schools of Septyl. Auburnises focus on inner peace. Motto: To love is our gift. Emblem: A naked male and female elf offering a garland with larks flying above, cast in gold on a brown field. The Chair of Auburnis is known as the Pilgrim.

AUREPHAEN

Feast day of the Luminari, commemorating Auriel and the dawning sun. Celebrated on the 15th of Aurenth, the spring equinox.

AZURELLE

One of the seven Schools of Septyl. Azurelles focus on the advancement and training of the erendinth. Motto: The zealous soul must be temperate. Emblem: A naked male and female elf wielding the powers with a dragon behind, cast in gold on a blue field. The Chair of Azurelle is known as the Blue Dragon.

BELIN'S WATCH

An Evellion city in the Vespien Mountains comprised of humans and dwarves. Named for Belin, the dwarf who sheltered Thellion refugees in their greatest hour of need.

BOREPHAEN

Feast day of the Eldinari, commemorating Boriel and the sleeping sun. Celebrated on the 15th of Borenth, the winter solstice.

BOWL OF THENIEL

Sea set apart by the merpeople as sacred. The place where Theniel brought the waters to Teraeniel.

CENTAUR

Anacordel dedicated to protecting the forests of Eklean, particularly the Illumined Wood. The upper body is like an elf's but broader and more rugged while the lower body looks much like a four-legged horse.

CEURENDOL

The Jewel of Life. Created by the Luminari by placing their life essence within seven jewels of incredible brilliance which allowed them to share their immortality with every race in 1.3a (7085.3E). Also known as the Light Diamond, the Lieben Stone, and the Heart of Hearts.

CEURENDOL WAR, THE

A cataclysmic war instigated by the Erynien Empire which began over a philosophical difference over the Jewel of Life and whether immortal life was proper for the 'lesser races.' The war divided Eklean in two factions, those faithful to the Luminari and those subjugated by the Erynien Empire. As the fate of the war grew clear, emissaries and merchants from other continents withdrew from Eklean, fearing the Erynien Empire. 322-500.3a (7407-7585.3E).

CEURENYL

City founded by the ei'ceuril. Home of the Temple of Ceur and Gwilnor Academy. The only city not to fall into Erynor's control when Krysenthiel was lost to the Shroud.

CEURTRIARCH

Leader of the ei'ceuril, known as High Archsteward and Arbiter of the Light.

CHANCELLOR

The head of Gwilnor Academy under the authority of and appointed by the Seven Chairs.

CHILDREN

When capitalized, refers to the proto-race.

CITADEL, THE

Seat of the Sha'ghol on Cyndinare.

Cor'lera

A small village in eastern Parendior and in disputed territory claimed by both Lucillia and Perrien. The vineyards of Cor'lera produce the coveted ice wine, the Cor'leran Blue.

Crimsyn

One of the seven Schools of Septyl. Crimsyns focus on healing and run many hospitals and infirmaries throughout Eklean. Motto: Through healing, hope is given. Emblem: A naked male and female elf dancing with a dog, cast in gold on a red field. The chair of Crimsyn is known as the Physician.

Cyndinare

Southern Skyland of the Cyndinari, one of the four elven kindreds. Lost to the Darkness.

Cynethol

Home of the Cyndinari, situated among the Kinzdol Islands.

Daereneth

Continent south of Ogren and west of Ja'Horan. Tropical continent.

Dawn Age

The time frame that the Qien Dynasty refers to following the period in their history where Tolvenol, the Dark Primus, ruled over the continent of Qien. The elves refer to this as the First Era.

Deurghol

The Cyndinari directly responsible for the Shroud. They are neither living nor dead. Also known as the Deathless.

Dorthl

Substance that manifests differently in the different realms, either as a solid, a liquid, or a gas. Nullifies the erendinth and boosts tenebrae.

Draelyn

A mixed race anacordel of dragon and elven origins.

Draelish

Native language of the draelyn.

Dragon

Legendary creatures bound to the erendinth.

Druids of Kweil Aitch, the

Secluded faction of humans who learned to walk Somaeniel, the World-in-Between early on.

Dwarf

Anacordel who sought the deep roots of the mountains.

Ealyn

Leaders of the draelyn of Tenethyl.

Ei'ana

An organized group of wielders. Since the Balance was lost during the Ceurendol War, there are only kiara wielders among the ei'ana. There has not been a kien wielder among the ei'ana for over a thousand years.

Ei'ana Counsels

A series of norms ei'ana are to follow in regards to wielding. The counsels prohibit men from becoming ei'ana due to their inability to wield safely after the Balance was lost. The counsels also require ei'ana to bring kien wielders to the Temple of Ceur for their own protection and the protection of their communities.

Ei'ceuril

A religious order, currently a majority of men, focused on serving Anaweh, the Creating Light. Because a kien wielder is not capable of wielding with control, every male ei'ceuril capable of wielding is confined to the Temple of Ceur.

Ei'denai

Elven lord serving as aryl with his spouse. Head of House.

Ei'ethil

Elven lord.

Ei'lythel

Elven lady.

Ei'terel

Elven lady serving as aryl with her spouse. Head of House.

Eklean

Continent where the anacordel first stirred as Children.

Elder Days

The Elder Days span from the beginning of creation until what the elves refer to as the First Era, following Ramiel being sealed away in the Void and the creation of the separate races.

Elder Ones

Anacordel that evolved from the Children before the Great Blessing, at which time the different races were solidified.

Eldin Wood, the

Home of the Eldinari.

Eldinare

Northern Skyland of the Eldinari, one of the four elven kindreds. Lost to the Darkness. The Eldinari were the first to evacuate their Skyland for the lands below.

Elemental Erendinth, the

Forces wielded to influence the elements. *See Erendinth.*

Elf

Anacordel who changed little when the different races were created. Because they wished to retain their original form, their immortality remained, and they were gifted the Skylands. There are four elven kindreds, the Luminari, Cyndinari, Aldinari, and Eldinari.

Elya

Powerful wielders born of any race who learn to wield instinctively and are not limited to the restrictions common to normal kien and kiara wielders.

Emradiel

One of the seven Schools of Septyl. Emradiels focus on beauty and life. Motto: Only the prudent thrive. Emblem: A naked male and female elf gesturing with open palms toward the beauty around them with a stag behind, cast in gold on a green field. The chair of Emradiel is known as the Tender.

Enthiel

Anadel dedicated to one of the seven irythil. The enthiel are very involved with the anacordel. A single enthiel guides an entire people.

Erendinth, the

The erendinth are the wielded powers believed to have created Teraeniel. Tradition says that there are seven powers, three transcendental: lumenys, animys, and umbrys; and four elemental: aquaeys, aerys, terys, and ignys. Much is forgotten or unknown about the full extent of the erendinth which are dependent on inner spiritual and emotional workings.

Erendinth Games, the

A game of wielding created at Gwilnor Academy, involving the wielding of all seven erendinth.

Faun

Short nocturnal anacordel with the hind legs of a goat from the navel down. Some fauns have horns.

Giant

Anacordel that were drawn to the frozen north. During the Great Blessing, their physical features became capable of withstanding the harsh tundra of Glacien.

Glacien

Northern frozen continent spanning the northern pole. Connects Eklean and Ogren.

Goblin

Anacordel native to the Kinzdol Islands. Known for their monetary shrewdness.

Goblin Guild

Infamous bank and guild of Eklean. Regulates the majority of Eklean's currency. The Goblin Guild is based in the Kinzdol Islands with branches in every city and most villages.

Great Blessing, the

Event recorded in the Theseryn where Anaweh blessed the growing differences among the anacordel and solidified their choices by making each their own distinct race.

Grilae

Red flowering fruit trees native to Cyndinare.

Guardian Knights

Order of knights once based in Krysenthiel that served and protected all the land from injustice. The Guardian Knights were largely composed of Luminari and were defeated during the Ceurendol War.

Guardian Senate, the

An international body, crossing countries and continents to ensure the wellbeing of Teraeniel. Disbanded toward the end of the Ceurendol War.

Gwilnor Academy

The foremost school dedicated to the education of wielders, located in Ceurenyl.

Holy Tomes

Volumes recorded by various ei'ceuril, some being prophets, and from which the ei'ceuril base their beliefs and practices.

Human

Anacordel that differ among themselves more than any other race. They traveled the furthest from the Valley of Saeryndol, migrating across the entirety of Teraeniel.

Ignys

An elemental erendinth. The essence of fire.

Ilithae

Silver leafed trees native to Aldinare. The only ilithae trees to survive the doom of Aldinare are found in the Wooded Hills of Thellion.

Illumined Wood, the

A vast forest with mysterious qualities and inhabitants.

Imperium

Selective school for Cyndinari youth. Its violent academic style educates the next generation of shadow elves.

Irythil

The seven anadel who, under Anaweh's guidance, introduced the erendinth, thereby creating Teraeniel.

Ja'horan

Continent south of Eklean. Inhabited largely by nomadic peoples.

Jahro Islands

Island chain in the Unarian Sea. Believed to be the home of pirates.

Jienzu

Heart, mind, and body practice of meditation, breathing, and body positions called forms, used by the draelyn and ancient elves to achieve balance. Largely forgotten.

Judges of Yanil

An order that once ruled beside the Yanilean. The judges are now a secret organization that strives to uphold law and order with limited influence.

Keeper

Head of the time wardens and possessor of the time key.

Kiara Wielder

A female wielder. Kiara wielders learn to control the erendinth easily but require a kien wielder to reach their potential strength. Because the Balance was lost, kiara wielders are not able to reach their potential strength.

KIEN WIELDER

A male wielder. Kien wielders reach their potential strength easily but require a kiara wielder to learn control of the erendinth. Because the Balance was lost, kien wielders are not able to wield safely, and if any male begins to show an aptitude to wield, he is sent to the Temple of Ceur where wielding is impossible.

KILNAE DEL

Order of mages native to Charren, headquartered in the Charrenese capital, Karithel.

KINZDOL ISLANDS

An archipelago in southern Eklean, homeland to the goblins and Cyndinari.

KIRENAE

Gold flowering fruit trees native to Luminare.

KWEIL AITCH

Island east of the Illumined Wood. The place where the veil is thin between Teraeniel and Somnaeniel.

LAY VOTARY

A non-clerical class of ei'ceuril.

LETHIEN

A mixed race anacordel of elven and human origins. Largely extinguished by Erynor during and after the Ceurendol War.

LORENDIL

Anadel that guard and protect individual anacordel. Some anacordel are known to communicate with their lorendil.

LUCILLIAN ALLIANCE, THE

An alliance of the Eklean kingdoms established to return peace and order to Eklean following Emperor Erynor's disappearance.

LUMAENIEL

The World-Beyond. Dwelling of Anaweh, the anadel, and those anacordel who have passed beyond.

LUMENYS

A transcendental erendinth. The essence of light.

LUMINARE

Eastern Skyland of the Luminari, one of the four elven kindreds. Lost to the Darkness. The Luminari evacuated their Skyland for the lands below where they established Krysenthiel.

MAR'ANATHYL

City on the Skyland of Luminare. Governed by the Lorenthien aryls.

MASTERS, THE (SEVEN MASTERS, THE)

Vigyl Vyoletryn, Cyrelle Azurelle, Lanielle Emradiel, Lyon Arantiulyn, Mainor Auburnis, Caelyn Crimsyn, and Saeyrn Albien are the founders of the Seven Schools of Septyl and Gwilnor Academy.

MERIDEAN CONCLAVE

Governing council of the merpeople.

MERIDEPHAEN

Feast day of the Cyndinari, commemorating Meridiel and the noon sun. Celebrated on the 15th of Meridenth, the summer solstice.

MERPEOPLE

Anacordel who longed for the depths of Teraeniel's oceans.

MIERVAE

Anacordel who longed to nurture Teraeniel's forests. Miervae are also referred to as Great Trees and begin their life as Settlings.

MINUM

The least of Eklean's anacordel. A short mixed race anacordel of goblin and human origins. Before the elves migrated to Eklean, they were enslaved, sold by goblins to humans.

NARIL

Anadel reminiscent of the seven erendinth. There are seven types of narils and they are commonly known as nymphs.

NYMPHS

See Naril.

OBSERVANT

Non-wielders who have dedicated themselves to one of the Seven Schools of Septyl.

OGRE

Brutish anacordel covering the vast majority of Ogren. Mixed race anacordel of giant and human origins.

OGREN

Continent east of Eklean and west of Qien. Mountainous land with a mixture of forests and deserts. Inhabited by giants, humans, and ogres.

Phaedryn

Those bound with a phoenix.

Purged Desert of Dwonia, the

A vast wasteland in western Eklean that was rumored to have at one point been fertile. Home of the Twelve Tribes of Dwonia.

Return

The final stage of formation of an ei'ceuril toward becoming a steward. Often occurring in the Illumined Wood.

Sanctum

Expansive complexes housing the aldarchs and their courts on Aldinare.

Schtach

Language of the dwarves.

Schtam

(1) A dwarven people. (2) The dwellings of the dwarves.

Schtamite

The eight dwarven schtams.

Seguian

A portal created to traverse space and time. Traversing time is restricted and only the keeper can use the time key to traverse time.

Septyl

(1) The order of Ei'ana composing the Seven Schools of Septyl. (2) The city of the ei'ana in Krysenthiel and now lost in the Shroud.

Septyl Knights

Order of knights dedicated to Septyl. The knights receive their training at Gwilnor Academy and vow to serve one of the Seven Schools of Septyl.

Seraph

Six winged anadel in Lumaeniel.

Servants of Shadow

Secret organization carrying out the orders of shadow elves and, in some instances, the orders of the Deurghol.

Settling

Tree-like creatures that wander about in their youth until finding an appropriate place to settle their roots and grow into a Miervae, also known as a Great Tree.

Settlings have unique vitality qualities.

Seven Chairs of Septyl, the

The leaders of the Ei'ana. Each of the Seven Schools elects its own Chair who leads his or her particular School and participates in the leadership of Septyl. Responsible for admitting student wielders into Gwilnor Academy and selecting a chancellor.

Seven Schools of Septyl, the

The order of Ei'ana, composed of Albien, Arantiulyn, Auburnis, Azurelle, Crimsyn, Emradiel, and Vyoletryn Schools.

Shadow Elves

Cyndinari who consume the spirit of others to prolong their own life.

Sha'ghol

Past rulers of the Cyndinari. First to communicate with Ramiel after her was imprisoned and wield tenebrys.

Shifting

(1) The ability to teleport in Somnaeniel. (2) The Phaedryn ability to teleport physically in Teraeniel.

Shroud, the

A diseased-looking fog placed by the Cyndinari over the entirety of Krysenthiel. It severed the Luminari from the Jewel of Life, cutting them off from their life essence and making them mortal, as well as any others who had benefited from it. An unanticipated result was that the Cyndinari also lost their immortality with that placement of the Shroud over the Jewel of Life. The Shroud's mysterious origin is one reason no one has been able to remove it.

Skylands, the

Four island countries, Aldinare, Cyndinare, Eldinare, and Luminare, floating in the clouds thousands of feet above the ground. The dwelling places of the elves before they were forced to evacuate to the land below.

Sojourners

The exiled of Dwonia who sought reentrance after forming an allegiance with the Erynien Empire.

Somnaeniel

The World-in-Between. A realm visited by dreamers. Gateway between Lumaeniel and Teraeniel.

SOPHILLIAE

Orbs that preserve knowledge.

SOPHILLIAN

Head Librarian of the Sophillium

SOPHILLIUM

The library of Septyl that houses the sophilliae.

STAR WARDEN

An elven military unit, typically ensuring the protection of their lands.

STELLENDAE

Remarkably large trees native to Eldinare that now dominate the Eldin Wood and serve as dwelling places for the Eldinari elves.

STEWARD

A clerical class of ei'ceuril with the ability to wield.

STEWARDS OF SHADOW

Ei'ceuril stewards who forsook Anaweh to support Ramiel.

TEMPLE OF CEUR, THE

Home to the ei'ceuril and pilgrimage site for the faithful. It is impossible to wield within the temple walls. All kien wielders are confined to the Temple of Ceur.

TEMPLE KNIGHTS

Order of knights dedicated to protecting the Temple of Ceur and the city of Ceurenyl. Some of the temple knights are men who were brought to the temple when it was discovered that they could wield. These temple knights are prohibited from leaving the temple.

TENEBRAE

An unrecognized School of Septyl intended to replace the other seven Schools. Its adherents focus on power and dominance. Motto: Might conquers. Emblem: A naked male and female elf standing triumphantly on seven broken emblems, cast in gold on a black field. The chair of Tenebrae is known as the Conqueror.

TENEBRYS

A corrupted form of the erendinth, unrecognized by the Ei'ana of Septyl as one of the erendinth and absolutely forbidden to wield. The essence of Darkness.

TENETHYL

(1) Jeweled city of the draelyn hidden in the Illumined Wood. (2) City destroyed by Ramiel's forces before the Great Blessing.

Teraeniel

The World-Below. Composed of the continents Daereneth, Eklean, Glacien, Ja'Horan, Ogren, and Qien.

Terys

An elemental erendinth. The essence of stone.

Theseryn

Holy tome recording the creation of Teraeniel and the anacordel, written by the first Ceurtriarch of the Ei'ceuril. The Theseryn states that seven irythil, under Anaweh's guidance, introduced the erendinth thereby creating Teraeniel.

Time Key

An artifact created by the Luminari to restrict the ability to traverse space and time. It was entrusted to the minums, the least of Eklean's races.

Time Wardens

A select group of minums entrusted by the Luminari with the ability to create seguians, allowing them to travel to any place and any time.

Tosk

City in the Void.

Transcendental Erendinth, the

Wielded forces to influence the ethereal realities of lumenys, animys, and umbrys. The ability to wield the transcendental erendinth is forgotten.

Tree Spirits

Narils who agreed to bond with the trees under Sariel's guidance.

Umbrys

A transcendental erendinth. The essence of shadow.

Vaer

Fruit native to the Illumined Wood.

Valley of Saeryndol

Birthplace of the Children, the first anacordel.

Verakryl

A crystalline tree within Mount Verinien which brought life to the world and is connected to Anaweh. Also known as the Tree of Life.

Verathel

Sprouts of Verakryl, the Tree of Life.

Verathn

Weapons of power.

Vespephaen

Feast day of the Aldinari, commemorating Vespiel and the setting sun. Celebrated on the 15th of Vespenth, the autumn equinox.

Void, the

A realm that existed before Teraeniel and Somnaeniel. Realm of Ramiel and the fallen anadel.

Vyoletryn

One of the Seven Schools of Septyl. Vyoletryns focus on justice and diplomacy. Motto: With justice, peace. Emblem: A naked male and female elf holding a staff with an eagle soaring above, cast in gold on a violet field. The chair of Vyoletryn is known as the Watcher.

Wielders

Anacordel capable of wielding the erendinth.

Winged Horses of Thellion

Ancestors of the grey coursers of Perrien.

Wise Ones

(1) Part of the Ei'ceuril hierarchy. There is no certainty how many are among the ei'ceuril. (2) Part of the Ei'ana hierarchy. There are seven wise ones for every School of Septyl.

Yanilean, the

The undisputed monarch of Yanil, always male. Used both as the monarch's title and as his name during his reign.

Days of the Week

(Based on the seven anadel involved in the creation of Teraeniel)

Gwynthaen–Thenaen–Uraen–Ramaen–Lerenaen–Saraen–Karaen

Months/Moons

(Based on the anadel attached to the elves)

Spring – Marenth, Aurenth, Delenth

Summer – Dynenth, Meridenth, Reventh

Autumn – Kyrenth, Vespenth, Orenth

Winter – Estlenth, Borenth, Lierenth

Currency

Goblin Guild currency – 16 iron angots for a copper lewt. 9 copper lewts for a silver jent. 13 silver jents for a gold crown. 3 golden crowns for a lumol.

Luminari currency – 8 kenols for a narol. 4 narols for a lumol.

Appendix B

Dramatis Personae

Aaron Roendryn

Luminari. Ceurtriarch. Prince of Lucillia, brother of Ellendren. Ei'ceuril.

Abbie Wintyr

Human with emerald eyes. Student at Gwilnor Academy. Druid of Kweil Aitch.

Aen Finamarc

Lethien from Cor'lera, squire to Alex Vaerin.

Agnelle Phanstienne

Luminari. Ei'ana and Chair of Auburnis.

Alesei

Queen of Tiel. Of the Royal House Ziera.

Alethea Lenwyn

Eldinari. Emradiel ei'ana and former Lenwyn aryl.

Alexander (Alex) Vaerin

Human from Perrien, whose family migrated to Cor'lera. King of Thellion. Betrothed to Diana Thellion.

Aliel

The first phoenix born since the fall of Krysenthiel, bonded Devlyn.

Amry Thellion

Former king of Evellion. Married to Queen Lara. *Deceased.*

Andrea Farneis

Human from Sudern. Septyl knight. Nephew to Duke Farneis. Known as Andrew.

Angennia (Ange) Soricci

Human from Yanil. Judge of Yanil.

Arbol

A faun searching for settlings.

Aren Lorenthien

Luminari. Led a rescue party to Aldinare and did not return. Now a Dark Phaedryn in service to Erynor.

Arlyn

Ei'ceuril steward from Cor'lera. Devlyn's uncle on his mother's side.

BASTIEN

Human from Sorenthil. Temple knight.

BERNARD

Human from Perrien. Ei'ceuril, librarian, and magister at the abbey school of Cor'lera.

BON LI

Prime Minister of the Qien Dynasty.

BYRON ROENDRYN

Luminari. Lord knight. Brother to Vernal.

CAIRN

Human. Chief of Tribe Laith. Son of Suin.

CATALINA TURLAN

Human from Yanil. Supreme Judge of Yanil.

CECILLE FARNEIS

Human from Sudern. Daughter to Duke Farneis.

CIAREN

Draelyn of the Gold House.

CLARA

Aldinari. Ei'ceuril, steward and abbess of the Monastery of the Poor Ladies in the Ashton Wood.

CLOVIS

Cyndinari. Attendant to Yloran. Known in Lankor as Bieto.

DANIELLE AERQUIN

Luminari of House Aerquin. Student wielder at Gwilnor Academy.

DAPHNE ASHTON

Human from Mindale. Lady of Ashton Wood. Emradiel ei'ana.

DAPHNEL

Human from Ceurenyl. Temple knight.

DEVLYN LORENTHIEN

Ward of Cor'lera's abbey school. Physical features indicate Lucillian ancestry.

DIANA THELLION

Princess of Evellion. Eldest daughter of Amry and Lara. Betrothed to Alexander Vaerin.

DOLAN LORENTHIEN

Father of Devlyn, Leilyn, and Liam. Husband of Evellyn. Son of Eldinari Lei-enya Lierafen and an unknown Cyndinari, although this is undisclosed. Raised in the human Telvin family of Cor'lera. *Deceased.*

EAGAN WINTYR

Human. Druid of Kweil Aitch, and Abbie's brother.

EALYNDOL LORENTHIEN

Luminari. Former Ceurtriarch. *Deceased.*

ELAYNE THENREL

Luminari. Guardian knight.

ELLENDREN ROENDRYN

Luminari. Princess of Lucillia. Student wielder at Gwilnor Academy.

EMDIAN

Human from Sudern. Ei'ceuril steward.

ENRICO DESILLIO

Human from Yanil. Noble in the Yanilean's court.

ENTIEL TELVIN

Human from Perrien. Ei'ceuril, steward, and abbot of the abbey school of Cor'lera. Devlyn's uncle on his father's side.

ERYNEL MERIDEN

Cyndinari. Former Sha'ghol and Erynor's mother. *Deceased.*

ERYNOR MERIDEN

Emperor of the Erynien Empire. Disappeared after Lucillia gave birth to the twins, Roendryn and Feolyn in 7857.3E. First Cyndinari born on Eklean.

ETIENNE JIETHEL

Human from Briel. Grand chamberlain to His Majesty, King Irvienne Haert of Briel.

ETRIEN FERNORIL

Aldinari elf.

EVELLYN LORENTHIEN

Luminari from Cor'lera. Mother of Leilyn and Devlyn. Widow of Dolan. Captive of Erynor.

FERINN

Merperson. Currently resides in Myrium. Consort and widower of the late

Queen Karina Larviere.

Forvl VIII

Dwarf and patriarch of Oern Schtam. Son of Oma and Forvl VII.

Fyona Orendi

Luminari. Student wielder at Gwilnor Academy.

Fyreh Glaeda

Eldinari. Azurelle ei'ana and magister at Gwilnor. Twin brother to Myrah, husband to Suella, and father to many children.

Galithinol

Dragon of the Gold Flight. Father to Weilyn and grandfather to Thien, Vivien, and Theseryn.

Genevie Dalieth

Human from Briel. Brieli knight and lieutenant.

Gordon Carvil

King of Torsil. Of the Royal House Carvil. Supporter of Erynor.

Hannah Torin

Human from Mindale. Azurelle ei'ana and chancellor of Gwilnor Academy.

Harnyl Roendryn

Luminari. Aryl of Lucillia. Married to Queen Vernal. Father of Aaron, Kaela, and Ellendren. *Deceased.*

Ianthol

Cyndinari. Shadow elf. *Deceased.*

Ilynor

Cyndinari. Shadow elf.

Indryl

Luminari. Tenebrae ei'ana, once believed to be a Vyoletryn ei'ana.

Irvienne Haert

Human from Briel. King of Briel.

Izara

Ja'horan Druid Elder.

Jaerol Solaris

Cyndinari. Former Erynien emissary. Student wielder at Gwilnor Academy.

Jaek

Luminari. Lucillian sentry.

Jaris Iln Desaris

Cyndinari. One of the Sha'ghol. *Deceased.*

Jax

Minum and time warden.

Jeanne Darkel

Luminari. First of the Guardians.

Jehn

Luminari elf. Ei'ceuril. Secretary to the Ceurtriarch.

Jenyd Tarneth

Daer of House Tarneth. Advisor to Senator Koth.

Kaela Roendryn

Luminari. Princess of Lucillia, sister to Ellendren and Aaron.

Kaelien

Elder One. Queen of Tenethyl. Aunt to Gael. *Deceased.*

Kaeyth Illiero

Luminari. Ei'ceuril novice.

Karina Lariviere

Former Queen of Sorenthil. Widow of the late King Dorian. Wife to Ferinn. Mother of Myranda. *Deceased.*

Karl Olney

Human from Perrien. Observant of Vyoletryn.

Kevn Weyvien

Luminari. Has studied to become either an ei'ceuril or an ei'ana.

Kiara

A mythical woman believed to be the first female wielder.

Kien

A mythical man believed to be the first male wielder.

Kyrendal Lorenthien

Luminari. First chancellor of Gwilnor Academy. Crafter of the verathn. Monk at the Monastery of Kyrendal. Son to Kien and Kiara.

Lacus

Human from Torsil. Ei'ceuril steward.

Lara Thellion

Queen of Evellion. Widow of the late King Amry. Azurelle ei'ana.

Lawrence Maroven

King of Mindale. Of the Royal House Maroven. Supporter of Erynor.

Leilyn Lorenthien

Sister of Devlyn, living in the Illumined Wood. Daughter of Evellyn and Dolan.

Lenora Hanaryld

Human from Ceurenyl. Ei'ana and Chair of Arantiulyn. *Deceased.*

Lex Telvin

General from Perrien. Leader of the renegade Perrien Militia. Brother to Entiel, Vine, and Dolan, who was adopted. Uncle to Alex. *Deceased.*

Liam Lierafen

Son of Dolan. Half-brother to Devlyn and Leilyn. Student wielder at Gwilnor Academy.

Liara

Dragon of the Red Flight bonded to Prya.

Lillianna

Human from Mindale. Ei'ceuril and formerly an Emradiel ei'ana.

Loral Vicalen.

Luminari. Attendant in the Narielle household. Father to Toryn.

Loretta Javie

Human of Sorenthil. Ei'ana and Chair of Crimsyn.

Lucillia

The woman who gave birth to the twins, Roendryn and Feolyn.

Lyren Fenthyr

Luminari. Attendant, formerly in the Roendryn household before joining the Lorenthien household to attend Devlyn Lorenthien.

Malind Koth

Daer Senator of the Upper Tier.

Mara

Elder One that lived in Tenethyl.

Melanie Birkwell

Human from Mindale. Ei'ana and Chair of Arantiulyn.

Mildred Thellion

Human from Evellion. Duchess of Cyril and widow of Talyian, the late Duke.

MYRAH GLAEDA

Eldinari. Albien ei'ana and magister at Gwilnor Academy; twin sister to Fyreh.

MYRANDA LARIVIERE

Queen of Sorenthil. Student wielder at Gwilnor Academy.

MYRASHA

Dragon of the Purple Flight.

NADIA DESUANI

Luminari. Ei'ana and Chair of the Tenebrys School; former Arantiulyn ei'ana.

NAITHOS

Dragon of the Blue Flight.

NATALIE

Luminari living in Cor'lera.

ODUIN DUR SETHARA

Cyndinari. One of the Sha'ghol.

OLIVER PENAULT

Human from Perrien. Septyl knight of Vyoletryn.

OMA

Dwarf of Oern Schtam. Stone seer.

ORANNA

Luminari. Azurelle ei'ana and former chancellor of Gwilnor Academy. *Deceased.*

ORENIEL

Centaur of the Illumined Wood.

PAOLO FARNEIS

Human from Sudern. Duke of Sudern.

PAUREL ROENDRYN

Luminari. Ei'ana and Chair of Azurelle.

PEVREL

Luminari elf. Attendant to Ellendren Lorenthien.

PHENDIEN SHENDIELLE

Eldinari. Ei'ana and Chair of Emradiel.

PRYA

Draelyn of the Red House. Bonded with Liara.

QIEN DI

Empress of the Qien Dynasty.

Qien Ji

Crowned Prince of Qien and Son of Empress Qien Di. Monk of Beishi Monastery.

Qien Kai

Cousin of Empress Qien Di. Azurelle ei'ana and magister of politics at Gwilnor Academy.

Raelinth

Cyndinari. Attendant to Yloran. Known in Lankor as Pico.

Raleniel

Elder One that lived in Tenethyl. Married to Weilyn.

Ramira Bir Ginthol

Human from Yanil. Supreme Judge of Yanil at the time of Nauto's Wrath.

Razcul Miethen

Cyndinari. Shadow elf disguised as an Eldinari assistant magister at Gwilnor. Known as Danyol.

Reia

Luminari. Arantiulyn ei'ana.

Renaud Lariviere

Human from Sorenthil. Temple knight. Royal cousin to Queen Myranda Lariviere.

Rusyl

Dragon of the Blue Flight.

Saecrien

One of the Children who watches over the Waters of Anaweh.

Saendre Liorith

Luminari. Student wielder at Gwilnor Academy. Assistant magister to Kai.

Sanjin al'Sanhir

Human from Charren. Crowned Prince of Charren of the Royal House Irithru.

Sara

Human from Briel. Auburnis ei'ana.

Selenya Waeyn

Luminari. Ei'ana and Chair of Albien.

Skimp

Minum and time warden.

STEPHEN

Human from Evellion. Temple knight.

SUIN

Former chief of Tribe Laith. Father of Cairn. *Deceased.*

TABITHA

Human from Sudern. Azurelle ei'ana.

TAEN TAERINIOR

Luminari. Ei'ceuril novice.

TARIEL

Phoenix bonded to Ellendren.

TERAN

Cyndinari. Uncle of Jaerol.

THERRIL

Ei'ceuril magister of theoreticals at Gwilnor Academy.

THIEN

Draelyn of the Gold House. Married to Loren. Son to Weilyn and Raleniel. Grandson to Galithinol the Gold. *Deceased.*

TIERA WELDON

Luminari. Emradiel ei'ana.`

TINDOL

Human from Dwonia. Member of the Sojourners.

TORYN VICALEN

Luminari. Lady of the Watch.

TRETHIEN NARIELLE

Luminari of House Narielle. Student knight at Gwilnor Academy.

TYE

Human from Dwonia. Member of Tribe Fendur.

VELARIA TREYVEN

Cyndinari born in Lucillia. Ei'ana and Chair of Azurelle.

VERNAL ROENDRYN

Luminari. Aryl of Lucillia. Married to King Harnyl. Mother of Aaron, Kaela, and Ellendren. Direct descendant of Lucillia. *Deceased.*

VINE VAERIN

Human from Perrien. Self-styled Queen Mother to the King of Thellion.

Viren Dekenurel

Luminari. Guardian knight.

Vivien

Draelyn and ealyn of the Gold House. Granddaughter of Galithinol the Gold, and daughter of Weilyn.

Waleisius

Merchant in Cor'lera, more commonly known as Walei.

Weilyn

Draelyn of the Gold House. Married to Raleniel. Son to Galithinol. *Deceased.*

Wyn Lierafen

Eldinari. Grandson of Dalenya and Fendryl. Star Warden. Emradiel ei'ana.

Xanth

Cyndinari. Shadow elf.

Yelaris

Dragon of the Blue Flight. Bonded to Velaria.

Yeniel

Phoenix bound to Aren.

Yloran Eth Gnashar

Cyndinari. One of the Sha'ghol. Known in Lankor as Enna.

Ythinor the Black

Dragon of the Dark Flight. Bonded to his half-brother, Erynor.

Yvonne Kardol

Human from Yanil. Crimsyn ei'ana and Magister of the art of wielding at Gwilnor Academy.

Zara

Cyndinari elf. Former servant of the Erynien Court.

THE SEVEN IRYTHIL AND THEIR ASSOCIATED ENTHIEL

URIEL – Lord of the Stars, whose name means Anaweh is my Light. Irythil who brought Anaweh's Light to Teraeniel.

> **AURIEL** – The Dawn Star. Guardian of the elves of Luminare.

> **MERIDIEL** – The Noon Star. Guardian of the elves of Cyndinare.

> **VESPIEL** – The Evening Star. Guardian of the elves of Aldinare.

> **BORIEL** – The Night Star. Guardian of the elves of Eldinare.

GWYNTHIEL – Lady of the Lorendil, whose name means Strength of Anaweh. Irythil who brought Anaweh's spirit to Teraeniel.

RAMIEL – Lord of Death, whose name means Arrogant toward Anaweh. Betrayed Anaweh and all creation. Irythil who brought shadow to Teraeniel.

THENIEL – Lady of the Seas, whose name means Anaweh Heals. Irythil who brought water to Teraeniel.

> **NAUTO** – Guardian of all humans living along the coasts.

> **AQUAE** – Guardian of the merpeople.

SARIEL – Lord of the Land, whose name means Command of Anaweh. Irythil who brought substance to Teraeniel.

> **TERA** – Patroness of harvest and nourishment. Often referred to as Mother Tera.

> **MUNDI** – Guardian of the dwarves.

LERENIEL – Lady of the Winds, whose name means Friend of Anaweh. Irythil who brought air to Teraeniel.

KARIEL – Lord of Peace, whose name means Who is Like Anaweh. Irythil who brought fire to Teraeniel.

SEVEN CHAIRS OF SEPTYL

CHAIR OF ALBIEN — Selenya Waeyn. Luminari. The White Owl.

CHAIR OF ARANTIULYN — Melanie Birkwell. Human from Mindale. The Orange Lion.

CHAIR OF AUBURNIS — Agnelle Phanstienne. Luminari. The Brown Lark.

CHAIR OF AZURELLE — Velaria Treyven. Cyndinari born in Lucillia. The Blue Dragon.

CHAIR OF CRIMSYN — Loretta Javie. Human from Sorenthil. The Red Dog.

CHAIR OF EMRADIEL — Phendien Shendielle. Eldinari. The Green Stag.

CHAIR OF VYOLETRYN — Paurel Roendryn. Luminari. The Purple Eagle.

HIGH LUMINARI HOUSES AND ARYLS

ARYL OF ARENTHYL AND EXALTED ARYL OF KRYSENTHIEL — House Lorenthien

ARYL OF LUCILLIA — Vernal (deceased) and Harnyl of House Roendryn

ARYL OF REINYL — Therrin and Zara of House Reyndien

ARYL OF OSTYL — Naesiv and Valerie of House Aerquin

ARYL OF WINSTSYL — Toral and Silvia of House Narielle

ARYL OF TENYL — Iridil and Enoria of House Taerinior

ARYL OF DELMIRA WOOD — Ciraenth and Aegian of House Ginielle

ARYL OF EANDYL — Enithil and Binoral of House Clarion

ARYL OF VERENTHYL — Kyiel and Fyona of House Lauriel

HIGH ELDINARI HOUSES AND ARYLS

ARYL OF LIERTHYL — Fendryl and Dalenya of House Lierafen

ARYL OF VIRATHYL — Naerelle and Eohire of House Shendielle

ARYL OF DRETHYL — Vanoreh and Elialen of House Illia

ARYL OF LADRITHYL — Indryn and Diera of House Allandis

ALDARCHS OF ALDINARE

GAEL OF QUEL'ANIR – The Reverend Mother, also known as the Nurturer. Her followers dedicate themselves to nature and caring for the ilithae trees, native to Aldinare.

ORIEN OF ELN'DINAI – The Just Father, also known as the Judge. His followers focus on upholding law in Aldinare.

NIALTH OF DUR'LINOS – The Philosopher, also known as the Learned One. Her followers dedicate their life to study.

THESERYN OF THAS'THALLAS – The Faithful Servant. His followers devoted their lives to worshipping Anaweh, the Creating Light. Theseryn left his sanctum of Thas'thallas to establish the Ei'ceuril order and became the first Ceurtriarch.

LERATHEL OF VAL'QUIN – The Artisan. Sister to Nialth. Her followers are practitioners of the arts and designed the great cities and sanctums of Aldinare.

ENDRUIL OF KIR'ENON – The Shepherd. His followers are caretakers of the alicorns native to Aldinare.

AERYTH OF AI'LYR – The Rogue. Her followers prefer to hide in the shadows and wield the fabled Aldinari bows.

IRITHEL OF MEL'INOR – The Smith. His followers develop advanced weapons and tools, often forged from aldaryl.

Ealyn of Tenethyl

Vivien — Ealyn of the Gold House. Granddaughter of Galithinol of the Gold Flight.

Daela — Ealyn of the Amethyst House. Granddaughter of Myrasha of the Purple Flight.

Torik — Ealyn of the Onyx House. Grandson of Jiertha of the Grey Flight.

Mellory — Ealyn of the Ruby House. Granddaughter of Vulgath of the Red Flight.

Niron — Ealyn of the Sapphire House. Grandson of Naithos of the Blue Flight.

Allister — Ealyn of the Opal House. Grandson of Ithinol of the White Flight.

Helen — Ealyn of the Jade House. Granddaughter of Fenoral of the Green Flight.

Dragon Primus

Lyvenol — Primus of the Gold Flight. Warden of lumenys.

Eilynol — Primus of the Purple Flight. Warden of animys.

Orythnol — Primus of the Grey Flight. Warden of umbrys.

Aerinol — Primus of the White Flight. Warden of aerys.

Caephenol — Primus of the Blue Flight. Warden of aquaeys.

Thereinol — Primus of the Green Flight. Warden of terys.

Fyrinol — Primus of the Red Flight. Warden of ignys.

Tolvenol — Primus of the Dark Flight. Warden of tenebrys.

APPENDIX C

CIVILIZATIONS OF TERAENIEL

ALDINARE

Remnant of Aldinari rescued from the Skyland Aldinare by Aren and accompanying Phaedryn. They are considered part of Krysenthiel.

Race: Elf

House/Aryl: Avign, Eraen, Kenoril, Threilen

AUDUN

One of the eight schtams composing the Schtamite. Situated at the westernmost edge of the Laudien Mountains.

Head of State: Patriarch Dridn IV, son of Dridn III

Race: Dwarf

BRIEL

River valley kingdom situated between two rivers forming the River Reifen and the slopes of the Dead Wood.

Capital: Briel

Head of State: King Irvienne of the Royal House Haert

Motto: Seek the message

Sigil: Black raven on a yellow field

Race: Human

BRUNST

One of the eight schtams composing the Schtamite. Situated within the Vespien Mountains. Close friends with the Eldinari.

Head of State: Patriarch Thraen, son of Anuun

Race: Dwarf

CHARREN

A kingdom spanning across two continents, Ogren and Daereneth.

Capital: Karithel

Head of State: King Sanhir of the Royal House Irithru

Race: Human

DAER EMPIRE

Oldest continuous human empire in Teraeniel and advocate of slavery and colonialism. Situated on the continent of Daereneth.

Capital: Daer

Head of State: Body of the Daer Senate

Race: Human

DWONIA

Desert country once controlled by the Twelve Tribes of Dwonia. Only two tribes refused to ally with Erynor and remained in the desert.

Heads of State: Chief Kodin of Tribe Fendur and Chief Genin of Tribe Vadir

Capital: Nynev

Sigil: Red lion on a yellow field

Race: Human

ELDINARE

Eldinari society secreted away in the Eldin Wood.

Head of State: Aryl Fendryl and Dalenya of House Lierafen

Capital: Stellantis

Sigil: White tree on a green field

Race: Elf

ERYNIEN EMPIRE

Cyndinari empire founded by Erynor Meriden, its sole emperor. Responsible for the Ceurendol War and enslavement of the Luminari.

Capital: Broid

Head of State: Emperor Erynor Meriden

Sigil: Bronze sun on a red field

Race: Elf

EVELLION

The mountain kingdom where the Laudien and Vespien mountain ranges meet. Original inhabitants were the refugees of Thellion.

Capital: Everin

Head of State: King Amry and Queen Lara of the Royal House Thellion

Motto: The pure will soar

Sigil: White eagle on a blue field

Race: Human

FRIETON

The free city-state of Frieton. Given to the minums on their release from slavery.

Capital: Frieton

Head of State: The Keeper (identity unknown)

Race: Minum

Gestoria

Fallen kingdom situated on the Plains of Orithil. Once great allies to Thellion and Krysenthiel. Obliterated during the Ceurendol War.

Capital: Quellion

Motto: Will triumphs pride

Sigil: White gold winged lion on a blue field

Race: Human

Glyol

One of the eight schtams composing the Schtamite. Easternmost and only schtam in the Illumined Wood.

Head of State: Matriarch Vylma, daughter of Toreldn

Race: Dwarf

Harol

One of the eight schtams composing the Schtamite. Situated in the Laudien Mountains.

Head of State: Matriarch Loewn, daughter of Brenola

Race: Dwarf

Ja'horan, Tribes of

Nomadic civilization on the continent of Ja'horan.

Race: Human

Ja'nalihn

Short lived kingdom covering all of Ja'horan.

Race: Human

Jopht

One of the eight schtams composing the Schtamite. Southernmost schtam in the Vespien Mountains and staunch defenders against the Shadow schtams from northern infiltration.

Head of State: Patriarch Oerth III, son of Oerth II

Race: Dwarf

Krysenthiel

The kingdom of the Luminari. Currently lost within the Shroud. Translates to land of the golden flowers, named by a human trying to speak Aelish, the language of the elves, to describe the countryside.

Capital: Arenthyl

Head of State: Exalted Lorenthien Aryl

Sigil: Seven golden kryseniels blossoming from a larger central kryseniel on a white field.

Race: Elf

Lucillia

Kingdom of the Luminari after gaining their freedom from the Erynien Empire. Named after Lucillia, the woman who gave birth to the twins, Roendryn and Feolyn.

Capital: Lucillia

Head of State: Aryl Vernal and Harnyl of House Roendryn

Race: Elf

Mindale

A kingdom east of the southern Vespien Mountains.

Capital: Binton

Head of State: King Lawrence of the Royal House Maroven

Motto: Mind over body

Sigil: Brown ox on a green field

Race: Human

Nunstol

Shadow schtam that was cast off by the Schtamite for their actions in Mount Cyngol.

Head of State: Patriarch Uriden, son of Urodrn

Race: Dwarf

Oern

One of the eight schtams composing the Schtamite. Belin belonged to Oern schtam and sheltered Evellion and his people as they fled Elothkar.

Head of State: Patriarch Forvl VIII, son of Forvl VII

Race: Dwarf

Parendior

A hilly country north of the Laudien Mountains and west of the Illumined Wood. Most Parendians are farming folk, and when Perrien invaded, they had no means of defending their land.

Motto: Protect the harmony

Sigil: Purple doe on a beige field

Race: Human

Perrien

A kingdom north of the Laudien Mountains where the citizens overthrew their monarchy and replaced it with a council and doubled their territory by invading Parendior.

Capital: Gneal

Motto: Swift to action

Sigil: Grey rider and horse on a white field

Race: Human

Qien Empire, the

Empire of the Hundred Kingdoms on the continent of Qien, west of Eklean.

Capital: Zhongshi

Auxiliary Capitals: Beishi, Dongshi, Nanshi, and Xishi

Head of State: Empress Qien Wei

Race: Human

Sorenthil

A kingdom along the River Meyien.

Capital: Myrium

Head of State: Queen Karina of the Royal House Lariviere

Motto: Flow with the waters

Sigil: Blue dolphin on a light blue field

Race: Human

Sudern

A city state on the Dagger's Point peninsula. After a bloody civil war with Josque, the inhabitants declared themselves independent.

Capital: Sudern

Motto: Hidden daggers

Sigil: Red ship and dagger on a white field

Race: Human

Thellion

The fallen Eklean kingdom covering all the lands east of the Vespien Mountains. Met its downfall through a civil war relating to succession.

Capital: Elothkar

Head of State: King Alexander of House Vaerin

Motto: Eternal wisdom

Sigil: Silver winged horse on a white field

TIEL

A southern kingdom bordering the Erynien Bay and the Unarian Sea.

Capital: Josque

Head of State: Queen Alesei of the Royal House Ziera

Motto: Eternal wisdom

Sigil: Orange serpent on a blue field

Race: Human

TORSIL

A weak kingdom with little influence on its neighbors.

Capital: Trest

Head of State: King Gordon of the Royal House Carvil

Motto: Stronger together

Sigil: Grey wolf on a red field

Race: Human

UNDOL

One of the eight schtams composing the Schtamite. Deeply religious and situated in the Laudien Mountains surrounding Lake Saeryndol. They have strong ties to the Luminari.

Head of State: Matriarch Miurel IV, daughter of Miurel III

Race: Dwarf

VORN

One of the eight schtams composing the Schtamite. Situated at the northernmost edge of the Vespien Mountains.

Head of State: Matriarch Tiltha, daughter of Tilma

Race: Dwarf

YANIL

Southern kingdom along the Erynien Bay. Yanil was once jointly ruled by the Yanilean and the Judges of Yanil.

Capital: Lankor

Head of State: The Yanilean

Motto: Deep as justice

Sigil: Black castle on a blue field

Race: Human

ZORIK

Shadow schtam that was cast off by the Schtamite for their actions in Mount

Cyngol.

Head of State: Matriarch Jiora, daughter of Jiorza

Race: Dwarf

About the Author

Ryan D Gebhart first started writing the Jewel of Life series in 2012 in Philadelphia, PA, shortly after concluding his undergraduate studies in philosophy. This unexpected passion evolved over the years and has remained a constant companion through his career changes, from a Franciscan friar, to a claims processor, receiving a graduate degree in Architecture, and now working at an architecture firm and teaching at the Catholic University of America in Washington, DC. Ryan D Gebhart is originally from Wilmington, DE.

Keep up with Ryan D Gebhart at www.RyanDGebhart.com